EXPOSED In The SHADOWS:

He Who Plays

A Paranormal Mystery Rekindling Lost Love

J. K. Grueber

Copyright © 2023 Jeanne K. Grueber. All rights reserved.

The characters and events portrayed in this book are fictitious. Any similarity to real persons, living or dead, is coincidental and not intended by the author.

No part of this book may be reproduced, stored in a retrieval system, or transmitted in any form or by any means, electronic, mechanical, photocopying, recording, or otherwise, without express written permission of the publisher.

Mystic Ridge Publishing, LLC

Mysticridgepublishing.com

ISBN: 979-8-9878673-6-5 (Ebook)

ISBN: 979-8-9878673-7-2 (Paperback)

ISBN: 978-1-965796-11-5 (Hardback)

Cover design by: Anne Graff, Andrew Grueber, and William Grueber.

Contributing cover photo editor: Sanderson-Decello Design, LLC.

Printed in the United States of America.

*Mystic
Ridge
Publishing
LLC*

J. K. Grueber

The Envy Series:
COLORS OF ENVY: A Paranormal Romance Mystery
FACES OF ENVY: A Paranormal Romance Mystery
ECHOES OF ENVY: A Paranormal Romance Mystery

The MacDade Brothers Mysteries:
EXPOSED IN SHADOWS: He Who Plays.
A Paranormal Mystery Rekindling Lost Love
EXPOSED In The CROSSHAIRS: He Who Rides
A MacDade Brothers Paranormal Mystery
EXPOSED By The RIVERSIDE: He Who Lives
A MacDade Brothers Paranormal Mystery

The Vampire Tales:
Cursed At Conception: The Vampire's Henchman
Damned By Death: The Vampire's Hammer

DEDICATION

Remembering Elizabeth "Betty" H. Summers, 1938-2022.

I still hear your accolades over my first published novel, as welcome and wonderful then as in all other milestones throughout my life. Thank you for being my big sister. I know you rest in the palm of His hands with Mom, Dad, and our three brothers, but know that you are missed.

PROLOGUE

Darkness had settled some little time ago, and the night had only begun to come alive with an abundance of people still out and about. Not a bad neighborhood. A few too many bars existed. Neon lights boasted all manner of pubs scattered liberally between corner delis, homespun grocery stores, and pizza parlors. Rather like the city where he'd grown up, the familiar clatter-clank of a nearby train vibrated beneath the raucous of rock 'n roll blaring from open doors. The sounds echoing on the summer breeze further reminded him of his childhood and the years he'd spent crowded with his brothers and sisters in a one-room flat on the poorer side of the tracks.

He hadn't been born with a silver spoon, not like the lot of the MacDade clan—this younger generation in particular.

Damn it. He'd taken a chance coming this early. Even tucked in shadows, adequately concealed despite the nightlife waking behind the neon lights, he suffered second thoughts about arriving this early—early enough to change his mind. Not that he figured he would. He'd already put too much time and money into this ordeal to back out now, and he wasn't likely to get another opportunity.

A crease slid across his brow. His attention shifted to the neon glow of the marque beyond his sight to the distant left. From where he stood, he could see the entrance clearly enough. Not a five-star by any stretch, but then, the neighborhood wasn't boasting any signs of tourist attractions. The bars probably kept that motel in business, although he hadn't witnessed any evidence of that sort of shenanigans. Probably still too early to see any ladies plying a trade in that direction. From what he'd seen, no one appeared to be hurrying to hit the sack.

No more than ten feet away, an aging couple ambled past the narrow opening, near enough for him to hear them discussing where to let their toy poodle piss. Luckily, they opted not to utilize the slot where he stood. Even with the dark now fully descended, he felt exposed.

Battling an urge to check the time, either on his indigo watch or cellphone, he continued to study the entrance in his line of sight. He'd taken a gamble—one hell of a gamble to stand this close to that lighted entrance, but when the time came, he could sprint the short distance to the alley that paralleled the street ahead. Rather than broadcast his out-of-state status via his personalized license plate, he'd rented an economy car and stashed it in the shadow of overhanging trees two streets back. He could reach that car in under thirty seconds . . . but then, he had no intention of running, not tonight.

Once and for all, a certain arrogant fellow needed chopped down a peg or two, and with his thought, he lifted his cigarette pack while likewise checking the time. Only after he drew a puff and the end flared did he consider his recklessness. If someone spotted that glow . . .?

The wait was almost over. Probably under thirty minutes before that limo arrived . . . and if all went as planned, less than two hours after that, all hell would break loose.

With his thought, he cupped his cigarette behind his palm and drew a puff while spying toward the black slot directly across the street from where he stood. Doubtfully anyone stood in that alley just yet, but he shuffled a sidestep, improving his angle of the wider black opening toward his right. He should have a bird's-eye view of the entire show, and it would take all his great willpower not to trot across that asphalt and add a few lumps, which was the least of what that fellow deserved.

A pity that, not being able to take credit after all his careful planning, but only a damn fool would broach that thought. And he was no fool, as this evening would surely attest.

Once and for all, this big son of a bitch would pay . . . For Natalie, for the kids. Hell, for the whole blasted clan.

He just needed to be patient now and watch the chips fall.

PART ONE

With Fire

1

The Castaway Lounge was crowded, but not to the point of losing the nautical theme. Like a heavy fog rolling off the high seas, cigarette smoke swirled through the heavy rope netting that draped from the ceiling, and rowdy laughter enhanced the ambiance tenfold, threatening to break into a swashbuckling song at any moment. Around the high tables nearest the bar, a crowd of patrons mingled, swilling drinks with fancy names like the Tempest or Ed Fitzgerald or chugging beer with imported labels. These weren't fishermen or pirates despite the waitstaff's attire of britches and vests, puffy-sleeved blouses. An eclectic consortium, from young executives to beach bums, comingled in fine good humor.

A Friday night

Music blared; voices and laughter rose to match the decibels thundering off the walls.

Sitting in a corner furthest from the bar, Natalie watched the mayhem with a discerning eye, and despite the raucous, she clearly heard the rich baritone laughs cutting through the din as effectively as a trombone in a band. No mistaking that fellow. By size alone, he stood head and shoulders above most others. At six foot six, his wild blond waves rose above the masses, and even in the smog, those unruly locks caught and refracted the light in perfect harmony with the buoys and life preservers dangling within the fishing nets overhead. Like a great Highlander lord of another era, he stood at the bar, the ends of his rakishly long hair brushing against the black lamb's wool collar of his suit jacket. Oh, and when that head tipped to receive a whisper in his ear, the arrogance in his pose could be no more revealing. As handsome as the devil himself, his mustache curved in a perpetual smirk no matter his mood, and the stark blue eyes, near the color of cobalt, shined like neon to suggest an abundance of mirth.

Was it any surprise Liam MacDade could walk into a crowd and be surrounded by blasted women? And men? He was the epitome of male charisma, from the breadth of his shoulders to the cut of his handsome jaw, refined and rugged in one fell swoop, and he carried himself like a blasted Scottish laird!

Well, enough was enough. Once and for all, Natalie needed to know what her unruly husband was up to. As if she needed more proof. For months, he'd been making this trip to New Jersey. A business venture, he'd said often enough, and at least part of that was a fact since Mason Eldridge, the family advisor, and Artair, Liam's personal bodyguard, had made the trip with him. At a glance, she'd recognized the dark-haired fellow. Only slightly smaller than Liam, Artair lingered casually within the crowd at the bar, his dark eyes sprinting over the laird's immediate circle. Formidable, this Artair, who needed to divide his attention between his share of the ladies and his occupation. At first, and probably second glance, they could pass for friends as easily as cousins, as much by the cut of their jaws as by the cut of their clothes.

The Pendleton deal, Natalie had heard often enough, and recognizing Frank Pendleton joining Liam outside the Castaway added another degree of merit, although she might consider that detail an opposing point. After all, Liam and Frank's friendship stemmed from their college days. What better excuse to cover his infidelity than visiting an old chum? And if the greeting that she'd witnessed from the backseat of a cab was any indication, they'd remained close. Between Liam's size and his long jacket, Frank had disappeared as if swallowed in Liam's embrace, and even now, the sleek fellow was lost in the crowd under the netting and smoke.

College. That seemed like such a long time ago. Those years had been so full of promise. Natalie had intended to land a law degree. Had meant to rally for the underprivileged, a defender of truth. Idealistic . . . and foolish to her own ears now. As near as she came to the poor was the food drive at Christmas or sponsoring benefits at the Club for the Woman's Shelter in Lexington.

Whether Natalie was angry or merely heartsick, she watched her husband dip and land a kiss on the woman plastered under his jacket. Either way, she was annoyed. Far too clearly, familiarity and intimacy lingered between them.

This was not a chance meeting or first encounter, and Natalie would have realized that truth without the damning evidence currently resting in her safe in her bedroom closet at home.

Across the smoky room, the woman nuzzled against Liam's broad chest as if it were her personal territory, and perhaps, she wasn't so slender as she first appeared. Rather like a Barbie Doll on steroids, her tiny waist magnified the overabundance of glowing mounded flesh presented to Liam like a blasted banquet feast on a platter.

The niggling at the nape of Natalie's neck hadn't abated. If anything, that sense of a spider tap-dancing under her hairline had only increased since she'd landed in Le Guardia a short time ago. A single call to his office verified his flight and schedule. Clarice Chambers, his personal secretary, had been more than happy to share his itinerary; after all, Liam had nothing to hide . . . other than the obvious. Only a select few knew that one Natalie MacDade had kicked one Liam MacDade from their marital bed several months past. So why now? Why did she suddenly have this wicked sense of doom? As if she should plow through this crowd, grab him and run?

The photographs?

With the waiter, dressed in a pirate costume, stepping alongside the table, Natalie's muscles lurched; an instant later, panic gripped her as the black-clad body slipped onto the bench beside her, obliterating what remained of her view of the bar.

"How we doing here, miss? Uh, sir? Can I get you anything?"

Natalie had barely touched her Hurricane; Mason held a half-full tumbler in his capable hand. Quivering a smile to be caught spying on her blasted husband and her reaction to the same, Natalie shook her head with her glance at the young waiter. "Fine, thank you, hon."

Mason—typically grim and somber—shook his head and tilted his glass. "Fine, lad."

For as far back as Natalie's memory allowed—spanning at least twenty years—Mason Eldridge had been a part of the MacDade dynasty. Forever, he'd stood at the eldest MacDade's right hand. A rock, a solid fixture, or foundation stone with his handsome features chiseled in granite. Salt and pepper, he wore his hair in a trendy business style, and if he'd ever worn anything other than a dark suit, Natalie couldn't recall the occasion. Spying him sideways through clear panes that she suddenly felt silly for wearing,

Natalie quivered another smile, and Eldridge studied her as if she were daft, which only enhanced her amusement.

"Don't suppose I need to wonder what you're doing here, lass," he said at a volume to be heard just beneath the raucous of another blaring nautical tune. His gray-blue eyes carried a touch of sorrow to betray his knowledge of the circumstance.

Sobering nearly on the instant, Natalie lifted her drink unconsciously and glanced toward the bar where her unruly husband's blond waves tipped at an angle to suggest another lip-lock on his blond consort. Glimpsing at Mason, Natalie shook her head and nearly cursed the sting in her eyes. Cigarette smoke, damn it, nothing more than cigarette smoke burning her eyes.

Mason glanced to the bar to assure himself of Liam's preoccupation, and for an instant, he appeared as angry as Natalie felt. But he tempered the heat behind genuine concern. He was one of the few who knew about their separation, and doubtful he held Liam fully accountable for his current behavior. After all, the MacDades were a randy lot, and Natalie had known that at the onset.

Lucius MacDade, her father-in-law, was, perhaps, the only faithful male in the clan, and probably only because Megan MacDade would accept no less. There was no end to the tales of uncles—and aunts—and cousins whose exploits spanned the globe. Even before Lucius had settled in America, the MacDades had been wealthy, and possibly, that image of Liam in this nautical environment wasn't too far off the blasted mark. As Natalie had heard, many of his clan had braved the high seas long before ships had boasted engine rooms.

Had she truly believed, under the circumstances of their marriage, that marrying the rake and bearing his children would put an end to his carousing?

What kind of fool did that make her, then?

Every kind of fool, she answered silently and swilled another gulp of the bitter drink to squelch the lump rising in her throat.

As if sensing her distress, Mason touched her denim jacket sleeve, drawing her focus to the understanding in his eyes. "Why don't I call you a cab, dear? Do you have a room here in the city, perhaps? Or should I make you a reservation?"

She hadn't thought that far ahead, and did her oversight reflect an ulterior desire to spend an evening in her husband's bed? They'd traveled well and often in those first years of marriage, and she could never mistake his attentiveness in bed. He could take her to that wondrous edge without half trying and never left her wanting. Whether the same could be said of him, she was never positive. He always appeared sated after their tempests and never claimed to be less than content. But how the blasted hell was she to know? Before Liam, there had been no others, and in a moment of crystal clarity, she knew there would be no others after him. Not another man alive could compare with this blasted nobleman.

With the pressure on her forearm sleeve, Natalie realized she hadn't answered Mason. Distracted, she glimpsed at him and shook her head. "I have a cab waiting," she said at a pitch barely to be heard despite his proximity.

He'd leaned closer, apparently attempting to block her view of the bar, with his not-inconsiderable width. Like all the men surrounding the clan, Eldridge was not slight-of-build. Even in his advancing years—nearer to sixty than fifty—he appeared as fit and capable as ever, but the wisdom in his eyes betrayed his age. He would spare her what he could.

"Why don't I see you safely to it then, dear? I'm guessing you are alone?"

Considering the complexity of her mission, she couldn't have invited a friend. Or dragged either of her sisters or brothers along—even if the thought had crossed her mind. Too easily, she could imagine Heather and Linnie engaging the blond bimbo in a catfight; and John would foolishly stand on his honor to fight Liam with the proof across the room. Tomas—in his innocence—might have remained neutral since he idolized Liam; unfortunately, he was too young to bring him into this atmosphere.

In good conscience, Natalie couldn't create a public scene to disgrace either of their respective families, and she could just imagine Kirk Callahan's reaction if he caught wind of this situation. Lucius MacDade might enjoy the tale. Doubtful, the patriarch of the Callahan clan would appreciate the fame to follow a good old-fashioned donnybrook in this fine establishment. And Natalie wasn't naïve about such an event becoming public. Whether Liam's infidelity or the fight would hold dominion, it wouldn't matter one wit; Kirk Callahan wouldn't suffer the humiliation silently. The only salvation thus far was Liam's discretion. Very few of his exploits ever reached the tabloids, and before five months ago, Natalie had believed that most sensible people would consider those photos tabloid-worthy sensationalism.

Safer, much wiser, to handle this affair solo, and in an odd moment, Natalie wondered if Mason meant to shuffle her out before she created just the sort of scene she'd meant to avoid. For the sake of their families, however, she'd depart as discreetly as she'd arrived, though she wondered if Liam would even care to find her here in witness to his infidelity.

"I'll be fine, Mason," she decided and drained the last of the Tempest, setting the glass aside in the universal sign as a prelude to departure. Realizing Mason's disheartened gaze, she forced a faint smile. "Truly, sir. If you can just see that the lout remains busy for a few more moments, I'll leave quietly. This is neither the time nor place for the discussion he and I shall have soon."

"I can't, in good conscience, let you leave alone, my dear. This is by no means a sordid part of town, but still nowhere for a lady to travel alone." Fleeting another glance to the bar, appearing more dismayed, he decided, "I'll just see you to that cab and direct your driver to the Baymont. By the time you arrive, you'll have a room."

Arguing would be futile, and she might eventually need a room. "Fine then, but ehm . . . if you could refrain from mentioning my presence here this evening, I'd appreciate it, Mason."

"Your secret is safe with me, dear," he assured her and began sliding from the booth.

Within shadows, Natalie slipped from the booth and remained behind a curtain of swaying and bouncing bodies. As if the laughter and song were water and herself the duck, she swam through the growing crowd and managed only another quick glimpse of the giant tipped low and otherwise engaged with the tart under his lapel. For a fleeting instant, Natalie considered the confrontation, wondering at the satisfaction of ripping a handful of blond locks by the roots and flagging the scalp as a trophy.

Fuming, despite her best effort to remain composed, Natalie escaped the mayhem at the entrance. Mason on her heels, she set course for the cab idling across the lot. Like the interior, the exterior of the Castaway carried the fanfare of a dock, from woven rope barriers between thick jutting posts to wooden planks in a rendition of gangways. In abundance, coach lights and lanterns dangled from iron poles, and nautical flags waved in the soft evening breeze. Shrubs and trees crowded the pavement, countering the soft glow of neon and creating deeper shadows on either side of the walkway.

With the noise faded, Mason spoke in a natural pitch as he caught up to walk at her side. "I am sorry you bore witness to this, my dear, but I should mention in his defense, I'm sure she's nothing more than a distraction. We truly are here on business."

"No need to explain, Mason," she said with a sigh and offered another faint smile to offset his apparent dismay. "I'm not ignorant of my husband's exploits. I suppose I should be only grateful that he's reasonably discreet and not flaunting her for a society page."

"Aye, well, I don't think you need worry about that then," Mason said grimly and turned his attention to the cab driver, offering directions to the Baymont as Natalie slid into the rear compartment.

She truly hadn't planned this trip well. Her single overnight bag still rested on the rear seat where she'd tossed it when climbing into the first available cab, not more than three car lengths behind the limo to carry her husband to this blasted bar. Perhaps, she should have hired a car as well, but doubtful she'd have remained anonymous in her pursuit. With a brief wave to Mason as the cab pulled from the curb, Natalie suffered yet another prickle beneath her collar. Before rational thought could intrude, she glimpsed Mason passing beneath shadows en route to the entrance, and before he disappeared in the crowd, she leaned forward. The driver's name she'd read earlier, she used now. "A change in plans, Mario," she said lightly. "Do keep the meter running, still, and find us a slightly less conspicuous parking space, will you? I'm not quite ready for the evening to end."

"But uhm . . . Miss, that fellow just paid—"

She slipped her hand over the seat and flashed the hundred in the light at his side. "I should think this is your lucky day, sir. You might consider his money your tip, but our mission hasn't changed. I should like to see where that limo stops next."

Nearly muttering, his voice barely reached over the seat. "My wife, she's no gonna believe this. Not for a minute. She's gonna think I'm playing the ponies again."

In the shadows of the rear seat, Natalie suffered a strained smile. Mrs. Mario was lucky if that was her only fear in her husband's regard. If only her own life were so simple. Bad enough, she need worry over his indiscretions, now she need worry over his blasted safety. As if a fellow who stood six-foot-six and held a black belt in karate, need worry about a thing. Still, she couldn't shake the feeling, the blasted persistent feeling that something was terribly wrong . . . and according to her gram, when a McCuddy woman started suffering the pricklies, it was not a good omen.

Ach well, and the taste was bourbon. That was something, at the least.

And she was certainly still attractive and more than willing.

What more could any able-bodied man want than a sweat-slicked body pressed against him, a sweet taste of Kentucky bourbon on his lips, and his hands amply occupied?

Sprawled atop the tangled sheets, watching the orange glow of the hotel sign flicker across the ceiling between a slice of dull beige curtains, Liam MacDade rested for the first time in several hours. Long blond hair tangled in the matt of blond fur at his muscled chest, labored breaths drew into a more natural rhythm, and a wry smile slipped into his mustache as he canted his head to spy the pixie face asleep over his heart. She'd given her all. More creative than on any prior encounter, and being honest, he gave her an A for the effort. The little lass had worn herself plum out with that last bit of tangling. Over and under, under and over, she'd seemed bent on a marathon of gyrations that left him more befuddled than sated.

Now and she slept.

Supposed he couldn't hardly blame her. A glance at the digital on the nightstand verified Liam's thought of the hours. Not late by normal standards but just past midnight, and they'd arrived in her suite—and there was a term misused even to his own mind—at just past nine. That he'd promised Frank to visit his Da's manor—

Damn it. Father. The English word was 'father,' and just the thought of that Scottish dialect slipping through his mind was enough to enhance the smirk on his lips. Too long in his own da's company. After weeks of reviewing the contracts and grants alongside his father, it was no damn wonder he was now thinking with a brogue. For forty years, Lucius MacDade had lived on American soil, and still, the fellow refused to forfeit his dialect. But then, Megan MacDade was just as guilty; when her hot Scott's blood fired, she let fly that brogue as if she were standing on the moors.

Why the bloody hell he was thinking of his parents with his latest paramour draped across his naked anatomy, he hadn't one good reason or excuse—but that he was, spoke volumes in his mind. As much as he enjoyed the young woman's company on his brief trips to New Jersey, he knew the affair nearing an end, and perhaps, she sensed that end, too, which might explain the past few hours of exertion. Young and supple, Alecia Helms had fulfilled his physical needs for the past four months, and she had yet to make her demands. Those would come, though, sooner or later. And he suspected this one would only cost him about five grand—plenty enough to keep her in sequined shoes and fishnet stockings for a time. Aye, and the cost of his indiscretions.

Sighing, Liam slipped his hand to his nether regions, found her fingers still lying possessively over the family jewels, and with an economy of motion, slid himself free. She stirred only a fraction, emitting a sigh off her parted, slightly swollen lips. He'd kissed her senseless, and with a wry smirk, he recalled the taste of bourbon sipped off her lips as often as his glass. His smirk notched deeper.

She would need lip balm in the morning.

Meandering, he gathered his clothes in the subdued light, pausing now and again to admire her plump behind aglow in the shadows. For such a slight woman, as most women were slight compared to his considerable size, she possessed rather long shapely legs . . . but for an instant, those weren't the legs he saw, and the image blindsided him. Natalie's legs were, without a doubt, stunning; the legs of a fairy, a mile long and as willowy as an ivory sculpt.

Damn his unruly nature! To find himself quickening while attempting to zip his fly! Still, the image he'd seen a thousand times continued to scroll through his mind. From her aerobics-toned thighs wrapped tightly about him, whether encircling his hips or his waist, to the wild abandon of her auburn hair with just a hint of red highlights to lance fire, she arched above him . . .

Nearly cursing aloud, he looked upon the sleeping woman and caught himself comparing her to a scullery maid of yesteryear. While at the same time, thinking to wake her at least once more to cure the ill growing against his zipper.

He would need to be awake and alert in the morning if he fully intended to meet with Frank's father. Clearly, he remembered Frances Pendleton from a dozen encounters during his and Frank's college days. A bit of a stuffed shirt. It was a wonder Frank had any fun at all, what with that fellow breathing down his neck and demanding his adherence to family values. Like him and the MacDade dynasty, Frank was being groomed to take the reins of the

Pendleton fortunes, but at least Lucius MacDade possessed the good sense not to hold those reins too awfully tight.

'Make it er break it on yer own, lad. Dinnae let me interfere.'

Well, so far, so good. At last count, Liam estimated his personal wealth had doubled, and the family fortunes had turned a tidy profit in the past fiscal year. Between him and Gregor, he suspected they could keep the dynasty afloat for a few more years. Aye, and then there was Lucas.

As he let himself into the dimly lit hall, Liam's natural smile wavered as much dismay as pride flashing through his mind. What exactly any of them had done to alienate the youngest of the three MacDade brothers, Liam had yet to discover. Eight years separated him from his youngest brother, but that age gap shouldn't be insurmountable. Regardless, any attempt to bring Luke back to the family fold failed miserably. The bugger was as stubborn as ever a MacDade to grace the earth.

Annoyed on every level, Liam glimpsed the faded gold carpet and lemon-colored walls, which had struck him rather funny upon arrival. Why Alecia Helms insisted on these seedy hotels, he could never decide. She surely knew he could afford a few luxuries, only beginning with a clean bed, and he'd offered to personally book their accommodations on more than one occasion. Just another of her idiosyncrasies. Or some warped sense of humor to see him on her level.

Stepping off the elevator on the first floor, Liam bypassed the main lobby and the rear entrance to the parking lot. A second entrance opened to the street, and toward that end, he was destined. Parking a stretch limo in the Fairlane Hotel lot would be akin to broadcasting his intentions in neon lights. Less than three blocks away, past a few rowdy bars and an abundance of darkened storefronts—boasting everything from delis to barbershops—shade trees and residential houses offered at least a modicum of discretion to conceal the limo.

Setting course for his ride, Liam considered the late hour again with rock n roll music blaring from at least two neon-lit openings on the next block. Vehicles lined either side of the street, whether accommodating the bar crowds or the residents behind darkened windows on the upper floors. A single cab rested at the curb on the next block, apparently awaiting his next fare to come stumbling from one of the neon-lit openings.

Pulling his jacket closed against the unseasonable night chill, Liam drew a clear breath, appreciating the cool air after the past few hours of stale cigarette smoke and old sex. Living in the country his entire natural life had certainly spoiled him to the cloying scents of engine exhaust and crumbling brick. He doubted he could ever truly adjust to living in a city . . . and no sooner that thought crossed his mind when he heard the footfall behind him, sensed the presence.

No amount of bourbon could alter his innate ability to sense danger. Too swiftly, too deliberately, this fellow—or fellows as the second scrape of soles indicated—advanced on him. Undoubtedly, they'd stepped from the narrow black slot between the buildings he'd just passed. No more than walking-space-wide and black as pitch, those spaces. And the gaping black mouth of an alley opened just a few paces ahead.

"You need to stop there, dude."

Even expecting the confrontation, Liam hadn't anticipated the friendly tone in the gruff voice. Thinking he'd misjudged the circumstance, he paused his stride and managed a half turn before the unmistakable jab of a gun barrel pressed into his side, making contact despite his jacket. Well, and he could understand the weapon. Though their faces remained in shadow, they both needed to cant their heads slightly to look up at him. An unlikely pair of muggers. Perhaps no more than teenagers by his estimation, though he could be wrong, merely judging by their diminutive size, dingy jackets, and jeans.

"Gentlemen," Liam spoke in his natural deep pitch. "You might want to reconsider yer intentions here."

The barrel jabbed. "Keep moving, dude. Up here to our office."

Well, and he did warn them. Sidling, he continued to the alley entrance, but he had no intention of entering their 'office.' In a single motion, Liam spun, and an instant before the gun flashed, he realized the pair had multiplied. How many others had joined the fray, there was no time to wonder. With a backhand, Liam sent one flying, and a fist took another, but they were like flies. Swarming. And Liam glimpsed steel slashing as he pivoted, using his jacket as a shield. That he might lose never crossed his mind. Slamming a jaw, kicking a knee, he heard the cries and yips, more in mind of a pack of wild dogs than humans. White hot, the pain flashed in his side as angry voices ran together in a litany.

"Get him!" . . . "Shoot the mutha fucker!" . . . "Hold him!" . . . "Yooou're a deaddd mannn . . .!"

Not yet, he might have mentioned as he clasped an arm and snapped it with a single stroke. The scream resounded in the narrow space, and the yips became snarls as ten years of Karate lessons took control of every ounce of his two hundred pounds. Like rag dolls, he tossed them, one after the other, landing them against the walls and on the alley floor. That he was leaking occurred to him as he slammed yet another rather large body into the black brick, but he had no time to waste. Another fire lanced his arm, flames ignited in his side, and still, they swarmed around him, landing their combined weight to ram him against a wall. Raging like a wounded bear, he collected his balance and spun, propelling the mass off the wall, but either the lights or his sight was failing. What little light shone from the street wasn't enough to judge a single feature of another body arriving. He recorded only a glimpse in silhouette and grasped the numbers stacked against him.

And alas, it occurred to him . . . he might lose.

"Miss . . . uhm, is that yer man there?"

The strange voice rousted Natalie from a doze, and she awoke confused, needing a moment to remember why she was sleeping in a cab smelling of heady pine scent. In seconds flat, the reality slammed her, and her attention riveted in time to see two men step from the shadows at Liam's back. Her heart hammered a quickening beat; the hair at the nape of her neck stood on end. From three hundred feet, a half-city block between them, she knew what one man held.

Already reaching for her door handle, she snapped, "Call 911! The police!" An ambulance, she screamed silently as she heard the distinct spit of a gunshot.

Wearing her running shoes, she lengthened her stride, not certain of else than a need to reach that alley. They'd disappeared into that blackness as if a phantom had whisked them off the sidewalk and swallowed them whole. Not even the sounds reached her with the crashing drums and screaming guitars of a live heavy-metal band booming from a neon-lighted doorway ahead. At the last second, she veered to avoid ramming a patron stumbling from the neon-lighted entrance and glimpsed the fellow twirling and staggering against the building in her wake.

Closing on the opening, she saw one, then another body sailing from the black crevice and knew an instant of relief that her husband was alive and well in that alley. Then another body spun and staggered, and she heard the scream echoing from the darkness. Not just two—not just two men! Already, she counted four, and by the continued sounds to begin reaching her, there were still more. Voices, shouts, the sounds of a raging bear . . . hurt! He was hurt! She knew that sound!

Without first—or second thought—she entered the fray, grasping at a body staggering toward her. Catching a wad of hair and kicking with a banshee cry, folding the fellow at the middle, she sent him stumbling toward the street. Another came her way, and as if she were merely a springboard, she propelled the body toward the light. Cast in a surrealistic glow, he was still afoot, pressed against the wall, her Highlander with his wild blond locks scattered above the heads, his blue eyes as midnight blue as a night sky. Wickedly quick, he spun off the wall, black cape swirling, spinning like the eye of a tornado, driving the last of his assailants to slam the wall in his stead.

That they might believe an army of harpies descended on them, Natalie knew only their combined shouts to "Run!" . . . "Leave the Bastard!" . . . "Let's get outta here!"

In the stopped instant, as the footsteps fled into the darkness, Natalie almost feared the moment when Liam would turn from his frozen stance. He'd seen her there, but for an instant before he raged off the wall. She heard his breath, heaving, now. Saw him sway . . . and he was falling. In two strides, she reached him. Still too late to save him. He slammed to his shins, and with a grunted breath, hurt sound, he continued falling.

She clasped him, taking his weight against her to lay him down gently. "Oh, m' God . . . Oh, m' God, Liam," the litany huffed uncontrollably off her lips. The absence of sound off his lips started a cry in her throat as she feared that silence like no other in her life. No! Not for an instant would she believe he could be gone! Unconscious, not dead! He was hurt though! With him folded against her, tears streaming, slipping the heavy glasses on her nose, she cradled his head, barely aware of the sounds of sirens approaching and anxious voices arriving.

Mason was there then, tugging anxiously at Liam's coat, uttering, "Oh my God . . . Liam . . . Natalie? . . . Liam . . ."

"Helllp himmm," Natalie pleaded, demanded.

A groan lifted from the shadowed head; the body shuddered and started a scramble despite Mason's effort to halt him. Against Natalie, Liam struggled and rose only partway to one knee before folding, collapsing into himself.

"Hell . . . ah helll," his deep voice uttered, huffing in hurt breaths.

"Shhh, darling. Shhh," Natalie pleaded softly, folding over him as if she could somehow hold him and take the pain from his voice. Against his ear, she whispered, "Shhh, you're okay . . . be okay . . . Shhh, baby . . . I have you . . . Still—be still, m' love."

Whether he was calming or passed out again, she neither knew nor had time to discover. Spotlights flashed over them; headlights blasted the blackness, blinding. Abruptly the alley was thrown into a different chaos with police and paramedics swarming around them. Uncontrollably, Natalie struggled against the hands to grab her until Mason's voice registered. Gently, firmly, he drew her away to grant the medics access. Belatedly, the tremors wracked her at the sight of the blood glistening at his waist, the lax slant of his head, his handsome face already too pale against the black gravel. All things sped up then. The medics snapping orders, the stretcher arriving, hands lifting him, strapping him secure. Natalie broke from her hysteria to follow the stretcher, unwittingly, blindly plowing toward the ambulance. Again, Mason Eldridge caught her, cradling her and promising they would follow in the limo, and he was as good as his word.

Within the confines of the back seat, Natalie sat forward, keeping the ambulance in view, mesmerized by the flashing red lights, aware only of the running dialogue, silently reciting every prayer she'd learned as a child. By the time she identified the Emergency entrance lights, only one litany remained, a single string of words, "Let him live, God. Let him live . . ."

The limo barely stopped when she yanked the handle, flew from the car, and raced up the ramp as the stretcher drew from the maws of the van. Already, he'd undergone a change. An oxygen mask covered half his face, concealing the natural smile in his mustache, turning him younger by a decade. The pale gray Oxford shirt that he'd worn in his travels had been ripped or torn from beneath the band at his broad chest. A mound of bloodied cloth bulged at his middle . . . and too clearly, Natalie glimpsed the red river pooling near his motionless arm. As the breath lodged in her throat, holding back a cry, the paramedics attempted to shuffle her aside, already wheeling through the open doors.

"Get back, miss," the words droned, and only one thought surfaced as she identified the man racing alongside her. "Heee's mmmine." Only another dozen strides, she clasped Liam's hand, raced at his side, before the chaos erupted yet again. Doctors and nurses poured from every direction, and

Natalie shuffled aside as they descended on Liam, surrounding him and snapping vital signs, orders. ". . . blood type . . . transfusion. . . OR . . . surgeon . . ."

The entire consortium passed through a set of gray doors, and a hand clutched Natalie before she could follow. A short, redheaded nurse spoke as if Natalie were a daft child. "You need to wait here, miss . . ."

Mason caught up to her, clasping her shoulder, and in his drawn profile, Natalie found solace. The pain on his chiseled features surely reflected her own; his eyes shined like silvered glass as he drew her into his capable arms. The dam broke. Clinging to the elder man, buried within the rich male scents of expensive tobacco and cologne, Natalie lost her tenuous grip and sobbed. Reality. Her husband could be dying. No fool was she to ignore the gravity of those voices and faces rushing that stretcher into the hall. He was badly hurt. She could lose him. Her lover . . . her friend. Oh, and he was both, no matter what he might believe. The father of her children . . . and with that thought, she found strength to begin recovering.

"There . . . there now, dear. He'll be all right . . . He'll be fine," Eldridge spoke in a litany, and it seemed he vibrated around her. "There, now . . . He'll be all right . . . ."

He had to be all right . . . Those were the words Natalie heard belying the elder man's dialogue. The heir to the dynasty, the clan . . . and there were calls to make. In her own words, she regained solid ground. He wasn't just her husband, not just a father . . . He was a son, a brother, a crown prince to an American throne. Clumsily, she found the useless glasses still clinging to her nose and nearly sent them flying in her haste to wipe her eyes. Whether she caught them or Mason assisted, she found the horn rim in her grip as she discovered the silly cap askew over her brow. How she'd kept either, remained a mystery, and she suffered the foolishness of her disguise, now, as she found Mason studying her more critically.

"We—" She drew breath and swallowed, realizing aloud. "We need to call his father and mother. They need to be here."

With a slight lift in his brow, he studied her more carefully, keeping a hand on her shoulder, fearing her collapse. "It's done, dear. I phoned from the car."

And he believed she'd heard him make that call, but those minutes were lost to her. He might have called God down from the heavens, and she might not have heard. She was lost suddenly.

"They're on their way," he added and seemed to look over her skewered disguise. A strained smile quivered on his lips. No mirth touched his eyes. If he'd ever affected the affliction of mirth, this was not that moment. "I uhm . . . They were going to stop for you. Under the circumstances, I told them you were here, dear. We uhm . . . we might tell them you were both making an attempt at reconciliation. A weekend getaway mixed with business?"

Appearances. Reality. At light speed, she realized what Mason had already determined. No matter the circumstances, they must keep up appearances. Poise. She was as bred and reared royalty as Liam was, and it wouldn't bode well to have either of them traipsing around a seedy hotel on a questionable side of town, any town. She needed to change . . . and just damn Mason Eldridge for hitting so close to the truth! In her bag—her bag! Natalie flashed a glance at the emergency entrance doors as if she might see her faithful cab through the glass. What she saw, halted her panic and renewed her faith in mankind.

For the past several hours, she'd been glimpsing a narrow swatch of those dark eyes and bushy black brows, had viewed the New Jersey cab company logo on the hat turned backward over black curly hair. She hadn't once seen Mario afoot or in natural light. Short and stocky, the fellow stood no taller than her 5'7", but he stood solid, despite his rather sheepish worried smile. He held her bag dangling at his side, a Louie Vuitton overnight bag in perfect contrast to his faded jeans.

With her relief, she collected her thoughts, and the fellow seemed gifted with an innate understanding to start toward her. At nearly the same moment, a woman approached, holding a clipboard, bouncing glances between Natalie and Mason. She barely started to speak toward Natalie when Mason touched Natalie's shoulder. "I'll handle the paperwork, dear."

Natalie started a protest when she grasped the futility. This was Mason's job. It's what made him invaluable to the MacDade dynasty. He handled things. Whether setting up business meetings or tempering the personal affairs that could tarnish the family name—as if the latter had ever been a serious concern. The MacDades, the lot of them, did whatever they damn well pleased, and if the world intruded now and again, to hell with the world.

Mixed and muddled, as torn by fear as anger, Natalie left the paperwork to Mason and met Mario partway into the waiting room. Surreptitiously, she peeled another hundred from the wad in her hip pocket and handed it to the worried fellow as he offered her bag.

"I uhm . . . you forgot this, miss," he said somewhat nervously, and at the glimpse of another hundred, his eyes rolled to her with disbelief. "I donna need that, miss. You covered my fare twice over."

"Take it, please. You've been a godsend this evening." In more ways than one. Had she not been there, had Mario not awakened her . . .. A ghostly shiver slid through her as she collected the bag somewhat clumsily. "Thank you."

"You er welcome, miss, and if'a you need a ride again, you call, and you ask'a for Mario, eh?" The offer and smile were genuine, but worry flashed across his dark eyes as he glanced toward the gray doors. Heartfelt, he met her gaze again. "I hope'a he's all right, miss. I'll say a prayer, huh?" By no surprise, he knew—he understood the past several hours.

"As many as you can, sir," she said, and if she said more, the words were lost. Reality. Her husband lay somewhere beyond those doors fighting for his life, and there was nothing she could do for him now. Distracted, she glanced about as if searching for a purpose, belatedly waking to her surroundings. She stood at the fringe of three rows of battered chairs, more than half occupied by an assortment of people ranging from a young mother holding a whimpering little girl in her arms to an elder black man holding an equally aged black woman against him, their frosted black hair mingling. The woman was ill, the child was ill, but others paced or stared, sniveling, coughing. Dozing. Nothing moved fast now, as if someone had turned a dial to slow the pace. Offbeat, someone yelled, and another staff woman called out a name. Surrealistic. Natalie suddenly felt as if she had stepped onto the set of a hospital series, though none of these faces bore any resemblance to the doctors or nurses she might recognize. A daytime soap, perhaps. She'd never seen more than a commercial for one of those daily ditties.

To the nurse approaching Mason, Natalie's attention riveted, and for a split second, she wondered what the hell he was doing on a TV soap opera. Her thought shifted before the woman spoke.

"We're taking him into surgery now, sir. If you'll come with me, I'll direct you to the surgical waiting room—"

"I want to see him," Natalie stated, already in motion.

"Nat—" Mason started and clasped her elbow, halting her.

She hated her name shortened to that degree as if she were some pesky bug, a blasted gnat! Rather she be called 'Nate'—like her unruly husband seemed bent on calling her when he wanted a rise—than 'Nat' like a damned

insect. Something of her irritation undoubtedly surfaced as Mason continued hurriedly.

"Let's let them do their job, dear."

"Yes . . . let's," she said hesitantly. They needed to do their job and keep
him alive long enough for her to pound the stuffing out of him! How dare
he land his big unruly self in this fix and drag her along to have her worrying
so!

Railing as many silent curses as she'd railed prayers a short time ago,
Natalie accepted the escort to pass through the gray doors. Behind the curtain—like the Wizard of Oz—the inner sanctum of the hospital bustled, and
only for a moment, she thought to drag at the curtains and search for the
single face she needed to see. They had already taken him from here. She
needed only a glimpse of the fleeting gazes to know her Highlander had made
an impression when passing through these halls. In the elevator, she glimpsed
at Mason, who wore yet another peculiar expression as he glanced at her bag.
He truly hadn't been too blasted off the mark in his fabrication; the proof
rested in her designer bag. Blast him! And blast Liam for being just as randy
as she had feared.

2

A cannon exploding could be no more effective than the computer ping to snap Lucas McDade from a dead sleep. Already turning, focused, he found the glowing digits of his utilitarian clock on the nightstand next to his head, and what remained of his sleep-induced haze vanished. No one sent an e-mail at 1: a.m. unless it was an emergency.

His parents—Lucius or Megan MacDade—something had happened to one of them.

Up and moving, he took two steps to land in his office chair, reaching for the buttons to ignite his screen and open his e-mail. Gregor. The message originated in the MacDade estate. Gregor's personal account. Short and direct, 'Liam's been hurt. On his way to surgery. Southern General, Trenton, NJ. Taking the jet. Should be there by 3:30. Come if you can.'

Liam? Hurt?

For a moment, Lucas stared at the screen, doubting the words. Not 'Liam got hurt'—as in a car accident, a plane crash, or falling out of bed. 'Liam's been hurt'—implied that someone else hurt him. And at 6' 6", it was pretty damn hard to believe someone else could do him damage. The blasted giant had been taking karate lessons since he could walk.

As if ice water poured over him, the implication struck with the epiphany—there were plenty of other ways a man of Liam's size could be hurt, only starting with a god-blessed gun.

Up and moving, Luke reached his compact closet in two strides. Snatching a pair of jeans off a hanger, he compiled the immediate details. Pack a bag. Arrange transport—

And there, his thought stopped as surely as his actions. For the first time in over a year, he stood within a stone's throw of the estate—close enough that he might reach the municipal airport and catch a flight in the family jet.

'Come if you can.'

He could beg off . . . could make an excuse as he'd been making excuses for the past two years on those rare occasions when he was forced to acknowledge an invitation. He'd missed births, birthdays, baptisms, communions, and more weddings and funerals than he cared to consider. He'd never even set eyes on his youngest niece, who would be one year old at Christmas. He'd only seen pictures sent via Gregor's e-mail. The MacDades didn't post pictures in public forums, although the paparazzi had captured them on film at least once, right after the baby's birth. In freeze-frame, Luke saw Liam clasping Natalie's shoulder, her resting in a wheelchair with their new babe in her arms. They'd emerged from Lexington General, their smiles tempered by the camera despite their apparent joy. A rare moment that, as the MacDades were all adept at avoiding tabloids or the like.

"Damn it," Lucas muttered as he stuffed his garment bag. If the past two years had taught him nothing else, he'd honed his skills at speed-packing. One never knew when the urge to fly might strike, and Luke had been flying solo for quite some time. He should just roust Kev Mills from bed and have him fire up the chopper. From Lexington to Trenton couldn't take too long, and Kev knew how to keep his mouth shut.

Stalling, damn it. Even knowing he was mentally stalling, Luke couldn't quite settle the decision in his mind. He could join his family at the airport . . . his family. If they were piling into the MacDade jet then the situation was serious.

Growling a curse, he finished dressing and packing and passed through his shadowed efficiency apartment like a phantom on the run. Snatching his car keys from a rack at the door, he let himself out and continued down the carpeted hall to the stairwell. Keeping a flat this close to the MacDade estate had seemed risky at first, but for as often as he stayed, it was worth the cost. Three rooms—bedroom, living room, eat-in kitchen—supplied more than sufficient accommodations when he needed to conduct banking business.

A home base, Lexington, but that might change soon. If all went well with his latest endeavor, he might be transplanting southeast soon. And he would probably relocate the bulk of his business to that little town, Freemont, at the base of his mountain.

His mountain. He liked the sound of that. And it might be close to accurate if his latest purchase closed.

On autopilot, Luke found the rented Lincoln at the curb outside his building and slid behind the wheel, trying not to consider his actions. If he had been in Chicago or San Antonio, he wouldn't be racing to join his family at the blasted airport. He would have a legitimate reason to book a commercial flight—

'Come if you can.' Gregor wouldn't have added that tag line, would never have suggested a reunion of any kind, without a damn good reason. Liam dying . . .? Not possible! No way in hell could his oldest brother, heir to the blasted MacDade dynasty, be dying. Injured, maybe . . . Seriously, injured.

Come if you can.

Uttering another curse, Luke stepped on the gas, glad the streets were empty. Most of the streetlights were blinking at the late night hour. Without the need for directions, he navigated the highway, racing through patches of vapor lights and hoping not to wake any snoozing patrolmen en route. What he would say to his family, he wasn't even certain. 'Hi—I'm home,' might get him clouted from the big guy himself . . . or maybe not. According to his mother, his father might have gotten over his raging, but Luke would rather avoid lending the fellow any reason to rant.

Two years was a long time to pass without speaking, but then—even before that, they were not exactly on speaking terms. This would probably be the same. Mum would welcome him. Probably Gregor, too. Liam . . . Liam might not want to see him either. Unconsciously, Luke eased his tennis shoe off the accelerator, letting the car slow. He hadn't seen Liam in over two years, and Liam was a hell of a lot like Lucius MacDade. So why the hell was he racing through the night to catch a flight where he was neither expected nor likely wanted?

The thought nearly halted him altogether, but his foot pressed down of its own accord. He elevated the Lincoln to hotrod status on the four-lane. If there was no room on the jet, he would book a commercial flight. Regardless of what his father or brother might believe, they were still family. If nothing else, he needed to know—to see for himself that his brother was all right. He would like nothing better than to reach the airport and have Gregor tell him it was a false alarm, a mistake, maybe, and to apologize for scaring the shit out of him.

The surgical waiting room was not entirely empty despite the hour. In the furthest corner from the courtesy phone desk, half concealed by the high-backed vinyl chairs designed kindly to offer privacy, a collection of people gathered. Natalie lent nothing more than a cursory glance at their subdued voices. The window directly across from the doorway drew her like a magnet, and her thoughts spun in erratic circles as she turned a blind eye to the city street below. He must live. No other thought surfaced more clearly than that single benediction. Liam MacDade could not pass into the great unknown—not as long as Natalie MacDade drew breath.

"Umm, Natalie," Mason intruded.

In reflection on the glass in front of her, she spied him.

Head canted, his eyes searched her face at an angle. Like all MacDade males, this one wore arrogance in his posture and rugged jaw despite his advancing years. He wasn't truly that old. Perhaps, slightly younger than Lucius MacDade, and a presence in his own right.

A cousin or uncle in the maternal MacDade line, but even after all these years, Natalie was never positive where anyone fell in their lineage. No differently than in her own clan, it seemed at every celebration—whether a baptism, marriage, or funeral—more relatives climbed from a closet.

Too many to keep track of, though Natalie was sure that a family scribe existed somewhere in the world to keep the records straight.

"Might I ask, my dear," Mason continued as if only to draw her from her daze. "What uhm . . .? What were you doing in that alley? I . . . I seem to recall sending you safely to a hotel. And yet I vaguely recognized that fellow downstairs."

Tired suddenly, Natalie turned enough to lean at the window ledge and met his critical gaze. "I needed to know, Mason," she answered simply, honestly.

Not well could she hide the pain, but she tipped her head and saw her own profile in reflection. She no longer wore the silly glasses, but her golf cap rested at a skewed angle, and loose locks jutted from beneath the cloth. Lord, but she looked a mess . . . and at least that much, she could remedy.

With a sudden thought of the clan descending on this hospital, no doubt in record time via the MacDade jet, she pushed more fully afoot. "I . . . I suppose I better find a restroom. If we're going to be convincing, I need look the part."

"Believe there was a restroom just around the corner, but I could surely find you a private room or staff lounge—"

"I won't be long," she promised and strode toward the door. Reconciliation. 'A mutual attempt . . .'

A one-sided attempt, she corrected silently, and her thoughts carried her into the restroom around the corner. At least it wasn't a communal room with a dozen stalls. Surprisingly clean despite the simple, utilitarian design, the sink provided enough space for her bag. What had she truly been thinking when folding that little black dress so neatly in the depths? Or tucking that slinky negligee at the bottom? A fool's mission. If she'd found him in his own room in the Baymont entertaining businessmen—? A fool's dream. She'd known when embarking on this blasted adventure that she would find him in the arms of another. And yet herein lay the proof of her ulterior motive. Securing the door, she began stripping and needed to stop a dozen times while flashing images of her Highlander laughing and dipping to kiss his blond consort . . . And wiping more tears, she found her spooked shine in the mirror as she fleeted images of her Highlander crumbled in her arms. If he passed—

With every ounce of her willpower, she refused to buckle to the fear or panic at the edges of her mind and called upon the poise drilled into her since birth. If not yet, then soon, a dozen reporters would begin holding court outside—or inside this facility—and it wouldn't do at all to be seen with mascara trailing black tendrils down her cheeks or with her hair spiking in every direction. Slowly, meticulously, she transformed from the teenage style to the sophisticate. Spiked heels and black nylons replaced the jeans and tennis shoes, and in a stopped instant, she recalled packing those items, along with the slinky black dress designed with the sole purpose of seducing the rake. If not much else, she knew he favored her long legs and seemed most often content when she wrapped them about him and held him firm. More than once, the unruly devil had mentioned the success of her aerobics classes and promised to keep the coffers full if only she'd keep attending those classes.

Perhaps, only to spite him, she'd stopped attending formal classes, and the thought brought a tainted smile to her lips. What the rake didn't need to know was her continued daily routines and the benefit of infomercials.

Not needing more than a touch-up of makeup—as she'd drawn the line at stepping into public naked—she brushed and pinned her hair with the diamond comb to send her long locks spilling over one shoulder in a seductive style guaranteed to catch an unruly fellow's eye. And that fellow might not even wake to notice.

The threat of tears stung the corner of her eyes, and she swallowed against a lump. Surely, they should know something soon. And with her thought, she scanned her reflection and decided—that was as good as it would get despite the red haze in wicked contrast to her hazel eyes.

Stuffing her disguise in her bag, she suffered a momentary fear of stepping into that waiting room. If Mason appeared even slightly more distressed—

Nothing had changed. The fellow rose from the arm of the nearest chair, drawn from a pensive pose, and in his swift appraisal and approving grim smile, Natalie knew she had succeeded in the intended fabrication. Perhaps, only Mason would know the extent of the lie they would share—at least only until he found the privacy to share the details with Lucius. No one, least of all her father-in-law, would refute the fabricated lies.

With her thought, Natalie joined Mason and glanced about, verifying that no one stood in earshot. "Have you a thought about how we might explain being at that alley? It's uhm . . . It's not as if I would entertain even a wild notion of visiting the Fairlane Hotel with him."

With a visible appreciation of her clear thinking, Mason considered and wondered. "Were you aware of Miss Helms before this evening?"

Her heart ached. Helms. By Mason's familiarity, this woman held some significance in her husband's life, as if Natalie needed more proof. Should she admit the truth? Or feign ignorance? "I suspected," she answered cryptically.

"I don't know if the young lady will come forth, my dear, but if she should, we might just say he stopped there to break it off with her." He shrugged, rather indifferent. "Otherwise, we might just admit, honestly, that he was supposed to meet someone there. We needn't elaborate details as our lad tends to keep his dealings private."

"You will confide in his father, won't you?"

He appeared apologetic. "I won't have a choice, Nat."

She nodded, oddly relieved by that fact. It was one thing to dupe the public and an altogether different matter to deceive the patriarch of the clan.

In record time, Luke reached the municipal airport, slightly surprised to recognize the sleek black limo speeding through the gates onto the tarmac just ahead. Wheeling into a parking space in front of the small office complex, Luke grabbed his bag off the seat and slipped from the car, already running toward the gate before he considered his actions. Doubtful airport security would shoot him, but they would likely take aim. Still, unless he hurried, he would miss the flight. Already, the sizeable private craft had taxied onto the runway, engine whistling. Steps lowered, lights flashing, the open portal door glowed, and several suited silhouettes milled near the sleek silver bird. The limo's taillights blazing red neon brake lights as it drew near the waiting Cessna.

Cursing, Luke poured on more speed, drawing from his field and track training to sprint through the closing gates, spotting the security man stepping from a booth to his right. "I'm with them!" he shouted as he passed and might only have escaped a bullet by the lights reflecting off the Louie Vuitton logo on his garment bag.

Already, the limo had stopped, and under the brilliant vapor lights, Luke recognized the various shapes and sizes, blond heads of the bodies emerging. His immense father turned. His petite mother received his father's hand as she launched from the limo. Another larger male paused to assist another woman—not Natalie. This stout young woman carrying a bundle was not Natalie but rather the nanny whose name eluded him though he might have seen her a time or two when Liam and Natalie had first lived on the estate. At the fringes of the arriving party, several of the private security men poised to act, already looking his way, but Luke's attention remained on the nanny. That he might see his niece, his two small nephews, hadn't occurred to him. The last time he'd seen either of the boys, one had been barely five, the other three. Seven and five now, they appeared impressively tall and capable as they hurried at Gregor's flanks toward the steps.

What made Gregor pause and look, Luke was not altogether certain, but as his brother halted in the half turn, looking in his direction, Luke considered turning, fleeing. Instead, he slowed, nearly walking by the time he reached the group.

"What the bloody hell'd ye do, lad? Invent a time machine?" Gregor asked with the quirky lifted brow that all MacDades seemed to inherit.

"I was in the neighborhood," Luke said in a breath, bouncing his gaze to see his father poised at the bottom of the step, looking toward him rather than following Megan up the steps. At least his mother hadn't spotted him yet. He could still run—

"Let's go then," Gregor stated, nudging the taller, wide-eyed boy toward the plane, shifting his vacant hand to touch Luke's shoulder as carefully as a man might handle dynamite. Even in the artificial light, his pale blue eyes conveyed the tension, just shy of terror, and his voice, even with the heavy brogue, vibrated with emotion. "We need hurry."

Nothing more needed said. Accepting the signal, Luke started toward the steps and nearly bulked again when finding his father still looking toward him, stopped at the steps—maybe to bar entry. Doubtful his father could mistake him for someone else, not with Luke's white-blond waves glowing neon. That he looked like Liam—could pass for a twin if he were older—had determined Luke's decision to wear his hair long and grow a beard to match his mustache. Luckily, despite his Scottish heritage, his facial hair remained more brown than red—almost as golden as Gregor's hair—and still not much of a disguise.

Before Luke could decide on his flight, Lucius turned at the steps and followed the nanny, reaching his hand to her back to offer balance and escort.

"Uncle Luke?" the young voice came hesitantly, and Luke dropped his gaze as he accepted Gregor's nudge and again started toward the plane.

"I am," Luke offered and might have continued with the reintroduction if not for the smaller boy clasping his hand, drawing his gaze. Where the older boy could be Liam's clone—and his own—with his white-blond curls, the younger boy favored Natalie with soft honey-colored curls blowing in the warm breeze and his more hazel eyes aglow. Still, the MacDade genes hadn't skipped him; only the coloring was different. The shape of his nose, the natural curve in his lips, and his almond-shaped eyes were inherent.

"My daddy's been hurt," the boy spoke while tugging as if this were the most natural reunion in the world and accepted the stranger on sight. "We need a hurry."

Apparently, he wouldn't need to book a commercial flight, and his brother wasn't taking any chances.

At the steps, Gregor sent the boys—and Luke—up ahead, apparently condoning and appreciating the youngster's acceptance.

Stepping into the cabin, Luke suffered the doubts yet again, spotting his immense father not far enough away, but before he could react, his mother turned.

No turning back.

In an instant, the tears flashed over her light green eyes, and for such a little woman, she moved like lightning—maybe like a pixie—launching toward him and throwing her arms over his shoulders. "Oh God, darling, I'm glad you're here . . . It's your brother—" And she couldn't finish. Whether she needed to withhold a sob for her benefit or to spare the children, she swallowed the sound against his neck.

"Let's we get seated," Lucius spoke in a tempered tone, and perhaps, that low volume verified the seriousness of the situation.

Over his mother's strawberry blond locks, Luke found his father's stark blue gaze, and the last of his reservations vanished as his father offered a slight nod, a greeting of acceptance—as if he had expected nothing less.

Shuffled into a window seat with his youngest nephew landing beside him, Luke lost his bag into the hands of a slender young steward who managed to appear pleasant and all-business at the same time. Like all MacDade staff, this fellow had probably been hand-selected by the head of the clan, probably boasted Scottish heritage, and would work well under fire. Before the steps and door folded, several more bags and a small security detail came aboard. Bags were stowed, seatbelts checked, lights dimmed.

Across the aisle, past the older boy, Gregor rested at an angle, gazing toward Luke with an odd tight kink in his golden mustache. Despite the worry etched across his brow, he appeared dumbfounded, and the questions loomed large in his pale eyes. Without a doubt, he was considering the time between his e-mail and Luke's arrival, likely wondering how long Luke had been in the vicinity.

Tilting his focus through the portal as the jet taxied onto the runway strip, Luke reconsidered his decision yet again, deciding he would part company with the clan as soon as he knew his brother's condition. Catching this flight had been foolish. Inevitably, his father would begin searching again; his mother would likely be hurt that he hadn't contacted her for a visit. He did call her though. At least every two months, he called to speak in person, and between times, he communicated via the Internet. Not with any consistency, to be sure, but he generally responded to Gregor's messages.

That he was not big on communicating with anyone from the clan shouldn't truly bother them one way or the other. He'd spent most of his life in a boarding school, more familiar with most of his teachers than his parents, closer to friends than ever his older brothers. Too many years between them, he'd decided long ago and simply accepted that fact.

The jet shot down the runway and launched, and Luke glimpsed his nephew plastered in the seat, his expressive eyes more thrilled with flying than worried, but for such a young face, the sobriety remained fixed. Bright boy. He knew this was no pleasure trip . . . but just how the hell bad was it? And where was Natalie? Gregor hadn't mentioned her, so she couldn't have been hurt. So, what the hell had happened, here?

Luke barely considered asking for details despite the children's presence when he heard a cell phone ping and glimpsed his father pushing off his seat. The jet was large enough to seat ten people comfortably and boasted reclining chairs, a table, and a bedroom in the rear compartment, ideal for transatlantic flights. Still, the plane was not large enough for Lucius to walk out of hearing range, even if Megan wasn't gripping his arm.

"Aye, Mason . . . Uh huh . . . Aye . . . And . . .? Good God almighty, where the fuck were you?"

Uh oh. Only that thought echoed in Luke's mind as he recognized the descending tone. And that was not a word the chieftain of the MacDade clan would bandy about, let alone in the presence of his wife and grandchildren. Unless the fellow had changed a great deal in the last two years, he was usually in more firm control.

Far lower, he growled, "And Artie? Where the hell was . . .? Bloody hell, Mason . . . Aye, we'll be there . . . Aye, send the bloody limo to the airport for us . . ."

The phone clapping shut sounded more like a gunshot, and apparently, even Megan decided she better wait for the details. Turning, striding between the seats, Lucius navigated to the kitchen area, bypassing the steward to collect a bottle of liquor from a fully stocked cabinet.

Hesitantly, the steward asked, "Can I get that for you, sir?"

"I have it," Lucious stated. "Tend to the others."

Tense, only more tense with that low pitch, Luke wondered as much about that phone call as about the circumstances. What the hell had happened here? Just how bad was Liam . . .? And why did it sound as if Artair MacDade, Liam's personal bodyguard, wasn't with him? Before Luke could more than catch Gregor's likewise tense gaze, the steward intruded, asking for orders.

Both boys asked for colas—the older one broaching the request, the younger following suit in an amusingly adult voice—but Gregor intervened in a strained, lighthearted tone. "Think m' lads here would prefer milk or juice if we're well stocked, Hank. What say, boys? Maybe a cocoa?"

"With whipped cream do you think?" the older boy, Jamie asked.

"What say, Hank? Whipped cream?"

"I do believe we can accommodate the young lad," Hank stated, giving away his heritage.

"Aye, then. Whipped cream it is, and a bourbon for me and my brother if ye don't mind."

"Coming right up, sir," the fellow agreed as if truly happy to be of service. He apparently already knew Megan's preference for tea and needed only a second to collect the nanny's order.

For a moment, Luke thought about stepping out of the seat and greeting the nanny so he might glimpse his niece, but his nearest nephew, Micheal, intruded.

"If you dinnae like bourbon, sir? You could have some cocoa," the boy offered politely.

"The bourbon will do, but thank you," Luke said as he eyed the bright eyes. As quick-witted as ever a MacDade, the boy was well aware of these dire circumstances but in inherent MacDade form, vowed to be brave. With a thought of how the boy had probably been awakened and shuffled into traveling clothes, Luke suggested, "You could probably drink your cocoa, then rest for a little while. I'd be glad to wake you when we land."

"Well, I might then," he said and dashed his gaze across the aisle, apparently seeking his older brother's guidance.

At the same time, Luke caught the dark blue eyes—Liam's eyes—studying him from across the aisle, and whatever the boy was pondering remained a mystery, though he appeared to be working out a puzzle. Far too old and intent, those eyes, and Luke grasped the simple truth—he was looking at the future chieftain of the MacDade clan. This boy, like his father, probably already knew his place in the world, and when the time came, he'd take the helm. The younger boy, too, would be groomed—like Gregor—to take his place if ever his brother fell.

Was that the tension and fear haunting Gregor's pale blue eyes? A fear that he might be forced into the role until this young boy could reach the proper age?

As if a weight had dropped into Luke's stomach, he felt suddenly gut-punched with the revelation that his older brother might truly be dying. They were here—his brother's children rousted from their beds in the quick of night, being flown across three states—to see their father for the last time?

He needed the bourbon by the time it came, and although it wouldn't have been his preference, far more comfortable with a blasted beer, the liquor offered a balm on his tight throat. No matter how he might feel about his family—or failed to feel—the thought of losing one of them was a reality check. Invincible, they were not—any more than they were blasted immortal, no matter that they lived like blasted gods.

3

Between the drone of the jet engine and the silence, Luke was nearly dozing when the motion woke him. He oriented on the instant as his mother passed in the aisle, joining his father at the table behind him. Across the aisle, Gregor appeared awake and aware. Between them, the boys slept, their chairs leaned back; they curled toward each other, backs to their uncles. They were close, these two. Like Liam and Gregor, bouncing off each other through thick and thin—

"What did Mason say, love? Has he heard anything?" Megan asked, barely above a whisper.

"They were taking our lad to surgery," Lucius answered in an equally low pitch.

"What was that about—where was he, Lucius? Does he know what happened? How?"

"I don't know the way of it, Meg m' love," he said grimly. "The details were fairly muddled."

"You know something," Megan persisted.

"Aye, I know our lad was on his own when these dirty bastards mugged him," Lucius said in a lower tone. "Aye, but not entirely alone, as it turns out. Somehow, our Natalie was there with him, and it was her, our Natalie, that probably saved his life, according to Mason."

"N-Natalie was there, Lucius? With him when it happened—not in a hotel—"

"I truly dinnae know the extent here, Meg," Lucius said carefully. "Somehow, Natalie was there, supposedly in a hotel, and Artie seeing she arrived there safely . . . Next, she's in the bloody alley, fighting alongside our lad and saving his life from a dozen muggers. There's what I know, m' Meg. And it's not a hell of a lot."

"Wh-where was Mason? Did he say?"

"Aye, in the bloody limousine two blocks away," Lucius said grimly.

"I-I don't understand, Lucius," she strained on the brink of a sob. "How . . . how could this even happen? He and Artie—Mason—they're always together."

"Not always," Lucius spoke with such soft care that the implication was clear.

The only reason Liam would ditch his bodyguard and personal assistant would be if he were stepping out on his wife. So, what the hell was his wife doing in an alley with him?

By now, Luke would have thought his brother would have sowed enough blasted wild oats. The arrogant bastard had been at it since he was ten or eleven years old—his exploits legendary—and apparently, marriage hadn't changed a thing. With a wink, a smile, a snap of his fingers, Liam could probably tempt a blasted nun, and no one thought any less of him, so long as he was discreet—which he was, as a rule. Only once or twice in the past eight years had Liam slipped up.

Just about two years ago. Just after graduation, Luke recalled, himself escaping the tabloid-worthy news of his commencement and Liam head-lining one of those grocery store tabloids—the giant ducking from the paparazzi with a stewardess under his arm and a laugh on his mustached lips. Aside from that, he'd once been captured kissing their movie star cousin, Carmin McCullum, on the cheek. That gossip made a splash only until Carmin's boyfriend/manager threatened to sue the tabloid—not that it hurt Carmin's career. Having an affair with a married heir to a billion-dollar empire hadn't harmed her reputation one iota, and she'd milked that bit of sensationalism for all it was worth. According to Megan, Natalie had gotten a kick out of it, too. Allegedly, she and Carmin had shared a good laugh and posed for other paparazzi together, arm in arm. Luke had never heard what transpired after the stewardess pictures, but he doubted Natalie had laughed.

Anyone even remotely close to the MacDade clan knew that Liam wasn't the most faithful bloke on the planet, and even if he was innocent, his face was a little too well known to be ignored if he stood within a dozen yards of a beautiful woman.

God knows, Luke had needed to duck from his fair share of the paparazzi before he'd grown his hair and beard. First, the recognition, then the snapshots, then the revelation that he was the youngest, not the oldest heir to the MacDade dynasty. And the questions bombarded him anyway. Even after he'd changed the spelling of his last name, he'd suffered his share of nosy parkers.

Had Liam's indiscretions somehow led to whatever the hell happened here? And how the hell was that even possible? His brother, if not faithful, was discreet, else more pictures would be circulating.

Questions, only more questions. And the main one hadn't even been answered. An alley? A fight? A fistfight that Liam had lost—or would have lost without Natalie?

There was a whole lot more to this story than Luke was hearing, and not even Gregor appeared ready to enlighten him.

An intruder. He'd always felt like an outsider in the MacDade clan, and this wasn't the exception. If he wanted to learn the details, he'd need to hang close and listen—and there were seconds on end when he wondered why he would even bother to seek explanations or details. He had his own life, his livelihood. He'd stopped depending on the MacDades, financially or emotionally a long time ago, and he'd just as soon leave it that way. And he was certain, they felt the same.

Through a drunken haze, Liam struggled to awaken, not certain of a thing save for the odd soft flutters at his head and the distant stuttering of mechanical sounds.

"Shhh, rest, darling . . . You'll be all right . . ."

He had heard that melody before this moment. Soft lyrical words, the quivering voice of an angel, and lips brushing against his ear. In fuzzy glimpses, he drew the memory to the surface and tried struggling to rise, to ward off an attack. A hand pressed firm but gently at his shoulder; another halted his head from rising, forcing him onto the pillow. And a feat too great to combat against either. Huffing a breath, Liam drew his world into focus, half expecting to find an Amazon woman hovering over him. At an angle, he found the face and struggled to make sense of his memory.

In a fleeting instant, he recalled a moment in shadows, a single flash of a child—no child. Despite the conflicting images in his mind, he was nearly certain that a woman had swirled in that alley. A willowy woman dressed more like a boy, with odd reflections where eyes should be, and a warrior by no other definition. Pivoting, spinning, she'd sent his assailants sailing on a fierce wind. . . and the gentle words, the soft lyrics . . .

"Are you near to waking, honey?"

Oh, and this voice was gentle, too. Like a familiar song to soothe the rising panic behind his eyes. Clearly, he recognized her slender face, her livid hazel eyes the color of a freshly budding forest. She was a wonder, as lovely a woman as ever to grace the earth, and for the life of him, he couldn't decide why she might be hovering over him, stroking his forehead, smiling ever so slightly. When last he'd seen her . . . she'd been curled like a minx on a daybed in their solarium, reading a book, barely acknowledging his parting amenity. Head canting more, his senses floating in a weird wonder, his focus wavered over the cascade of her auburn hair. In a curtain, the silky waves spilled over her bare shoulder and lanced fire in the neon light. And still more to discover. Black silk parted in his line of sight—carefully parted to contrast beautifully with a mere hint of the smooth white orbs concealed therein. If he had the strength—his thoughts halted with the reality.

She'd kicked him from their bed . . . So, for whom was this feast provided? Even in the fog, he knew an odd outrage.

"Aye . . . and there's no sense in this," he muttered, closing his eyes and forfeiting even the effort to rise.

"Just rest, darling . . . You'll be all right."

Opening only one eye to verify the vision above him or the absence thereof, he grasped something of reality. He had survived. He rested in a hospital . . . and his estranged wife hovered above him, looking for all the world as if she'd spent the night on the town. Perhaps, he was not awake. "Errr uhm . . . ye a mirage? Er, a . . . vision yet to carry me away to some . . . otherworldly. . ." Talking hurt. His voice—even to his own ears— sounded like sandpaper scraping wood.

Her glossy lips quivered. A hint of familiar laughter danced in her hazel eyes, but the worry flashed nearly as quick. As if she were a sprite to flicker here and there, she seemed one moment above him and in the next, dousing his parched lips with a cool sponge.

Afraid she might disappear if he blinked, he watched her more closely, not certain if she moved like lightning or if his thoughts dragged through mud. "Ye-ou arrre a quick li'l sprite," he decided and saw the glimmer of laughter yet again, not certain of a thing else the strangeness of this moment. "Wh-where the bloo-oody hell am I?" he wondered.

"You, sir, are in Southern General Hospital," she said gently. "But you're going to be fine—" Perhaps, she sensed his desire to rise. She pressed his shoulder again, and worry flashed through her blood-riddled eyes. "Stay down, love," she said smoothly, and perhaps, only the endearment slipping off her lips halted him. "You need to stay still, Liam. You're hurt. You'll be all right, but you have over a hundred stitches . . . I don't know how much you remember . . ."

He twitched his head, certain what he remembered was faulty. "I dinnae think much."

The smile quivered on her lips again as she studied him. "Aye, and ye've spent a great deal of time with yer da, lately."

Damn. That dialect slipping off his tongue was not a fabrication in his mind. That he might be even more confused occurred to him as he sought the sanity in her smile. "Yer . . . speaking in tongues," he decided and tried swallowing nails.

Again, the sponge dabbed at his lips, and he watched the sobriety in her eyes as she managed to spill cool drops of water on his tongue. Appearing truly sorrowful, she caught his gaze and smiled faintly. "The nurses should be back in soon, honey. Until they say differently, I'm afraid this is all you can have. I don't know if it's helping—"

Belated, he flinched at a burning sensation flashing through his waist and lower.

"Don't! Blast you," she snapped suddenly, pressing at his shoulder. "Just lie still. Are you in pain? Do you need something for the pain?"

Well, his own fault, that fire; he'd tried to move, if only to grab that blasted sponge that looked more like a lollipop in her hand. He was not a child, not his daughter nor one of his sons to need a lollipop for a doctor's visit . . . and that was no lollipop. Water. His focus sailed to the cup in her other hand, aware on some distant plane that she'd dipped that sponge several times to sate his parched throat. With a mere glance, she seemed to grasp his need and dunked the sponge, lifting it dripping to his lips. More grateful than he could put into words, he found her watching him closely, and for a moment, they were young again . . . children as oddly conflicted as ever in the past.

"You'll be all right, Liam," she said gently. "Truly, hon. The doctors assured me, you'll be all right. It was bad . . . but you'll be all right. . ."

Natalie knew the instant his eyes closed, he'd fallen under the effects of either anesthesia or pain. He needed to rest. According to the surgeon, Dr. Emerson, they'd spent the past several hours sewing him back together where that blade had pierced and torn. Only by the grace of God, the knife had missed any major organs, but if he were a lesser man, he would've been eviscerated. Even in hindsight, Natalie shuddered with the thought. Emerson hadn't pulled any punches while addressing her and Mason. Liam MacDade was one lucky young man. An eighth inch in any direction, that blade would have struck his kidneys or main artery or scored his stomach and bowel. He was intact. Fully. And would make a full recovery with only battle scars to remain in evidence . . . so long as he heeded doctor's warnings and remained still.

Sighing, Natalie brushed gently at the blond silk at his temple. Barely above a whisper, though no others stood in range to hear, she told him, "Rest, my own . . . just rest easy." For himself, for their children . . . for her . . . he need rest and recover.

And for his parents and siblings, she added with the flashing memory of Mason hurrying from the waiting room.

No more comfortable in his family's company than at the onset, Luke fell into step alongside Gregor en route to the limo and slid into the seat furthest from his father with his mother and oldest nephew between them. Across the slight aisle, the nanny rested holding the still-sleeping baby, but even in the shadows, Luke caught enough of a glimpse to see the cherub face, pixie nose, and tussled blond curls. Arabella. Arabella Megan MacDade. She was beautiful, in no uncertain terms, and Luke smiled his appreciation, still smiling faintly when the nanny returned the slight greeting with a nod. He should have taken a moment on the flight to greet her and see his niece, and he wasn't sure what had stopped him. Vaguely, he recalled citing a plethora of reasons to avoid rocking the boat by moving around that cabin—only beginning with waking the boys or baby. That he preferred not to stir his father's ire probably accounted for his feigned sleep throughout that blasted flight.

With the tinted glass adding to the night, Luke watched the gloomy scenery passing, unconsciously sizing up the property value against the visible urban decay. Not bad. Not a place where he might buy a dozen houses and erect a strip mall with any tremendous profit. The houses appeared well-kept, lawns well-tended with flower islands and boxes adding curb appeal. A nice neighborhood—not likely a place where a 6' 6" giant would get mugged even if he were walking alone after midnight. Anyone with any good sense would run from a guy Liam's size, let alone tangle with a fellow who walked like a large lethal cat, all grace and arrogance.

Even before pulling into the neon glow of the emergency entrance, Luke noticed the news van at the curb and suffered the instant dread with a thought of the paparazzi. If not already, the instant the hospital or police released Liam's name, the media circus would begin . . . or maybe not, he dared to hope. This wasn't Kentucky where the MacDade name might be instantly recognized and the news people eager for any hint of a story. With any luck, they could all remain invisible.

Deciding against making a scene to collect his bag from the limo's trunk, Luke vowed to return for it as soon as he knew Liam was all right. Falling into step with the younger nephew finding his hand again, Luke spared the boy a glance even as he heard a bored reporter fire a question toward them.

"Are you here about that mugging victim?"

"Humph," Gregor growled as he drew the older boy into the space between them. "Not the brightest bulb in the socket, that one, eh?"

"Good sign," Lucius commented in a lower tone. "Means they dinnae know who he is yet," he added and ushered Megan and the nanny ahead through the electronic doors.

In the early morning hour, only a half dozen people lingered in the waiting room, one of whom was a woman standing, rocking a baby with the slow steady rhythm that all natural mothers perfected. A security man came to attention as Lucius cleared the door, and the triage nurse nearly jammed a thermometer up a young black man's nose.

"Hey—take it easy, lady!"

Lucius barely started. "I'm looking for my son—"

The gray doors burst open across the room, and to the sight of Mason Eldridge, Lucius veered away from the security man. To his credit, Mason kept coming, and Luke questioned the fellow's sanity for not turning and running with the giant bearing down on him.

"Where's m' lad, Mason?"

"In surgery," Mason stated as he flung his hands forward, one reaching for Lucius, the other to Meg, clasping hand and shoulder, respectively. Tears washed over his darting pale blue eyes. What little color remained in his generally sturdy cheeks drained as the emotions ripped new lines beneath his bearded cheeks.

Feeling even worse the intruder to see Eldridge breaking, Luke hung back and still too close, he saw the tears leaking, bearded lips quivering. Uncle Mason's once sturdy frame seemed to collapse before their eyes.

"It's bad, Luciusss," Eldridge broke, pleading. "It's baaad. He lossst sooo—"

"Hush, Mason," Lucius commanded in a voice three octaves lower than normal, then looked over the gray head, locking on the nanny, lancing off his grandsons. "Keep the li'l uns here for a moment," he said and again, looked down at the stricken round faces. "Stay with yer nan 'til we find ye m'aither."

Just that quick, Lucius took command, needing only a glance and nod to station two of their private security men with the nanny. Lancing Gregor—and Luke—in a firm glance, including them both in a nod, he directed Mason toward the doors and drew his wife under his arm. A MacDade would never break in public. Protocol dictated that they hold it together, and Mason got the message, struggling for composure as he hurried ahead.

Who made those rules, Luke wondered as he grasped the ice spilling down his spine, the first genuine case of fear sliding over him. Mason Eldridge was not a man to panic. The fellow had stood at the chieftain's righthand longer than Luke had graced the earth. He wasn't some simpering bureaucrat pencil pusher to collapse at any bad turn. His reaction, his breaking, was far worse than his words could ever be.

Gregor clasped Luke's arm, his elbow, and Luke saw enough in the spooked high shine to understand, Gregor needed that connection to hold himself together as much as he meant to offer comfort. Together they passed through the automatic doors that either the guard or nurse had engaged.

Before the doors ever shut behind them, Lucius held Mason against the wall, the lapels of his black suit crunched in his fist, and the man nearly stood on his toes. Megan, slight and sleek, clasped her husband's arm, but whether she meant to thwart his rage or add to it, remained a mystery.

"You will tell me, now, Mason," Lucius spoke in flawless American English, which was not a good sign, not a good sign at all. "What the fuck happened to my son, and how badly is he hurt?"

Stammering, Mason managed, "He was mugged—a gang—a street gang the police are saying . . . forced him into an alley . . . kn-knives . . ." And he was breaking again, tears spilling down his cheeks. "Luciusss I'mmm sorry. Sh-shoulda been meee—"

"Pull your God damn self together, man."

If Lucius MacDade was not holding him jacked against the wall, that order might be easier to accept, but Luke decided not to mention that detail, preferring to remain slightly out of reach. He'd never liked standing too near his father, not even on a good day. Easier, safer, keeping an arm's reach away—and his father had a long reach. Luke considered backing another step or two, but the doors had closed. This hallway was too narrow—not more than ten feet wide. If Lucius decided to pound Mason to a pulp, there could be casualties, over and above the nurses, who had stopped, stared, apparently trying to decide if they should call security.

Surprisingly, Mason drew breath and might have tried collecting on his toes. Lucius seemed to notice and lowered his hold accordingly. "I'm—I'm—sorry."

"Aye, such I heard. Now tell me if these bastards been caught."

"They—they ran, Lucius," Mason said while heaving for breath, still too wrecked to speak normally. "God almighty, it's . . . he's bad, Lucius," he repeated and nearly buckled to the vibration in his voice. "He—they don't know how many times—places, he was stabbed, but—but he lost s-so much blood."

After a moment, Lucius decided, "M' lad won't let a few cuts or the like get him down, Mason. We'll not believe else." With his words, he pulled the slightly smaller man off the wall and into an embrace, offering him the comfort of an embrace as if only now remembering they were friends and family. "All right then. Pull yourself together," Lucius spoke in lower pitch. "I'd like to see our Natalie now . . ."

Once they passed from the emergency department, the utilitarian beige hallways were empty, but even without Mason leading the procession, doubtful they would need directions with the overhead signs charting their path to the surgical area. Unlike the busy hum of the emergency rooms, only the whisper of treads on the tiles broke the silence as they rounded turns and passed through electronic double doors. Passing through the surgical department doors, Luke spotted the tall man standing sentinel at another set of doors labeled 'Recovery.'

For as far back as Luke could remember, Artie MacDade had shadowed Liam, a polar opposite in coloring from black hair and mustache to dark eyes with a propensity to appear dead when he was on point. A bodyguard, an attaché, a friend when they were off duty, as quick to share a good laugh and a drink as a trip to the motherland. Presently, the fellow appeared as rigid as a bronze statue, turning only his blank black eyes to identify the intruders. Nothing changed in the man's demeanor, not a flinch or tick to suggest the nervous posturing that some of the guards had always exhibited when the elder MacDade arrived on scene. Only as they drew near, Luke recognized the tension about the eyes and kinked mustache, doubting the fellow had gained age lines over the past few years since Luke had last seen him, and he was not much older than Liam. Dressed in jeans, black tennis shoes and a casual suit jacket, no doubt to conceal his weapon, he hadn't been engaged in a formal capacity when this situation developed. More like a night on the town, Luke considered with distant memories to make the assessment. From the time the fellow had completed his formal police training and returned to the estate, he and Liam had spent as much time carousing together as working.

So, what the hell happened this evening? Could Liam truly have sent his bodyguard off to escort his wife to a hotel then went about a casual affair?

"Artie?" Lucius spoke in a low tone and need not continue.

"He's out of surgery, sir, and Mrs. M. insisted on seeing him in recovery," Artair answered with a natural reverence. "According to the surgeon, the operation went as well as could be expected."

One does not beat around the bush when addressing the patriarch of the MacDade clan, and those last words weren't lost on anyone present. Luke gripped internally as fiercely as his mother gripped his father's hand. '. . . as well as could be expected.' Not 'good.' Not 'great.' Not 'he'll make a full recovery.'

Liam wasn't out of the woods yet, by any stretch.

"We'll just step into the room here," Lucius decided, turning as he signaled toward the designated waiting room which they'd just passed.

The room was empty at the predawn hour. At least two dozen high-backed lounge chairs, couches and single chairs with tables in the mix, spread out through the rather large room. A room wide enough to accommodate a small conference meeting at first glance, conveniently equipped with a coffee station, not yet in operation. Toward a circle of comfortable chairs, Lucius directed Megan. As she settled on the edge of a lounger seat, he turned to one of the remaining security men. "Go get the nanny and bairn, Ben."

"Aye, sir," the fellow spoke as he accepted the command and reversed course.

Lingering aside, Luke considered sitting with his mother, but caught himself moving away, gravitating toward the courtesy island. A step up from a vending machine, an industrial machine offered a hot water carafe on one burner, coffee on the other. Absently, he set about turning the machine on, finding the coffee, while at the same time listening to his father console his mother, offering assurances that they both knew could be wrong. Gregor had settled alongside their mother, and he too, offered encouraging words.

"He'll be all right, mum. You'll see . . ."

"Mason," his father spoke then. "Let's we step over here, now, and have a chat."

The absence of that Scottish brogue sent a prickle down Luke's spine. He'd heard it just often enough in his youth to know he'd rather not stand too near his father now. Poor Uncle Mase wasn't off the hook yet, not by a long shot.

They'd traveled far enough from the door not to be overheard, and Luke chanced to wonder if his father might have forgotten he was present for as clearly as he heard the words.

"Start with what the police are saying and let's we go from there."

"They don't know much, Lucius," Mason said on a breath, his voice leveling toward a more natural business tone. "But they think Liam was targeted because of money—his wedding ring and the uhm . . . his signet ring. There's a Det. Harbinder assigned to the case, and him saying it's too early. A few witnesses saw several men fleeing the alley, but there's no good descriptions yet."

"Mm hm," Lucious murmured, apparently collecting more in what Mason hadn't said. "So, it wasnae the nicest part of town m' lad was in then?"

"Honestly, Lucius, I wouldn't have thought it that dangerous, which I pointed out to Harbinder."

"Aye? And what else did ye tell him, Mase. Let's we start there, now."

"I . . . uhm. Well, you know the lad and lass been separated, aye?"

"Aye, for a few months, now, and you told the police that?"

This was something new, and clearly evidenced Liam's discretion as that tidbit of gossip would've drawn the paparazzi like flies on shit.

"I didnae make it sound like a few months," Mason said carefully. "Led them to believe was more recent, and well, they knew Liam was in the Fairmont Hotel, and that's not a five star, Lucius. I couldn't well say the lad was conducting a business meeting there at midnight so I might have alluded to Liam and his wife reconciling and Liam breaking it off with a mistress."

Oh, bloody hell, a 'mistress?' Like some god damned lord of a bygone era? Girlfriend or hooker might have been more fitting if Luke was catching the gist of this.

"I asked for their discretion, Lucius—the police, and they assured me, the press wouldn't hear it from them . . . but to be honest, I wouldn't count on it. I . . . I don't think they've quite figured out who Liam is or his connection to High Land, Inc."

"So, what then? These Mc-bitches just got lucky mugging my lad for his jewels?"

"I think that's exactly what this Harbinder's implying after seeing the limo," Mason said in disgust. "Think they see him as a young man in the wrong place at the wrong time."

"All right then," Lucius said in a lower tone. "So, now, and you need mention how m' lass got pulled into this—and how the bloody hell did she end up fighting alongside him?"

"She uhm . . . I don't know exactly the details, Lucius, only that she suspected Liam's indiscretions and decided to find out for herself, as near as I can determine," he said as if truly puzzled. "She showed up at a lounge where the lad met up with the Pendleton boy—wearing a peculiar disguise that might have worked if I'd not caught her watching Liam. The look on her face, Lucius . . . She just looked more sad than furious, but uhm—" He decided to hurry. "I didn't want any scene there in The Castaway, so I talked to her then led her out to a cab she had waiting—"

"You put a bloody heiress to a bloody fortune in a cab—"

"Lucius, I didnae know what else to do. Liam was already getting ready to leave with his blasted mistress. I paid the cab driver handsomely to see that she reached the hotel safely, then I booked her the penthouse suite in the Baymont where we were staying."

"Aye . . . and sent Artair after her."

"He was off the clock, but aye, I sent him to see that she arrived safely," Mason said worriedly. "But she never checked in. I thought maybe she went back to the airport, and I had Clarice checking the airlines and cab companies."

"Aye, so let me get this straight," Lucius said in a discreet dark tone. "I had an heiress running aboot in a blasted taxicab and an heir diddling a mistress in a seedy motel . . . and you didnae think to call Gillis?"

"It's not the first time Liam saw that lass, Lucius, and they're generally discreet about their rendezvous. I didnae think we needed to involve Gillis as it was not as if Natalie advertised her identity. The way she was dressed—more like a tomboy—doubtful anyone could have recognized her, and Liam can generally take care of himself. I just didn't see the danger—"

"You get paid well to see there isn't any danger, Mason," Lucius said in low warning.

"I'm sorry, Lucius. If . . . if he doesn't recover—"

"What exactly did that doctor say when they took him for surgery?"

Tense, wanting that answer as well, Luke continued making the coffee on autopilot, dropping a premixed pod of grounds into the filter basket, setting the machine to brew, and searching behind doors for Styrofoam cups and whatnots.

"He . . . he was stabbed, Lucius. At least four times that they knew for sure as he has cuts on his arms and hands, but one . . . one was bad," he strained. "The-ey hit him in the gut. They . . . he lost a lot of blood . . . and they nearly lost him in the ambulance. That's when I called you . . . When we got here."

"Aye," Lucius said distractedly and maybe needed to concentrate on the details. "So, our Natalie followed m' lad to that hotel and somehow managed to see him in trouble."

"I . . . I think she has the knack, Lucius. That's the only way I can explain it."

Bloody hell, now that, too. *The knack.* The gift of second sight. Of course, these old Scottish devils would blame the mystical. No matter which way the winds blew, fairies, pixies or mystical gifts would be blamed for either Liam's demise or recovery, and poor Natalie would be forced to endure a lifetime of 'fey,' just like Gram MacDade whose talents were legendary. It couldn't possibly be that Natalie figured out Liam was cheating on her—no matter their separation—and decided to catch him in the act and confront the unruly reprobate. That would be far more true to form in the MacDade family history.

Luke had grown up hearing about the infamous exploits of MacDades from randy spouses to pirates to IRA supporters. Hell, even his father had been accused of joining that cause, and Luke couldn't say he'd be surprised. God knows, the MacDades had never fully broken ties to the blasted Motherland. Even he'd been dragged across the pond to meet a few of the clansmen and women in the Highlands.

As if his father were following his own thoughts, Luke heard the low command.

"You need make the call o'er to Cyrus and the others here in the states, Mason. Let them know our lad's been injured. Have them spread the word. Then get on the horn with Craig Cavenaugh, have him arrange for Liam's transfer to a private hospital. I want him moved closer to home as soon as it's safe."

His father paused, possibly only to watch his grandchildren arrive and hurry to sit with their grandmother before he continued, "Then call Gillis if you huvnae already, and get a full security team here before morning."

"I already called him, Lucius," Mason said grimly. "I sent for a team and I had him start a private investigation. He might already have spoken with that Det. Harbinder. We should hear soon."

"All right then," Lucius said distractedly. "So then—better get on the phone with Marion and have her put together a press release. I think we're already on borrowed time, here, Mase. As soon as a few industrious reporters figure this out, we'll be in for a siege."

Why exactly Luke braved his father's wrath to carry him a Styrofoam cup of black coffee, he couldn't have said, but he landed under his father's intense scrutiny while handing over the cup, delivering one to Mason as well. Belatedly, if only by his uncle's startled eyes, Luke realized he had been invisible, and something in that revelation struck an odd hurt chord inside of him. God knows, he'd never been the most social MacDade before his graduation two years ago, but he'd never been a phantom in their midst.

"Uncle Mase," he managed by way of a greeting, and before the bewildered man could find words, Luke turned and returned to the small alcove where several other empty cups waited. His mother drank tea, never coffee, but after a second's search, he realized the improbability of finding her imported brand and settled for a generic bag. Setting the tea to brew in a cup of hot water, needing the busywork even if he were reduced to butler status, he found hot cocoa mixes in the dry goods box and prepared the cups before pouring his own and Gregor's coffee. Odd, the little things to be retained in the subconscious, like his father's preference for strong black coffee, his mother's tea brand, his brother's tolerance of coffee if one added enough milk and sugar to wonder what he truly preferred—coffee light, or milk dark.

For a few moments Luke was busy mixing and delivering drinks, but he drew the line at waiting on the nanny who was free to serve herself when Megan collected the still sleeping cherub. How the baby managed to remain asleep through this entire ordeal, he couldn't quite grasp and wondered if the nanny might have dosed the half-filled bottle of milk being tossed about for the past few hours. He'd noticed, the child barely whimpered when that bottle landed in her mouth, and for a few idle moments, watching the pretty pink lips suckling the nipple, Luke wondered if the little girl might be daft. Not unheard of. Two handsome, intelligent parents could produce a freak of nature, dumb as a box of rocks, by some random clash of perfect genes, but if Arabella was dull, no visible signs were obvious. She truly was lovely with long thick lashes fanning over delicate round cheeks and perfectly heart-shaped lips.

"Would you like to hold her, darling?"

Damn. He'd been caught studying that child. His gaze lifted, locking on his mother's intent, troubled gaze—her thoughts undoubtedly conflicted between fondness for him and terror for his brother. Managing a slight smile, Luke shifted his hands in the universal sign of retreat and decided, "She looks content where she is, Mum. Maybe later."

Despite the situation, his mother quivered a knowing smile, and let him off easy. "Maybe later then," she agreed, possibly encouraged by the suggestion of a 'later' in Luke's regard.

He couldn't blame her for doubting that he'd stay for any length of time, not when the thought of leaving held priority in his mind. The sooner he learned of his brother's condition, the sooner he could slip away again. Too much association with the MacDade clan had never gone well for him.

4

Waiting room time was not like ordinary time, Luke decided as it seemed like they had already been in the conference room for hours when it couldn't have been more than one. As ordered, Mason had retired to the deep end of the room to conduct his business and start the wheels in motion, and Lucius had gone to stand in the hall, either to guard the door or ambush the first passing nurse or doctor. Even on a good day, Lucius MacDade wasn't the most patient man, and there was nothing ordinary in hanging around a hospital in the middle of the night with the occasional codes disrupting the silence.

Refilling his coffee cup, Luke glanced toward the window, unconsciously gauging the time nearing daylight. At least some little time had passed. Gregor had stepped out, maybe to find the restroom. Both boys were dozing again, one on either side of their grandmother with the baby cradled on her lap between them.

Funny, he'd never truly thought of his mother as a grandmother before now. She never aged, not in his mind or in appearance. Sleek and sophisticated, she carried herself with the essence of a model though she probably stood about six inches too short for a runway. How a woman barely 5'4" could produce three sons over six foot was another of those unsolved mysteries, as difficult to fathom as the strawberry-blond-haired woman posing as anyone's grandmother. She barely appeared old enough to be the mother of adult sons . . . and Luke's attention inevitably trailed to the doorway where his father appeared to be holding up the doorframe against which he was leaning.

Six foot five at the least, Lucius stood with the impressive build of a bodybuilder, and only his tailored black suit, impeccably styled, lent thought of his position at the helm of a multi-billion-dollar company. With his neatly styled waves barely hinting at a gray strand or two, his impressive auburn beard sporting a salted streak, Lucius MacDade could pass for another heir, not the magnate with the savvy to build the conglomerate of High Land, Inc.

Whether the sound of an electronic door or Lucius easing off the door-frame alerted him, Luke knew someone approaching, but judging by his father's indifference, this wasn't a medical practitioner.

"Excuse me," the husky, slightly lofty voice erupted. "Trenton PD."

Judging by his father's slight nod, at least one of the MacDade security men had stepped into the officer's path. Luke stifled a harrumph at the thought of the indignant policeman, and the probability of a clash on the horizon.

At the doorway, filling the doorway, Lucius stood firm, merely canting his head to look down at the fellow in the hall.

"I'm looking for Mason Eldridge," the newcomer announced. "He said he'd be here."

"He is. And you are?"

Another more tempered voice commented, "We're Detectives with Trenton PD. Todd Lenmar and my partner, Glen Harbinder. Any chance you're one of the MacDades?"

"Every chance," Lucius said and sidled. "Come in, lads. Let's we have a chat."

As if inviting them into his private office, Lucius stepped back and ushered them into the room, deliberately steering them away from Megan and the sleeping babes and toward Mason across the room—which placed Luke nearly in the center once again. Always an avid listener, if not an eavesdropper, Luke leaned at the counter, knowing he could be seen, deciding not to be heard.

"Mason," Lucius ordered while ushering the police toward the deep corner, and in an uncomfortable moment, Luke caught a fleeting glimpse of his father taking note of him. Rather than signal him away, the giant turned his full attention to the policemen. Not invisible, after all, and it seemed a subtle indication of acceptance of his presence in that glance.

"What have you learned, detectives?" Mason asked, hanging up his phone and turning his full attention to the visitors.

"We have a few more questions, Mr. Eldridge," the broader, more rumpled man of the pair stated shortly. He appeared middle-aged with a mid-aged bulge pulling his wrinkled shirt taut under a more wrinkled open jacket. A black tie lay askew over his white shirt, his trousers sagged, his black shoes could use a good buffing though the wear creases and scuffs would likely remain. Sporting a receding hairline in perfect contrast to his partner's full scruff of brown hair, Harbinder looked like the dowdy partner in a comedy routine. Lenmar, who might not be younger, appeared collegiate by comparison with a collarless beige shirt, brown sports coat, and khakis.

"Ask then," Mason said while leaning to land his hip on the table at which he'd been sitting a moment earlier. "How can I help?"

"You can start by telling us about High Land, Inc.," Harbinder stated with an edge of accusation.

"What would you like to know?" Mason asked.

Leisurely, Lucius backed a pace, leaning against one of the high-backed chairs as if merely there to observe.

"First off—what is it? We know you rented that limo under a corporate account. So what business is it in and what position does our victim hold in the company?"

"I'm not sure it's relevant," Mason said pensively but with a slight signal from Lucius, he continued. "But it's a furniture manufacturing company, among other things, and its currently listed on the list of top five hundred companies in the U.S. Liam's currently the COO—the Chief Operations Officer of record."

"So, it's a corporation?" the partner asked.

"It is, aye, but family owned and operated," Mason stated.

"What's your position?" Harbinder wanted to know.

"Something of an attaché," Mason commented. "Have you learned anything, gentlemen? Have you found any of the men responsible?"

"We're hoping your boss can tell us a few things when he gets out of recovery," Harbinder said with a tone that might not bode well on future relations. A little too snide in Luke's opinion and judging by the slightly darker tint in his father's eyes on the detective, that tone wasn't appreciated. "We heard he came through the operation—but in the meantime, you being an attaché and all, maybe you can tell us what you know about this woman, Alecia Helms? What's her story? You called her a mistress. Is she his hooker, Eldridge?"

"As I mentioned earlier, detective, Liam's seen Miss Helmes a few times, but he was breaking it off with her tonight. He and his wife are working on mending their marriage—"

Lucius cleared his throat discreetly and with a glance toward his wife and grandchildren, made his thoughts known before ever speaking in his low, guarded tone. "I think we'll leave that subject closed for the moment, gentlemen,"

"It doesn't work that way," Harbinder said boldly. "And you are, Mister . . .?"

"Lucius MacDade, Det. Harbinder, and it sure the hell does work that way," he said in a lower lethal tone. "We are discussing my son, and his sons are across this slight room. If you have any intention of pursuing this line of investigation, you will do so with care and discretion unless you would prefer public service as a city janitor." Barely pausing, he continued, "Do you have anything constructive to tell us at this time?"

Before Harbinder could speak, Lenmar hurried, "Not yet, sir. It's too early in the investigation, but we need to know about this uhm—woman. Only your son's name was listed at that hotel, and it seems the woman's vanished. Anything you can tell us, Mr. Eldridge, would certainly help."

"I'm afraid I can't be much help in that regard, detective," Eldridge said, maybe lying though it was difficult to tell with the soft edge in his low tone. "Maybe when Liam wakes, he can offer you some answers."

The conversation cut short with the motion at the door, and Luke's attention riveted as swiftly as his father's recognizing the green surgical scrubs, if not the lean, dark haired fellow who hesitated before striding confidently toward the small enclave. No longer leaning, neither Lucius nor Mason, with Megan already rising as well, lifting the baby, and ignoring the nanny, Luke stepped forward, unconsciously putting himself in the way of both detectives, backing them from the closing circle without a thought.

"Mr. Eldridge, Mr. . . . . MacDade?" he guessed and gained a quick nod, offering his hand with the introduction. "I'm Dr. Emerson. I'm head trauma surgeon here at Southern General. I think they already told you, your son pulled through the surgery but I'm not going to tell you it was clear sailing. Honestly, the next twenty-four to forty-eight hours are crucial. Right now, he's in critical condition and I'm having him moved to the ICU as soon as we can move him—"

"We'll be taking him home as soon as we finish making the arrangements, doctor," Lucius said in a cool tone. "Meaning no offense, here, mind, but I have our personal physician and a trauma team waiting."

"Sir, I wouldn't recommend—"

"How bad was he hurt, doctor?" Lucius asked directly, standing erect that only his head canted to eye the shorter man in a cobalt shine.

"Sir, he sustained multiple knife wounds, one of which punctured his large and small intestines and came too close to several vital organs, including his stomach and bowel. He has ninety-two stitches closing that wound, and another twenty-three between his hands, and arms. He's lucky, Mr. MacDade. He was very nearly eviscerated and if that knife had traveled even an eighth inch in any direction, we might not have been able to save him. Right now, our major concern is blood loss and possible infection, but it's imperative that we keep him as still as possible. Honestly, sir, with as much damage as he sustained, we need to watch for any hemorrhaging. I truly wouldn't recommend trying to move him until we truly have him stable."

"Then, I suggest you get him stable," Lucius said simply, unconsciously accepting Meg's hand circling his arm, holding on. "We're taking him home as soon as he is. Now, when can we join our lass and see him?"

"Your . . ." Emerson seemed only now to realize Natalie's absence. Glancing about and deciding, he wisely decided to skip any mention of a breech in policy. "I'll send a nurse out as soon as they have him in a room—"

"You are not listening, doctor," Lucius spoke in a lower tone. "I won't have him moved into the mainstream ICU. If you have the monitor's and equipment in that recovery room, you need to keep him there, and if need be, post a qualified nurse to attend him until we leave."

The poor doctor appeared caught between a rock and a hard place, but he was no fool. There were enough dark suits already gathered in this waiting room and adjoining hall to lend him more than ample evidence of the forces against him. "I can do that," he decided. "Give me a few minutes and I'll send someone out for you."

As Emerson turned, Luke caught sight of his nephews standing several paces away, both wide awake, but well enough groomed to be seen and not heard. Clever boys, these two, sprinting their gazes between the departing doctor and their grandparents. Worry etched across their young faces as apparent as their fear and the littler one broke first, hurrying behind the nanny who reached to take the baby, clasping his grandmother's free hand squeezing as the tears leapt over his hazel eyes. "I want to see my daddy now, kay, Grammy? Can I see daddy and mummy now? Please?"

"Soon, darling," Megan cooed and blinked against tears, managing a smile as she freed her hand from her husband and swiped the tussled auburn lock off his brow. "We'll see them both in a few minutes, li'l love."

"Me, too, Grammum?" the older boy asked hopefully.

"You, too, love," she promised then added. "You'll need be patient though. We'll need make certain your daddy's awake enough to see you . . ."

And there was a whole lot more to those words than the obvious, Luke grasped for the first time fully considering—his brother might not survive this.

If ever Megan MacDade appeared more distraught, never more than this moment. Only a day past, Natalie had seen her, but she'd aged since they'd shared a laugh in the clubhouse lounge. Pale and gaunt, her hazel eyes flashed off Natalie to her son as she hurried the last steps to his opposite side. On her heels, Lucius hovered, taking in the length of his son beneath the sheet before reaching the bedside.

In a hushed voice, Megan asked, "Has he awoken?"

Relieved, as much by the MacDades' arrival as her words, Natalie managed, "Just a few moments ago. He's been fading in and out. The nurses said that's normal."

Whether Lucius had received the full accounting from Mason, he seemed to know something as he looked from his son to her, asking, "Are ye all right, lass?"

Lord, how she loved them—as much if not more than her own flesh and blood if truth be known—and with the memory of the brogue slipping off her husband's lips, she couldn't help but smile just a little. "Aye, yes, sir. I am now."

"How could this have happened?" Megan asked the question she might have been asking herself for the last several hours. Her attention riveted on her son; her hand fluttered at his opposite shoulder, needing to touch to be certain of the life beneath her fingertips. In a quick gentle stroke, she moved the hair off his pale brow, no differently than Natalie had a moment ago. Her soft lips quivered, as near to weeping as could be, and her pale eyes shimmered with a well of tears. The question wasn't meant to be answered, not by another human, but as was her way, she would rail the God above for that answer. How could He have let her son be harmed?

Natalie shook her head, needing that answer, too, as she looked upon his too-handsome face so blasted pale against the white pillow. She'd reviewed those seconds a million times in the past several hours, and still, she was no closer to an answer. In fact, she'd become only more confused with every passing moment.

At first, or even second glance, she wouldn't have mistaken that street for a haven of thieves and muggers. For hours, she'd rested within that cab, two blocks from the Fairlane, watching all manner of people wandering on the sidewalk. Lone walkers, small crowds, elders, and children. She'd arrived early enough on that street to see people patronizing the delicatessen halfway down the block, others coming and going from the pizza shop near the hotel, and still others strolling to and from the various apartment buildings. In all that time, not a single body had seemed alarmed or on alert, and she'd witnessed no acts of violence—not even a drug deal if what she watched on late-night television could be an indicator. No pimp or street punk stood on a corner; no hooker plied her wares to the various cars to pass . . . aside, perhaps, from the one who'd sashayed at Liam's side at the onset. That one dressed like a lady of the evening. If her fire-red skirt had risen much higher on those black fishnet stockings, Helms might have been cited for indecent exposure lest she wore a bikini swimsuit rather than a thong.

And with her thoughts still turning, Natalie caught her father-in-law watching her. She truly hadn't reached a conclusion which troubled her even more. Something was wrong with this entire ordeal—over and above Liam lying so near the pearly gates—something was terribly wrong, and the prickling under her hairline only verified her thought. She wished she'd thought to speak to Mario, wished she'd thought to ask if he'd noticed those men before Liam's arrival. In retrospect, however, she was certain what that fellow would have said. If he'd seen anything, if that cabby had noticed a single thing out of sorts, he would have awoken her sooner if only to carry her away or set up an alarm. Too clearly, she recalled him rousting her, privy to the object of her interest, and he'd probably guessed the relationship as well. No dunce, that decent little fellow, and depending on what the police discovered, she might be calling for a ride sooner than later.

A soft, uttered groan slipped off the mustached lips, and once again, the hand started to lift as if to reach for the oxygen tube near his nostrils. Clasping his hand, twining fingers through his loose grip, Natalie saw Megan likewise occupied, halting his started struggle.

"Shhh, darling," Natalie whispered, landing her free hand on his forehead as he flinched and started to move. The pain was hitting him. As if it were her own to bear, Natalie suffered the fire in his side and saw the wince spread across his strained face. Flashing a glance at Lucius with an innate knowledge of his authority, she half pleaded, "He needs something for the pain. Please make them hurry—."

"Up!" the single word became a snarl with the rasping timbre of his voice. "Up!"

Neither Natalie nor Megan could stop the bear from rising if he so chose, and the blindness in the vivid blue eyes struck Natalie a fierce blow. In an instant, she laid over his chest, pressing her lips to his ear, hissing, "Ssstop, Liam. Ssstop! Lie still, m' love. Lie still—"

Against her neck, his breath huffed in ragged, hurt sounds, but he was stopped. Only his head attempted to rock against her cheek. His fingers closed in a bruising grip, locked, and pressed between their heaving bodies. Still, she held him, suffering the quakes to roll through him, and move him, move her. Not for an instant would she grant him the freedom to move. With every ounce of her strength, she pinned him down, and knew the extent of his injuries by her success. Not for an instant could she have stopped him if he weren't so deathly ill. With her sobs threatening to break against his ear, she continued to whisper to him as the activity swarmed around them, and she knew the moment the sedative entered the IV line. Beneath her, he calmed, melting, and she could be only grateful as the quaking became quivers. How? How by all the Saints above, would they keep him calm enough to heal those stitches? Tears swimming in her eyes, she lifted and brushed a kiss on his cheek, glimpsing the murky blue eyes attempting to follow her. The eyes of a child . . . he could appear no more confused or hurt if he were but a babe in arms, and never more than at this moment could Natalie see the eyes of her children beneath the long damp lashes.

Drifting, his focus swam toward his parents, but whether he recognized them remained a mystery as his murky eyes listed further and his lashes sagged.

He was asleep. By no means, naturally. Even under the drugged oblivion, the strain of pain troubled his brow, and his breath uttered in hurt spurts.

Feeling as if she'd run a marathon, Natalie eased back, keeping his fingers laced loosely within her grip as she halted her collapse on her forearms. Unbidden, the tears flashed over her eyes, and she tipped her head further to hide the spill. For just a second, she wished she could lower the rail and crawl under the sheet alongside him, wished she could feel the strength of his long lean anatomy pressed against her. She'd like nothing better than to forget these past dozen hours. From the madcap dash to and through two different airports to the moment she'd seen Liam's collapse. Like a giant oak falling in the forest, he'd listed and tumbled, and it offered no solace to recall herself standing witness to such an event years ago.

He'd taken her with him—a busman's holiday, he'd called it when inviting her to join him. There was no arrogance in his offer, no attempt to impress her with the vast MacDade holdings. As natural to him as breathing, he'd simply dragged her onto the family jet, then on to the Ozarks where they'd boarded a helicopter to finish the journey. Barely 20, he'd stood on a bluff overlooking the forests and panned his gaze over the emerald blanket with a pensive set to betray his youth. He was not, even then, a man to take his responsibilities lightly. No matter his carnal appetites, he wouldn't risk life or limb on a whim.

Liam MacDade had believed himself safe on that street, and he should have been.

No other thought held more firmly in Natalie's mind, and that simple benediction lent her strength to begin recovering. Whatever that madness, it wasn't a natural turn. Those men had been waiting for him. If nothing else she knew the truth of that revelation. Her husband had been ambushed in that alley. And whether he'd been meant to survive, remained the only question—a question to strike horror in her mind.

Someone had attempted to kill him; the proof lay before her between the bleep-bleep of a heart monitor to the IV and oxygen tubes draping away from him.

The whirlwind courtship and subsequent marriage of Liam MacDade to Natalie Callahan had made the international news stations eight years earlier. And if Natalie had dressed then as she was dressed now, the courtship would have been even shorter. His sister-in-law was a stunning woman at nineteen; at twenty-seven, she was drop-dead gorgeous, and Luke decided his older brother was a fool for stepping out on her. In a short, simple black dress and black nylons, she possessed a set of long slender legs to match any Radio City Rockette.

What the hell was going on here?

She hadn't fought off a gang of street thugs wearing a cocktail dress and high heels, and her long honey-golden hair, flowing over one nearly bare shoulder, hadn't suffered even a gentle breeze, much less an alley fight. So, who the hell was Mason trying to fool? The story he'd told Lucius MacDade had more potholes than a Pennsylvania highway, and the only truth seemed the end result lying prone, as pale as the sheet to cover him.

Scanning his brother from scattered white-blond waves to the immense covered feet forming twin white peaks past the footboard, Luke barely glanced at the IV bags hanging above Liam's head. Pale beige electric leads trailed beneath the sheet, reporting a steady beat on the monitor on the offside. An oxygen tube attached to his nostrils . . . and suddenly, this was far too real.

If his own heart were hooked up to a machine, it would likely sound like a drumbeat in a rock 'n roll band. This was, and was not, Liam MacDade, the giant who'd once lifted Luke off his feet and sent him flying halfway across their Olympic-sized pool in their backyard—then dove in to rescue him.

'There's m' li'l cannonball!'

Laughing . . . the sound of his laughter rang out of the past, and Luke swallowed against the sudden fear gripping his throat in a stranglehold. Somehow, he hadn't anticipated feeling another gut punch at the sight of his brother. He'd seen enough hospital scenes on TV to know what to expect, but this . . .? Nothing could have prepared him for the sight of Liam MacDade splayed on a too-short bed, and even with several paces between them, Luke's attention fixed on the gauze wrapped hand, the bulge of white gauze on the arm. Blood stains caked in the manicured fingernails—both sets locked in a lover's hold somewhere near Liam's chest.

He should have stayed with his nephews, Luke decided, and nearly backed from the room as Gregor continued forward. Whether he felt more connected or more like an intruder, he couldn't decide. His mother had invited him to join her and his father when the nurse had come for them, but he'd begged off, postponing the inevitable by suggesting he would wait for Gregor. Where Gregor had gone, Luke wasn't certain, but the red streaks in the pale eyes upon his return were telling—Gregor had needed a few moments to collect himself. Belatedly, Luke recalled the youngest boy speaking before dozing off, asking Gregor, 'Is my daddy gonna die, Uncle Gregor? Do you think he's gonna die?'

'Ach, no, lad. Your da's too fierce to die . . .'

Looking at his two older brothers—one splayed unconscious on the bed, the other gripping the bedrail and landing a hand on his sister-in-law's shoulder—Luke suddenly felt more like an outsider than any time past. He didn't belong here. Had no right to be witnessing their pain when he hadn't even seen his oldest brother in person in nearly two years. He needed to collect his bag and get the hell out of here.

5

"Good God almighty," the low voice intruded, drawing Natalie from her daze to see Gregor and Lucas sidling into the room. If not for subtle variants of shade between eyes and hair, they could be triplets, one as handsome as the next, though Gregor more closely mirrored Liam if only by their ages. Perhaps, only two inches and two years separated the two oldest brothers, but where Liam's hair was a shade lighter and his eyes a shade darker, Gregor wore a more golden mane and mustache. Lucas, at barely twenty, wore his surfer-blond locks longer than both others and already sported a shag of beard on his chiseled jaw. His blue eyes, though, shined like neon with an intensity to betray his years.

That Lucas was even here was a surprise. Of all the MacDades, he seemed to dance to a different drum, and as Natalie heard more than a time or two, he was becoming more estranged from the clan by the day.

Less than a year ago, in one of their rare moments of shared confidence, Liam had mentioned Lucas striking out on his own. Lucas had refused even to consider attending college, which had vexed the entire clan, the eldest of whom had ranted extensively. 'The worst part of this,' Liam had confided while suffering to appear amused at their father's rant, 'The boy's smarter than the lot of us. The devil's been reading since before he was two . . .'

Well, and he was here now. And Natalie needed only a glance to witness the fear as livid in his eyes as in all others. On Gregor, the fear was far more vivid. His expression was tortured as if he shared Liam's pain. As he arrived alongside her, his hand landed naturally on Natalie's shoulder, offering support and strength. Flashing his gaze from Liam to her, to his parents, back to her, he was nearly manic in his fear. "How is he—how are you? What the hell happened, Lee?"

He was one of few people who could drop that nickname and sound respectful, and meeting his searching eyes, she suffered the reality in a wicked blow. She was not all right. The fear and exhaustion slammed her to rise the tears yet again. "I-I don't know," she stammered and swallowed.

"Good God, you look exhausted," Gregor uttered and flashed his focus to his father. "Have you talked to a doctor yet? Do we know anything?"

The elder stood with his hand resting on his wife's shoulder, and it occurred to Natalie that the fellow had remained unnaturally quiet since they'd entered. He was not in shock, not on the verge of collapse, but behind his blue eyes—eyes his eldest had inherited in spades—he was fuming. Just the flash of his cobalt blue eyes lancing at his sons was enough to send a shiver down Natalie's spine. Far easier to bear if this immense man were raging; it would be more natural than this quiet seething—rather like a volcano boiling red hot beneath the surface.

That she wasn't the only one to suffer under that stark gaze, Natalie had sense to notice as the fear enhanced in both younger men's faces.

"Aye, we know ye brothers not out of the woods yet," Lucius said in a low quiet growl. "He has a hundred stitches holding his intestines in and another dozen er more in his arm. When it's safe to move him, we'll be taking him home."

"Home to our house? Or home to Lexington?" Gregor wanted to know.

"Home," he answered and apparently caught Natalie's stunned surprise, meeting her stricken gaze head-on. "We're making the necessary arrangements, lass. You and the wee bairns will be coming along too. I dinnae want him getting shuffled aboot this place er another of its ilk, and I dinnae want him dodging cameras er his picture landing in some blasted tabloid with tubes hanging aboot."

If he expected an argument, he was disappointed. Only relief flared in Natalie's mind as she considered how vulnerable Liam could be in this public institution. Far too clearly, she imagined some industrious reporter or photographer sneaking through the halls or bribing a nurse. And the thought of an ambush confirmed her decision. "Did anyone say how soon he might be moved, sir?"

"Not yet, lass, but we have more lads coming soon to join Artair and Ben ootside that door."

If she weren't still holding his hand, doubtful, she would have seen the shudder through Liam. He was trying to awaken. Worry flashed in her mind as she realized the improbability of those drugs wearing off already. Studying the strain across his brow, in his lips, she felt an almost desperate need rising as she looked to the elder MacDade, who apparently read the same signs in his oldest son. "The pain meds aren't helping—not holding him. He's only struggling more." And the increased bleeping from the monitors confirmed her words.

"Aye, I'm seeing that," Lucius growled and looked to his next oldest son. "If ye see him trying tae come off that bed, yer land one on his beloved jaw and knock him senseless."

"Da?" Gregor spoke in as much exasperation as doubt.

"Aye," Lucius said and lanced his youngest son. "And you help hold him, too. Not bloody likely the ladies could hold him down, any more than those damn drugs."

Later perhaps, Natalie would find the humor in the elder MacDade losing his brogue in his anger when the opposite held true of his sons. Currently, she remained more concerned with her husband's struggle to rise from his drugged oblivion. As Lucius turned, Natalie glimpsed Lucas sideling toward the end of the bed, heading for the opposite side. Determination haunted both younger faces. They would obey that command to spare their brother a greater ill, but devil bedamned, she wouldn't stand by and watch them clout their brother, no matter that they intended to save his blasted life. At the hurt breath and growled huff, Natalie spun her attention as the thick black lashes quivered to lift. Brows knitting, his hand lifted. Without a second thought, she ducked over him, sparing him his brothers' wrath and landing her lips against his ear as his face swung toward her. "Still! Lie still . . . Enough, Liam . . . enough. Rest . . . Just rest, darling, m' love . . . Be still . . . Still like a mountain lake . . . Still like the mountains . . ." He was calming, stilling beneath her, his breath quieting.

"Och, well, and that works, too," Gregor said in a low musing voice.

"Lucky for us, I think," Lucas muttered.

Far away, Liam heard the voices, but only one voice—closer, now—brushed against his ear and reached into his cluttered senses. The voice of an angel or a fairy to sprinkle a calming dust on his raging senses. He wanted to rise. That much he grasped . . . and the pain. Aye, he understood that fire smoldering at his waist, felt the sparks igniting to move him. If he could move . . .? But a greater force held him, and like a hand to stroke the pain away, the lyrical sounds brushed against him. In waves, his senses floated, images rising and drifting on a wicked foggy tide, and the fires sparked, moving him. "Bl—oody hell . . . hurts."

"Shhh, darling . . . I know it hurts . . . Still, lie still . . ."

And when he barely thought to move, the hands stilled him, one locked in his grip and pressed at his chest, the other stroking his hair, oddly comforting, stilling. That he tasted honey on his breath, a taste of honey and scent of jasmine . . . a familiar essence to start his senses rising anew. He knew these scents . . . and in odd floating moments, knew his wife hovered over him. Her soft fiery locks brushed against his lips; her voice whispered at his ear. If this was a dream, he wouldn't mind lingering, but the faraway sounds drew near. He was waking. Not easily. But waking to the fire flashing in his side, gripping him in waves to clasp the fingers more tightly, to tip his face into the fragrance and draw wisping breaths.

"Still, Liam . . . You must lie still . . ."

"We can try a different drug but short of starting him on a morphine pump, I'm just not certain how effective it will be. That shot should have held him longer than this. He wasn't completely out of the anesthesia."

"Still, Liam . . . That's it, darling. Just lie still . . ."

"Lee, how's he doing?"

"I . . . I think he's nearly awake . . . Honey, can you hear me?"

"Uh . . . huh," he managed, though he wasn't altogether sure. Floating, his senses swam in odd twists, positive this was Natalie . . . and yet he knew the improbability. Great gaps weaved through his waking mind. A warrioress in shadow . . . a gun . . . knife . . . voices . . . a fight . . . a fairy whispering in his ear . . . a blond sprawled on rumpled sheets within a weird pulsing neon glow. No—he wasn't awake in any ordinary sense, but he heard his mother's voice cooing, felt her hand on his shoulder, and his estranged wife resting over him. Her hand, he held. Her fingers twined through his and held him flat. Perhaps, that thought alone lent him pause to grasp reality. She was strong . . . but he suddenly feared breaking her slender fingers in his grip. And yet, her grip held his more firmly.

"Shhh, lie still, darling . . . You need to lie as still as stone. As still as your mountains . . . Don't try to rise, baby. Please . . . please just lie still . . . You can't move. You have stitches . . . remember? I told you about the stitches," she huffed softly, sounding close to sobbing against his ear, and that too, stirred him. She would cry for him? "Wake, m' love . . . but don't move . . . Please, don't move . . ."

That endearment again halted and disoriented him. Not ever in his life had his wife called him such a thing—her love. Perhaps, this was a dream . . . "Aye," he uttered and drew pained breath as another wave of fire rippled through him. "Dream," he hoped. But the flames were real and rippling more like watery waves. Only more confusing, those waves. Never had he suffered pain such as this, to slam and retreat, slam and retreat. "Uh . . . uh . . . What tae hell . . . did they . . . give me . . .?"

Ever so slightly the auburn silk lifted, and at close range, the hazel eyes, near to amber in his swimming mind, looked into him. For an instant, the mirth danced in the green depths, but just as swiftly, concern flashed across the lovely brow. "Please, Liam . . . Tell me you know me. You can hear me. You understand."

"Talking—too fast—sprite," he strained against the nails in his throat, against the fire flashing in his side. "I am here."

A fireworks display ignited in her livid hazel eyes; the smile quivered in her glistening lips. "Oh, darlin', that is good to hear."

Perhaps they were still friends . . . or whatever they had pumped into him for pain had affected her as well. Even in this weird awakening, he knew his wife suffered an odd affliction of the Highlands. She knew things. Felt things. Like his own Gram, his wife had the knack . . . Or the ken, as he'd heard upon a time. She was here . . . holding his hand in a fierce grip, feeling what he was feeling. "Aye," he uttered and managed to nod his head a notch without losing sight of her eyes. "Aye . . . ta drugs have ye too . . . w'ar stoned."

For a stopped second, she spied him with neon surprise. Her lips parted and quivered, and she stifled a near-girlish giggle, dropping the silk curtain over his sight as she vibrated a sound at his ear.

She was laughing. That much he could tell, and belatedly, the quiver started into his lips. Oh, but it reached no further when his mere thought of moving stifled her laugh and strengthened her grip. The fire flashed anew, and he might have moved, but her hand stilled him. And his other hand was caught now, too, held in a far tighter grip. His wife was out of hands. One in his grip, one on his head . . . and he wasn't sure who held him. Barely, he thought to move again when the pain drove a raspy snarl from his lips.

"Shhh, darling . . . Be still . . ."

"C-canny fight . . . the fire . . . and the drugs," he heaved softly against her ear, and something of his meaning touched her. Breath hitching behind the pain, he caught her gaze as she lifted, and nothing could he hide of the battle raging inside him.

"I can't let you fight this, Liam," she said softly, and a hint of tears glistened at the edges of her long lashes. "I can't, darling. You're hurt . . . You need pain medicine. You can't keep fighting against it. Do you ken? You have to let the medicine work—"

"Not—though," he huffed as another wave of fire sailed through him. "Ahh . . . God, Nate . . . make it stop," he pleaded as the tears rose uncontrollably, drowning her image. His hand vibrated with the effort to control the pain, and again, he feared breaking her fingers, but he couldn't release her. Like a lifeline, he knew if he let her go, he would go. The pain would take him. "Plee-ease, no . . . drugs," he heaved and tipped his head further into the silk, breathing in the honey scent, the floral scent . . . the heady scent of the morning dew on the moors. "Ahhh." And she was helping him. He knew it as surely as he knew himself to be Liam James MacDade . . . She was helping him, calming him, spreading balm on the flames, sprinkling fairy dust on the fires.

"I dinnae ken what you're doing, lass," the low voice uttered. "But whatever it be, keep it up."

"Dad?" another low voice intruded. "What's . . ."

"He's calming," Megan MacDade said simply, smoothly. "And waking, I think now."

Liam was waking, breathing in the wild scents from the moors, not clear of much else as the flames ebbed, tempering to a heat he could manage. Oh, and she was a blasted wonder, this wood nymph of his. If only . . . well, and he was breathing again. As she lifted yet again, he found her watery eyes, belatedly realizing the tears were in his own eyes. As if she sensed even that mild discomfort, she slipped her hand off his brow and brushed the heel of her palm over his lashes, taking the tears away. For whatever reason she was here, he could be only grateful.

"Still," she said gently. "You need lie still, Liam. Do you ken?"

"Aye," he strained softly. "Still."

"If you move even a finger, I'll make them knock you flat," she threatened in a tone to remind him of his mother, as fierce as ever a woman to walk. "Do you ken?"

"Aye." When she used that old word, she surely meant business, and he couldn't help but quiver a smile. "Uh-huh," he added, hoping to counter the determined fire in her green eyes. "I—woon't move." But it was hard not to move when he wanted . . . wanted to taste those glistening lips as if that alone might quench the desert drying in his throat.

"M-maybe you'll have to move just a little . . . I think you might be allowed a few sips of water now."

"I—widnae mind—draining our pond," he suggested.

"Coming around then, are you, brother?"

Barely shifting his head to find Gregor hovering over Natalie's shoulder, Liam struggled to remember if he had seen any of them before now. There seemed a wide gap in his memory, but Natalie still wore the black dress she'd worn in his memory. Truly struggling, he managed to shift his head enough to find his mother, father . . . It was his father's sturdy hand locked in his grip, pressing his hand to the mattress. And Lucas? Perhaps, he was dreaming, after all. His little brother might be a mirage. The lad hadn't graced their presence in more than two years. To have him here, hovering at the end of the bed, seemed the greatest proof of his serious ailment. "Aye," he uttered and sought Natalie's eyes. "Was knock-ing on . . . heaven's door."

"Too blasted close, darling," she attested gently and brushed the back of her fingers across his forehead, shifting the unruly locks off his brow. Her eyes clouded as she studied him. "You've had me scared witless," she started and might have said more if not for the chaos erupting in the room.

First and foremost was an incredibly brave nurse intending to empty a syringe into an IV line despite Lucius MacDade stating, "That willnae be necessary, lass."

"Doctor's orders, sir. It should help him rest—"

"That will not be necessary, lass," the fellow spoke simply, and even in Liam's altered state, he suffered the chill of that tone. The absence of a Scottish brogue was not a good sign either. "Send your Dr. Emerson in here when he has a moment."

"Really, dear, do as he says," Megan intervened in a deceptively gentle tone. "Perhaps, you should just take our Liam's vital signs and the like before you go."

In an odd position to see the young woman bouncing her glances between the collective MacDades, Liam took pity on her, asking, "Water?"

Looking down at him, she stole a glance at Natalie, who was likewise studying her with a startling intensity, and something in Natalie's gaze started the woman hustling toward the door while sliding that injection swiftly into her white smock pocket. With a subtle squeeze of Natalie's fingers, Liam drew her heated shine, and even in his lingering fog, he was slightly startled by the ferocity of her gaze. Had that nurse attempted to touch that IV line, she would have been laid low. "Easy . . . lass. Easy," he strained softly, repeating the word he'd heard more than a time or two recently.

Her glare softened on the instant, and she brushed his forehead in a natural rhythm. "Are you certain you don't want something for the pain, darling? As much as I know you like to keep your wits about you, this may not be the time to test your great strength. It was bad, Liam. There'd be no shame in needing a pain reliever."

"Aspirin . . . er Tylenol, then?"

Gregor commented, "You don't have the damned flu, Liam. Were I you, I'd opt for whatever she had in that syringe, especially when dad about wrung that doctor's neck to order it."

"I didnae sooch thing," Lucius interjected, sounding almost himself for the first time, but the glitter in his dark blue eyes betrayed him. "Was but a wee bit of persuading," he said as he looked down at Liam, sober on the instant. "But if that ache starts to get the better of yerself, ye need ask for that shot. No sense in suffering if ye dinnae need to."

"Aye—Da-ad," he managed, and to his dismay, noted another nurse arriving with an all too familiar cup. At least this one carried a spoon rather than a lollipop stick, and when the nurse might have assisted, Megan Mac-Dade merely slipped the cup from her grasp. Offering a smile to soften the blow, she commented, "We'll handle it from here, dear."

So began the torturously long process of melting ice chips on his tongue, but there was no sense arguing with either his mother or estranged wife. That he might be wearing thin occurred to him only as he snapped from a doze and might have jarred his entire anatomy save for Natalie clasping his fingers.

"Liam, you need to rest," Natalie spoke softly.

He was tired—bone weary tired—as if he'd spent a week trekking through the mountains. But there were things he needed to do. Something niggled at the back of his mind . . . Something he needed to know . . . And again, he envisioned that shadowy image twirling in the shadows . . . heard that soft uttered voice at his ear . . . an alley. Two wee lads had ushered him into that alley at gunpoint, and the weapon had spit fire. Others . . . more than a half dozen other lads had waited in that alley . . .

His eyes snapped open, and his head tipped, landing, locking on his father's gaze. "The . . . police. Did you . . . talk to them?"

"Briefly," Lucius said as though he'd merely awaited the question. "Mason spoke with them at length, but they'd like to talk to yerself as soon as yer able."

"I din-on't know . . . what I can tell them—" Especially not with his estranged wife in the room. It was one thing for her to suspect his infidelity but to cram it down her throat. . .? A whole different kettle of fish. He would truly not like to hurt her in that way. No matter their differences, she was still his wife.

Lord, what a mess.

And no relief to know his mind clearing and still far too muddled. The images drifted like flotsam in his head. He'd been with Alecia . . . at the Fairlane Hotel. In sequence, he recalled leaving alone . . . And on the second block . . . an ambush. A mess. And he needed to talk to Mason, and perhaps, Gillis, before he spoke to the police. Rather doubtful Mason had admitted the nature of their visit to Bender Ave, but those details would not be impossible to discover. Not with the blasted single-star hotel a block away.

Damn it.

A mess.

"Are ye feeling up to that chat, lad?"

He shook his head slightly, more confused than he cared to consider with his wife hovering at his side. No matter what he said, she could be hurt, would no doubt hate him for creating this tabloid-worthy drama, and whatever this odd turn to stand her beside him . . .? Selfishly, perhaps, he would rather not change it yet. His thoughts turning in weird circles, Liam knew only a greater befuddlement to find her watching him still. Perhaps, the drugs hadn't worn off. He would dearly like to know why she stood in this room—dressed to the nines. Had she been meeting someone for a night on the town? And just that thought stirred his blood.

Perhaps, she followed his every thought. She leaned on the bedrail, head tipped and hair streaming to one side. Whether she wore her curiosity or concern more vivid, Liam couldn't be certain. She studied him, however, and it took a moment for him to consider what might be going through her mind. Either she knew or sensed his turmoil, and how much might she already know about this mess?

Not even sure if she had stood in this room, as he suspected, before all others . . . Well, and she was his wife. She would have been granted entry before his parents. Shaking his head, hoping to clear the picture, he barely started to move—maybe his hand, maybe his leg. He might have meant only to shift his knee—and the fireworks ignited in his center. Uncontrollably, he grunted and tipped his head further, gripping both hands as if preparing for a wicked rollercoaster ride,

"Shhh, honey. Still."

"Ah . . . ah . . . g-goo-d . . . God," he heaved and gained no relief with his voice clearing.

"Steady, lad," Lucius ordered.

"He needs that blasted shot," Gregor stated in irritation.

"Drugs weren't helping," Lucas commented with an indifferent tone.

Another hand brushed at his head, this one his mother's. "Shhh, baby."

He needed to move, needed to stop this wicked whirlwind . . . He needed to know how much his wife knew about this ordeal . . . He needed—

Against his ear, the whisper came. "Still, darling. Lie still . . . you need to rest. Everything else can wait."

Only at the fringes of awareness, he understood the urgency, but he wasn't receiving a choice. Everything else would need to wait. If not for the hands holding his with equal strength, he would be folding if only to douse the fires. No choice there, either. In lightning-quick flashes, he remembered the instant that knife had impaled him, a wicked thrust and twist . . . Hell's fire ripped through him, then and now. The pain would take him . . . If he held Natalie's hand much tighter, he would surely break her slender fingers, but if he let go . . .? He let go.

6

The instant Liam's fingers sprung, his muscles gripped . . . and he melted beneath her touch. Tears flashed over Natalie's eyes as she gleaned the intensity of the pain to take Liam MacDade under. He was every bit his father's son. As fierce and strong as any man alive . . . and as stubborn, too.

Behind the curtain of her hair, she wiped the tears from her cheeks and drew a sighing breath, lifting enough to see his handsome face in repose. He'd passed out. Plain and simple. He'd buckled to the pain and passed dead away. Only the heart monitor's steady beep verified the life within his long lean frame. Well, and she wasn't about to wake him. And with a sense of Gregor reaching toward him, Natalie lashed her freed hand and caught his wrist. Tipping her head to find his startled eyes, she shook her head, needing to swallow before she tried to speak.

"Lee, I think he's—"

"Resting," she said softly. "He needs to rest, Gregor."

"Honey, he needs those pain meds," he said carefully.

"He needs to rest," she sighed with the weight of her decision wearing on her weary mind. If only she believed those meds would help him, but she'd felt the battle raging inside him. "He can't fight the pain and the drugs," she said as she looked down at his handsome profile. Her Highlander. A wild and unruly rogue, if ever there was one. "What am I to do with you?" she whispered. If only life could be simple. She could let them load him full of sedatives and let the healing commence. Nothing simple. She'd known when she met him at the alter eight years past, life with this blasted MacDade would never be simple.

With the start of a crease across his brow, Natalie reached over the rail, landing her palm over his hand. Weaving her fingers through his, pressing his hand to his chest. He'd scraped his knuckles. Specks of blood stained his digits though someone had attempted to clean him while tending those minor wounds. Reality. He had been engaged in a fight for his life, and sooner or later, they would need to speak to the police.

With a thought of where that battle had begun moments ago, Natalie wondered if he were considering the details. More than once, she'd caught him searching her, attempting to solve a puzzle. Not in a single lucid moment had he found the sense to ask why she was in this room or in that alley. Although about the latter, she doubted he would. Sooner or later, however, she might need to enlighten him.

How to say what needed to be said . . . with his father, mother, and brothers in the room?

How not?

The story Mason had alluded to fabricating for the elder MacDades was the same story he'd concocted for the police, with slight exceptions. Too clearly, she recalled Mason departing her company in the waiting room and returning with a musing grim expression. 'I'm not going to heaven, lass,' he'd begun simply. 'I uhm . . . might have suggested that yourself and Liam were reconciling and uhm . . . he was breaking off a tryst at the Fairlane. . . I think it prudent to keep most else to ourselves. I uhm . . . omitted your arrival in that alley. Might have suggested we were waiting in the car together.'

'What happens when Liam awakens, Mason? He certainly knows the lie.'

'We'll need to be certain he comes to his senses . . .'

Whether Mason had meant reaching a clarity of mind to perpetuate a lie or come to his senses and turn the fabrication into a reality, Natalie had cause to wonder. And looking upon Liam's pale face, she reached only a single conclusion. She wasn't ready to boot the unruly devil to the curb. As if he heard her silent proclamation, his long lashes lifted; his dark eyes shined more black than blue with the pain lurking therein. "Good morning, darling," she whispered if only to lend him pause.

It worked well, derailing the start of motion. A single eyebrow lifted, and his concentration enhanced. "Mo-orning."

With the raspy timbre of his voice, he was either questioning or merely responding. Either way, he needed ministrations. "Ice?"

"Wa-ter?" he managed with a tenuous hope.

"Ah, well, and wish that I could, darling," she said gently and glanced over as Megan produced the cup. That neither would gain a moment to fulfill his needs became apparent as the nurses descended on him, and perhaps word had already spread in this surgical wing. They came in a set, careful and quick, checking the monitor and producing a thermometer to stick in his ear, which gained them a peculiar glance from the giant in their care.

"How we doing, sweetie?" the perky stout woman asked as she clipped an oxygen gauge to his finger, careful not to move his caught hand from Natalie's grip. "Do you think we might try sitting up a little?"

Bewildered, Natalie asked, "Are you daft?"

The woman's focus shot upward and halted. "We . . . we . . . He should be . . . He needs a breathing treatment."

Somehow, those thoughts seemed to follow one another, but Natalie failed to find the connection. "My dear, his breathing is fine so long as we don't jostle him about. If you would like to be useful, you could bring some aspirin, a glass of water and a straw. Or at least another cup of ice."

"Nat-alie," Liam managed, and she dipped her gaze to find a slight kink in his mustache, the merest trace of amusement in his eyes. "Eas-sy."

For even the glimmer of his normal self, she was grateful and quivered a smile. "Ah, well, if you'd behave and take your blasted medicine, darling, I wouldn't need to be giving these ladies such a time."

"He could probably have more pain medicine, now," the woman offered hurriedly.

"Aspirin," Natalie said and heard the word echoing off his lips. Dropping her gaze, she shook her head. "You do know you need more than that, Liam. What say we compromise, and they bring you something that won't knock you out?"

"Ahh-wl, right then. With—water."

Rather quickly, the nurse jotted the oxygen reading and hurried from between the elder MacDades. "We'll be right back."

When they'd both ducked into the hall, Gregor commented, "I dare say this won't take long."

"Word's spread," Lucas said idly from across the room where he leaned near the door. "Lunatics in recovery."

"Well, recover to be the main word," Lucius idled, and drew Liam's gaze. "You need do as yer told, now, lest yer wife need clout these lasses. And if ye land yer m'athair in a donnybrook o'er the same, I willnae be too pleased."

Liam appeared slightly confused, and Natalie sensed the underlying battle waging against the pain. Swiping his brow, noting an almost cold clamminess, she knew enough to be worried. For all his great strength, he wasn't handling this well. Squeezing his hand at his chest, she drew his haunted gaze. "They won't be long, love." And there it was again, the confusion she'd read a time or two in the past few hours. Could he honestly doubt—even after all this time—that she loved him?

"M—morning . . .?"

"I uhm . . . I'm honestly not certain, darling," she said and glanced at her in-laws to find Lucius checking his gold watch.

Whatever he saw surprised him before he nodded and offered, "Aye, morning, just, lad. Not that it need con-sarn you." Looking to Natalie, speculation keen in his eyes, he wondered, "Dinnae guess yer ready for a rest, yet, are ye, lass."

"Not yet," she said and found Liam's troubled gaze. "Maybe when you're resting, I'll do the same."

"We . . . need to . . . talk," he managed, though he appeared more troubled with that thought.

"Yes, I'm certain we do," she said quietly, knowing they were, perhaps, on the same wavelength. That he could appear even more distressed by that discourse, struck a chord in her mind. Brushing her hand over his brow, if only to smooth the troubled lines, she managed a gentle smile. "Just lie still, darling. They shouldn't be long."

An understatement, that. In record time, the perky woman returned with a tall male nurse as backup; however, he appeared no more comfortable than his female counterparts. Darting his glance over the exceptionally large males in attendance, he decided Natalie was the least likely to belt him. unfortunately, he needed to pass Gregor. "I uhm . . . if you'll excuse me, sir . . .?" he spoke politely, attempting to sidle past Gregor. "I can help lift him a little to take those pills."

Unmoving, Gregor commented, "As can I."

The man paled considerably and glanced at the worried woman across the bed.

"Gregor," Luke sighed. "Let the poor guy do his job, will you? I'm sure he'd be more careful than you in your present frame of mind."

Innate to every MacDade, Gregor eyed Lucas with a single arched brow, and across the bed, the elder MacDade sent an identical glance to his youngest son. As if mirror reflections, they both stood with arms laced across their chests, the arrogance not disguised in either one.

Appearing immune to the combined gazes upon him, Lucas shrugged his indifference and maintained his casual lean at the wall. "They're trained to be careful."

Perhaps, only to indulge his younger brother, Gregor stepped back a pace and flagged a hand for the nurse to continue. But by his direct glare, he left no doubt of the outcome if the fellow proved any less than capable.

Far more nervous, the nurse sidled toward Natalie and encountered his second roadblock, clearly unprepared for the resistance. "Uh . . . ma'am? If uhm . . ."

Rather than release Liam's hand, Natalie shifted on her feet, granting access to her husband's upper half, but she remained close enough to judge the integrity of the careful treatment. Almost amused, she noted both medical practitioners treating her husband like delicate crystal, much to his obvious annoyance.

"Just lift—the damn—bed," Liam nearly growled.

"Well," Gregor huffed with a bemused note. "There he is then. The real Liam MacDade."

Natalie suffered a smile, catching Liam's irritated flash toward his brother.

"I was truly beginning to fear we'd lost you, brother," he said, perhaps more sober than he meant to portray. "It's damn good to know that's not the case. You'll be back to yer normal ornery self in no time."

"Aye," the elder stated, likewise lifting a brow and quivering a smirk in his salt and peppered mustache. "And impatient as ever, I'm seeing for myself."

Despite his impatience, Liam was not quite as prepared to be moved as he let on, but perhaps, only Natalie sensed his pain and felt the quick grip on her fingers. Still, he managed to free his right hand and accept the pills, likewise the sips of water. That the motion might have laid him low became apparent only after he accepted the breathing apparatus and blew into the tube. Like a chain reaction from the gates of hell, he started a cough, choked on the pain, and half buckled on the elevated bed. All three MacDade males descended on him as if they were of a single mind. Natalie knew only relief as father and brothers clasped wrists, shoulders knees to halt Liam in a twisted pose. Still, the choked sounds continued to heave and grunt as his body convulsed and shuddered beneath the sheets.

Tears flashing over her eyes, Natalie stood in silent witness as the patriarch of the clan clasped Liam's curly head and held him, whispering, "There, lad

. . . Just catch yer breath now. . . No need for fretting so . . . Aye, just hold steady, m' boy . . . ."

And behind Lucius, Megan stood clasping her arms, holding herself together as the tears flowed unchecked down her cheeks. Like Natalie, she'd known the futility of calming or holding all six-foot-six of solid muscle.

But theirs weren't the only tears. Gregor's eyes shined like blue crystal before he ducked his head to rest his forehead on his forearms, and Lucas appeared far younger than his twenty years, no longer indifferent but nearer to terrified as he pressed his brother's knees to the bed. Within the tangle, a choked breath broke on a sound too near a sob.

"Aye, and that's a wicked pain," Lucius growled as he cradled his son's head and shoulder, looking as if he would rather lift and hold him completely. "Just ye catch yer breath now. We'll just rest here a bit and let those pills take hold. Nae need to fret . . ."

Into the mix, the lanky Dr. Emerson arrived, and on his heels, Mason Eldridge. "Oh, lord," the doctor huffed. Then, "Mr. MacDade, we need to give him something to help him through this. We'll be lucky he hasn't already ripped those stitches."

"Aye," Lucius growled. "Get it then, doctor—"

Within the fold, something of the words registered, and Liam started a protest and another struggle to throw them off. Near to snarling, he started another choking fit.

"And make it strong," Lucius added, holding Liam steady against his struggles. "I dinnae want to see him suffering this again."

Not again would Natalie interfere. Feeling helpless, she could only be grateful for the indomitable presence holding Liam's struggles at bay. Not a moment too soon, the nurse hustled into the room, and Dr. Emerson snatched the syringe from her hands, personally, sinking the needle into the IV port. In mere seconds, the struggle ebbed, and the choked sounds became wisps of rasping breaths.

Recoiling, Gregor eased backward, resting his elbows on the rail, his fingers twined in his golden locks, holding his ducked head in trembling hands. "God a'mighty," he heaved, straining against a sob.

Unconsciously, Natalie touched his shoulder, feeling the vibrations through his system as he drew a ragged breath.

Lucas was gone.

Through a film of tears, Natalie verified that sudden thought, though she had no idea when he'd fled. Megan stood at her husband's side, touching his shoulder. Lucius had eased backward slightly but continued to hold Liam's sweated locks to the pillow.

Dr. Emerson stood aside, merely studying his patient as if he might judge him healthy or unhealthy from a distance, and he seemed to know when it was safe to speak. "I'd like to check that incision, Mr. MacDade, then if I could have a word with you?"

"Aye, have at it," Lucius said, sounding wearier than ever in the past. Without losing his grip on Liam's head, he eased aside and granted access.

No fool, this Dr. Emerson. He set upon Liam personally, undoubtedly to the three present nurses' relief, lowering the bed, moving the sheet, and manipulating Liam's arms and legs with the utmost care. Carefully, methodically, he checked the IV site, the bandages at the muscled biceps, the oxygen tube, the wide white band at Liam's waist, and the catheter. When he was satisfied, he rearranged the sheet and blanket, then straightened, and there could be no mistaking the gravity of his thoughts as he looked up at Lucius. "A word now, sir?"

"We're family here, doctor," Lucius spoke in a lowered tone. "If ye want to have yer nurses step out, I widnae mind, but the rest stay." As he spoke, his focus shifted, and for just a second, he was searching for Lucas—a heartache there and gone—before his attention landed on Eldridge at the end of the bed. "Mason?"

"Taken care of. Artair's still outside, and Gill's sending a half dozen more lads," Mason responded grimly and flashed a glance toward the door.

Following that glance, Natalie gained only a slight impression of a dark shadow just out of full sight, and she understood at least part of what Mason might have handled. Gill—Gillis MacDade, head of security. No stranger to bodyguards or heightened security, she could be only relieved to realize the presence now. Whether Lucius had reached the same conclusion that she had or merely took the precaution to thwart publicity seekers, the added security was welcome. Just the sight of the departing nurses veering, shying as they departed, lent a modicum of relief. Artair was as good as a palace sentry and as formidable as all other MacDades cut from the same ilk. They were as clannish as her own family and would leave naught to chance.

"Sir," Emerson began carefully. "I know we talked about transporting him earlier, and with that in mind, I merely intended to offer the alternative.

I had a private room prepared upstairs with all the necessary equipment to be considered an intensive care unit, along with a highly trained staff to care for him. Under the circumstances, I don't think he's ready to move. I'd like you to reconsider taking him from here until he's truly stable."

"Well, then we're thinking on the same plane here, doctor," Lucius said grimly and dipped his gaze to see Liam looking up from beneath his hand, his blue eyes as murky as smoked cobalt. "Aye, ye need rest, now, and quit yer fighting. Ye won that battle, and ye dinnae need to go this one alone." His focus shifted to the doctor. "I'm nae meaning to offend ye here, doctor, but I'll be sending for our physician to oversee his care while he's here. And I willnae mind a list of names of those on yer staff to be tending him." Without a doubt, he would screen that list personally.

Emerson appeared only relieved. "I'll have it for you, sir."

"Good then. How soon will ye move him?"

"We can have him moved now."

"Good then," he said again and idled. "Probably should mention, we've taken the liberty of posting security outside the door, and they'll be traveling with him. They willnae interfere with a thing lest they need to."

For a moment, Emerson considered rejecting that stipulation, but the steady dark gaze changed his mind. "Which reminds me, sir. We have a bit of a situation downstairs."

Lucius lifted his brow, the only indication of his curiosity.

"The Press. I'm not certain how exactly, but at least a few details of last night leaked, and we have about a dozen reporters and news vans gathering outside."

Lucius looked toward Mason for verification.

Mason nodded, appearing disgusted. "A fact, Lucius. They're being a nuisance."

"Any we know?"

"None so far, but I contacted Marion. She's preparing a statement."

Emerson interrupted. "Ed Turner, our Chief of Staff, is likely to call a press conference, and I wondered if you and Mrs. MacDade . . . or uhm, both of them, would like to join us. We won't offer any details of your son's condition, only to say that he was injured and currently listed in critical condition."

"Is he?"

The question came from Gregor, who had recovered enough to look at the doctor.

"At this moment, yes," Emerson said with a worried glance at Liam, then back. "He is."

"Let's we get him moved and comfortable," Lucius decided. "Then we'll see about yer press conference."

Navigating only as far as the ultra-modern lobby, Lucas rested on one of the vinyl-cushioned chairs, listening to the canned piano music emanating from a faux baby grand. With the top hatch propped open, the audience could watch the rods piston the chords of Bach's Concerto No. 4. Doubtful Bach had imagined this setting when creating his music, however, and likely he'd anticipated an audience greater than one. People were coming and going. The normal business hours had already begun with the lobby doors opening and closing, visitors and patients arriving and departing.

His brother rested on the second floor. Might—or might not—be awaiting transfer from the recovery room to another floor or another hospital several states west. Resting, forearms on his knees, head sinking nearly to his folded caught hands between his knees, Luke tried to decide between returning to that room or racing out the door to find the limo and his bag. He could leave the bag. He could collect his belongings later—like in the next year or two.

Too much. Too much and too many. Either too much bad coffee, too many hours of awareness . . . too much and too many MacDades.

MacDade overload.

Stress overload.

Leaning, staring at the Terrazzo tile beneath his tennis shoes, he marveled at the ungodly gold flecks and suffered an odd surprise to find he wore a matched set of white Nike's. Considering his race across the tarmac, he must have dressed prepared to run . . . as he considered running now. The problem was simple—he felt as if he'd pulled an all-nighter, maybe sucking down 16 ouncers and pretzels at his computer. A hangover could hurt no worse unless he tacked on the unyielding tension gripping his muscles even now.

Liam MacDade was going to die.

Gregor should have told their nephew that his father was too stubborn to *live*, not die.

If the big jerk refused the medicine again, or the drugs ran through his massive system like greased lightning as it appeared, they would never hold him down long enough to heal.

With the memory flash of his brother buckling, bucking, and nearly breaking loose under his considerable might, a shudder spilled from head to heel like ice water pouring through his hair follicles. Those nurses would never hold Liam MacDade to that mattress. They would need to strap the fellow to the bed, and Luke could imagine how that would go over with the big jerk. He would probably pull himself apart trying to break the blasted straps.

All things at once, Luke drawing a shaky breath while pushing off his forearms, the piano changing its tune in a background hum over a wave of voices through a briefly parted door, a dark-clad body halting four steps away. Before fully lifting, Luke knew someone poised, studying him. He'd sensed a body approaching and believed he would recognize a familiar face in the form of a MacDade security man.

The dark-clad fellow appeared vaguely familiar. He wore his dark hair in a business cut, neatly styled, although he wore casual black slacks and a gray polo shirt rather than a suit. Startled warm brown eyes accompanied the bewildered kink in his mustached lips . . . and he was not a security guard.

Another few seconds passed before Luke dredged the memory from the past and recalled the sculpted face in any number of situations—from a brief visit to Liam's college dorm a million years ago to Liam's wedding eight years ago. Pendleton. The roommate and apparent friend. Had this situation already made the national news?

As if launched off the balls of his shiny Italian leather loafers, the fellow continued forward, his bewildered smile enhanced behind visible tension. "Luke . . . you have to be Luke MacDade," he said with the lyrical soft rhythm of a soprano straining to be a tenor. An odd combination with the damp eyes and taut smile. "I'm Frank. Frank Pendleton. A friend of your brother's," he offered while swinging onto the next chair, sitting sidesaddle and apparently struggling not to reach over. He gripped a fist on his knee to halt that action. "I can't believe how much you look like him. Liam, I mean. How is he? I tried calling, but they wouldn't even admit he was here. I know he's here, but they won't tell me how he is."

Either this fellow was ADHD or sailing on amphetamines. Luke couldn't decide which and then wondered at his own delayed thoughts. He'd tried smoking weed once. It felt like this. The world in delay. Exhaustion. Considering the wakeup call at 1: am, the past six or seven hours of tension, on top of jetlag, accounting-lag, and play-lag . . . he was lagging.

"Luke? Lucas?"

Refocusing, almost amused at how easily he'd faded into his internal kibitzing—much to this fellow's apparent chagrin—Luke managed a slight smile, shaking his head as he acclimated, glancing over the quiet lobby. Not too much people traffic yet. An elderly woman had taken residence behind a tall Information Desk, and an equally elderly couple stood, barely tall enough to peer over the counter, undoubtedly asking for directions. Dayglow spread through the dual sets of double doors, with the sunlight blocked by the roof of a portico-covered drive. Several patients had already escaped through that glass cove, but even as he assessed his own escape, he noticed the van parked at the end of the main stairway entrance. Morning sunlight sprinted off the windshield . . . and illuminated an odd gathering of people just beyond the entrance ramp and steps.

"You look exhausted, Lucas," Pendleton intruded.

With a serious effort to collect his thoughts and his mental balance, Luke looked at Pendleton, truly looked at the patrician nose, soft lips, and warm worried eyes, and grasped the man's genuine distress and concern.

"I think that café's open, now," Pendleton spoke carefully, undoubtedly, wisely believing he dealt with a man on the edge. "Why don't I buy you a cup of coffee? You probably haven't had breakfast yet, either. We could both go, or I could just bring you something if you prefer?"

He must look as bad as he felt. Only that thought held firm, but before he could respond, the brown eyes flashed terror behind a sudden watery sheen.

"Lucas? Liam—how is he?" the man stammered. "Please, he's—he—he's not—"

Dead. That was the word caught on the fellow's tongue, creating fear in his manic brown eyes. Belatedly, Luke realized his silence had just hiked the man's terror. "He came through the surgery," Luke offered quietly. "He's in ICU—or going to be. He's in recovery. Might get moved to a room or—or transferred to a facility in Kentucky."

Relief, like a liquid mask, poured over the tense face and softened the damp shine in the eyes. In a breath, needing to swallow, Pendleton huffed,

"Thank God. When I heard that news broadcast this morning—I was so afraid . . . Thank you."

Luke nodded as he considered adding that the relief could be premature. The fellow apparently hadn't heard the mention of ICU or chose not to acknowledge the severity. Sighing, glancing toward the door, Luke's attention caught again on the activity through the glass. A crowd. The news? Pendle ton had heard about this on the news? And just happened to be in the vicinity? Or was Pendleton the reason Liam was in Trenton, New Jersey? Before Luke could decide on his question, the logo on the van registered. A news van. WKBN. A television station van. "Shit," he uttered, considering the probability of his father's forecast. Looking at Frank, he dared to hope. "They mentioned him by name? On the news?"

"They did," Frank said as his quick brown eyes darted from the doors to Luke, following his thought. "And they've started broadcasting updates," he said with a hint of concern.

"Shit," Luke repeated absently and spared another glance toward the glass doors. The chance of him escaping unnoticed had just thinned.

"Were uhm . . . were you coming in or going out?" Frank asked hesitantly.

For a moment, Luke wasn't entirely certain. He'd needed out of that room, away from his family, away from the possibility of his brother not surviving . . . and apparently, something of his confusion surfaced all too clearly. "Out," he decided.

Frank reached, touching his shoulder not too unlike Gregor had reached to comfort Natalie. "You look exhausted, Lucas."

"Just Luke," he offered absently.

"Luke, then," Pendleton said with a soft smile. "I know a back way out of here, and my car's in the garage across the street. What do you say we get you out of here for a little while, and I find you someplace you can rest for a few moments?"

Luke reconsidered his need to move for a half second, but at the burst of sound, he glimpsed the glass doors opening. Even without ever seeing her before or noticing the microphone clutched at her side, he might have recognized her celebrity status by the clip of her high heels, the polished glossy shine to her pixie face, and her coifed blond hair. Doubtful a good breeze would shift a strand off her brow. The expression of wide-eyed wonder was as fake as the hairstyle with the kind of pasted appearance perfected by any decent actor. Already up and moving, making the decision even before he heard her addressing someone over her shoulder, Luke headed for the first hallway, bypassing the open café and a gift shop.

"... Isn't that one of them?"

Them. The MacDades. He felt odd—as if he were some rare, exotic bird being hunted and spotted in the Congo... 'One of them fancy birds.' A parrot, maybe. Or a prairie dog on a Texas plain... no mistaking that critter. 'One of *them.*'

"Damn it," he muttered as he passed through a set of double doors, only vaguely aware of Frank Pendleton following. He was getting slap-happy, worrying about hunting fucking prairie dogs—why not a jackrabbit? Or hell—a seagull in Tennessee? 'One of them there birds you see at the ocean . . .'

He should be catching an elevator, returning to that recovery room, or the waiting room where his nephews were awaiting the trauma of seeing their father hooked up to machines with blood caked at his manicured nails. Liam was probably a good father. He'd always tried to be a good brother with what he'd had to work with. Neither boy was shy or backward. Like their father, they seemed outgoing, friendly, and polite—they were polite even under these wicked conditions. Liam had done well with them—Natalie, too, Luke guessed. He'd never really gotten to know her. He'd been twelve when they'd married; too young to be involved in either of his brothers' lives by then, much less of age to hang out with a young couple in love.

They were still in love by the looks of them. Even a blind man could have identified the love in those voices, the closeness they shared . . . so what the hell was Liam doing visiting a *mistress* in a seedy hotel?

And what the hell did it matter? What the MacDades did behind closed doors was not his concern or business. He had enough trouble keeping track of his own life without becoming involved in family secrets.

Lost in his private thoughts, as surely as he was now lost in Southern General, Luke halted before passing through another set of doors. Belatedly, he found Frank stopped at his side, watching him with a faintly bemused, curious smile. "I . . . you mentioned a backdoor?"

Frank glanced at the closed door and back with a peculiar expression. "You seemed to know where you were going," he commented. "We can reach the garage through here."

"Good," Luke decided and continued forward, passing through the doors into a brightly lit corridor—a short corridor with a bank of windows offering a fine view of the side street and parking garage entrance. By habit, he spotted the security camera in the corner above the door and flashed a smile, refraining from a wave. His mug on film was as good as a phone call to announce his departure. Inevitably, his father would order Gillis's men or Mason to check the security footage when Luke failed to return to that room. It wouldn't be the first time that Luke McDade waved or nodded to a camera, knowing his father would receive the message. The big guy only thought he was being clever by keeping tabs on one wayward son, and Luke had learned to tolerate the occasional surveillance. When it was necessary, he slipped from sight and sometimes managed to remain invisible for several weeks or months at a time.

"This way," Frank offered, directing Lucas toward the ascending ramp.

Not many cars filled the visitor slots, not yet anyway. Luke spotted the black Lincoln partway up the slope, matching the sleek ride to his escort, half wondering if he should try finding the limo. It might still be near the emergency room entrance, which, if he read the signs right, existed on the opposite side of the hospital.

"There's a limo floating around here somewhere," Luke commented as Frank used a remote key fob to unlock the doors at their approach. "Any chance you saw it?"

"I did," Frank said as they parted at the rear of the car, him looking over the hood as he reached the driver's door. "If you mean the same one Liam was in last night, it was parked near the emergency entrance."

"That's the one," he said and slid into the sleek bucket seat, appreciating the elegance. He'd always loved cars—any cars—from luxury liners to hotrods. This one reeked of class and sophistication, as clean as his father's antique Rolls-Royce Silver Cloud. Wood grain console, digital controls, the ability to switch from manual to automatic shifter with paddles discreetly, conveniently placed on the leather steering wheel. Admiring the car, Luke barely lent Frank a thought until the fellow spoke.

"Do you uhm . . . do you want to stop at the car? Maybe leave a message or something?"

"Did you notice a driver there?"

"I did, and he was," Frank said lyrically, his mustache kinked in what might be a permanent smile, his brown eyes intent rather than amused.

"If we can circle that mob out front, I wouldn't mind stopping at the car," he admitted, deciding he would rather not mention his reason. This fellow might frown on the decision to leave the hospital—as well as the area—in the rearview mirror. Liam's friend might not appreciate a younger brother fleeing the scene before the situation fell one way or the other.

Listless, Luke gazed through the side window, trying not to think about what could be happening in that hospital room. If anything happened, turning on the local news would enlighten him, and he might prefer hearing it secondhand. If he believed his presence in that hospital room would make a difference, he would return, but he knew better. For as far back as he could remember—which spanned his lifetime—he'd been more of an afterthought in his family's lives. Not exactly a late-life baby, but close enough. Probably, just more like an accident.

Far more comfortable than the recovery room, the private suite boasted several vinyl couches, two recliners, and two wood-trimmed windows with sunlight pouring almost vertically through slots in the heavy beige drapes. Ultra-modern lamps occupied three wood-grained end tables, suggesting a living room motif with a wide television across the room. Monet prints in stark wood frames decorated the pastel beige walls, adding to the illusion of a homey ambiance. The scent of disinfectant, the steady bleep and hum of hospital machinery, the utilitarian tile floor . . . and the single bed situated between the windows aglow under neon lights countered the effect.

Standing alongside the raised bed, gripping the iron rails to remain afoot, Natalie studied the handsome face for telltale signs of discomfort. Even without the tubes at his nostrils, there was no mistaking his condition. Far too pale, those sculpted features, in sharp contrast to the long, thick black lashes.

"He'll be all right, Lee," Gregor said confidently, but the bravado was feigned. Too clearly, he was worried, as his glance at the bed indicated. He might as easily have said, 'He has to be all right.'

Natalie nodded and might have returned the comfort, but the motion past Gregor drew her focus. On the fringes of her mind, she glimpsed Mason, but Lucius's gaze and his approach held her attention.

Halting just past the end of the bed, he glanced off his sleeping son, then to her with a calm blue gaze. "Do ye think we might have a word, lass?"

The press conference . . . she nodded and fleeted a glance to Mason's troubled expression before turning, touching Gregor's hand in reassurance. "You should rest, hon. We've none of us had a short night."

"Thar's a private room, just this way," Lucius said and motioned toward the door.

The homey atmosphere continued into the hallway with wood-trimmed doors and wood-framed photos on papered walls. The VIP wing, no doubt, with the family waiting room appearing more like a compact living room sporting another large screen TV and more couches with floral pillows to offer comfort. Other than the sentinels outside Liam's door, the floor appeared deserted, and the waiting room was empty.

Behind them, Mason shut the door as Lucius motioned to the small table and chairs near the window. "Ye need rest. Let's we sit."

As much as she knew she'd rather stand for whatever her father-in-law meant to say, she wasn't about to argue. Settling on the chair nearest the window, she glanced through the glass to identify another hospital wing in her immediate view. Mere swatches of sunlight reflected off the string of windows, high and low. A blue sky above, a hint of white clouds. That she might still be stuck in the shadows of the evening past occurred to her as her gaze listed to Lucius already seated across from her, studying her intently. Mason had settled into a chair, forming the point of a triangle despite the round table.

"Lass, I willnae beat aboot the boosh," Lucius began quietly, no malice in his dark blue eyes. "Was a thing I questioned when Mason phoned me in the wee hours. Aye, and I didnae want to question too deeply. But a fact, I wondered if it was a bit muddled."

"Lucius," Mason started, appearing slightly worried.

"Mase," the elder said calmly. "I can appreciate yer help here, but I think my fine daughter shood tell this tale." His gaze returned, calm and consoling. "I'm naw believing quite all I heard and nae of this to go any further. The facts as I know them. On separate flights, yerself and himself arrived though nearly at the same times. Aye, and Mason to tell the police detectives ye were with him in the limo. That ye're dressed for reconciling, I've nae doubts, but my wonder . . .? Was the lad there and gone at that hotel? Or there and occupied for a time?"

Leave it to this great bull of a man to hit upon the facts. Natalie sighed and resigned. "There and occupied, Da."

"Aye," he stated grimly. "Was more my fear. And yerself?"

"I had to know," she said and tilted her gaze through the glass. Exhaustion was, perhaps, the only salving balm. She need not feign the weariness of her thoughts.

"Aye, and was yerself following him then."

She nodded, meeting Lucius's gaze. "I was in a cab a block from the hotel."

"I dinnae know what worries me more, lass, thinking of yourself sitting in a blasted cab and confirming yer suspicions, er yourself in the bloody cab alone on that stretch of road."

"I've thought about this," she said, and in a glance added Mason, who appeared rather ill. "And I don't think it was such a bad part of town. I've reviewed the facts a hundred times, and I think we need to speak to the police. It was an ambush meant for Liam."

Alarm flashed in Lucius's dark blue eyes, and he glanced to Mason as if searching for that possibility. "Did you leave something out of yer telling, Mason?"

"I don't know how I could have," he answered, alarmed as he looked at Natalie. "What makes you think so, dear?"

"We need be honest," she decided. "I don't care what nonsense we feed the press or the police, exactly, but the fact remains, that street didn't seem dangerous. There weren't gangs or pimps or prostitutes on the corners. I was there, Mason. I . . ." She looked at Lucius. "I'll not deny I was there for several hours, and it was a thought of clouting him when he rallied to keep me there. Was a thought of ambushing him, my own self, to cross my mind, then I saw the two men step from that black nook and follow him. No more than twenty or thirty feet to that alley, I think. And he had to know they were there. But they weren't alone, and I . . . I heard the gunshot when they stepped into the shadows."

"A bloody gunshot?" Lucius asked and lanced Mason with a far more heated shine. "A bloody gunshot and you failed to mention it?"

"I swear by the almighty, Lucius, I heard er saw no such thing," he said warily as he looked to Natalie. "Are you certain? You couldn't be mistaken? What with all that noise from those bars?"

"I know what I heard," she said quietly, glancing between them and settling on Lucius. "And I know my blasted husband wouldn't have walked into that alley on his own. No fool is he, sir," she added honestly and recognized the pride in the elder's eyes. "It was no more than a pop. Not the sound of a hunting rifle or the like . . . More like the snap of a firecracker."

"And you ran toward it anyway?" Mason asked with a rising note of incredulity.

"Well . . ." In hindsight, Natalie realized her foolishness, supposed she could have been shot, but the prickling . . .? "The danger was to himself," she decided and shrugged, seeing an almost bemused shine in her father-in-law's eyes before he turned his gaze to Mason.

"Where the hell were you, lad?"

"In the blasted limo," he said in irritation and held his gaze steady on Natalie. "So, that was truly you, I saw flying down that blasted street?"

"Uhhh, well . . . probably," she said carefully, feeling slightly foolish now, but knowing she would do it again. "He . . ." Her gaze caught and held on Lucius. "He was in trouble, Da."

"Aye, he was fey," he spoke in a lower tone, a simple benediction to offer his clear understanding and, perhaps, for the first time, admitting his knowledge of her ilk. In his own family, there were rumors of the knack passing from one heir to the next. His own mother was said to have the talent. That he appeared slightly more shaken, perhaps, only Natalie could attest. In that single little word, he confirmed his grasp of how close his son stood to death's door.

With a subtle nod, Natalie acknowledged his belief.

Leaning back in his chair for the first time, by no means relaxed, he tipped his bearded face toward the window to either collect his great balance or weigh his words.

This was how Liam would look in twenty or thirty years, she considered in an odd moment. A wild and wondrous cross of Highlander Lord and sophisticate, as handsome then as now, no matter the webbed laugh lines at his temples or in his lips.

Sighing, Lucius brought his gaze about and seemed to take her measure, possibly to judge, for himself, that she was unscathed. "You joined that fray, aye?"

"He had them well in hand by then, and I uhm . . . Well, I didn't do much, to be sure."

"Mo nighean, I dinnae know if you're being modest er honest here, but for yer presence in that blasted alley, I'll be only grateful. The problem is . . ."

His gaze shifted to Mason and back. "We've already muddied the water with the police."

That his brogue slipped on and off his lips was not a good sign, though who would take the brunt of his rage remained uncertain. It seemed Mason Eldridge wouldn't escape unscathed.

"Lucius, what I gave the police was more like supposition than fact."

"You put my daughter in the limo," he said in a lower tone. "May be hard to say you only thought she was there with you. And I'm likewise near to certain my son knows that to be false."

"I'm sure he'll see the wisdom in letting that detail stand," Mason said carefully.

"Aye, providing his fine wife widnae still like to clout him when his head clears," Lucius said intemperately and eyed her with nothing short of admiration. "Mine only hope is you rein yer temper until his head is truly clear."

"Well, I've not clouted him yet," she said absently, and Lucius harrumphed a sound like a laugh, his blue eyes sparking for a second.

"The lad's been blessed twice over," he muttered and sobered, yet again, studying Natalie intently. "War back to the boosh, daughter, and myself not meaning to be insensitive, but uhm . . .? Did ye know about this tart he was visiting?"

"I don't suppose she was the first," she said in weary resignation, averting her eyes as though she might hide the pain of that admission. "Seems I need only visit a supermarket a time or two to discover my husband's latest exploits. Those tabloids keep me apprised on occasion." On rare occasions, she could admit.

"Lass," Lucius said quietly. "I dinnae think I'd put much stock in those. The lad's generally discreet."

And she had kicked him out of their bed, he need not mention. With a faint, tainted smile, Natalie nodded. "He is that—until now. Is there a means to keep this from the tabloids, do you think? I should rather not have our little ones hearing these details."

"A thought here," Lucius decided. "It's not a known fact that you and my son were having marital problems. Perhaps, and therein lies our salvation. Confiding thus to the police—this reconciliation fits our purposes fine enough. They can investigate this uhm . . . woman and judge her participation—" His gaze shifted to Mason. "Has she turned up yet?"

"Not that I'm aware, but Gillis is looking for her. We'll find her."

"Believe we'll let the police handle her." Lucius decided, his thoughts elsewhere momentarily.

Mason started, "If she runs to the tabloids—"

"I dinnae give a bloody damn," Lucius growled. "Will be the word of a loose woman over that of a MacDade lady." His gaze caught Natalie. "Providing yer willing to admit you were in that blasted limo, waiting for yer fine husband attending a business meeting."

Well, and she knew the waters could be muddied more. "For the press, this fabrication, not the police, I should understand?"

"The police have what they need," Lucius attested. "I dinnae think they'll need to speak with you at all. Could be Mason was too upset to recall the possible sound of a weapon firing last evening whence running to that alley, but himself to be thinking clearer today." His focus shifted to Mason. "They need that information, Mason. If there's a bullet er shell in that alley—" *Or in my son.* "They need to find it."

"I'll phone them as soon as we're through here," he agreed.

"Now, lass, is there else you can think of?"

"Not off hand, Da," she said lightly.

Speculating, he glanced over her again, and a slight smile flickered under his mustache. "Would em . . . ye mind to attend that press conference with Meg and myself? I dinnae expect you'll need speak, but it's a fine presentation you'll offer those devils just as you are."

Dressed to the nines and haggard. "Lord . . . I don't think I could look much worse."

"My dear, trust me," he said smoothly. "Just the sight of you will have those lads—and lasses—drooling. Tis no mistaking, you have spent a night feart far yer husband's life."

Not a fabrication or feigned presentation, he might have added, and Natalie understood. No amount of cosmetics or change of clothes could alter her distressed image, and how much more believable could the truth be?

"Lucius, she's exhausted, man," Mason said.

"You set us on this path, Mase," Lucius countered, the brogue gone, his blue gaze like molten cobalt. By the time he spied Natalie, the color had cooled. "If yer against it—"

"I'll join you," she decided. "But uhm . . .? I should like to beg a favor of you when we're through."

With a lifted brow, prepared for the worst, so it would seem, he stated, "Name it, lass."

"I uhm . . ." Almost genuinely embarrassed, she hesitated. "I didn't plan this trip well," she admitted in dismay. "I should like to find a change of clothes and a shower. And I'd like not to go far."

With his relief, he let fly another harrumph and sparked his amusement. "That, mo nighean, would be my pleasure to correct."

The main entrance of the hospital presented a pleasant ambiance. Bushes bordered the half-moon ramp leading to the wide cement stairway. With the sun lancing between the collection of buildings of the hospital's connecting wings, a warm breeze carried the lingering taste of summer along with the drone of voices. As Dr. Emerson had attested, a sizeable crowd had gathered with news vans parked at the curb and more than a dozen reporters poised to record the breaking news. Bystanders had gathered as well, collecting outside the conglomerate of camera crews and loitering in the street. Police cars—intense blue lights revolving and piercing the natural sunlight—blocked traffic at either end of the hospital's frontage, and, perhaps, only curiosity over the police presence drew the crowd.

A press conference, Natalie considered and suffered as much surprise as dismay as she was shuffled onto the steps. Never would she have imagined such an immense crowd, and she wasn't the only one suffering the confusion. Megan's hand gripped hers in a momentary vice, and at her flank, Gregor huffed a soft, "Good God"

Until now, Natalie hadn't believed they might be considered celebrities, not of this magnitude or under this circumstance. Granted, she'd ducked her share of paparazzi in the past, and one persistent fellow had needed to be escorted from their wedding ceremony years ago, but to be bombarded to this extent seemed far more than unnatural. Was it that or else to stir the short hairs at her nape and send a shiver down her spine? Or some other sense of doom to press against her? The weariness had taken its toll. No longer could she decide if it was her sixth sense or merely common sense of so many eyes upon her. Tense and shivering, she feared the goose pimples would look like freckles to an unforgiving camera, and with that in mind, she drew the simple black shawl closer to her shoulders. Unprepared. The word applied to her wardrobe as well as her frame of mind. To bring only a lacy shawl to replace that silly denim jacket . . .?

And it seemed the camera flashes never ceased even as the first speaker, no other than the Chief of Police, Chief Tarpon—a fellow who barely reached Lucius's shoulder—began to speak.

So, and Natalie heard the fabrication unfolding for the first time.

". . . I can offer you the details as we know them at this moment . . . At approximately 12:30 a.m. this morning, Liam James MacDade was assaulted while leaving a business meeting in the Renfrew District. We know there were at least eight assailants, and Mr. MacDade suffered multiple knife wounds as a result . . .

"As most of you may already know, Mr. MacDade is the oldest son of Lucius MacDade, lumber magnate and entrepreneur . . . We're asking for the public's help on this one. We have a hotline set up, and the MacDade family is offering a ten-thousand-dollar reward to anyone with information that leads to an arrest for any or all of the men involved . . ."

"Chief! Do you have any leads!" someone shouted.

"This is an ongoing investigation. We're not giving out that information."

"Do you know if this was random—or was Mr. MacDade the intended target?"

"We believe the act was random—"

"Have there been other assaults in that area—"

The questions continued to fire at the chief for several more moments, voices overlapping and vying for decibels to be heard.

A senior agent of the Federal Bureau was introduced next, an AIC Parsons.

Startled, Natalie's attention riveted, and her insides shook for reasons she couldn't begin to fathom. Why would the FBI be involved in a mugging? Was it normal? Or did they believe this was an act of domestic terroristic attack to warrant their attention? Was it the high-profile nature of this assault? Fear . . . fear niggled at the edges of her hair follicles.

". . . asked to assist . . . working in conjunction with the local authorities . . ."

Some of the questions Natalie had asked were shouted by the throng of reporters who appeared to be pressing closer on the steps. Why was the FBI involved . . .? If it was an isolated act of violence . . .? "With the nature of the assault . . ."

". . . Terrorist attack?"

". . . Do the MacDades have government contracts . . .?"

". . . Is Liam MacDade involved with the government . . .?"

". . . Did he serve in the Armed Forces . . .?"

At her side, Gregor uttered, "God. They're about to turn him into a spook."

Undecided if he was amused or disturbed, Natalie canted her head to meet his eyes and remained undecided despite the kink in his mustache. "Seriously?" she whispered.

He favored her with a distressed glance and slight shrug. "Seems where this is headed."

"God," she muttered and panned her gaze over the crowd, all too aware of the cameras flashing and film rolling. At least one of the Action News cameras was broadcasting live, and an overwhelming urge to turn and tell Liam some foolish thing about becoming a movie star sailed through Natalie's mind before her muscles gripped. This was Gregor, not Liam hovering over her shoulder—and the sudden revelation struck like a punch in the stomach. That she flinched, started to buckle, and moved her hand as if she might hold the pain at bay occurred to her only as Meg pivoted her worried eyes. Through a sudden blur, she recognized Meg's enhanced worry, and the cameras were rolling.

POISE, she screamed silently and ducked her head aside, drawing clear breath, appreciating Meg's hand clasping her in a half turn. Oh, how she wanted to cry suddenly, for herself, for Liam, for her babies . . . For the wicked fear that he might truly not recover. Just something so simple, sharing a musing confidence . . . When he was beside her, his attention never wavered, his eye never wandered. But how much of that attentiveness was learned and drilled into him as surely as the 'poise' to demand her recovery? How his eyes could glitter with mischief on a moment's notice . . . and he would find this blasted gathering amusing—more so if he knew himself to be the focus.

Unconsciously, she brushed at a loose tear and drew a calming breath, finding Meg watching her still, worrying, and at her back, Gregor's hand clasped in support. Over Meg's strawberry blond locks, Lucius spied Natalie as well, his concern for her as apparent as his worry for his son.

The Chief of Staff, Dr. Ed Turner had begun to speak, and at the fringes of her mind, Natalie heard the amplified words as if from some distant place. "... Multiple knife wounds ... extensive damage ... blood transfusions ..."

No mention of a gunshot wound, thank the good lord, but she'd heard those words before. Already, she'd lived through the pain of those words spoken by the Chief of Surgery, Dr. Emerson.

"... Stable ... Critical condition ..."

"... Life supports?" Someone wanted to know.

"... Conscious ..."

"... Regained consciousness ..."

Her stomach hurt, and in slow degrees, illumination surfaced through the cobwebs in her brain. Not a natural pain! Not her pain! Liam! Clasping Meg's hand, Natalie drew the pale hazel eyes, and something of her instant panic shot into Megan's awareness. "I have to get to him!"

"Go, dear," Megan said and flashed to Gregor. "Go with her!"

Without a thought, Natalie spun. With Gregor on her heels, she plowed a path through the suited bodies between her and the glass doors. Whether they were police, bodyguards, or hospital security, she knew only a need to wade through them as if breaking through a watery tide. The sliding doors barely parted as she strode through en route to the elevator, aware in every second of his pain advancing, increasing.

"Lee, what's wrong?" Gregor asked as the elevator doors shut.

"He's waking."

For a half second, he studied her before the belief struck. "Oh God." His focus shot heavenward to the lighted button, willing it to ignite faster. "How bad?" he asked when he might have asked, 'How the hell do you know?'

"Hurts," she managed and refrained from buckling to the fire at her core. The instant the doors opened, she flew and barely noticed the sentries jolting, both reaching for a weapon before recognizing the mad woman dashing toward them. Natalie swung through the open door and nearly skidded on her heels to find the attending nurse merely pausing to look over with a pleasant smile.

"He's doing fine, ma'am—"

"Like hell he is," Natalie snapped unnaturally and continued forward, vaguely aware of the young woman's alarmed backward step. Barely reaching the bedside in time to catch his hand flying toward the oxygen tube, Natalie laced her fingers through his and pressed his hand to his chest. His lashes lifted, and the murky blue orbs tried to focus. A single groaned breath escaped under his mustache, an attempt at speech. "Hush," she stated, and his focus riveted. "Enough, Liam . . . Enough. You need to stop this . . . Stop fighting the blasted drugs. Do you hear me? Enough. You need to behave . . . To get well, you need to behave . . ."

"Mmm—try 'n," he heaved in a soft breath, and in his eyes, in his voice, he pleaded for relief.

"Oh, God, what am I going to do with you?" she half begged as the tears swam over her eyes. "I can't leave you for a minute."

"D-d-din-nae gggooo."

Belatedly, the nurse seemed to catch on, huffing, "That's not possible. He was . . . It's not time for another shot."

"Lass," Gregor growled. "The lad's six-six with the metabolism of a thoroughbred. I dinnae think you can judge his needs by ordinary measures. Check your blasted charts or orders or what have you. I think you'll find my brother's to get those blasted shots far more regularly than most."

"Nnno," Liam groaned and tried moving his hand, but Natalie held him quick. Barely his injured arm lifted, and Gregor appeared in a flash, locking a grip in an arm-wrestling pose.

"Hold on, Brother," Gregor ordered, sounding more like their father than ever before. "Just hold on. We'll have you resting easy in no time."

Liam wanted no part of resting easy. He tried pulling his hand away, tried skidding his hand down his chest where the flames were rising.

Without a first or second thought, Natalie drew his hand, likewise his arm over his head to the pillow above his tangled blond locks. Dipping downward, she landed her lips over his started protest. Well, and that stopped him. Whether in shock or confusion, he ceased to move, merely parted his lips more and tilted his head, availing himself to her ministrations. A sound—other than pain—escaped him, rather like the sound after a taste of warm soup. That she hadn't kissed him—or been kissed by him in some time touched her fluttering senses as the familiar heat started in her lower regions. Blast him, anyway! Treading at the pearly gates, and he could still turn the tides in an eyeblink. She drew a breath and lifted enough to find his murky eyes looking at her with an odd sort of fascination. "Now, blast you. Lie still," she uttered, and his lashes dipped to effect confusion.

At the edges of her vision, she glimpsed the nurse at the IV line alongside Gregor, and Liam barely seemed to grasp the same before the plunger sank. But for a second, hell's fury ignited in the cobalt blue depths, but the medicine rolled over him like a tidal wave, taking him under.

With the hand turning limp in her grip, Natalie knew a moment of regret and sorrow, and drew a breath against the lump.

"Lass," Gregor said hesitantly. "That was mean."

Lifting her damp eyes, she barely suffered the pain of those words.

"Aye, but the quickest, most painless means to the end," he added and quivered a smile, glancing at his sleeping brother and back. "If he retains that memory, you may be in trouble when he's back on his feet."

"I uhm . . . Well, I doubt he'll remember," she said while recovering and finding the worried nurse watching them now. "Please, find out how closely you can give those sedatives. It seems to be holding him for no more than three hours. We need to keep him quiet, or he'll surely rip those stitches to pieces."

"I'll call Dr. Emerson, ma'am, and I truly am sorry. He seemed to be resting quietly. His vitals were all good."

"He's a wily devil, to be sure," Natalie admitted, taking pity on the woman, 'Kerry D.,' according to her nametag. "You probably won't know he's waking until he's near to exploding, and then he'll fight you to avoid taking any medication.

"I uhm," Gregor stifled a laugh and looked to the worried nurse. "I widnae suggest using his wife's tactics to derail him, though, miss. Now, if it was me in his stead," he started, and with the flash of a dimple at the end of his mustache, Kerry D.'s attention riveted, herself derailed.

"Rogues, the lot of them," Natalie muttered and glimpsed the innocent flash in Gregor's eyes. Anything but innocent—that impish grin and sparkling eyes. She shook her head, smiling more naturally at his wink. A flirt . . . Even more so than Liam, this middle son was a flirt, but he retained the common sense thus far to remain single. His exploits, tabloid-worthy, to be sure, were of vast interest to as many society pages as gossip rags. But he hadn't a thing to hide. As Natalie had heard often, any woman would be only flattered to catch his roving eye, and none had ever suffered an ill at his hand.

.'He's like a blasted bee,' Liam had once said of his brother's conquests. 'He flits from one hen to another like a blasted bee pollinating flowers.'

Natalie recalled laughing and fearing, 'Hope that's not meant in the literal sense. Were it true, he might go broke paying child support.'

'The lad has the good sense to be careful,' Liam had mused. 'So far as I know, not a single bairn to his credit . . .'

Sighing yet again, more than weary, Natalie brought Liam's hand to rest more naturally at his chest, then ducked and brushed a kiss on his cheek. "Rest, my love, as will I for a bit." She needed to sit. If only for a moment, she needed to sit, and she reached only the nearest recliner before kicking off her heels and lying back on the cushion, dropping into oblivion.

8

How exactly he'd come to be sitting in the shadowy dining room, Luke couldn't quite decide. He might have dozed in the car. The last thing he clearly recalled was stopping at the limo and waking the driver to grab his garment bag from the trunk. He'd mentioned finding a hotel, and Frank had suggested breakfast. Now, here he rested, taking up space at a formal, lace-covered table with carved legs as wide as his own and a candelabra centerpiece of museum-quality crystal. Old money, but new, compared to the MacDades, Luke decided while glimpsing at the uniformed woman pushing a cart into the room. The smell of bacon reached him despite the silver domed lids. The MacDade estate housed a surplus of waitstaff, but nowhere in Luke's memory had he seen more than a similar apron to suggest a servant status—and his mother had often worn an apron when she decided to concoct an old family recipe.

Listless, Luke continued his scan, acclimating to appreciate the woodwork within this single long room. Old money. Old architecture. From high, tintype ceilings to dark walnut frames and etched crown moldings, the style was period Victorian with all the trimmings. Old lace draped the tall, narrow windows and the French doors; hand-painted, porcelain plates stood behind beveled glass china closets. With the morning sun slanting through the lace, an odd haze lingered in the room, and belying the bacon, the scent of sunbaked wood and dust permeated the air.

At one end of the table, a rail-thin woman sat as prim as a schoolmarm, her silver hair coifed as if for a bun but cut short to frame her slender, cosmetic-dusted face. She wasn't that old, not to account for the hairstyle, and Luke recognized enough of Frank's patrician features to know this was his mother. If they'd been introduced, Luke had slept through it and decided not to repeat the ordeal. Across from him, leaned back and lounging, Frank wore one of his more peculiar smiles as if judging an odd specimen under glass. Belatedly, Luke realized his old habit of navigating on autopilot. If he tried, he could recall every second of the past hour—or two—but why bother? Even indisposed, he generally functioned well enough, and if he needed to know—the memory would come.

Frank's mother's name was Cheryl—pronounced Sher-ell, he recalled, and the patriarch's name—an older, more worn version of Frank—Frances.

An accomplishment that. Now, if he could recall why he'd agreed to come to this house . . .?

The paparazzi. Frank had offered refuge rather than risk drawing the paparazzi by letting him check into a hotel. In record time, the fellow had gained his parents' approval to offer his buddy's little brother a guestroom for a good night's sleep.

Sleep wasn't a bad idea. And breakfast wasn't too bad either. Feeling like a charity case, if not a basket case, was different . . . or maybe not too. As a child, he'd once imposed on three separate friends to spend his vacation time rather than return to the MacDade estate. By Christmas, his father had been mad enough to send an entire security detail to escort him home. Luke hadn't intentionally waged war on his father. He'd just decided it was prudent to steer clear of the big guy for a while after their summer-long feud. Even now, Luke couldn't understand why his father had set to raging; after all, graduating three years early had seemed only sensible after stacking up enough credits to qualify at the age of fourteen. Anyway, those last few years turned out to be a blast. So maybe someday, he'd find grace to apologize and thank the big guy for the experience.

That day hadn't come, however.

"Luke? Why don't I show you to that guestroom if you're finished? You look about out on your feet."

Autopilot, Luke confirmed, looking over the dredges of bacon, eggs, and toast crumbs scattered on the flowered plate. Hopefully, he'd managed to use his fork. The cloth napkin rested on his lap. That was a good sign. Looking toward the woman who wore the same quirky smile as her son—without the mustache—Luke managed a smile. "If you're certain it's not an imposition, I wouldn't mind accepting that offer."

"It's no trouble, dear," she said pleasantly, and Luke decided she was the yin to the patriarch's yang. Where Pendleton senior was stodgy, she was stoic and probably possessed a fine sense of humor.

To the swish of the French door opening toward the inside of the house, Luke's attention riveted to watch a gaunt, middle-aged fellow stride into the room and cut an angle toward Frank. The fellow had opened the front door when they'd arrived, and Frank had addressed him with a simple 'Carl' before waving him aside like a bothersome fly. The butler, but of course. Luke glimpsed the darting eyes sprinting in his direction before Carl arrived alongside Frank.

"Sir," he began in a droll tone. "Your father suggested you and your guest might be interested. There's a press conference about to air on WKBN regarding Liam MacDade's condition—"

"Now, do you mean?" Frank asked while rising and lancing Luke, not awaiting an answer. "This way—"

Possibly only spurred into motion by Frank's manic rise, Luke collected his napkin, wiped his mouth as he rose just in case he caught some crumbs in his beard, and addressed the somewhat startled woman. "Thank you for breakfast, ma'am. It was marvelous." Marvelous? Not just good? Idiot, he nearly chastised himself aloud until he grasped the older woman's appreciation for his impeccable manners and apparent lofty arrogance. At times, his ability to read a person or situation and act accordingly baffled even him.

"You're most welcome, dear," she offered. "I'll have a bath prepared when you're ready."

"Excuse me, then," Luke said with a nod, excusing himself and joining Frank at the opposite side of the table. The butler led the way, offering escort in case Frank forgot the location of the nearest television in his parents' house.

They traveled only as far as the front foyer and then passed through another set of French doors into a room that might have been a receiving room in another era . . . Or the same era, Luke corrected. Parlor chairs and Duncan Feif end tables adorned in silk-shaded, blown-glass lamps scattered about the room. A brick fireplace stood against the outside wall with skylight windows heavily draped to either side. Crossing the room, the butler leaned and opened a cabinet, exposing the TV where it hid like an unwanted stepchild. At Frank's manic gesture, Luke accepted one of the chairs near the console set, almost surprised to see Carl deliver a remote control into Frank's hands. He wouldn't have been surprised if the butler had leaned and turned the channels with a Bakelite nob at Frank's command.

"Can I bring you gentlemen your coffee here, sir?"

"That would be fine, Carl. Thanks," Frank said offhandedly.

With the screen erupting in livid color, Luke's attention riveted. The camera was positioned outside the glass entrance of the hospital, and not surprisingly, the sleek blond woman, whom he'd narrowly escaped in the hospital lobby, stood front and center, speaking.

". . . as you can see, crowds are already growing," she spoke as the camera panned at her signal.

"What the . . .?" Luke started as he impacted the details within the camera lens. A crowd had formed, but not just reporters and paparazzi. Directly front and center of the horseshoe drive, a sizable collection of ordinary people had gathered, and a mound of offerings—from roses and carnations to hand-drawn signs of well-wishes—had already accumulated. A memorial? A shiver skittered down his spine, and he tensed, far more poised as he bounced his glance over the faces, young and old, mostly women. What the hell was this? Liam wasn't dead! Or was he? Was this a memorial? Had Liam passed?

". . . the people of Trenton began this outpouring of love and support shortly after we aired the news of Liam MacDade's condition early this morning . . . For those of you just tuning in, this is the scene outside Southern General Hospital this morning where the heir to the MacDade family fortunes lies fighting for his life after he became the victim of a vicious assault late last evening. We're about to receive an update on the young Mr. MacDade's condition . . ."

The screen split and Liam's face erupted on half of it.

Of all the pictures that might have surfaced, this one certainly explained the 'outpouring of love and support.' Three years ago, the photo had aired—capturing both Liam and Natalie arriving on the red carpet to support their cousin Carmin for her Oscar nomination. At 6' 6", Liam looked like a God among worshippers. His wavy neon-blond hair scattered and contrasted perfectly with the stark black suit; his blue eyes turned near to cobalt under the camera flashes; his mustache enhanced the infamous MacDade smile that could turn warm or cold on the instant.

Liam almost always smiled, Luke remembered absently, flashing images of his older brother in a hundred freeze-frames. Even when he was raging,

Liam smiled, and that one could put the fear of God in the unsuspecting—or a little brother.

Damned their Scottish heritage to make them prone to that lunacy.

"Damn it," Luke muttered, refocusing as the blond reporter returned center stage again. Behind her, several dark-suited—and white-smocked—bodies emerged through the glass doors. Police uniforms, suits . . . Lucius and Megan MacDade. They weren't weeping, but the stoic expressions on their handsome faces lent creed to the gravity of the circumstance. They were something, these two. They moved with the natural elegance of royalty with the added touch of several familiar bodyguards flanking them and escorting them toward the podium area.

"Here's the MacDade family, now," the reporter—Molly Anderson, according to the trailer scrolled at the bottom of the screen—announced. "Mr. and Mrs. MacDade and several family members arrived during the night on the MacDades' private jet . . . We understand that his wife—here she is now, Natalie MacDade being escorted by Liam's brother, Gregor MacDade--was already in the area with Liam last evening. We don't know if she was with him at the time of the attack . . . We know she hasn't left his side since he came out of surgery. . ."

"Oh Lord," Frank huffed. "We should have gotten you back there right away."

Luke spared him a stunned glance, wondering, "Are you daft?"

"You should be there with your family," Frank stated.

They had stopped being his family quite a while ago, Luke might have mentioned, but refrained, turning his gaze to the screen as the local police chief, Jack Tarpon introduced himself. It might be interesting to see what kind of spin the MacDade clan put on this situation, but Luke wasn't entirely sure he wanted to know. In fact, within the first few seconds of Chief Tarpon's speech, he knew enough—Liam was still fighting for his life—or death if he fought too hard.

Maybe Luke would rather not know how the MacDade machine was working.

By now, word of Liam's condition had probably spanned the globe, and Luke wouldn't be surprised to learn the airlines were jammed. His mother's parents were still alive, tucked up in the Highlands and refusing to travel in deference to their age; both of his father's parents had passed, but enough uncles, aunts, and cousins existed to fill a dozen commercial flights if they all chose to visit at once. Considering Liam's position in the clan, that was more than possible, and Luke confirmed his decision to steer clear.

Only half-listening to the continued speeches, several keywords sparked his interest and curiosity, and he caught himself thinking yet again about their relatives across the pond. Just how many of those folks would arrive to join this apparent vigil outside Southern General? With his focus glued to the set, he watched while recording faces and words.

Scan and go. He'd always hated watching television. The scenes moved too slowly; the words seemed to drone on and on in useless dialogue. Decidedly, he was finished watching and looked over to see Frank frowning at the screen.

In profile, the face was far more patrician, sculpted to appear soft and sleek as if from another era to match the furniture. The film of tears glistening under the thin black lashes wore well with the quiver in the mustached lips, and Luke knew abruptly—this fellow was in love with Liam MacDade. Luke would make book on it. Far more than simple friendship appeared in the taut lines—more like devastation. And what did that mean regarding this situation?

Luke nearly uttered his internal humph. What, indeed. What the hell was Liam doing in some sleazy hotel with a woman who had disappeared directly after the attack?

Trenton, NJ. Was it a coincidence that Liam had landed in a hospital less than a dozen miles from his old college buddy's family estate?

His thoughts turning in weird, rapid circles, Luke considered and rejected a dozen scenarios before deciding—his brother might step out on his wife with a mistress—but unless the fellow had undergone a lobotomy, he wouldn't step out with another man.

Far too clearly, the memory surfaced. Rather than the sunbaked scent of old silk and wood, Luke smelled the familiar aroma of fresh sawdust and hay. He'd loved the stables—had always loved the scents and sounds of horses happily chomping fresh-cut hay, content after a morning run or afternoon workout. Gregor was always in the stables or arena. Always near the horses for as far back as Luke could remember. Gregor was set on becoming an Olympian . . . had mapped his course toward that goal, either practicing his dressage or sailing over the complicated series of jumps that forever decorated their immense indoor arena. White rails, flower boxes, fences taller than Luke's head . . .

The lyrical young voice echoed from the past. '. . . If we put a flowered hat on yer head, squirt, ye just might be the right height for my next course . . . What say, bairn? Do ye think ye could stand still long enough for me and Jacone to jump over you?'

Teasing. Gregor was always teasing, even more so than Liam, and Luke knew better than to fall for the gest. Instead, he'd offered to run to mum's garden. 'I'll pick some roses and glue them to one of Mum's straw hats if you'd like.'

For a moment, Gregor had maintained an air of speculation, then chuckled turning his attention to mounting the big bay Andalusian. 'Better just sit this one out, Lucas. Least till I know Jacone can clear three feet without ever nicking a rail . . . Mum would take my head if I knocked yours off . . .'

What a joy to sit on the bench and watch through the observation window as man and horse—or boy and horse—became one fluid motion through the course and sailed effortlessly over the jumps. Luke had been visiting the stables without Nan Em for at least three years and paying close heed to Uncle John's instructions to Gregor. Uncle John, who was actually Cousin John, was old, maybe as old as the hills, like his father said sometimes, but the elder man sure knew about training horses and riders. Gregor's lessons were so much more exciting than his own. Uncle John most often just ordered Luke to post about the arena on Duchess, his little black Hackney pony . . .

But Uncle John was gone now. Luke considered with the sadness washing through him even as he watched Gregor sailing over the rails. Uncle John had passed dead away in his sleep some time ago, and a new man was running the stable, now. Mr. Chandler sure knew his horses; he'd lived and worked on a racetrack forever, according to Uncle George, who'd brought him to the estate.

'Down on his luck . . . Lost his wife in an accident ponying a horse to its morning workout . . . It's just him and a wee bairn, and I dinnae think he can stand being around the track right now . . .'

'George,' Father had said, sighing in his deep rumble. 'I need someone to continue Gregor's lessons. M' lad's set on becoming an Olympian, and John believed he cudnae only compete but win it if he tried.'

'You might find someone with that talent at Keeneland, but it won't happen overnight, Luche. In the meantime, ye might give Chandler a try.'

'You know him that well? Well enough to vouch for him knowing our stock?'

'He knows his horses, Lucius. I've had him training some of mine over at Laurel for some time now.'

'I'm happy with Grafton handling the ones I send to the track.'

'I'm nae saying hiring him there, but you have what—about thirty or forty head here . . .? Milt's looking for a fresh start. Maybe get his lad off the backside. Might work oot well all around. The lad's big enough to muck stalls or clean tack. Could get two for the price of one . . ..'

The boy came, too, Luke considered as he tried shaking the memory from his mind and on dual planes, saw the television, saw Gregor sailing over the rails within the arena—an Olympic-sized arena. Mum wanted Gregor to turn his sights to the swimming competitions instead . . . They'd all learned to swim in the immense in-ground pool, but Gregor spent far more time in the arena . . ..

Like with Liam and the pool, pretty girls had always hung around in the arena when Gregor trained. But unlike Liam, Gregor rarely paused to chat with them with his concentration on his horse and his ride.

Liam was at the pool. Surrounded by another batch of girls who'd begun visiting along with Lettia Rhoades, Liam's latest girlfriend. When they left, Luke meant to return to the pool—a guy could only tolerate so much blasted hair tussling, and Lettia's town friends liked to tease him about his curls. 'Just like your big brother . . ..'

Watching Gregor was far more fun, and maybe today, Gregor would carry him astride Jacone for a few minutes. Even if Gregor held the reins, sitting on that powerful Andalusian stallion was a thrill beyond measure, and Mr. Chandler, Gregor's newest trainer, never minded, either, so long as Gregor held onto the stallion.

'Whachu doin' over here all by your lonesome?' Jimmy asked while scooting onto the bench alongside Luke.

'Just watching,' Luke answered, not entirely comfortable to be caught by Jimmy. The Chandlers had been living on the estate in the little house where Uncle John had once lived. Probably for almost seven years, now. And Luke knew better than to be rude. Mum said they needed to treat people with respect, even those less fortunate, and Jimmy qualified—him not having a mother. And Mr. Chandler wasn't a nice father. Even his own father had never shouted at him. Not like Mr. Chandler, always ordering

James about and yelling at him . . . even hitting him once that Luke knew about. Still, something about this boy was disturbing—over and above him always smelling like horse manure and sweat.

'Ain's no fun in that,' Chandler said offhandedly. 'I got done with my chores early. How 'bout we go on over ta the pond for a dip? Or we could just go fishin' if ya want.'

Despite all the warnings and threats of dire consequences, Luke had been hiking to the pond just over the hill for quite a while. And he had a feeling, looking into Jimmy's big, mousy brown eyes, that Chandler knew it. That sly smile was an indication, too. The boy had followed him and spied on him.

'I don't think I better,' Luke decided, more uncomfortable with the thought about what Jimmy might have seen.

Only this past summer, on one of those rare hot, muggy afternoons in July, Luke had stepped out of his tennis shoes, shorts, and shirt and taken a quick dip. But surely, he hadn't been followed that day. He'd only done that once. He'd stashed a fishing pole over by the pond as much as two years earlier, which, apparently, Jimmy had witnessed to mention fishing. Luke sort of liked to fish. It was something he could do while reading without needing to waste time just sitting.

'Come on. It'll be fun,' Jimmy said in a whiny voice.

Beneath Jimmy's left eye, under a smudge of dirt, the blackeye had faded, but Luke had noticed that bruise several days earlier. He'd caught Jimmy watching him then, too, rather than mucking the stall across the aisle from where Luke had been brushing his pony. Jimmy worked hard for a boy, but then, he was just a little younger than Gregor, and Gregor worked hard, too. If Gregor wasn't riding or grooming his horses, he and Liam were taking karate lessons from Uncle Gillis, or honing their golfing or tennis skills with other instructors. There was no end to the lessons they were all taking, and it was hard work learning a new skill.

'Come on, Luke,' Jimmy pleaded again, a different tone in his voice as if he were suddenly anxious over Luke staring at his eye.

Slightly embarrassed to be caught staring, Luke glanced through the glass window, watching Gregor take the double jump, barely skimming the ground between leaps. Gregor was probably almost done . . . and Luke spotted the three young ladies, scantily dressed in sundresses over their bathing suits. He wasn't getting a ride today. Dang it. And if Gregor joined the group at the pool, Luke might as well forget swimming, too.

Sighing, Luke looked to the intent brown eyes and decided, 'All right, James.'

With a smile spreading on his puffy lips, Jimmy huffed, 'Good. We can maybe take some snacks from the breakroom, huh?'

The breakroom was actually a lounge, Luke nearly thought to correct, but let that pass as well. A 'breakroom,' Jimmy had once confided when Luke had wondered why the boy called it that, was the room where jockeys, pony riders, and grooms hung out between workouts. According to Jimmy, halfway between the daily morning training at the racetrack, the outriders sent everyone off the track and let the tractors level the churned-up ground. With nothing to do for a half hour, a lot of the backside workers headed to the breakroom for coffee, smokes, or snacks . . . If not to the kitchen for a quick breakfast.

Luke wouldn't mind hearing more about life on the racetrack. Jimmy made it sound exciting, but he was never too keen on talking about it. Jimmy was little, maybe only seven or eight when his mother was killed on the track, but he'd admitted once to being there, seeing her and two horses carried off the racetrack. Luke couldn't even imagine that horror in his young mind, but he recalled Jimmy saying, 'It happens.' As if it was no big deal.

Lying atop a flowered quilt, Luke gazed at the shadowy lamp within his line of sight. He rested on the second floor of a stranger's house, lingering in that half state of consciousness where he knew himself awake within the dull light. The distant hum of car engines passing on a nearby highway penetrated the drawn drapes. He heard a fire whistle—or the whistle of a teakettle . . . a sound from the past, that. The whistle of a teakettle emanating from the immense industrial-size kitchen of the MacDade mansion . . . and it was as if he were still there, locked in the past of twelve or thirteen years ago.

He'd gone to the pond with Jimmy . . . Personally, he'd collected cans of soda from the well-stocked refrigerator in the stable lounge and snatched a box of cookies and a bag of chips from the cabinet. Food and drinks were never far away on the estate. Not like at the boarding school where he wasn't supposed to stash snacks, not even candy bars, though he managed to sneak in contraband at every opportunity. In the MacDade stable lounge, no one needed to sneak food, but Luke had discovered early how Jimmy feared ever to help himself. With good reason, Luke knew, having seen the elder Chandler take a belt to Jimmy right there in the lounge just for eating a candy bar. Luke collected a few candy bars as well, adding them to the empty feed sack that was no longer empty.

Maybe visiting the pond wasn't such a bad idea after all.

In another month, Luke would return to St. Andrews, and for the first few weeks, he would miss the freedom to hike the woods and mountain climb, or fish in the abundance of streams and ponds on the MacDade estate. If there was one thing Luke MacDade loved—had always loved—it was the forest. Any forest. Mountain terrain or lowland planes, he loved the scents from pine to birch, from blackberry bushes to wild laurel. He would live in a forest someday, someplace like his parents' estate, surrounded by forest. Like a mountain man, he would live off the land . . . at least mostly. He might keep a fully stocked cabinet of snacks close at hand just in case he made friends with the local deer and rabbits. He'd never harbored any great desire to hunt, regardless of learning to shoot at an early age.

Jimmy was waiting, sitting on a log at the designated spot, deep enough within the forest to avoid notice and further concealed in thick, tangled briars. His eyes brightened with delight and laughter at the overstuffed bag on Luke's back. 'Gees, did you leave anything there?'

'Course I did,' Luke nearly scoffed at the implication that he would ever do else. Now that he'd decided on this adventure, he'd applied himself to the details with the same determination that he might engage for an exam. He'd always been a stickler for details—whether watching Gregor's hand and foot placement as he sailed over a jump or scoring through a dozen books to learn the vein pattern of a particular leaf or tree indigenous to an area he might occupy.

In companionable silence, they strode in single file, Jimmy leading and sparing Luke a few scratches by holding briars aside with his gloved hands. Like Luke, Jimmy wore shorts and a t-shirt, though Jimmy's shorts probably began as a pair of holey-kneed jeans with the tattered fringe dangling at his knobby knees. Low, that fringe, and Luke prickled with an odd embarrassment to notice the end of an ugly red welt below the ragged tapestry. He knew about stuff like that. About kids who were beaten or battered if only through Mum's volunteer work at a shelter in the city. She'd taken him along sometimes, letting him hand over his personal bag of clothes and shoes that he'd outgrown or discarded. Just once, Luke had suggested that Jimmy talk to Mum, but the boy had threatened to run away instead. Maybe running away was not such a bad idea.

Uncomfortable, Luke heard the first trickle of water, indicating the stream and slight waterfall that fed the pond. A 'froog' pond, Liam had called it once after a month-long trip to the motherland, and the name had stuck with help from Gregor and his natural brogue. Froog Pond. Even if Gregor wasn't attempting to mispronounce frog, the word would be *froog*. As if Gregor intentionally defied his American heritage, he preferred speaking with the accent in direct reflection of their father—and their mother when she was mad.

Of the three of them, Gregor sounded as Scottish as their overseas cousins, and Liam said it was because Gregor was conceived on Scottish soil. Their father insisted it was the opposite—Liam in Scotland, Gregor in America—but Luke wasn't convinced it mattered either way. He doubted a baby in the womb could learn to speak with a Scottish accent.

Froog Pond was just large enough, with the forest on every side, for sunlight to glisten over its sprawling center. A dozen yards out, visible through briars, Luke recognized the ripples of fish bobbing for bugs or air, already enjoying the sparkling light show despite an odd chill down his spine. A light show. . . He'd been here before, with others—with his brothers. They'd come here fishing and even swimming, though not too often. Liam only seemed angry when they came—or annoyed, maybe, that he needed to babysit. Too well, Luke knew how his brothers could become annoyed when he snuck after them—probably more often than he should. They preferred being with people their own age. Only tolerated him because Mum and sometimes Father insisted.

Well, not today. Today, Luke was here with someone closer to his own age.

Jimmy was almost thirteen . . . or maybe just twelve and a half . . . And sometimes, like now, he seemed younger, worrying about getting caught with the snacks.

Jimmy had led them to the very clearing on the bank where Luke had stripped to his undershorts and where he usually fished. Not a coincidence in Luke's mind. The boy had deliberately led them off the more direct deer path, taking the narrow, bedraggled path to reach this small, isolated cove.

Setting his sack aside, Luke withdrew his gaze from the pond, not even certain what disturbed him, but when he looked at Jimmy, the sense of foreboding intensified.

From sheepish to intent, the brown eyes held firm, and the focus lowered then rose as if sizing up Luke's wardrobe, maybe making the same comparison—or contrast—to pass through Luke's mind earlier. With his own name-brand tennis shoes and matching shorts and shirt ensemble, Luke couldn't blame the boy for appearing almost angry.

'Think I'll get my pole,' Luke decided and hurried just a little, half thinking this might have been a bad idea to come here with Jimmy. He could've come alone if he wanted an adventure; after all, he only had one pole. Tucked down under weeds and a jutting flat rock, protected from the elements, Luke had further safeguarded his pole, separating the shafts and tucking them into a long plastic case that had once housed a tennis racket. Bringing it to the mossy embankment, he settled on his shins, glancing to find Jimmy sitting, leaning on a black bolder—the same bolder where Luke had set his folded clothes a month earlier. 'I only have one pole here, but we can share. We just have to dig around the rocks there to find worms, or if you want, we could catch some crayfish. If we cast out far enough, we can probably catch a trout.'

'Come here a lot, huh?'

'Not too,' Luke admitted, setting about retrieving his rod from the bag and affixing the parts. 'I like to fish, though,' he added and glanced up to find Jimmy smiling again. Something was not quite right there. Luke was more sure of it and wondered if he should just pack up and return to the stable. He could probably find something to do inside until the teenagers abandoned the pool. Lettia would need to get back to work . . .

Something was wrong.

Unconsciously, Luke rose, landing on the side of the bed, clearing his focus—if not his mind—to spy the shadows spilling at a different angle on the drawn blind. He rested in a stranger's house—the Pendleton house—and the memory threatening to break at the edge of his mind was wrong—something wrong. Out of sequence. The Froog Pond . . .

He hadn't begun visiting the pond until he was around nine . . . and Lettia Rhoades had died a lot earlier. He couldn't have been more than five or six when the young woman had crashed her car down on Kernel Rd. at the base of the mountain, and the Chandlers had already lived on the estate for three or four years before that. Liam . . . Liam and Lettia had been friends, or maybe more than friends. In hindsight, Luke knew they were probably getting it on. Liam's exploits were already legendary by the time he and Jimmy had walked to that pond . . . and that was the last time Luke had ever trekked to the pond.

Shaking his head, collecting his balance on the side of the bed, Luke spotted his garment bag hanging on a hook outside the closet door. Accommodating, these folks. Or they preferred he not go snooping around to find his clothes.

The second point of interest landed his focus on the phone—his cell-phone rested in plain sight and reach, and belatedly, he recalled setting it there—right after phoning the hospital for an update. His name wasn't on the list of people who had a right to know about Liam.

Calling the nurses' station had verified Liam's status in the living realm, and the woman on duty had offered to locate a family member.

Time to go, Luke decided. He could probably learn as much on the internet as he would from Molly Anderson reporting for WKBN or the nurses at Southern General. He might swing by the hospital . . . depending on the crowd. Some kind of vigil—a candlelight vigil scheduled for this evening.

By now, Liam had probably made the national and international news, and the information would be spotty at best, but the underlying details would be true. If Liam didn't survive . . . it would make the news.

Reaching, lifting his phone, Luke flipped the case open and pushed the buttons that he'd mentally recorded when finding the hospital phone number in the Pendletons' phone directory. With few words, he called for a cab, then pushed off the bed. Stuffing the phone in the back pocket of his jeans, he continued to the closet door, unzipping his garment bag. He'd packed in a hurry, but habitually. A few cotton shirts, a black Armani, pressed jeans, a sports jacket appropriate for casual dining . . .? Where the hell did he think he was going? A pleasure cruise?

Shaking his head, Luke pulled a clean shirt off a hanger, then thought better of pulling it on and retrieved his personal case from the garment pouch. Automated, he made use of the attached bathroom. As the lady of the house had promised, a bath had awaited him earlier, and he remembered scrubbing the disinfectant and antiseptic smell from his pores.

He hated that smell, the smell of a hospital. His Grandfather MacDade had died in a hospital—John Hopkins in Maryland—sixteen years earlier, and that blasted smell had stayed with him ever since. At times, instant recall could be a curse.

Donning fresh clothes and returning his dirty laundry to hangers, Luke pulled on the sports jacket and finished packing. Momentarily, he considered his next move, then lifted his phone from his pocket. Calling his cell carrier's information, he gained the airport number and booked a redeye to Virginia. Glancing off his Rolex, he collected his bag and flipped the strap over his shoulder.

Wide awake, he left the room, appreciating the flow of museum-quality antiques, from the ancient oriental runner to grace the hall to the side tables weighted down with Tiffany lamps. The smell, he was certain, would never leave him. Like the hospital smell after all these years, he might never stand near another antique without thinking of the Pendletons and this brief visit.

Descending the spindle-railed staircase to land in the center of the parlor, strategically perpendicular to the ancient front door, Luke set his bag on the curved step, leaning rather than hanging it on the walnut newel post. To the sound of soft television voices, Luke crossed the foyer to the open French door. By no surprise, the butler greeted him even as he spotted the elder Pendletons sitting at opposing chairs to either side of the console television.

"Please, do come in, sir," Carl offered, not seeming to notice that Luke was already halfway inside the room or, perhaps, making a point to sound indignant.

"Thank you, sir," Luke said politely, and the man blinked as if bee-stung. Either the fellow wasn't accustomed to common courtesy, or he'd fully intended an insult—miffed by Luke's indifference.

"You look a little more rested, dear," the woman said with a pensive smile, her posture ramrod straight despite the plush Victorian-style chair.

"I am, thank you, ma'am," he said as his attention distracted to the scene and words of his father on the television. It looked like the same press conference he'd seen before retiring to the upstairs room.

On the set, Lucius stood front and center, Megan under his arm, and cleaved to his side at the podium. His stark blue eyes were a reflection of Liam's—and with Liam's Oscar photo cropped and filling half the screen, there was no mistaking the likeness. Mirror images, with the older, grimmer MacDade animating. "The person—or persons responsible for assaulting my son will be apprehended and duly processed," Lucius promised in his natural deep tone, and the heat in his cobalt eyes reinforced the threat.

From somewhere out of sight, another reporter called, "Do you believe your son was targeted because of his position in your company?"

"I cannae speak to the details of the investigation, but I can't imagine a reason why he would be in that regard—"

Frances Pendleton interrupted in a droll tone. "They've been playing parts of that news conference all day."

"Please, come sit, dear. Dinner should be ready shortly. Or would you prefer another breakfast?"

"Neither. Thank you, ma'am. I have a cab coming in a few minutes."

"We could have our driver take you wherever you'd like to go," she spoke as if she needed to hurry the invitation before her husband could interject. "Our Frank should be back shortly, though. He went to meet his fiancée for an early dinner."

Was that last mentioned with purpose?

"I'm sure he'll want to see you before you go," she added.

Her thoughts seemed even more convoluted than his own, and he wondered if he had found a kindred spirit in this elder woman. "I'll be glad to leave a number where he can reach me, then, and please, extend my gratitude."

Pendleton Sr. pushed off his chair and glanced at his butler, "Do bring our guest a brandy," he said as he came forward, appearing to shun the television in his wake even as another flash launched Natalie and Gregor into the limelight.

Luke's attention riveted, watching Natalie's bright amber eyes turning to glass as she glanced off Megan and spoke. Her words were lost, but the expression on her face was clearly tortured. And Luke had seen that expression this morning as she'd lay over her husband, holding him against the pain as if drawing it from him, into her.

". . . Our hearts go out to all of them," Molly Anderson said with a heartfelt tone that could win her an Oscar on the silver screen. "We're told that Liam MacDade's condition remains critical and that every hour, now, is crucial to his recovery."

"Molly—" The camera cut to a dark-haired man seated behind the apparent news desk at the station. "It looks as if the crowd's growing behind you. Can you tell us if there are any updates on Mr. MacDade's condition?"

Absently, Luke commented, "She just did, dolt. He's still critical."

"According to our sources, he's regained consciousness several times, but they're keeping him heavily sedated . . . And the crowd *is* growing, Dan. People have been coming all day, delivering flowers and cards, and as I mentioned earlier, there's a candlelight service planned for this evening . . . Several of the local clergy are scheduled to speak, and I believe there's a prayer service to be led by our own Catholic Priest, Father Don Murphy as we know the MacDades are of the Catholic faith—"

"Mum's going to love that—an Irish priest," Luke said offhandedly and realized he wasn't standing alone in some hotel room across the country. The Pendletons probably believed they were harboring a madman. With a grim smile, Luke looked to the matriarch. "She's pretty fussy about things like that."

"You're not Catholic, then?" the woman asked.

"Of course, they're Catholic," Frances said as if she were daft. "Liam attended St Vincent's, after all. That's where Frank and he met."

"Yes, we are, ma'am," Luke answered her as if Frances hadn't spoken.

On the screen, Molly Anderson continued, "We're told, Dan, that several of the MacDades' relatives have already arrived from as far away as Scotland and Ireland . . ." And apparently, some faceless, nameless producer ordered a 'cut—roll footage.' The screen split to show an earlier clip of three stoic bodies ascending the steps to the hospital. They looked, for all the world, like ordinary American citizens until Molly Anderson stood two steps ahead of the first leisure-suited man and still needed to cant her head upward along with her microphone.

"Sir? I understand you've just arrived from Scotland . . . Can you tell me how you're related to Liam MacDade?"

"Aye," Uncle Ulysses started, then continued in a mix of Gaelic and English. Taller than Liam, the fellow stood proportionately tall and sturdy, rather like an oak tree. The last time Luke had seen him in person, the fellow had lifted him to his shoulder and nearly given him a concussion on one of the doorframes in MacDade manor. Uncle Ulie hadn't aged much. Maybe a little grayer in his longish hair and bushy mustache, but his dark eyes shining through the camera lens, carried the same spark of wit to afflict all other MacDades.

On the screen, Molly Anderson's eyes seemed to cross with her confusion, and her lips parted on whatever question she meant to ask.

She missed her opportunity—both to ask more questions and to capture any more faces on film. The other two men passed behind Uncle Ulie and disappeared through the glass doors, leaving only fading impressions of males wearing dark jackets and slacks. With the golf caps on both heads, not even their hair color remained visible.

"Humph," Luke muttered and quivered a slight smile as he considered the probability of evasive tactics. Either uncles or cousins, the fellows had deliberately avoided the cameras, and apparently, Molly Anderson only figured it out after Uncle Ulie sidestepped and continued up the steps. The camera captured her dumbfound an instant before the camera panned to the crowd. The next news clip showed a small group ascending the steps and suggested they were foreign visitors. Luke almost felt sorry for Anderson as he recognized one of his cousins from Chicago . . . and the circus had only begun to come to town.

At the motion at his side, Luke accepted the offered tumbler, managed a 'thank you,' and caught up to his actions as he tasted the brandy on his tongue. Not a fan, he refrained from pursing his lips and swallowed the thick liquid, recalling a similar experience on the plane. At least that blasted bourbon was top-shelf and smooth as honey. Old money. Old brandy. And maybe past its shelf life.

Time to go. The cab should arrive soon.

Taking a few more swallows to be polite, Luke turned from the set, already deciding to forgo a stop at the hospital. Whether the sight of his relatives arriving or the mob growing for that vigil was worse, remained a mystery. Either way, he intended to avoid that scene.

Handing the glass away, passing a parting amenity to the seated woman, Luke started to the door with the elder Pendleton, who seemed to be eyeing him more critically.

"You were going to leave your number for Frank," Pendleton reminded him as they entered the foyer.

The number for his answering service, Luke corrected silently and agreed, "I will if you have a pen handy."

At a signal, Carl fled into another room and returned as Luke slung his bag over his shoulder. Reciting the number, he extended his gratitude to be added to the note and offered Pendleton Sr. his thanks while heading for the door.

Outside, the air had cooled with the onset of evening. Already, the cobbled drive lay in shadows from the heavy overhang of trees that suggested an evening shade might last all day beneath the foliage. Appearing recently neglected—as if the gardener had taken an extended holiday—weeds sprouted through patches of grass and flowerbeds sprawling between the hedge-enshrouded wall and covered porch. As Luke drew a relieving breath of fresh air, already descending the steps, the cab pulled through the open cast iron gates. A sense of escaping a crypt stole over him, shivering him internally. Not nice. Not very appreciative. But the Pendletons might relieve part of their stodginess just by opening a blasted window.

When he built his own house, his cabin in the woods, Luke intended to install windows floor-to-ceiling—and maybe skylights, too. What good would it be to build a cabin and erect walls to block the view? He preferred the sight of tree-covered mountains and wide-open sky despite how cleverly the walls would be constructed of shined polished pine. And he'd already decided on the exact spot for his cabin—providing the paperwork cleared. He owned most of the land on the mountain already. He just needed to finalize the last fifty acres before breaking ground.

Climbing into the cab, Luke considered a half dozen details before ordering the driver to deliver him to the airport. If, as it appeared, relatives were flying in from around the world, he would need to trade his sports coat for a windbreaker. Maybe buy a hat and cheap sunglasses, maybe some cheap loafers . . . and he better check his bag at the airport. The last thing he wanted or needed was to bump into any familiar faces before boarding his flight.

And in the back of his mind, a thought niggled, distracting and annoying almost as if . . . as if he'd already seen a familiar face. Somewhere in the news feed or in passing, he'd already seen someone or something alarming. A turned word. A face in the crowd . . .? Something.

9

Barely through the arches of the Pendleton estate, the phone blipped in Luke's pocket, and he identified the number of his answering service. A push of a button and two rings later, Luke identified himself and received a simple message from Frank Pendleton.

"Call me. Please, Luke. I need to know that you're all right. And I'd like to know about Liam."

The Pendletons must have phoned him before Luke cleared the first porch step.

Weighing options, Luke fidgeted with his phone to block the caller ID, then pushed the buttons to dial Frank. All too clearly, the fellow's concern was genuine, but whether that underlie his reason for his hospitality—the probability of learning Liam's condition—the results were the same. Pendleton had offered refuge, no questions asked.

"Hello?" the lyrical voice erupted hesitantly, almost warily, as if he feared to answer.

"Hi, this is Luke. You called?"

"How are you? Where are you?" Frank huffed, sounding relieved and anxious. "Mother said you left in a cab. I could have taken you back to the hospital. Is everything all right? Did you need to leave in a hurry?"

When Frank drew breath for the second round, Luke interjected with a faintly bemused note and tone. "As far as I know, Liam's hanging in there. I'll let you know if I hear anything, which I haven't yet, except what the reporters are saying."

"Are you on the way to the hospital?"

"Actually, no."

"Hey, I'm not too far from the house. I have to meet someone, but if uhm . . .? I could join you for dinner."

"Where are you?" Sounded like a restaurant or bar. And he had four hours to kill. It might be better not to arrive at the airport too early and risk running into anyone he knew—or knew him. Dinner. A beer to wipe out the taste of cough syrup on his tongue . . .? Not an altogether unpleasant solution.

"It's a little place—Well, it's called The Emerald Club. It's uhm . . . We could meet somewhere else," he decided abruptly. "There are a few decent restaurants not too far. How about the Rivers Inn?"

"Sounds good. I'm sure my driver can find it. What say? Maybe an hour? Would that give you enough time?" To meet someone—like his fiancée for an early dinner? Either Frank was a glutton, or he'd lied to his parents. The Emerald Club. . . sounded like someplace Frank would prefer not to meet anyone, much less his fiancée.

Frank sounded relieved, huffing, "That would be great! I'll see you there."

Not if I see you first, Luke nearly spoke aloud and rang off, catching his driver's eyes in the rearview mirror. "Change in plans," he said needlessly. "Do you know a place called The Emerald Club?"

"The strip joint?" the skinny driver asked with a quirked brow, a kink in his thin mustache. He looked like an older version of Ricky Ricardo, the fellow who'd played opposite Lucille Ball in that old sitcom—minus the Spanish accent. Dark, slicked-short hair, dark brows, and sharp-cut features. A shoe-in.

"That would be the one," Luke answered, understanding the fellow's amused skepticism. After all, he'd just picked up his fare in an austere neigh-borhood. *The rich and infamous like to play, too*, Luke mused silently before turning his attention to judge the passing scenery.

The Pendletons lived in one of the oldest and probably the wealthi-est parts of town, where the houses were brownstone and red brick, with their lawns enclosed behind elaborate cast-iron fences and immense bushes. Mid-summer blooms exploded from ornate cement planters and urns to mark porches and driveways. Fantastic topiaries lined the short drives and fringed the French windows. With the sun listing toward the west, evening shadows had dulled the vivid colors.

Almost relieved to leave the tree-shrouded lanes behind, Luke appreciated the more natural light of the suburbs. Sporadically, immense trees spilled shade over patchy grass lawns where children played in abundance. With an eye for detail, Luke identified the first signs of degeneration, from paint chipping to broken windows, and he'd spent enough time walking on city streets to recognize the area on the cusp of change.

At the sight of a strip mall just ahead, Luke decided, "Stop in there, will you? That bargain store?"

Whether the idea was his or a page stolen from his sister-in-law's playbook, Luke handed the driver enough cash to keep the meter running. Slinging his garment bag over his shoulder, he strode across the pavement. Mason had mentioned Natalie's odd disguise, her intention to pose as a boy, but Luke drew the line at shaving and posing as a girl. He'd done that once. With the memory, a wiry smirk tipped his mustache as he strode into the bargain outlet. He'd taken a bit-part as a female to see if he could pull it off, and according to his drama instructor and fellow thespians, he'd succeeded admirably.

Luckily, his voice hadn't completely changed at the time, or it might have been a different story.

At the cluttered men's aisle, Luke found a bulky silk windbreaker, a brimmed hat that might have served as a prop in Casablanca, and a pair of shiny black loafers—the kind with thick stitching and a fringe tassel over the arch. A classic, timeless style. Dressing down had always served its purpose. He finished the look with wire-rim glasses that might have been considered sunglasses if the lenses were more amber than yellow. If he thought he could change into a pair of cheap jeans in the backseat of a cab, he might try it, but the cabby might take offense. And if he truly wanted to get creative, he could dye his hair and streak his beard—he'd done that too once.

Doubtfully, he would need go to extremes. The Emerald Club probably wasn't a place to boast spotlights or white neon lights.

Red neon lights were a different story altogether. His disguise in place before departing the cab, he slung his garment bag over his shoulder with the LV logo turned under. At the shadowed entrance, Luke paid his admission fee to a bored young woman sporting tattoos up her spindly arms to clash with the spaghetti straps of her flowered, clingy halter top. In the red glow, he couldn't determine where the tats began, and the cloth ended. The legs were the same, he noticed in a downward glance to judge the fringe of her short shorts barely covering the more intimate tattoos.

She caught him looking and smiled snidely.

"Nice tats," he said with a hint of admiration, feigned to be sure, but her smile softened and eyes keened. "I'm supposed to be meeting someone here," he lied smoothly. He'd rather not attract her interest, especially if she was one of the dancers. "Mind if I look around?"

"Not at all, sweet thang," she drawled. Either mocking his accent or searching for common ground. "What's she look like?"

"A brunette the last I saw her," he said distractedly. This was the type of place where hair colors could change daily. "She's probably with a dark-haired guy. An upscale guy. Sort of preppy-looking, if you know what I mean?"

"Oh, sounds like Frank," she said, and her expression intensified even in the weird dull light. She seemed to be studying him, looking through him. "You sort of look like Liam," she said in a lower volume as if she preferred not to be overheard despite the pounding drumbeat from the stage. "Are you a relative? Or are you . . .? You're not with the police," she decided.

"Shit, you know Liam," he said as if distressed, and this once, he didn't bother to act.

"Frank said he's in critical condition," the young woman said while searching his face. "Are you one of them? His relatives?"

"I am," he admitted, not elaborating and feeling as if he were tiptoeing through a virtual minefield. "Have the police been here already?"

"They were here this morning," she offered. "They were asking if we saw Alecia or if Liam and her were here last night."

"Were they?" he asked while wondering what the hell he'd just stepped into.

"Nope, not last night," she said and might have added 'thank God.' "I haven't really seen him in here since they started dating. I mean, you probably know all about it, but I can tell you, it's pretty wild. I mean, I don't think anything started in here—last night, I mean. Tyler wouldn't put up with no shit coming down in here. Anyway, Alecia usually meets him over at the Castaway, which is what we told the police this morning. Liam has too much class to hang out in a place like this." She barely drew breath. "Frank, either, for that matter. I just don't get that one at all. I guess they just liked slumming it sometimes 'cause face it, this ain't a place somebody like them would hang out."

Information overload. "I don't know," Luke said thoughtfully, flashing his gaze toward the deeper shadows and dull glow within. Even in the early hour, a haze of blue smoke lingered above the scattering of occupied tables. Front and center stage, three brass poles stood in a regimental V formation with a spotlight on the center pole. The first act had already begun. A somewhat plump woman made love to the brass, blond locks streaming down her arched bare spine, not quite reaching her round rump—or at least they might be blond locks. Maybe blood red under the neon. This truly wasn't the type of place that the heir to the MacDade dynasty would patronize to pick up women. "It's sort of private," he offered and looked to the skinny woman, who was again looking at him a little critically.

"Are you uhm . . . Are you meeting them here, too? Frank and Alecia, I mean."

"They're already here, then?"

"Think they went downstairs," she offered, signaling toward a dark well to the right of the bar. "There's another show down there."

Frank wasn't meeting his fiancée. Only that thought held firm as Luke thanked the hostess and headed toward the steps. If nothing else, he wanted a glimpse of Liam's mistress, Alecia. A stripper.

Shaking his head slightly, he managed not to lose the hat and advanced on the stairwell a little more cautiously. If implications of top floor and bottom basement were any indication, he wasn't altogether certain he wanted to catch this second act. The top-shelf performance was an eye-opener.

Music blared just a few decibels higher than upstairs, and the acoustics were undoubtedly designed to clash mid-stairway and recede in either direction. The lighting was different. Lower, darker, and the smoke thicker. On the silver pole—a single pole—two women wearing nothing more than G-strings gyrated in unison to a slow, seedy rhythm, and for a few seconds, Luke wondered how often they practiced to remain in perfect sync. Again, shaking his head, he tried stepping into his brother's shoes to wonder what Liam had seen in a place like this. Neither of these women could boast a pair of legs to compete with his sister-in-law's long, graceful limbs and elegance. Liam must have flipped a cork and buckled under the stress of his position in High Land, Inc. or flat-out gone blind—deaf, too, if he lingered long in this environment.

Sidling into the shadows, fleeting glances over the silhouettes within the gloom, Luke identified a half dozen lone males before honing in on a corner booth at the deep end of the room. Without appearing interested, he strode toward the corner, dropping his garment bag off his shoulder in case Frank looked over. With his hair pulled into a ponytail, discreetly tucked under the silk collar, doubtful Frank would see enough under the brim to recognize the white-blond strands. Why exactly he preferred to remain incognito, Luke couldn't decide, but he slid into a booth where he might hear rather than see the couple currently engaged in an intimate discussion.

Funny how background noise could become just that—a background noise to hum beneath the more prominent notes of a conversation. Movie producers used that technique—a soft static drone to fill the silence and build tension beneath a dramatic exchange. Luke had learned to separate those sounds on stage quite some time ago.

"... I'm telling you, Frank, I think I'm being followed."

"And I'm telling you, we should go to the police," Frank hissed worriedly "They just want to talk to you, dear. They need to know if you saw anyone or heard anything—"

"Franky, please," the woman whined softly "I can't. You know I can't."

"Alecia, if you know something—"

"I dddon't," she whined. "I just know I can't go to the police. I took a chance even coming here. If Ty was working tonight—I wouldn't even have come this close. According to Glen, the police have been here on and off all day. I can't go back to my apartment. I . . . I need some cash, Frank. I have to get out of here, At least for a little while—"

"You know Liam's in bad shape," Frank said with a soft, accusing edge.

"I knnnow," she whined softly, an almost nasal southern drawl slipping in her tone "And they won't e-even tell me how he is! I tried calling the ho-ospital," she hiccupped on the verge of sobs.

"Of course, they won't tell you anything," Frank spoke as if weary and disgusted. "They're not offering any information about his condition, but I spoke to his brother a little while ago—"

"Gregor?" she whined. "You talked to him? What did he sssay?"

"I haven't talked to Gregor—You know Gregor?"

"Nnno," she whined, sounding like a bad actor in a B-rated movie. "Just L-Liam," she hiccupped. "Talked about him sometimes and—and I saw on the news—them talking, the whole family! She—even *she* was there. His wife! She should 'na been there! Should 'a been meee Frank."

"Don't be daft," Frank huffed, then seemed to soften his tone naturally. "Really, Alecia, you knew it would never last forever. Liam . . . there's no way he'd leave his wife. He's too honorable to ever leave his wife and children, no matter how much he might want to. He takes his responsibility too seriously even to consider it."

"Buuut she dint wannnt him, Frank."

"She's the mother of his children, Alecia," Frank said sorrowfully. "And . . . and there's no way she'd ever leave Liam MacDade. Surely you knew that—"

"I—I need to get away from here, Franky . . . Please. I can't be seen as the other woman," she whined. "I'll—I'll phone the police and—and talk to them but I—I can't stay around here. If his—his family finds out about me . . . I mean that guy—Mason—he scares me, Franky, and I—I just can't go to the police. It wouldn't be good for Liam . . . I mean for me to show up. The reporters would probably plaster us all through the mud, and I—I just can't do it, Franky. I didn' know who else to call . . . I mean nobody really knows about us, and my friends tried helping some with money and stuff, but I gotta get outa here for a while."

"You . . . you'll honestly phone the police?"

"I will, I promise. Just as soon as I get someplace safe."

Safe from what? From whom? The police? The paparazzi? The MacDade clan?

"All right . . ." Frank sighed heavily. "I didn't have much liquid capital on hand, but I managed to scrape together five grand if that will help? Just till this blows over though, Alecia. And you must phone the police. If there's anything you can tell them, you must call them. Liam . . . He's in bad shape. That's no lie . . . and the police don't even have any leads yet."

"Y-you talked to them? You told them a-about me?"

"I didn't have to," Frank said, sounding sorrowful. "Mason already gave them your name and mine, but I didn't mind. I did talk to the police—a Det. Harbinder. He's handling the case."

"Wh-what did you tell them? I mean, about me?"

"Nothing more than they knew," he admitted. "They already knew you were a dancer and that you'd been seeing Liam for a little while. It's not like I know where you live or anything," he said as if exasperated by that reality. "You need to come forward, honestly, dear. For Liam's sake, you need to speak with them."

"I told you," she whined. "I don't know anything. . . I was asleep, and I woke when I heard the whistles . . . Liam was already gone so—so I got out of there."

After a moment, with only the drumbeat and cymbals clamoring, Frank hissed, "Shit. I have to get going. I'm probably already late. Here—take this. I know it's not much, but it should keep you somewhere safe for a few days. Promise me, though, you'll phone the police?"

"I promise, Frank, seriously, as soon as I get safe."

Luke glimpsed at Frank slipping from the booth, and dipped his head at an angle, chugging a few swallows of the beer he hadn't thought about ordering. The bottle sufficiently covered his beard and mustache; the hat brim covered his brow. Frank was hurrying to meet him, Luke knew. He glimpsed the fellow passing in somewhat of a hurry. If he hadn't tipped his head at that precise moment; however, he might not have glimpsed another face averting in the shadows across the room. The recognition wasn't instant, but before the woman followed Frank from the booth, Luke had scored his memory banks to recall another of the MacDade security men from the distant past. His father almost always started his security men on the estate before turning them over to Gillis's regime. This fellow, Albert, had been with MacDade Security for at least ten years, which wasn't all that uncommon. Once accepted and trained accordingly, these gentlemen committed for life.

Keeping his head down, Luke glimpsed the woman who passed him and he felt slightly better about his brother's mental condition. Not very tall, pretty enough with slender features, big busted with the tanned mounds lifted and presented, barely contained within a tight V-neck T-shirt. She might have purposely stuck them out there to draw the eye to her endowments rather than her face to avoid being identified. Her facial features certainly took a rear seat to her bosom.

Remaining seated as she fled past the booth, Luke watched surreptitiously as the middle-aged fellow across the room. Casually, Albert slipped from his bench, dropped several bills on the table, and followed the woman at a discreet, leisurely pace. Half expecting the fellow to veer and stop outside his booth, Luke wondered if Gillis's team might be slipping when the fellow strode to the steps.

Waiting, finishing his beer, Luke considered the possibility of the hostess mentioning him to Frank, not that it mattered. The rear exit wore a neon sign missing two of its four orange letters.

Someone had turned on the television at a low volume. To the sound of Lucius MacDade commending the police for their service and the hospital staff for their exemplary care, Liam awoke. On some ethereal plane, he knew better than to move and reveal his position. Instead, he lay as still as stone, listening, not certain of else than the voice of his father emanating from the flat box across the room.

Then, in a more natural rhythm, closer, the same voice spoke in a low musing tone, "Well, and they've run that segment intae the blasted earth."

"It's your fine TV presence, Da," Gregor mused.

"Not vera likely," the elder growled quietly. "More than likely, the image of your m'athair to keep them running that clip. Not a finer woman to be seen on that set."

"Aye, and there's the other shot they're too blasted fond of showing," Gregor said in a low voice.

The female announcer's voice overlapped the voices shouting on the set. "I can only imagine what that woman's going through. So far, there haven't been any changes in her husband's condition, but we'll keep you updated as information comes in."

"Good God," Gregor growled. "Where do they find these people?"

"Well, that's sadly what sells their airtime."

"Lee's not going to be happy with that when she wakes," Gregor mused. "If we're smart, we won't let her see it."

"Not the most flattering pose, but there's no denying, no matter her distress, she's a striking woman, our Natalie."

"Certainly, no denying that," Gregor mused. "Too bad her sisters aren't quite so fair."

"Humph, the Callahan lasses are each one as fair as the next, and if ye had a stitch of good sense, you'd pick one and settle down."

"Well, s'pose I asked for that," Gregor groused.

"Aye, ye did, indeed."

Sighing, Gregor commented, "I couldn't imagine myself with Kirk Callahan as a father-in-law."

"I'd think the two of you would hit it off. The man likes his horses."

"Humph. Apples and oranges. His track and my field."

Not entirely sure if he were awake, his senses floated in weird, eccentric circles. As still as the highland hills, Liam lay listening to the canned voices from the box highlighting some mention of football games . . . NFL.

"Wonder if they're airing that conference on that other channel. As I recall, quite a few news stations were represented out there. Not the least of whom was our own Tanya Richards."

"Aye, naw surprise you noticed that one."

"Well, I uhm . . . don't suppose I should mention, I'm having dinner with her later this evening, then, should I?"

"The bloody hell ye—"

"Kidding, for God's sake, Da," Gregor mused. "Was all your blasted brooding getting to me," he said in a more tempered voice. "He's going to be all right, you know?" he said quietly. "Might not be ready for any marathons anytime soon, but he'll pull through this. It'll take more than a few hapless blokes with a knife to put him down."

"Yer knowing there were over a dozen?" Lucius commented.

"So, I've heard, and that's still not an even match. If not for the blasted knife, Liam would be the only one standing," he barely paused. "Which makes me wonder, did they have any luck checking hospitals? Have you heard?"

"Not so far."

"You have Gillis working on it?"

"Aye, but there's too many of those Goddamn free clinics where these bastards can get treated," Lucius growled. "God pity the poor bastard to ring me up fur a donation fur one of them in the future. Might be more inclined to pull the plug than donate a cent."

"Not exactly fair, Da, but if you were so inclined—"

"No."

Blast! That word had slid off his own lips. Liam lifted his lashes enough to glimpse his father and brother, sitting a short distance away, both looking toward him now rather than the set.

"Well, bloody hell," Gregor uttered and glanced aside while pushing to his feet.

Following that glance, Liam needed only to tip his head slightly to see Natalie lying rather oddly limp on a recliner, a white sheet draped nearly to her shoulders. That he feared for her safety suddenly, struck him a wicked blow and nearly started him rising. Her honey-colored hair lay askew on the sheet and her shoulders, and by the thin black strap, she still wore the black dress that had appeared so often in his dreams. Her head rested crookedly as if her neck had snapped, and her long lashes fanned over too-pale cheeks—

"Wake her!" Liam demanded as Gregor stepped into his line of sight. Lifting his focus, he rasped, "Wa-ake her!"

"Brother, she's barely had two blasted hours of sleep," Gregor hissed softly. "You've run her ragged for the past dozen hours. If you're truly awake—which you damn sure shouldn't be—then you need to settle and let her rest."

Catching up to the words, though not certain why his brother should be so irritated, Liam wondered, "Car-rousing again?"

"Oh, and there's calling the kettle black," Gregor nearly growled in greater irritation.

"I uhm . . . deserv-ing this?" Liam wondered.

"Well, no, not exactly," Gregor decided as his irritation sailed toward concern. In flashes, he glanced over Liam from his head to heels and landed his gaze on his eyes. "You're lying still for a change. I'm half afraid to ask how you're feeling."

"Thir-sty," he rasped.

"That, I can remedy," he said and barely turned, halting. "No need to panic, lass," he said, and Liam's attention spun, anticipating Natalie. Instead, a pixie-faced little woman loomed alongside him, seeming to move too fast for mortal sight. He'd experienced this before. Seeing her on one side, then the other. In one instant, she produced a cup, in another he barely swallowed, and the straw was gone. "Blast—sl-ow down, woman. Yer giving me whiplash."

The sigh drew his focus then, and his mind stilled. She rose from the blanket like a slinky black cat, sliding the white cloth away and slipping her stocking feet to the floor. Aye, and she wore the black stockings to set an unhealthy man's blood afire. Tipping his head more to gain the total picture, Liam found her eyes already looking into him, through him, with that weird light that seemed mystical even without the added effects of whatever swam in his system. "Ahhh."

"Humph," she retorted, rising fully to glide toward him. "I thought I recognized that growl and all you can say now is—ah?"

"A-ye—I . . . yes."

Gregor harrumphed a sound, then, "Well, are you bloody well satisfied, brother? You woke her."

Despite his swimming senses, he quivered a smile. "Ah-aye . . . I did."

"Any particular reason," Natalie asked and barely stifled a yawn, touching her hand daintily to her lips.

On those lovely lips, his attention fixed for a second—or an hour in his mind. When Liam managed a glance upward, he forgot the question, lost in her liquid green eyes. "Hi."

She studied him with a more peculiar expression, and a smile quivered slowly into her lips. "Are you saying hello, darling? Or stating a fact, I wonder?"

"Yer uhm . . . trying to . . . confuse me, eh?"

With her fingers gliding over his brow, something of his rising distress ebbed. "You wanted me awake, darling. Are you in pain again?"

"Aye-I am be-having," he managed with a fleeting thought of the importance, but again she quivered that tiny smile. "Aye . . . and there's that."

"There's some sense to these thoughts, my darling, but I'm not following."

"You were—sleeping."

"I was, yes," she said, and even in his altered state, he recognized the weariness in her eyes. "As you should be, darling."

"You could uhm . . . go back to sleep."

"Uh-huh," she idled. "You woke me to tell me that?"

"I did wake you," he managed, almost smoothly, and flickered a glance at the tiny woman hovering at the opposite side of his bed. "She did."

Lifting a brow and fleeting a glance at the startled woman, Natalie looked back down at him with a sober gaze. "Perhaps, I should clout her then in your stead. What say you, darling?"

"Clout Gregor," Liam suggested, sounding reasonable to his own ears. "He widnae mind."

"Here now, did I hear that right? Mine own name mentioned?"

Natalie flashed him a smirk. "Indeed, Gregor. He's volunteered you to take the clouting for waking me, and I'm considering it since I'm not altogether certain that I'm truly awake. I couldn't be held accountable under these circumstances."

"Yer awake," Liam confirmed. "But you could s-sleep now." If her speculating gaze were any indication, he could be in trouble here. A smile quivered on his lips, feeling like a fly to tingle there. Carefully, he skidded his hand and brushed a knuckle over his mustache, maybe bumping his nose . . . and bumping the oxygen tube affixed to his nostrils.

A smile quivered on her lips then, and she shook her head. "Lord, but you are just asking to be clouted . . . and if I wasn't reasonably certain that you're stoned, I would oblige you."

"Aye, stoned," he decided.

"Yea, well," Gregor mused. "You have enough tranquilizer in you to knock down a horse, so it's no huge surprise. That you're even managing to form words is impressive as all hell, Brother."

"It . . . is difficult," he admitted and lost the battle to keep his eyes open. For just a second, the shutter dropped, and as quick as a blink, he lost time.

"Fairy dust," he decided as he opened his eyes to find the world changed. His wife was there, hovering over him, but the black dress had evaporated, transformed into a pale green jacket of a color to match her eyes. Ethereal, she stood within a soft white light, her head tipped and fire dancing on the waves spilling over her shoulder. Otherworldly. Just the mere whisper of her hand across his brow confirmed his belief. "Aye . . . and the . . . faery herself."

A smile slipped onto the glossy lips; the stunning eyes sparkled with a rainbow of color. "Awake, again, are you then, darling?"

Just the whisper of her words stirred him oddly. "A-ye-I . . . don't think so."

"Well, that's good then, because you should be sleeping."

"With you."

Her hand stilled; her eyes steadied.

He had said something wrong— troubling—but his mind floated with the mere effort to collect a thought. Something wrong. Something he should know. Perhaps he wasn't awake. This seemed like an odd dream. A dream where he could be swimming underwater, and when he closed his eyes . . .

"Was that his voice I heard," the lyrical voice floated through his mind, and Liam grasped the familiar notes of his mother's voice.

"Yes, mum, but I'm not sure he was truly awake."

"Probably for the best at the moment, dear."

"I know . . . but with all this blasted publicity . . . we'll need to bring the boys here in the morning. . . ."

Twenty minutes after leaving the Emerald Club, Luke strode into the Rivers Inn. Hat, glasses, and windbreaker tucked in his garment bag, Luke asked for Frank by name, and as anticipated, he received a quick escort through the subdued, classy ambiance. High-backed cushioned booths contrasted beautifully with the cracked vinyl seating of the Emerald Club. The music played a soft symphony in line with the uniformed waitstaff and cloth-covered tables. Slipping into the booth across from Frank, Luke needed only a glimpse of the intense, curious brown eyes to know the waitress had mentioned him—probably to ask if he and Frank had connected.

Wearing one of his more sheepish grins, Luke commented, "I went to that other place—the Emerald Club. Thought maybe I'd catch up to you there. That tattooed lady said you were downstairs, but I didn't see you anywhere."

"Anita," Frank offered. "She mentioned talking to you."

"Guess I missed you already," Luke commented while donning a more peculiar smile. "Please don't tell me that's your favorite haunt, Frank . . . or that your fiancée works there."

Frank's eyes flashed wider with surprise and sounded as baffled as indignant. "My fiancée—? Certainly not!"

"Shit, that's a relief," Luke said good-naturedly. "When your mum said you were meeting your fiancée for an early dinner, I thought I'd get to meet her, but . . .? Well, it caught me off guard. You don't hang out there, right?"

"Humph," Frank managed, and the smile quivered into his thin mustache. He appeared just nervous enough to be a man returning from a clandestine meeting. And he wasn't a fellow prone to deception. Far too much expression brightened his soft brown eyes and creased his lean sculpted features. "I was a little worried about meeting you in a place like that, and no—I don't hang out there."

"Wew, that's a relief," Luke huffed. "I'd hate to think of my brother patronizing a place like that too often."

"Actually," Frank began and surprised Luke by continuing. "We have been there a few times. Think Liam liked being incognito. Sometimes family pressures can be a bit much."

Was there an underlying meaning and understanding in that comment . . . as if possibly the fellow new damned full well Luke had no intention of joining his family or gracing that vigil? "You . . . you're planning on attending that vigil this evening?"

"I am. And you're welcome to come with me," Frank offered.

The moment of truth. Luke leveled his gaze on his brother's old friend. "I'm flying out this evening, Frank," he said simply, honestly. "If I thought there was even one thing, I could do to help this situation, I'd stick around. But there isn't."

"Luke—"

"Look, I appreciate all you've done today. Truly," he continued and ignored the soft understanding in the warm damp eyes. This old friend understood nothing. "Fact is, Frank, it's a fluke that I was even here today. And I need to be somewhere else tomorrow."

"What if something happens, Luke?" Frank asked in the same sorrowful, near-desperate voice that he'd used with Alecia.

"Me being here won't change anything," Luke said without an ounce of inflection. "When he pulls through—when he's well enough for a visit—I'll stop back." He needed only a flashing memory of the confusion and panic in his older brother's eyes to confirm his decision. Whatever Liam had been seeing, thinking, it hadn't been good. The fellow had taken one look at Luke and appeared to decide he was dead or dying.

They weren't close. They hadn't been close for a very long time, but to be considered an ill-omen—the grim reaper or angel of death . . .? A little much even for him, and in twenty-twenty hindsight, Luke knew he'd determined to leave at that very moment. He might not like his family much, but he still loved them. No way did he want to live with the guilt of sending his brother through the pearly gates.

"Luke—"

"Frank, I have to leave," Luke decided and reached for his bag at the deep end of the bench seat. "I really just wanted to thank you for everything you did today," he admitted. "I'm glad you were there."

Frank hesitated, then seemed to realize the futility of attempting to change his mind. "I'm glad I was there, too, Luke. I just wish there was more I could do to help you."

"You've done more than enough," he said lightly and started off the bench. "Truly."

"Wait," Frank said while rising as well. "You haven't eaten."

"No worries. I'll catch something at the airport after I check in."

"The airport . . . do you need a ride?" Frank persisted. "That's the least I can do, Lucas. At least let me make sure you get there safely."

Frank was a worrier as well as a genuinely compassionate fellow and good friend. Considering that he would need to call a cab and wait, Luke decided he could kill two birds with one stone—relieving Frank's concern and reaching the airport with time to spare. "If you're sure it's no trouble, I'll take you up on that offer."

10

Striding through the tunnel to reach the plane, Luke felt oddly like the apostle Thomas, who'd denied Christ three times before the crucifixion. First, at the ticket counter where he'd checked his bag—after donning the hat, glasses, and windbreaker—the fellow had eyed Luke with a peculiar shine, and Luke had wondered if he'd worn dirt on his face or carried something stuck in his beard. 'You sorta look like that McDade who got mugged near here last night. Are you a relative by any chance?'

'I think they spell their name, M-A-C Dade,' Luke pointed out, and the ticket attendant quickly apologized.

Then, in the restaurant where he'd deliberately chosen a shadowed corner booth, the waitress had studied him—apparently ignoring his ball cap, beard, and hair—commenting, 'You have to be related to that guy who was hurt last night. A brother, maybe?'

'What guy?' he'd asked, and the woman had deflected her mistake by falling into a five-minute dissertation and update, enlightening Luke about Liam's ongoing critical status.

'They're saying it's still touch and go,' the waitress had professed with an exasperated sigh. 'You do look like him. I mean—his picture's been all over the TV all day, and he's really handsome.'

'I think I should take that as a compliment then,' Luke had said with a wry smile.

She eyed him more critically, and Luke decided he better learn to scowl more as she spoke ponderingly. 'Yes, you should.'

Learn to scowl? Or accept her comment as a compliment?

Either way, he'd been glad to finish eating. He'd dropped cash on the table and kept his card in his wallet. If he'd used a charge card, he might have needed to point out the missing A. In twenty-twenty hindsight, he should have changed his name four years earlier and used something simple like Smith or Jones. Dropping the A had been a mistake—and not even his own—and not even entirely official, although it now appeared on most of his credentials. It had begun at the driver's licensing bureau four years earlier when his name had been misspelled on his permit and perpetuated when he applied for his official passport.

Technically, his name was still MacDade on his birth certificate, but that was the only place it appeared. With practice, he'd slaughtered his original flowing script and learned to scribble an almost illegible 'A' on official documents—like property deeds and car titles. He guessed if it ever became an issue, he could be in trouble, but hell—it worked for now and generally kept him from the spotlight.

Strike three—the ticket taker at the tunnel entrance had looked at his ticket, at him, at his ticket—and decided to ask, 'Are you related to that Liam MacDade on the news, hon?'

'Think those folks spell it M-A-C-Dade,' he'd said again, not exactly lying or denying a thing. Still, he felt like Thomas—the one who needed to poke the holes in Jesus's palms before believing He'd arisen and who'd given rise to the old saying, Doubting Thomas. Was that next? He would poke holes in Liam to see if he were dead or alive?

If he needed to know, it would come to him, like most things came to him.

Need to know.

Settling into his designated seat, Luke spent a few moments fiddling with his seatbelt and turning off his cell phone. Belatedly, he spotted the topsy-turvy position of the magazines and barf bag in the pouch in front of him. No way could he stare at that mess for five minutes, much less two hours. Muttering a curse, he released his seatbelt, leaned forward, and arranged the magazines, the bag, and the card bearing directions in the event of a plane crash. Satisfied, he sat back and affixed his seatbelt for the second, maybe third time. Luckily, the stewardess hadn't wandered by during his fussing, or she might have called one of the federal marshals who'd begun riding on all commercial flights after 911. Details. Damn it. He couldn't afford to be 302'd. With his luck, he'd land behind locked doors in Southern General, a floor below Liam.

The paparazzi would love that.

Damn it, he needed to settle down and relax regardless of how badly flying distressed him.

He needed to be in Roanoke in the morning to meet with the realtor, and hopefully, in the afternoon, he'd meet with the architect.

He should have called the hospital again before shutting off his phone . . . or just thrown in the damn towel and called Gregor directly. He had the damn number for his next older brother. He could have phoned at any time during the day and blocked the caller ID. Why he preferred not to be connected directly with any MacDades, he couldn't even decide except that the email system worked out fine for all concerned.

That tiny beep at 1 a.m. had sounded like a blasted bomb detonating—and it might have been exactly that.

'At approximately 12:30 this morning, Liam MacDade was the victim . . .'

12:30 a.m.

Gregor had emailed him at 1: a.m.

Had it taken his brother a half hour to remember he had another brother? Like an 'oh shit' moment—'Oh shit, I need to message the runt . . . .'

They'd called him that—the runt—among other fine names like 'rug ape,' 'curtain-climber,' 'bairn' . . . or 'wee bairn' when they were feeling, particularly, large and old.

Luke had never minded those nicknames, not from either of his brothers . . . right up until Liam had landed a swat to turn his ass into a solid welt. As if a spectator, now and then, Luke remembered his brothers cornering him in one of their mother's gazebos—the big white one with the rose vines climbing the six ornate lattice pillars . . .

He should have known better than to sit and try reading surrounded by the ancient roses, the kind that still carried the heavy scent. Inevitably, he'd sneezed and might have gone into an asthma attack if he'd lingered too long.

He smelled it now, tasted it. That rose scent settled on his tongue like heavy oil . . . and here they were, his brothers, cornering him—wanting him to go to the stable, ride with them . . . He hadn't been to the stables in a long time. Wanted nothing to do with the stables . . . Except late at night when he snuck out of bed and visited Duchess, his Hackney pony.

'Settle! Stop! Lucas! Stop!'

Echoes, like echoes through a valley, those sounds volleyed through his mind, but he couldn't stop, knew only he needed to escape—and the fire exploded on his behind, snatching his breath, halting the scream in his throat . . . and reality struck.

He'd kicked his oldest brother in the family jewels, and his oldest brother needed the family jewels to produce another heir!

"I'm sorry," he muttered aloud, remembering in freeze frames. A spectator now, he saw himself crying and choking, begging for his older brother's forgiveness. The rising blisters and smoldering embers had taken a backseat to his fear and sorrow. The entire clan could be destroyed—

"Excuse me?" the stranger intruded.

Luke blinked the images from his mind and caught up to the plane already leveling at a safe altitude.

The woman was a stewardess. Or were they flight attendants now? Tall and sleek, she wore a pleasant, somewhat curious smile.

"I'm sorry to be a bother, but I wonder if I could trouble you for a drink?" Luke improvised, hoping she didn't offer brandy—or bourbon.

"What would you like, hon? We have a nice selection of wines and liquors, or we have sodas, coffee or tea . . ."

"Any chance I could get a beer?" Technically, he wasn't old enough to buy one, much less drink it, but that hadn't been an issue since he grew his beard. In twenty-twenty hindsight, he should have changed his birthdate when dropping the A. Even a single-digit difference would have simplified things. Most people thought he was older anyway, which worked out well in most negotiations and did wonders for getting served on airplanes and in strip joints.

The stewardess rattled off a short list, and delighted, Luke ordered an import. If a fellow was meant to break the rules, he might as well break them with a hardy, dark German brew. Unfortunately, it came American style, chilled rather than room temp. Luke decided not to quibble and popped the cap, ignoring the plastic cup and chugging a few swallows from the can while turning his focus through the black portal. At some point, he'd dimmed the overhead light. He found his own dull phantom image reflected on the black glass. Brimmed hat tilted gangster style on his forehead, hair skimming the dark silky collar of the windbreaker, mustache, and beard hiding the half-smirked grin . . . he would never pass for Bogart with the hair. More like a blasted rock star or Jesus freak. No wonder people were lending him a second glance—

I really like your curly hair.

The young voice slipped from the past, the image erupting full-force with the forest scents and odd semi-stagnant odor of pondwater. They were sitting on the smaller boulders, the kind to poke like mushrooms from a blanket of moss. Soda cans open and propped in the moss. A few empty candy wrappers were already stacked in a neat pile alongside the rock, and a bag of cookies stood open between them—directly centered within either of their reach. The fishing pole, too, poised, propped, and braced between them. Luke had overturned enough rocks and dirt to collect the worms; Jimmy had begged off the search, claiming he saw enough of the slimy things while mucking stalls. A lie, of course. The stalls never stayed dirty long enough to collect worms.

Jimmy was a little strange about stuff like that—*lying*.

'I do, ya know? I think your curly hair's pretty.'

Considering how often those dang curls got tussled, Luke was no more fond of his hair than his height—him being about the shortest MacDade on the estate, if not the planet. He blamed both for the near-constant barrage of head scuffing, not unlike their two Irish Wolfhounds that always begged to be scuffed and stood at a height to be obliged by any passing body. Why his parents insisted on Irish hounds rather than Scottish terriers, he'd never decided. Someday, though, he was going to own a mountain dog—maybe one of those Bernese Mountain dogs, black and tan, like a furry Doberman with white markings. Dobermans came from Germany. He might need to check an Atlas and find out where the Bernese Mountains were located.

"Switzerland," he remembered.

"Excuse me?"

Damn it!

The stewardess stopped in a half turn and clasped the seat with a hiccup of turbulence, an automatic response to maintain her balance, although she didn't appear old enough to be seasoned. With blond hair pulled into a ponytail and a tuft of curls around her pert little cap to match her one-piece navy-blue uniform and big blue eyes—she put Luke in mind of that reporter, Molly Anderson. If he'd remained in Trenton, he might have offered her an interview. She wasn't the type to be married or have any kids either. And the stewardess—Peggy, as boasted on her gold clip—was here.

"Planning my next trip," Luke said with a slightly sheepish smile, one he'd perfected in drama classes years ago. "Any chance you rotate on transatlantic flights?"

"Yes, I do," she admitted with a pleasant, relaxing smile. "I've flown into Germany a few times, but never Switzerland."

"Ever fly over the Alps?"

"I have," she relaxed more, and either she had time to kill, or she catered to the idiosyncrasies of first-class passengers . . . or she cued in on his mild distress and decided to offer comfort. "I've traveled north and south, and the views are just as awesome as you'd expect. Do you plan on hiking?"

"Love to hike . . . and climb," he added with a wry smirk. "I really don't mind heights."

"A bit of a control freak, huh?" she asked with a bright knowing smile.

"Just a little," he conceded, amused. "I think I need to take flying lessons sometime soon. I wouldn't mind flying if I held the yoke."

Her head tilted; her eyes sparkled. "Something tells me you might already know a little about flying," she only half teased. "Most people call it a steering wheel."

"I read it somewhere," he mused, not lying though the memory was lost. "Impressed?"

She huffed a soft laugh, her gaze more intent. Interested if not impressed. "It's possible."

"Any chance you have a layover in Roanoke?"

For a second she hesitated, but her blue eyes darted over him, and she decided. "As a matter of fact, I do. Is that where you live?"

"I'm thinking about it, but not yet," he admitted. "I'll probably only be there tomorrow."

"Where are you staying? What hotel?"

"Actually—" He offered the sheepish smile again. "I didn't think that far ahead. I'm hoping to find a room after I pick up my rental. . ."

Some things came way too easy. About twenty-four hours after departing Lexington, Luke escorted the slender young woman into a hotel room and wondered if he were taking a page from his brother's book. Not exactly a sleazy hotel or a strip joint. Only vaguely, Luke recalled another snapshot reaching the tabloids a year or so ago by the paparazzi . . . his brother captured, front and center, laughing with a sleek, attractive woman under his arm. Not many shots like that existed, but the woman had worn a uniform like the one Luke was currently slipping off the silken, tanned shoulders in front of him.

Slow and easy, he whispered kisses from her hungry lips to her neck, catching glimpses of her bright blue eyes filled with as much anticipation as delight. At least twice, she'd mentioned never doing something like this before now—never bringing a strange man into her hotel room before him. But her slender fingers, freeing his belt, twitching his cotton shirt buttons, told a different tale. Not that it mattered. If she asked, he might admit to slipping in and out of relationships as swiftly as he changed shoes. But she wasn't asking; he wasn't volunteering.

A fellow could move around the world invisibly if he knew what avenues to access, and aside from his various small flats, he hadn't paid for a hotel room in quite a while. He bought dinners, breakfasts, the occasional movie theater or opera tickets, depending on the city . . .

Two hours later, resting in the soft glow of parking lot lights slipping through a crack in the window blinds, Luke listened to the contented rhythmic breaths beside him. Thoughts adrift, he recalled that candlelight vigil and envisioned his brother lying under a sheet in a bed too short, with the sounds of a heart monitor and oxygen machine as a background hum.

Wide awake, Luke slipped from beneath the sheet, found the television remote, and held it under the light strip to familiarize himself with the controls. Turning the set as far from the bed as possible without sending it through the wall, he ignited the screen, turned the sound to mute, and engaged the closed caption function. A minute later, he rested on the single armchair, watching the candles flickering throughout the large crowd, reading.

". . . where more than two hundred people came together to show their support and offer their prayers to the MacDade family and friends . . . Molly Anderson of the local station, WKBN, was on the scene and spoke with some of the supporters . . ."

For several moments, the tidy blond—wearing the same flowery red dress to suggest she was likewise engaged in this vigil for the duration—held her camera to candlelit faces, capturing glowing wet eyes and quivering lips. Women. Most of this group were women ranging from teenagers to grandmothers, but quite a few men of various ages were present, too.

The mayor, according to the tagline below the picture, a sharp-dressed man with a naturally stiff upper lip and a firm jaw, spoke grimly. ". . . As you know, Molly, we're not a hotbed of crime here in our little city. We leave that to our big city counterparts to the east . . . We want those responsible for his assault to be caught and punished . . . and I've assured the family, we're putting all our resources to the task . . ."

The police chief was there as well, offering the simple fact, "We're tracking down every lead as it comes in, but as you know, the MacDade family has offered a reward . . ."

And the clergy—an Irish Catholic priest, Fr. Murphy began, "Let's we bow our heads and pray. . . ."

Luke's attention riveted abruptly as the camera panned over the gathering. A face in the crowd—several familiar faces, in fact. Frank Pendleton was there, a mere apparition in the sea of shadowed faces towards the rear. At least two of Gillis's men stood in attendance, their station apparent to the discerning eye by their interest in the faces around them rather than the speakers. Candles burned in jars within the flowers—a mound of flowers that had grown since this morning.

As the camera panned over the collection, a cold chill slipped down Luke's spine. Flowers. The flowers carried a funereal essence even in the cold light of the camera strobes and flickering candles. Votive candles. Luke's heart hammered a more leaden beat as the camera zoomed in on the red and blue glass flutes to be found in cemeteries. If Liam had passed . . . tears trailed down a few faces.

Heartbeat accelerating, Luke's throat squeezed against the started shout and demand. *Did he pass!*

As if the news anchor on the national network heard Luke's plea, the picture cut to the recorded scene from the press conference, and the words scrolled on the screen.

"Since the outpouring of support this morning, Southern General has been issuing updates to the local press, and although Mr. MacDade's condition remains critical, we are told that every hour is crucial to his recovery . . ."

"We have learned that his personal physician flew into Trenton this afternoon, and at this point, they're keeping him sedated . . .

"As we have learned, Liam MacDade is the oldest son of Lucius MacDade, the founder and CEO of High Land, Inc., a Fortune Five Hundred company that manufactures fine custom-built furniture. The company has since diversified from its original platform, and Liam MacDade, acting COO, is considered the driving force behind some of the innovations that are currently being launched on an international scale . . ."

As he continued to read and record the details of his brother's life and his family's history, Luke continued to scroll mentally through the faces he'd seen while scanning the crowd. Like balls dropping into slots in a roulette wheel, he caught the images, halfheartedly wondering if Natalie's family had been turned away at the doors like Frank Pendleton. Even in the shadows, Luke recognized Natalie's younger brother Tomas and the older boy John, who, if Luke remembered correctly, was about a year older than him. Doubtful, they had been turned away. More likely, the boys and the younger of the two sisters, Linnie, had merely stepped out to participate in the vigil, and so far, apparently, no one had recognized them. The Callahans weren't quite as well known as the MacDades—not in these northern territories. Maybe down south, with their main head-quarters and terminals in Georgia or South Carolina, they'd make the news.

"South Carolina," Luke muttered, collecting data while recalling the symbiotic relationship that his father had formed with Kirk Callahan. K. C. Trucking had handled most of the MacDade trucking and shipping even before the patriarchs had aligned their families with the wedding of the century.

What an extravaganza that had been, with over five hundred guests descending on Lexington. The wedding party had filled the front of the Cathedral, and the ancient pipe organ had echoed over the hills and vales leading the choir in hymns. Lucius MacDade had bought an entire hotel to accommodate all the overseas and out-of-town guests, then turned the first floor into a hall with different themes for different conference rooms. A half dozen bands and orchestras had played everything from symphony music to rock 'n roll with an impressive mix of Scottish and American traditional songs.

Luke remembered meandering from room to room to avoid all the head scuffing and cheek pinching. Eventually, he'd run into John Calla-han, who'd stood almost a full head taller and enjoyed proving it.

By the look of him on the television, John had topped off around six feet, and with a wry smile, Luke regretted departing. If he had stuck around Trenton a little longer—or risked stopping by the vigil—he might have gained the opportunity to look down on John. Foolish and petty, maybe. Luke had survived the boy's relentless taunting that day and managed to avoid him for the last eight years. John Callahan had been a bully then, and if Luke had released his anger back then, the boy might not have survived even to reach six feet.

No matter what Gillis MacDade might have thought at the time, Luke had never stopped practicing the moves he'd begun perfecting at five or six, and a fellow could learn a hell of a lot by watching and studying the maneuvers of a master.

Liam MacDade was a master at the martial arts, surpassing Gillis's skill level before turning thirteen, and Gillis had probably known it. The fellow had moved off the estate and taken his place in security around that time . . . But not before offering Luke basic lessons per his father's order. Unfortunately, Luke had already begun watching Liam and Gregor practice.

Gillis was fast and smooth; Liam was faster, with an elegance to defy nature and his already considerable height. Watching him, Luke had discovered how a body should move, large or small, perfecting the moves in the privacy of the nursery until the day Gillis decided to start teaching him.

'Just a few moves, aye, bairn? . . . Ye'll need pay heed here lest some idjit mistakes ye for a lass whit with all them pretty curls come a day.'

Luke's thoughts turned inward . . . He recalled aiming for Gillis's jaw, but . . . well, and he was barely a few feet tall. He might have misjudged that spin and kick by accident . . . but before Gillis recovered from howling and unfolded from holding his family jewels, Luke had perfected the art of running—and didn't stop until he was in his nanna's arms.

'He's going to kill me, Nan Em. He is,' he'd heaved and huffed, clinging to her slender body as if his life depended on it, which it probably had.

'Who, li'l love? Who's going to kill you?' Emma demanded, prepared to battle whatever monster might burst into their room. 'You just point him out to me, now.'

Exasperated and honestly terrified, he'd cried, 'Uncle Gill, Nanna. He's going to kill me. I know it. I'm a dead boy! I'm going to be flying to heaven with Grammy McDade, now.'

'Oh lord, Lucas, hush now,' Emma soothed and consoled, rubbing his back and smoothing the shakes. 'You're all right, baby . . . Your uncle's not going to be killing my little boy. Not so long as I have a say in it. . .'

What Uncle Gillis had done was almost worse, Luke remembered as he drew from the distant past. His uncle had reported to his father that his youngest son was nowhere near coordinated enough to learn the complicated moves and discipline necessary for martial arts. 'Might be better off getting the wee bairn ballet lessons to gain his balance . . ..'

At the time, Luke recalled hating his uncle for that suggestion, which his father had taken seriously, but in hindsight, it had probably benefitted him. He'd learned to dance, which had gained him the lead in a play a half dozen years later. And admittedly, he'd become just a little quicker and lighter on his feet.

If he'd engaged John Callahan eight years ago, he might have done some serious damage and probably ruined the wedding. . . and it would be worse now if the fellow was still a hard head and a bully. Doubtful anyone would have appreciated Luke putting John in a bed alongside Liam.

A bed Liam shouldn't be occupying.

On the television, some new footage finally erupted, and Liam caught his first clear look at the alley where Liam had been mugged. New footage and new information.

". . . As you can see, the spot where Liam MacDade was mugged early yesterday morning is still cordoned off with crime scene tape . . . Local and federal authorities are still scouring the alley for any evidence that could lead to the assailants . . . If you look this way, you can see the entrance to the Fairmont Hotel where—we understand—Liam was meeting a business associate before he intended to join his wife at the Bayfront Hotel . . . As we've heard, Liam was ushered into that alley at gunpoint where more than a dozen gang members lay in wait to rob him . . ."

And therein the entire premise fell apart.

A dozen assailants . . . armed with knives and now guns . . . casually await the possibility of a wealthy lone man leaving a what . . .? A single-star hotel?

And horses fly.

It was an ambush—pure and simple—and Liam wasn't meant to survive.

Lucius MacDade had suspected that detail from the start, which was the reason for tight security regardless that he proposed to thwart the paparazzi or overzealous reporters like this Molly Anderson.

"Damn it," Luke uttered with a sudden epiphany slamming him out of left field. This was Sunday morning. He'd been awakened over twenty-four hours ago, on a *Saturday* morning. On the second floor of the Pendleton chateau, he'd probably slept through a pro-golf tournament and awoken long before sunset of a *Saturday* night.

Sunday morning. This was Sunday morning dawning.

Not blasted Monday morning when he was scheduled to meet with the blasted realtors.

"Shit." He had an entire day to kill.

His gaze slid to the bed where the sleek, limber anatomy rested in gentle slopes beneath the sheets. Her name was Peggy, and her next scheduled flight wasn't departing until Tuesday morning, which he'd assumed would follow today.

Talk about jet lag. Damn it.

How he managed even to get from one moment to the next, much less one day to the next sometimes baffled even him, but maybe this wasn't an altogether bad turn. He could think of worse ways to spend a fine Sunday morning, afternoon, and evening. Touching the button on the remote to shut off the set, Luke pushed off the chair and made his way through the half-light, slipping beneath the sheet with a mere whisper of sound.

Yes. There were certainly worse ways to spend a day than to have a beautiful woman in his arms.

In the blink of an eye, his sons were here, and Liam lay drifting his gaze between the handsome pair at his bedside. Micheal's curly head hovered at a crooked angle, so much like his mother with his pensive set and curious tilt. Of their three children, Michael most favored Natalie with the willowy build and auburn locks . . . but his eyes were blue, nearly as dark blue as his older brother's. Jamie stood his ground, a capable small hand gripping the top silver bar and his piercing eyes near level with Liam's gaze. At seven, the boy was as solid as ever a MacDade, and as given to brooding as his grandfather.

"Are you dying, Da?"

"Jamie," Lucius spoke while freeing one hand from his youngest grandson. Landing his immense palm over the curls of the eldest, he drew the child's direct blue gaze. "Your da's ill. Not dying. Mind now."

"Not," Liam managed. "Dying . . . son."

The boy's blue eyes riveted and held steady, judging for himself as if he carried something of his mother's weird ways inside of him. "Good then," he decided in a voice too old for such a small body. "I dinnae want you to."

Too much time with his grandfather, Liam mused and might have meant to reach for his son's hand to reassure him, but the boy was gone. Just that

fast, there and gone, and a stranger swayed above him. Not merely hovering .
. . Liam had a sense of motion at his waist, prickling flutters to worry him—

"You're doing fine, son."

"Not doing." *And not your son*, he might have said aloud, but couldn't
be sure. He would know if this dark-haired fellow was his father. Weird
epiphanies. He rested at an elevated angle to view the odd room, to see slivers
of sunlight slanted across the white sheet covering his feet. Immense feet, to
his distorted vision. His own feet, he verified by asking his toes to move and
watching the white strip wiggle. A grand feat, that. His focus swam in search
of familiar sights and landed on the recliner where his wife had slept only a
moment ago. Disappointment flared in his mind to find himself abandoned,
barren . . . but he was not entirely alone. Another vaguely familiar round face
lingered at his side. And in another recliner, his younger brother sprawled,
resting rather casually with a raised knee, stocking foot wedged on the raised
footboard, one hand holding a Styrofoam cup balanced on the arm of the
dark brown chair. A natural smile remained on the mustache, the golden
head tipped to catch another strip of light and fire like molten gold. Curious
that Gregor should appear so handsome in repose.

"You should be married," Liam decided, uncertain that he'd spoken aloud
until the laugh idled off the golden, mustached lips and the pale blue eyes
ignited in mirth.

"Why am I not surprised that should be the first bloody thing off your
lips, eh?" Gregor idled in mirth. "Good to see you, Brother."

"Yer too handsome to be single," Liam managed in a struggle to maintain
a serious thought. Well, it sounded reasonably serious, though Gregor only
appeared more amused and emitted another humph, stifling a laugh. "It's
dangerous," Liam continued on a serious note. "MacDades should be married . . . dangerous . . ."

Above him, Gregor appeared abruptly, and Liam's senses swayed as he
found the more sober gaze upon him.

"Are you truly attempting to tell me something here, Brother? Or are you
just making small talk?"

A thought rolled around in his mind, but there and gone, on a carousel.
"I need . . . the carrousel to . . . stop."

"So, now I need to wonder if you're dreaming about a blasted amusement
park or actually trying to make some weird kind of sense that only you
are privy to," Gregor idled, studying him still. "These brilliant moments of

illumination are rather like trying to piece together a puzzle with too blasted many pieces in the box."

"Aye, that's business . . . building puzzles."

"Grand, now I'm getting either a lecture to be more involved in the family trade or receiving instructions to entertain your sons."

"Here."

"At least, that, I might ken. Yes—they were here. Several times, in fact." His amusement returned in full. "Micheal seems to think you look like Mr. Gadget or some such. And Jamie's likened you to Thor. Apparently, he's adopted a fondness for comic books." He paused but seemed to continue hurriedly. "Lee's planning to bring them back this evening. They're—"

"Natalie," he stated. "Her name."

"Good then, you remember," Gregor spoke simply.

Confused, as ever a moment past, Liam tried to grasp Gregor's sudden sobriety and barely held his own thought. "Her name . . . not Lee."

"She's been Lee to me since we met in grade school," Gregor commented. "She doesn't mind, and if you do, I'd say . . . tough shit, lad. That's who she is."

"Natalie," Liam stated again, not certain of his ire rising. Hard to think.

"Truly?" Gregor said with sudden sober curiosity. "It bothers you that much?"

What bothered him . . . something . . . there and gone.

11

Sooner or later, it had to happen.

"Ma'am? Will there be anything else?"

Distracted, Natalie snatched the tabloid off the rack and landed it atop the collection of snacks on the counter. Foolish, perhaps, but personally stopping to pick up a few things to keep the boys busy had seemed like the most natural thing in the world. Natural, yes, despite the blasted limo waiting for her around the corner and the blasted bodyguard idling inconspicuously near the entrance. The fellow wore a sports jacket and jeans, and unless one happened to notice how he moved, ambling but on alert, he'd look like a man with time on his hands. The dark eyes missed nothing regardless of his apparent attention on the ingredients of a cereal box, and suddenly, Natalie was more grateful for Artair's presence than ever past.

Looking down at that front page photo and seeing the headlines in bold print, she suffered a shiver.

'Wife of billionaire Liam MacDade suffers breakdown as husband lays dying.'

Caught for all posterity, she stood in grainy color, half-turned toward Gregor as if turning to him for solace when, in fact, she'd been pivoting towards the door. She recalled that moment, knowing and feeling her husband waking on the seventh floor. To deny her ability at this late date was a fool's dream. After eight years of marriage, the connection was bound to happen—the melding as if his blood ran through her veins.

Only vaguely aware of pulling the bills from her new purse, Natalie lifted the money to the young cashier and halted as the wider eyes rose from the tabloid.

The instant of enlightenment was followed by a breathless, "You're her."

"An odd likeness," Natalie started, as she had lied a million times in past years, but this young woman knew differently, and why hide it? "Yes, I am."

"Oh, man. I'm sorry. Are you—is he—they're saying he's still—Is he going to be all right, ma'am? I didn't make it to the vigil—I had to work Saturday."

Stopping for snacks had been a bad idea. Even with the precaution to park the limo on the side street, out of sight, this city was too small to remain invisible. "We're praying," Natalie managed.

"I will too, ma'am," the young cashier said breathlessly and looked as if she wanted to say more, as starstruck as if a celebrity stood before her. She hadn't even accepted the bills quivering in Natalie's hand, and she seemed at a loss as Natalie lifted the twenties higher to draw her attention. She looked at the bills but shook her bouncy short curls. Her hands quivered as she shoved the crackers and juice into a plastic bag.

As dumbfounded by the oddly disjointed protocol as the manic motion before her, Natalie watched the second bag fill. Absently, she wondered if she were facing a genius . . . one who might ring up the item prices from memory. That talent was not entirely unheard of. Liam could do it. But this young woman appeared normal enough, even sported an earring in her puffy lip—a wicked trend in Natalie's opinion. If Arabella ever thought about adopting this style . . .

That wasn't going to happen. Hopefully, this trend would peter out before Natalie needed to worry about stifling her daughter's free spirit.

The woman hesitated, then shoved the tabloid in the second bag and gathered the first, handing both across the counter.

"Miss, uhm," Natalie proffered the bills again, but the young woman merely shook her bouncy curls and handed over the bags. "But—"

Sorrow alighted in the young face, as odd as all else. "For your little ones," she said hesitantly and appeared more soulful, moisture rising in her eyes. "I saw them yesterday on the evening news. They're so doggone cute," she said with a tortured smile. "I can't imagine what they're going through. Just uhm . . . tell them it's from Marsha, okay?"

The news? Her *sons* were on the *news*?

With the revelation stirring turmoil in her mind, Natalie managed her thanks while suffering near blindness with the wash of tears flashing over her eyes. Clumsily, she gathered the bags, only vaguely aware of Artair coming to her rescue and escorting her through the door.

Feeling suddenly vulnerable, Natalie smashed the tears from her eyes and drew breath. Acutely aware of her surroundings, she blinked against sunspots flashing off a vehicle passing slowly on the street. a half-block away, a collection of children near her sons' age played on the sidewalk, dangerously close to traffic. A ball bounced off a porch post; her muscles lurched with the sound ricocheting like a gunshot. She'd seen this corner store a half dozen times or more. She'd chosen it for its obscurity rather than risk a crowded supermarket.

But far too quickly, she suffered the chill, the prickling—the wicked foreboding of something, someone, lurking just beyond her ken. She was not alone here and not as anonymous as she had intended. Cars passed, a young woman pushed a stroller, and a young man wearing the customary garb of a cyclist whizzed past the parked car at the curb. Further down the block, an older gentleman walked his Schnauzer, pausing to let it lift its leg at a telephone pole. Normal. All was normal until she turned toward the corner, toward where the limo should be hidden. Just past the side street opening, she saw the two elderly women looking her way, and directly across from them, on the opposite side of the street . . . a long black canister jutted from the driver door of a white van. For an instant, Natalie drew breath, fearing a gunshot . . . and in the next, the sunspots ignited on the wide circle of an immense camera lens. She gathered only a sense of a male behind that black contraption. A hallo of black hair appeared more like an extension of the camera in his hands. Not a live-action news anchor, this fellow! The prickles scored down her spine, as much a sign of outrage as fear.

Paparazzi!

And he could be responsible for her photo on that rag! Could be the reason that she needed a bodyguard to buy her boys some snacks! Could be the reason her husband lay in a hospital bed!

As unfounded as that thought might be, she suddenly held this single man responsible for all the ills upon them, and perhaps, it was the mere thought of her children being caught on video that flamed her brewing rage. Rather than veer into the side street, Natalie nearly collided with Artair as she started across the pavement, her attention level on the cameraman.

"Natalie?" Artair started, then seemed to follow her focus. He stepped smoothly into her path, but not before she glimpsed that interloper recoiling, drawing his camera into the open window and disappearing.

Natalie hadn't caught more than a glance, and before she could step past the human shield, the idling engine gunned, tires chirruped. Lifting her outraged glare to Artair, she snapped, "Why'd you stop me, blast you?"

"Ma'am, we can't stop them all," he said in a guarded, reasonable tone.

In that single sentence, Natalie found grace to pause. "You . . .? You knew he was there."

"Aye," he said gravely, and his dark eyes seemed now, never to stop moving, scanning the street fore and aside. Still, he managed to address her, sounding apologetic. "We've had that one with us for a time."

"But there've been others," she grasped.

"More than a few."

"I—I don't want my sons' pictures on the evening news or in some blasted tabloid," she said shortly. "Not today, or tomorrow, not next blasted month. I don't bloody well care if you must shoot the next anchorperson to attempt capturing my sons on film! I do *not* want to see—or hear—that they were the blasted star of the evening fucking news. Do you understand, sir?"

Brave man, this cousin, and bodyguard who stifled a taut smile while directing her toward the limo. "Yes, ma'am, but I should try not to make the news if I can avoid it."

By refraining from shooting an anchorman or woman.

Belatedly aware of what she'd said, Natalie suffered the start of a smile and shook her head, accepting his silent suggestion to start toward the car. How many others were following them though? Circling like vultures for that single money-making shot of her or her sons bursting into tears. They were waiting for that shot. For that news to make even more headlines. Officially, Liam remained in critical condition, and more than once, Natalie had heard of some hapless reporter or photographer trying to sneak onto the top floor. Barring a closeup, some had opted for photos of the exterior view of the hospital's upper floors. In fleeting memory, Natalie recalled catching that bit of a news segment where one ingenious anchorperson had directed her cameraman to zoom in on the seventh floor and pan the curtained windows of the VIP ward. . . . 'Where the MacDade family are keeping silent vigil . . .'

Albeit silent, Natalie had thought then and now, slipping into the back-seat with Megan and the boys, who both lit up at the sight of the stuffed bags. No, never silent, her boys. Though to their credit, neither shouted nor screamed even on a good day, let alone when they fully grasped the seriousness of their father's condition.

"Did you get me a comic book, Mum?" Jamie asked anxiously and slipped the tabloid from the bag before Natalie even recalled its presence.

"Jame—"

Far too quick, her eldest son. His blue eyes flashed on the headline and the sight of his mother on the brink of tears, and his panic flamed as he looked at her. "Mum! Is Da—"

"No, Jamie," she stated and slipped the magazine from his fingers as she glimpsed at Megan's alarmed curiosity. "Pay no nevermind to that nonsense, sweetie," she spoke calmly, catching his fingers that suddenly gripped her hand with the intensity of his fear.

"But it says Da's dying," he said softly, and tears threatened the corner of his eyes.

Younger, by no means slighter of intelligence, Micheal reacted now, too. No longer interested in the mysteries of the blue bags, his attention flashed off his brother, lifting to his mother for verification.

"Come here, sweetie." She tugged Jamie's hand and included Micheal, opening her arms to bring them both flying across the aisle into her embrace. Settling Micheal on her lap, Jamie at her hip, she looked between them. "Daddy's not dying," she said smoothly and hoped she wasn't lying. "We've talked about this, you remember? He was hurt."

"Bad men hurt him," Micheal said gravely, nodding.

"Yes, bad men hurt him, sweetie, but you know how strong your Da is."

"Aye," Jamie growled, sounding more like his grandfather than ever a child. "Like Thor, our Da. I think he put those bad men under."

Oh, lord. Under? This was not a concept an eight-year-old should understand.

"Grandad said our Da probably brained 'em simple," Micheal added.

Megan drew a short breath, and Natalie caught the bemused flicker in the soft hazel eyes. "Yes," Natalie said, trying to remain sober. "I think he might have."

"But now he's going under," Jamie said and gripped her hand more fiercely.

"Baby, it just takes time," Natalie said gently while squeezing his tense fingers. "Your da just needs time to heal. He'll be bouncing you on his broad shoulders in no time."

That they might be calming was a blessing; then Micheal asked, "Are you gonna divorce him, Mummy?"

Good God! "Baby, where did you hear such a thing?" Natalie asked and noted Megan was just as thunder-struck and alarmed by those words.

"Was a lady on TV said how could be you're gonna divorce daddy," he said grimly.

Jamie growled, "Told you that's nawt true, Micheal."

"Honey, when was this?" Natalie asked, reading the anger etched on her oldest son's young face, the gloom on the younger as he looked up at her, searching. "When, baby? When did you see this?"

Jamie growled. "Was last week, Mum. One a them dang shows Nan Irma likes to watch when she's rocking Arabella. Told him it was just baloney."

"But it showed da with another lady under his arm, and it said how there was 'trouble in paradise' for the MacDades . . . And now da's going to heaven." And the tears swamped his big blue eyes as his lips quivered.

"Oh, Lord," Megan uttered.

"Your da's not going to heaven—"

As if someone punched him in the stomach, Micheal swallowed a sound, and his swimming eyes grew even larger. "He's going to hellll, Mummy?"

"Lord a'mighty," Natalie huffed and realized Jamie was now holding onto his bravery by a thread. "Your father's not going to hell—or to heaven—or limbo. Your father's going to be fine." Unless she clouted him for putting her children through this horror!

"Are you gonna divorce him, Mum?" Jamie asked with careful rein.

Well, and how to handle that when the future remained so blasted uncertain? She'd never lied to her children, never would, but they were waiting, and she held no ready answer. "Your father's not going anywhere, baby," she said again, not lying. If divorce lay on the horizon, she and her children might move nearer to her parents. She would never take them from him, however, unless . . . ?

No, he was a rake and a rogue, among other things, but he would never deny his children or turn his back on them. He may not love her how a man should love a woman, but he loved their little creations incontestably.

"Nothing to fear, my loves," she said and hugged them a little tighter.

"Did you get us popsicles, Mum?" Micheal asked softly, sheepishly, looking up from beneath a lock of auburn hair that rested rakishly over his brow.

He looked so much like Gregor, Natalie couldn't help but smile.

"Dummy," Jamie growled. "Cannae have any popsicles. They'd be melting already"

"But I like popsicles," Micheal groused.

"Then we have to get them at the hospital, huh, Mum?" Jamie said smoothly, and it occurred to Natalie—her oldest never stayed irritated with his younger brother for long, not unlike Liam and Gregor. These two were close and thick as thieves.

Popsicles.

"I think we can probably find one or two," she decided.

"Whachu think, Grammy?" Jamie asked. "Think we could find some there?"

Hedging his bet, Natalie knew and shared Meg's amusement. Without a doubt, Grammy MacDade would move heaven and hell to find her grandsons a popsicle at that hospital, and the little imps knew it.

Reality intruded then, with the wide staircase to the hospital entrance coming into view outside the glass. Far more aware than at any time prior, Natalie noticed what she'd neglected to acknowledge over the past few days. An action news van parked at the curb just past the covered ramp entrance, and before the limo stopped, a woman stepped from the glass doors—apparently anticipating and merely awaiting the MacDades' arrival.

How did this work? Was there a surveillance team at the hotel, one paid to call this news team when the limo pulled from the underground garage? Did something like this, a personal tragedy, truly boost the ratings enough to justify the expense of a news network hiring someone to stalk their targets?

That answer was apparently simple. No other way could this woman time her arrival so accurately and position her cameraman for ultimate exposure.

Watching Artair step from the front seat, Natalie heard the woman directing her associate to "roll," but the door closed on whatever else she said. Rather than come to open her door, the bodyguard strode up the steps, and Natalie appreciated the cameraman backing a pace, two paces, as the tall, capable fellow positioned himself in front of the lens. Unbelievably brave, the perky skinny anchorwoman stood her ground and tried to lift her microphone, but Artair simply covered the mouthpiece with a single hand

and held it still. Barely two seconds passed before two other men stepped from the glass doors, and the limo driver cleared the top step.

"Goodness," Megan idled. "What do you suppose that's about?"

"Were I to guess, I believe we'll avoid becoming fodder for the evening broadcast," Natalie said lightly, watching as another pair of gentlemen, wearing leisure suits, stepped from the opening. The broader fellow reached reflexively and halted an elderly woman from tripping and falling down the steps when she recognized the news crew.

"Blast," Natalie hissed. *This could get ugly.* But with the cameraman blocked and the anchorwoman still attempting to dislodge her microphone, Natalie decided it was a good time to ascend those steps. Looking at Megan, she mused, "Ready for a mad dash to those doors, Mum?"

"Aye," she idled with understanding looming in her livid eyes. "What say, m' boys? Ready for a little jaunt?"

"Aye!" they spoke in unison.

"Jamie, grab that bag," Natalie directed and scooted Micheal to his feet before she gathered the second bag. Barely, she opened the door when another part of her security detail snagged the door, and she glimpsed the vaguely familiar face as she slid to her feet. As Artair had mentioned, they might not manage to stop every camera from flashing, but they could certainly limit a few, and apparently, Artair had phoned ahead. With dark-suited men to either side, the MacDade women and children were escorted—without a need to run—up the steps, through the glass doors, and directly to the bank of elevators. No, not all could be stopped, not when ordinary citizens carried phones with cameras in their pockets. One of two women waiting at the elevator doors attempted discretion while snapping a photo of Natalie holding Micheal on her hip and another of Jamie holding his grandmother's hand. Feeling as if she were standing naked, Natalie glimpsed several other people stopped now, watching them. The instant the doors opened, she ducked inside, and it was too late when she registered the sight of streaming blond hair.

Surely, that woman wouldn't dare show her face here! Surely a mistake. Just another woman with long blond hair like a million others.

Still, Natalie couldn't shake the feeling of familiarity, although she'd only seen the woman in smoky shadowed light. Cursing her foolishness, she realized she wouldn't recognize the blasted woman if they stood nose to nose. She knew her name. Alecia Helms. And she knew the woman had gone missing. Was it so much the blond hair? Or the way the slight, busty woman had spun away in a near graceful arc before Natalie could gain a clear glimpse. Was there an instant of intimate recognition, as if that woman might believe they shared the equal right to be present here?

"Mummy?" Micheal interrupted and appeared worried as he looked at her at close range.

Well, and she'd never been good at hiding her emotions. Undoubtedly, that flair of Scottish temper had alarmed him. Hugging him to her hip, she forced herself calm and in a fleeting instant, realized how much he'd grown. Too much for her to hold him much longer. Perhaps, he had reached the same conclusion; he made a move to slide aground, and she let him down, settling for his hand in hers before the doors slid open.

The hallway was empty except for the two sentries posted five doors away, and the rumor that Lucius MacDade had paid to keep those doors closed and rooms unoccupied was probably one of the few facts to leak from the hospital.

On route to the only occupied room, Natalie recognized an odd sense of her sons dragging their feet, but another thought struck just as swiftly to hasten her stride.

Liam was awake.

12

Not thrilled to be sitting, rather than lying, Liam heard the elevator doors opening down the hall, but he was far more intrigued by his father and brother's snoring. If anyone should be sleeping, it should be him, but the louts rested, one in either reclining chair, sprawled as though they hadn't a care in the bloody world. In perfect harmony, one breathed in, one breathed out, sounding like God-blessed bullhorns in either mode. Sitting up should be a feat worthy of their blasted interest as they were the ones to suggest it.

Perhaps, he wasn't exactly sitting up. Or being fair. But Liam was in no mood to be gracious when he lay against a lifted mattress that felt more like a gangplank. And the tiny woman standing alongside the bed, holding another blasted cup of red gelatin, dared to fluff the stone-stuffed pillows and suggest, "Comfortable?"

"Woman, I couldnae be less goddamn comfortable if I were sitting on a goddamn bed of thorns."

Her little round face paled, her lips parted—

And Natalie glided through the door, her livid hazel eyes glittering near amber in the bright morning light. A smile slipped upon her glossy pink lips, and she spared a pitiful glance to the startled nurse.

Before Natalie could utter a sound to chasten his temper, his attention divided to watch his sons freezing no more than two steps inside the room. One held his mother's hand, the other his grandmother's hand, halting both women effectively. In a stopped instant, Liam glanced between them, suddenly fearing that something wicked had happened to them. *They were daft!*

"La-ads?" he uttered, fearing that a loud word might strike them dumb.

"Da!" Jamie cried.

Liam jolted with enough force to send spikes of fire from his waist, but this once, he refrained from buckling, far more concerned with his son's mental state. The lad freed his grandmother and shot forward.

On Jamie's heels, Micheal cried, "Papa!"

All things at once, in fairy-dust time. Liam recoiled against the lifted mattress, taking in the sights in freeze-frame. Two odd little creatures flying toward him; panic lighting on both women's faces as they lurched to clasp the snazzy blue jackets; a startled growl from a recliner; Gregor launching afoot, growling and cursing, staggering to collect balance as the bottom of the recliner slammed his calves. And the little pixie nurse twirled like a top, maybe to escape the miniature tornadoes flying at her.

Oh, hell, this was going to hurt.

Barely, Liam ventured the thought when the soles of tiny tennis shoes squealed rubber on the tile floor, four tiny hands clasped the silver rail as if a prelude to vaulting, and both handsome faces stopped. Not certain what befuddled him more, their cessation or the tears in their eyes, the smiles on their faces . . . Liam released his held breath, and a smile quivered on his lips. "There 're my lads," he managed and reached a hand, catching one of either small hand under his single palm.

Natalie had held her breath too, Liam noted and heard her release as she hurried the last step and clasped a small shoulder in either hand. Her eyes lighted with as much amusement as worry, barely containing her laugh, commenting, "I was truly feart they wouldn't get stopped."

"Aye, was either under or over they were headed," Liam managed and enjoyed the surprise rising in her eyes.

"Da! You're awlright, now!" Jamie said in a more tempered, collected tone, though he huffed just a little as he fisted the tears from his eyes. "Aye! And that's a fine thing. Just look at you, then!"

"Mummy said you were nae going under," Micheal said gravely. With his bright, damp eyes peering over the rail, he appeared to take Liam's measure from head to heel. Locking on Liam's hand, his focus froze, regarding the IV port with an adultlike intensity.

Too late to retract that hand, no matter how that bulge of gauze, tape, and clear tubes might look to a five-year-old. "Uhhh . . . Micheal?" *What had he said . . . ? Going under?* "Your . . . mum was right, m'lad. I'm not going under.

Not any time soon." But lord almighty, he was getting weary again. Would this bloody roller coaster never cease?

"Mum brought us crackers and the like, Da," Jamie said lightly. "Would you like some?"

"Thank you . . . but not right now," he managed.

"We're getting popsicles, too," Micheal said while drawing his gaze from the gauze. "That would maybe help you feel better, Da. Do you want us to find you some, too?"

Lord, but he loved these little devils. Smiling slightly, Liam shook his head. "Maybe later, Micheal, but thank you."

"Mummy needs to kiss you now, Da," Micheal said bluntly, his glistening eyes oddly desperate as he added. "You're not getting a divorce."

Softly, Natalie drew breath. The only sound to follow that announcement. Liam lifted his focus, as stunned as he was stricken with a sudden pain. Had she told them she was thinking about it—

"Damned television," Natalie uttered, and lifted her gaze from Micheal to Liam with a genuinely heated shine in her eyes.

She was angry . . . and he was at a loss. Even in his lucid moments, no one had mentioned the details surrounding this ordeal, and he suffered only impressions of trying not to dwell too long or hard on the facts. Television. Not in some time had he heard a news broadcast. Reruns of old sitcoms, game shows . . . Hell, even a soap opera if he recalled even half moments clearly. Not a single news broadcast in any of his waking moments, not since some odd overheard conversation with his father's voice . . .

But he was thinking of the possible details now, and not happy with his thoughts.

Too clearly, he remembered leaving the Fairlane, leaving a blasted mistress asleep in that hotel . . . and his tentative separation hadn't become public knowledge. Even that blasted tabloid picture months ago, hadn't made a major splash in any worthy society page. It was certainly not the first time Liam MacDade had been photographed with another woman under his arm. Cicely . . . Amherst, he remembered. Just one of many, and even less newsworthy than some. It was not as if he jumped into bed with every woman he met. Cicely had been a stewardess, and he'd shared dinner and a hotel room with her, perhaps only once. He certainly attempted to be discreet, except that he'd been so blasted tired after that transatlantic flight . . .

The motion at his side drew him from his listing thoughts, and the fairy dust was at it again—the boys had moved—Natalie dipped, and her lips brushed his before he caught up to the action. Only more confusion lighted in his mind. Was that kiss for the boys' benefit? To confirm their belief that a divorce wasn't hovering on the horizon? He could understand that. The need to maintain appearances. Natalie Callahan-Mac-Dade had far too much class to suffer a divorce. She could hate him, and probably did, long before now, but there would be no divorce. By mutual consent, they'd entered this union, knowing damn full well it was little more than a farce created to merge two powerful clans.

Eldest son to eldest daughter . . . and too clearly, Liam recalled the day his father had taken him aside and suggested it. Fresh out of college, a master's degree in business tucked in his portfolio two years early . . . and his father—and her father—decided their blood should mix.

'You've known the girl since she was a wee bairn. It's not like yer blasted strangers."

'Marriage, Da? Have you lost your bloody mind? This isn't the flippin' Middle Ages! Hell, not the bloody Dark Ages. You cannae truly expect me to enter an *arranged* marriage.'

'You could do worse,' his father had said in quiet rhythm. 'Having seen this bonnie lass, m' lad, you could do a helluva lot worse . . . She'll give you fine handsome bairn to carry on the lines . . .'

'Jesus H Christ, you're serious,' he'd realized, stricken nearly dumb and numb.

'I dinnae see why yer fretting so,' Lucius had idled. 'I'm not saying you need spend yer every waking hour with yer wife. Say long as yer discreet, no reason you cannae continue what yer doing . . .'

'And you believe this young woman will go for this?'

'Her da's having a chat with her.'

'You're both mad as hatters! If you think any young woman in this modern age is going to enter a loveless marriage to produce heirs to a fucking dynasty—'

'Mind, son,' Lucius had said in dark, concise English. 'Rail as you will, but be it fact, the MacDade lines have run true for five centuries, and modern times willnae change that fact.'

'How the bloody hell did you get Kirk Callahan to even consider this?'

'There's not a clansman alive who widnae like to align himself with a MacDade.'

'My God, you're really not kidding.'

'Liam, nach eil a laughing matter, here.'

'Tell you what, Father, if she agrees to this arrangement, I'll do my part ...' And not for a moment, had Liam believed that Kirk Callahan would convince his oldest daughter to enter this arrangement. Only vaguely, he recalled seeing her a time or two, and a looker, he could attest.

Four months later, they'd stood at the altar, Liam remembered.

His gaze listed to watch his sons sitting on the couch across the room. Like mirror images, the two little gentlemen sat quietly, sharing a pack of crackers while watching cartoons turned at a low volume. The raucous had passed. His father, mother, and brother had stepped from the room. From the hall, their quiet voices echoed, but he couldn't make out their words. Waking to his wife leaning at the bedrail watching him, Liam sought some understanding. He'd never discovered how her father had convinced her to merge their families, had perhaps, always feared to learn of some barbaric method for which he'd need to murder his father-in-law. A matter of principle, that. If Liam ever discovered that Kirk Callahan had physically tortured this lovely woman into this arrangement, he truly would need to slay the devil ... And just that thought had held Liam at arm's length from his father-in-law. That Callahan seemed to fear him and kept his distance in most instances was probably a good thing.

Now here they were. Eight years later. She'd given him two handsome, unbelievably intelligent sons, and topped that off with an absolutely-stunning daughter—who had already started Liam thinking of how he might dispose of her suitors in a few years. . . And he'd done the unthinkable.

He'd brought disgrace to their doorstep. That neither his father nor brother had clobbered him was probably only a testament to how close he'd stood to the fey.

Barely above a whisper, his senses swaying badly, he uttered, "How do I make this right?"

In an equally quiet tone, she commented, "Had a thought we were going there."

In those few words and the concentration in her gaze, she confirmed her knowledge of where he'd been, what he'd been about when this disaster struck. She probably knew more than him now, which didn't bode well in his mind. But if the television had already begun mentioning a divorce on the horizon, then he truly had wrought ruin on the clan . . . Therein, his thoughts muddled. His father . . . Mason . . . neither would have allowed those facts to become known . . . and what about that damn black dress that stirred and fired his blood in odd conflict? She'd been dressed for an evening on the town . . . and abruptly, illumination.

He shook his head absently, holding her pensive gaze, denying what his mind perceived. Surely not . . . surely not even Lucius MacDade would concoct such a wicked scheme. Mason, though, like a dozen or more other MacDades, Mason was of a mindset to do whatever needed doing to preserve the family name. But how the bloody hell had they gained her . . . for the same reason. To save face. To keep up appearances and spare their children disgrace. In wicked turmoil, his thoughts spun on a slow tide, and her head canted with her curiosity as her brow furrowed. And oh, how those hazel eyes turned to amber as she scried him, the same shade to flame when she rose to the peaks of passion.

If she hadn't hated him before this moment, she surely should now.

"Liam," she intruded gently and touched her palm to his head.

"Don't, lass," he uttered, knowing he was neither worthy nor deserving of her calming touch.

"I feel your ache, darling," she said softly, studying him as she lifted her palm. "I'm not following . . . What are you thinking to be so distraught?"

"That black dress . . . was for me," he said softly and read the truth in her eyes, the distress not well hidden. Either Mason Eldridge or Lucius MacDade had dragged her into this scheme . . . dressed her to the nines . . . delivered her into this madness . . . and he knew why she'd oblige. To save face. To keep both clans from suffering a disgrace. To keep their sons from suffering any wicked truths . . . And still, at least one broadcast had put the facts in order if the word 'divorce' was being bandied about. For the boys' sake, she would perpetuate the lie, and renounce any rumors of divorce. They'd both come into this arrangement with eyes wide open, no illusions, and she'd determined to do her part.

How had they brought her so quickly . . . and that was the least of it, he knew on the instant. Perhaps in one of his lucid moments, he'd heard tell of the MacDade jet . . . but he needn't hear a thing to know that jet would have sailed the skies within an hour of a distress call. His father loved that blasted chariot. To spare his family name, he would sail the high seas, fueling the jet and setting a flight plan would have been child's play. In record time, they could have whisked her to the airport, brought her to this blasted hospital . . . and what of that other image?

A warrioress come to his rescue . . . and bloody fool that he was, he `1kjmwas probably already suffering the effects of blood loss, to start his mind twisting those details. Perhaps another man had come to his aid as he had believed in those first foggy memories. Even now, he recalled a hazy image of a body spinning, kicking, tossing other bodies about willy-nilly. And he'd believed his savior a woman. A woman, he confirmed, recalling a whisper at his ear, a gentle voice . . .

But, no. That voice, he had recognized and realized, he'd twisted those moments in his foggy mind. His wife had been here in this hospital when he'd come from surgery. His wife, his father, his mother, and brothers . . . brothers? Lucas had been here . . . but perhaps that was just another twisted memory from too many drugs. Only in those first memories had he believed he'd seen Lucas in the background . . . Aye, and probably more like an ill-omen to imagine his youngest brother hovering like the angel of death in the background when he'd been knocking at heaven's gate. Or wishful thinking.

"Liam," Natalie stated and again landed her palm to cover his forehead, brushing his hair off his brow before he could protest. "Stop," she said more quietly, flashing a glance toward their boys to be certain she hadn't alarmed them. "Just stop, now," she nearly whispered, the worry quick in her gaze. "You're tired. That I'm seeing far too clearly, and wherever those thoughts are taking you, it's not a good place to be."

"Talk," he said, remembering. "You said we need to talk." And he, too, shifted his gaze to be sure his sons were occupied. "We—"

She shook her head, favoring him with a gentle smile. "Not yet."

Things needed said. He would need to speak to the police eventually, unless . . . ? "Did uhm . . . did I speak with the police?"

"Darling, your father wouldn't have let you speak to the Pope in the state you've been."

A wan smile flickered on his lips as he considered that fact. "Aye, dinnae suppose he would."

"Liam," she said gently. "Rest. There's not for you to fret over."

Because she'd rallied to his aid, he understood and nodded, feeling some-how worse the lout for that single detail. How she could stand to look at him was a mystery. It was one thing for her to know he was unfaithful, but to have it crammed down her throat and drag her into the deception. "Bloody hell," he uttered as the weariness dragged at him. "Just uhm . . ." Again, he shifted to find his sons still across the room before looking into her lovely eyes. "Just tell me this," he near to whispered, half afraid to continue. Certain he must. "Do you want . . . a divorce?"

Her attention riveted. She studied him, her hand stilled on his forehead as he felt himself suspended under her touch. "Do you?"

That wasn't even an option in his mind—not in his regard. Never had a MacDade shirked his duties and divorced. One or two, male and female alike through the ages, had slain their partner if the tales held merit. But divorce had never become an option. If she wanted it, no matter the cost he would oblige her, and to hell with the repercussions. But he shook his head beneath her touch, admitting, "It would never be my choice."

"Nor mine," she said quietly. "Now, and you need rest, husband."

Not in the cards, he realized in the next moment as the pixie nurse-[] apparently escaped the clutches of the family outside the door. She scurried alongside the bed, lifting the torturous plastic contraption.

Flashing a winsome glance toward Natalie and favoring Liam with a bright smile, she announced, "Time for your breathing treatment, hon."

"If I were a—Hun—you would be dead, lass."

"Liam!" Natalie admonished.

"He rrreally doesn't like these breathing treatments," the woman mused, perfectly content being threatened.

"I breathe just fine—before you bring that wicked device."

"And it's this handy little thing to keep you breathing well, hon," she said.

"There should be laws against—perky women—and torturing sick men," he growled, and both blasted women stifled laughs.

"Quit being such a baby, Liam," Natalie said with a vibration still in her voice and her eyes flashing mirth—only until she realized their sons had reached the end of the bed, both drawn by either their curiosity or—

"I willnae be pleased if you hurt my Da, miss," Jamie said candidly. Recognizing the arrogance in the pose, the cant of the curly head, and the determination in the blue eyes, Liam lost his sobriety and started a laugh.

Hell's fire ignited in his side. He swallowed the pain with an iron will, refusing to buckle in front of his sons, but God be merciful, he couldn't halt the flash of tears over his eyes. In a split second, Natalie grasped his distress and sidled around the bed, clasping shoulders, and turning the boys. "Why don't we go find those popsicles, loves? Your daddy needs his medicine."

"But, Mum," Jamie said as he tried looking over his shoulder, clearly prepared to rally to his father's defense. "Was a mention of torture—"

"Your da was teasing, sweetie," she assured and kept them moving toward the door, though she flashed a worried glance over her shoulder, mouthing some silent words.

The words were lost with the blur over his eyes, and he released his breath with a grunt as he tried folding against the pain. The pixie nurse became an Amazon woman as she clasped his shoulder and arm, halting his collapse.

"Don't, hon. Don't try folding. Just take a deep breath. Try to relax . . ."

A breathing treatment without the apparatus; if not for the fire still flashing in his center, he might almost be amused by her coaching. Not amused, he lay heaving short breaths, and the only consolation was the lifted gangplank to lend him a partial ability to fold without fully caving in on himself.

"I think you're about due for your pain meds, hon . . ."

That he might truly need whatever this little Nurse Penny continuously pumped into his system via the tube at his hand had occurred to him more than a time or two. By the time the fires doused under the wave of whatever flowed through the tube, Natalie had returned, and it was her hand brushing a cool cloth over his sweated forehead, her eyes studying him through a film of tears glistening over her eyes. "Hi."

Her smile ignited, enhanced by the shine in her lovely amber eyes. "Uh-huh," she uttered. "Now, I know what that 'high' means," she mused. "And I need to admit, that pleases me, mine own. You're still in so blasted much pain."

"Get-ting better."

"Which also pleases me, darling."

"Your—own," he managed and belatedly considered his words, realizing, "I like being—your own."

She studied him closely, intently, despite the smile lingering on her lips. "I like calling you, my own. Aye," she said as if miming the brogue. "Mine own Highlander."

"Aye . . . and a baby, eh?"

"Figures you'd remember that," she mused.

"We—are, yer knowing."

"Are what, darling?"

"High-landers," he managed.

"I am knowing, m' love. Well I recall our visit to the auld country, and you showing me where the MacDade castle once stood. Do you remember that trip, love?"

He did now . . . tasting the cooled air of the lochs, feeling the whisper of wind fill his lungs. As if he stood on the Devil's staircase, he breathed in the scents of his motherland . . . And his wife was there, taking in the view with him, watching the mist filling between the mountains and slithering over the lochs . . .

She took him there, now, as he had taken her there, then . . . And in a cottage on the Highlands, they'd conceived their second son . . .

"That's it, my love . . . Just rest now and taste the mountains. Tis the high country. . ."

"Natalie, lass, can I have a ward with you?"

When Lucius MacDade wanted a word, the only question remained—how soon? Making certain Liam was still asleep and her sons remained occupied besting their grandmother at a game of Go Fish, Natalie accepted Lucius' escort from the room. Again, they made their way to the private waiting room. Shutting the door behind him, Lucius motioned to the table where they'd sat three days prior, and they settled into the chairs in front of the window. Unlike then, Natalie experienced an almost overwhelming desire to twist the blinds closed. She could imagine those telephoto lenses zooming in and enlisting a lip reader to record the conversation.

"I heard some of what ye endured on the trip o'er here this morn," he began quietly, eyeing her more intently, judging her level of distress. "Artie mentioned a mishap at that li'l store—then another blasted photographer."

"I don't suppose there's too much we can do about them," she sighed. "I just wasn't well prepared for any of it."

"Aye, and that tabloid didnae help."

She'd read the article, and even in hindsight, it irritated her to recall the words and the multitude of pictures within that rag. Her, her sons, the elder MacDades, Gregor . . . And the earlier photos of Liam, with his arm around the shoulders of an actress, alleging a sordid affair. Even a blasted picture of the vigil outside the hospital had been displayed, front and center. The article failed to remind the public that the actress was his cousin, and their encounter was purely innocent and completely aboveboard. Carmin McCullum had probably loved reading that tidbit of journalism . . . and might have called to share the laugh if not for a sense of waiting throughout the clan. When Liam was moved from the critical list to guarded condition, the entire clan would likely draw a collective breath and change the air currents on two continents.

"What uhm . . . are ye thinking?"

"Nothing of import, Da. Just thinking how our fair Carmin will find that tabloid amusing. If uhm . . . If not for Liam's condition and the blasted truth in that single detail, I might be a little amused again, as well."

"About that," Lucius said carefully. "Was just a bit ago, I spoke to Dr. Emmerson, and he's finally decided, our lad's stepping closer to the clearing. Not out'a the woods yet, mind, but close enough that our good doctor wants to make an announcement in time for the evening news, and our Dr. Cavenaugh finally agrees."

Relief poured over her mind with that simple proclamation, but she realized suddenly, "Oh, hell, another news conference. That's what we're discussing here, again?"

"Aye, but not one I'll ask yourself to attend. Mind, you have a presence those cameras love, but I'd not ask you to go through that again. Bad enough, we're barely staying a step ahead of those blasted cameras."

In that one statement, Natalie understood the evasive tactics that Lucius had implemented from the start. He'd tried protecting them, insisting that Natalie and the boys, Megan, arrive and depart from the hospital at odd times, never following the same routine, sometimes with him and Gregor, sometimes with one or the other. At every moment, security guards remained posted at the hotel, in the lobby, in the hospital. Meals were delivered, necessities delivered, phone calls screened, hotel staff threatened or tipped heavily to forget room numbers. Even taking the boys to the swimming pool the evening past had become an event with the hotel management posting signs that the pool was temporarily closed for repairs and 'Sorry for the inconvenience,' with vouchers provided for other guests to visit a pool at a sister hotel two blocks away.

"We truly can't stop them all," Natalie said with a quiet smile, appreciation in her gaze. "If you're serious though, and Liam's truly being moved to guarded condition . . .?"

Lucius nodded with a smirk to suggest that he'd known his son would survive, but Natalie had seen enough of his fear not to be fooled. They both knew just how close Liam had come.

"Then maybe they'll leave us alone soon, do you think?"

"We can hope, and therein my thoughts," he said lightly. "As much as I know ye have a lovely home, and it's reasonably safe and secure, I wonder if I might suggest the lot of you move into the big house with Meg and me. Not much has changed since the other eve, and I need to be certain you're all safe."

For a moment, she studied his unreadable eyes, and something of the gravity shined through. "Sir, what are you not telling me?"

"I did mention wanting to bring him home, and that stands. He'll need medical attention for some time."

Reasonable, that suggestion and offer, but there was something out of kilter. "Da . . . if it didn't concern me, I wouldn't be asking. But uh. . . what do you know about this attack that you're not telling me? Is it . . . it was an ambush, then."

"Blast ye women with yer damnable ken," he said in mild, genuine irritation. "Aye, lass, was an ambush, but more than that . . .? I cannae say, as I dinnae know. There are indications that more than a dozen men were waiting for him, and there was a blasted gun involved, as you well know. The police found the bullet just last evening. They're running it through their data banks, but nothing thus far."

"I uhm . . . I wondered the other day, but I didn't think to ask . . . Why is the FBI involved in this?"

"Natalie, yer too bloomin' smart for yer own good," he said with a hint of pride beneath his irritation. "Fact, I called in a favor and insisted on their presence, and greater fact, I want that woman found."

"Then you think as I do, she must have been involved, else how would anyone know where to find him. It's not as if his schedule's an open book. He generally tries to be discreet."

Lucius studied her with a far more brooding expression to lower his brow. "Daughter, tell me true. Do ye ever regret standing on that altar with him?"

Without hesitation, she answered, "No, sir." How could she? She had three beautiful children, and when he chose to be her husband, he was incredible. Financially, she would never want for a thing, not for herself or her children. Few women could say the same, and she was no fool in that regard. "I didn't bring up that divorce business," she said, assuming that had prompted the question.

"Aye, so my Meg mentioned," he said offhandedly. "I'm having that business investigated. If I understood, was something about a talk show or the like. About the time of our li'l Arabella's naptime. Ten or two, I'm thinking."

The leader of a dynasty that could probably make or break a small country, and the fellow knew the times of his granddaughter's naps? Natalie shook her head slightly with a bewildered smile. "Give or take a half hour, and I'd probably guess it was a morning program. I generally give Irma the afternoon off."

"That blasted husband of yers could afford to hire a second nanny."

"So, and he's offered more than once," she admitted with a fleeting memory of him nearly insisting on such an enterprise only a few short months past. For a time, he'd even conducted most of his business affairs from his home office, which had baffled and bewildered her for a time. She was well enough past that wicked bout of postpartum depression, now, to appreciate that detail. "But I rather enjoy spending the afternoons with her."

"Aye," he sighed. "And I'm not surprised. Mine Meg was the same way with all three of our bairn. Said she loved the smell of them, and I can't for the life of me figure that out. Was most often the smell of . . ." He rumbled a chuckle. "Well, and you ken."

"Do indeed," she mused, enjoying her father-in-law's sheepish expression, but a sudden thought intruded. Momentarily, she considered whether to mention it. With the nature of the conversation, she decided, "There's uhm . . ."

Lucius sobered as well, reacting to her sobriety. "Aye?"

"I wasn't sure I should even mention this, Da, because I truly can't be certain, but I thought I saw that woman. Alecia Helms."

His attention riveted. "Go on then."

"Was downstairs when we were getting on the elevator to come up, and I truly can't be certain. I never got a good look at her—I mean when I was uhm . . . following him. But this morning . . . It was the way she moved—or turned—and the hair seemed the same. It was more just an impression, which is why I didn't think to mention it sooner." She shrugged. "I could be mistaken. I rather doubted she'd be foolish enough to come here, I mean—under any circumstances, what with all the publicity. And now—if you believe her an accomplice, I can't imagine her showing up here. So, it probably wasn't her."

"Daughter, yer expending an awful lot of air to dispute a thing that I'm fairly certain, you know," Lucius said grimly. "I'd wager yer impressions of things to be spot on o'er an entire battalion of investigators. If you saw her, even a glance of her on yer clandestine mission, I'd further wager, you recognized her this morning. And it's blasted irritating that she waltzed in here with half the city's law officials searching for her."

"Uhm. It uhm . . . well. I wonder if that cameraman for that Live-Action news station might have caught her on tape. Seems to me he was still rolling footage—maybe mostly of Artair's chest—but he might have caught her on film. She was turning for the entrance when I saw her"

"Keep this up, I'm liable to hire you for mine blasted security firm," Lucius idled. "Seems yer make more progress than Gillis by coincidence than he is on purpose."

Natalie smiled slightly. "I don't think I'm cut out for that kind of work. I bungled my first attempt at investigations horribly. Mr. Eldridge caught me in the first ten minutes."

For a moment, he appeared surprised, then let loose a laugh. "Considering the circumstances, I'm extremely grateful you gave it a second go."

"Speaking of," she sobered, wondering. "How much has Liam been told of that circumstance?"

Likewise sober, he admitted, "Not much. As yer knowing, he's not been staying awake long enough to grasp much of a thing."

"We may need to change that soon, Da. There's too much confusion in . . . in his eyes. I don't think he's fitting the pieces together very well."

"Aye, mine fear as well, mo nighean, but I'm not sure how much he'll grasp if we do tell him. Seems to be fading in and out, and more out than in."

"He asked me if I wanted a divorce," she admitted, with the ache still heavy on her heart.

"Aye, and what did you tell him, if ye dinnae mind me asking?"

"No," she likewise admitted, but irritation niggled at her mind as she met Lucius's pensive gaze. "Five months ago, I received a phone call from a woman claiming that mine husband was having an affair and I should just give him a blasted divorce and step aside."

Lucius appeared surprised for the first time. "That's what uhm . . . why ye sent him to a nether room?"

"Yes," she said honestly. "I think I told him something to the effect that if he wanted another woman, he should have at her . . . but, well . . . he seemed truly bewildered. At the time, I was too blasted angry to consider that. The woman called on our private line, and it was about the same time that he began making these frequent trips to Jersey."

"Aye, he entered the negotiations with Pendleton about that time. A legitimate deal, mind. If he acquires the land in question, he'll make another fortune twice over just on the lumber alone, and there are development opportunities as well."

"I've heard him talk about it often enough to know that much to be true. It's just . . . a sense of something wrong," she huffed, close to admitting what he seemed already to know. "It's why I followed him," she said worriedly. "And I can't explain any more than that. Just a sense of something as if . . . as if we're being followed by something . . . evil," she admitted and cleared her focus enough to see Lucius MacDade far more attentive, and possibly alarmed, than ever in the past. "I'm sorry."

"Dinnae apologize for this. I'm thinking ye saved mine son's life with that bit of scrying . . . and my question now, was present tense you spoke just now. *Are*—not *were*—I heard clearly. So, and the trouble yer thinking is still following you?"

"Ahh, yes. I believe it is, but again, I can't be certain. Not when I know how wickedly close Liam's come to passing."

"You didn't know if he would live," he said as a matter of fact.

"I wasn't certain, no. And fearing the worst could be enhancing my . . . paranoia. All these blasted reporters and the like aren't helping either. We are being followed," she huffed in irritation. "And I just can't sort through it all."

"Aye, and therein lies the decision," Lucius decided. "After this announcement, we'll implement our plans to take our Liam home. And in the meantime, we'll make use of these empty rooms. When this is said and done, we'll probably have our name on one of these wings, but I dinnae think I want you, Meg, or the boys traveling beyond these walls til we leave for the airport."

"Our luggage—" A foolish concern, and the twinkle in the dark blue eyes confirmed her thought. The last time she'd mentioned the need for a few sundry items, she'd become the benefactor of an entirely new wardrobe. That arsenal of clothes and whatnots, along with her sons and their grandmother's luggage, would find its way to the hospital. "Doubt mine little ones will mind one bit. It's like pulling teeth to get them to leave Liam's room."

"Wee bairns see more than we want them to," Lucius idled,3 and there was something in his eyes to make Natalie think of Lucas. This was not the time to ask if ever a time would come. Whatever the falling out between father and youngest son, it had happened a long time in the past, and it seemed a wound that wouldn't heal.

Natalie barely thought to agree when her head cocked and her gaze tipped toward the door, alarmed.

"Lass?"

It wasn't a shout she'd heard, but it might well have been. Her senses were truly enhancing in her wily husband's regard. He wasn't awake . . . but something . . .? Rising off the chair, she only vaguely realized Lucius following as she strode from the room. Something was wrong . . . an impending sense of that second shoe about to drop reached her before she ever reached the room. On the surface, everything appeared fine. Micheal had fallen asleep on one of the couches, and perhaps, Nurse Penny had draped a blanket over him. The little woman doted over the boys like a mother hen, and Natalie had seen her in the hallway a short time ago. Jamie rested in a recliner with a comic book, compliments of his Uncle Gregor, open on his lap. Sensible, that little fellow, he'd chosen the chair most lighted near the window and closest to his father, by no surprise.

Nurse Linnie S. rested in the chair at the bedside, reading a novel under a strip of light from the opposing window. She offered a pleasant smile and glanced at the bed where Liam slept. Like the other two private nurses who'd been rotating shifts to care for Liam, Linnie S. was pleasant-natured, unobtrusive, and efficient. Barely above a whisper, undoubtedly fearing to disturb him, she offered, "Resting comfortably."

Resting . . . but comfortably remained to be determined. Natalie nodded distractedly and reached the side of the bed, searching his face. The top third of the bed had remained elevated slightly. He seemed to rest easier with that slight lift, and he rested in an almost natural pose, one knee lifted slightly beneath the blanket, resting against the iron rail. His hands in repose, one lying at his side atop the blanket; the other recognizable beneath the blanket, rested over his abdomen, lost somewhere between the mounded gauze and his nether regions. On that hand, Natalie focused even as her hand landed on his forehead. In an instant, she knew.

"Natalie, lass, what is it?" Lucius asked in a low, quiet volume.

"A fever," she said and pivoted to see Linnie S. setting her book aside.

Flashing another glance to Liam, Linnie S. offered a comforting smile, commenting, "I just took his temp a bit ago."

"I'm sure you did, miss," she said in a tempered voice. "Check it again. Now, if you please," she added curtly and returned her attention to her husband. He was resting, but closer to delirium than natural sleep, and it seemed, even as she watched, his breathing became more labored.

If only to indulge the anxiousness of a worried wife, Linnie S. brought the thermometer from the medical cart close at hand.

"What are you thinking?" Lucius asked as he searched his sleeping son.

"Infection," she said without a clear thought. "I don't know where, but," she looked up at Lucius at an angle. "We need to call Dr. Cavenaugh."

"Ma'am," Linnie said consolingly. "I'm sure he's—" But the thermometer beeped, and she withdrew it from his ear, taking a cursory glance—then riveting. "He is running a little high. Let me just ring Dr. Emerson, and we'll get another blood draw to see what this is about.'

"Yes, let's do," Natalie said, and so began the third wave of a battle Liam MacDade should never have needed to fight.

13

Hiking boots braced against a steady wind, Luke drew in the sights as clear as the mountain air to fill his lungs. In every direction from the edge of the ridge where he stood, the forest spread in an emerald blanket, appearing close enough to reach out and touch the distant peaks in one moment and inconceivably far—as far as the sun and moon—the next. Overhead, the blue sky stood in stark base relief, a cerulean canvas over which the cumulous clouds drifted, changing patterns and shapes before his eyes. *His*. His air. His view. His bedrock and moss. His briars and immense pines to whistle a soft tune with the air whispering through the draping branches.

From the moment he'd stood on this ridge nearly four years earlier, he'd imagined himself owning this view, free to come here whenever he chose to commiserate and commune with nature . . . Free to build his cabin in the woods.

A smile quivered into his bearded lips, his attention drawn to the caw of a hawk. Mesmerized, he watched the immense bird sail above the nearest pines in his view, almost close enough that he could stroke its golden-brown wings. A Redtail hawk . . . but only the beginning of the wildlife he would see if he stood still long enough.

Magnificent. No other word came close to describing this vista. High and low, the emerald hues changed, designating a valley or peak, and some of those peaks were even higher than the top of the mountain—*his* mountain as of 11:15 a.m. Bought and paid for, free and clear, and currently listed in the hands of Sky High Limited, over which he was, had always been, sole proprietor. He'd known, as much as ten years past, he had known that he would create a land-holding company. Toward that goal, he had been saving, investing, buying, and selling, but none of his past vestures had come close to comparing with this sense of accomplishment. Land. His land. Nearly eight hundred acres of pine, oak, cherry, and mahogany trees, and no one could cut a single limb without his permission.

To the distant sound of an ATV, Luke distracted yet again and drew another clear breath of the forest before turning toward the path from which he had arrived. His first genuine visitor to his new home. A wry smile slid into his mustached lips as he navigated through a wall of briars. Eventually, he might clear some of the deadfall and wild growth along the ridge, but he'd already determined where to build his cabin without disrupting the ancient pines. Those pines would provide an ample windbreak against the constant breeze and hopefully cushion his walls from the more wicked winter winds.

As Jim Colbin, the local forestry ranger, had been kind enough to mention, Skyler Peak was prone to blizzards starting as early as October and not letting up until May. 'You'll have about four good months for fun in the sun, providing you bring a windbreaker rather than suntan lotion.'

'If I wanted fun in the sun, I'd buy an island,' Luke had replied candidly.

Ducking beneath a low-hanging branch, Luke spotted the ATV bouncing over a rut of what might be considered a fire trail. As he'd been told, and charted for himself during a few recognizance missions, his mountain boasted a half dozen trails, most of them carved by hunters and hikers who followed deer and bear paths most often. Only one road traversed his mountain, winding upward with several switchbacks to lend an unsuspecting driver pause. That, unfortunately, would need to change, but Luke had already plotted the new course, deciding he'd keep the worst of his lane for his private drive to thwart unwanted visitors.

Reaching his Jeep—a bright red Wrangler that he'd bought an hour earlier in the thriving one car dealership town of Freemont—Luke waited alongside the fender, still smiling when Jim rolled to a stop in front of him.

Colbin killed the engine, returning Luke's smile as he glanced off the Jeep and scanned the sprawling natural clearing. Not quite thirty, the ranger wore the weathered look of a man accustomed to working outdoors. His chiseled jaw was dusted with a brown haze of day stubble; his dark mustache curled over his upper lip. If he let his thick brown hair grow and changed from his crisp uniform to a flannel-pattern shirt and coveralls, he would pass for a moonshiner, and according to him on one of their first encounters, more than a few of those fellows still existed back in 'these he'a hills.'

"You did it, huh?" Colbin asked with a strained-to-appear sober smile. "You bought this rock—lock, stock, and barrel."

"I own all the rights," Luke admitted, musing. "Guess I did."

"Smart, keeping the mineral rights," Colbin said sagely, eyed him a little more critically, and a laugh slid off his mustached lips. "Congratulations, kid. You have yourself a mountain, and it looks like you're pretty damned happy about it."

"I am," he admitted and scanned the clearing with its tall pines, underbrush, and barely passable entrance that disappeared a dozen yards away. He estimated about four hundred feet of open space, most of it sitting on solid rock with the slope rising in a gentle angle toward the deep end—the northern border. The south-facing end descended toward another clearing. A much more accommodating path existed nearly a half mile away. Far enough to offer him privacy on this upper ledge, close enough for easy access by foot, ATV, or snowmobile. He'd already decided not to connect the plateaus by either roads or wide paths. Two separate entities—his cabin and the Lodge. The Skyview Lodge.

"So," Jim interrupted, his smirk lingering. "How soon before you break ground? Providing you're still planning to turn this into a tourist trap?"

Colbin had started this bit of jesting right from the start, and Luke shook his head, not taking the bait. The Skyview Lodge might be found posted in a tourism magazine, but it wasn't a place anyone would find by wandering off an interstate. Exclusive and selective. And not many guests at one time. "I'm meeting with a contractor this afternoon," he admitted, shrugging as he met Jim's gaze. "I'd like to start bringing in equipment as early as next week."

"Not wasting any time, huh?"

"You're the one who said I can expect snow by Halloween," Luke reminded him and shrugged again, scanning the clearing, planning, even as he continued. "I'd like to move in up here by Christmas."

Colbin sobered, "That's pushing it, some. You might not even get the foundation laid before the snow flies."

"Your optimism is noted," Luke commented.

"I'm a realist, LJ," Colbin spoke simply. "This mountain can get pretty hairy in the winter, and I know I'm not telling you anything new. You did your homework. Hell, you probably know more about this damn mountain than I do, but this is rough country. You get stuck in a blasted blizzard, and your power goes down? It could be days before we reach you."

"I'll have a fireplace," Luke commented, somewhat touched by the fellow's genuine concern for his wellbeing. Seemed like a long time since anyone had given a damn about him—other than him. "And a few backup systems," he added and decided not to mention what else he'd discovered about Skyler Peak. If what he suspected was true, he could live off the grid for months without suffering a moment's distress. "I promise, I'll try not to be a nuisance, but uh . . . just in case. Who should I talk to on the town council? And how much will it cost me to be sure the road crews are up and running when I call?"

"Humph," Colbin fleeted a smile. "You're still planning that lodge, then?"

"Not this year, but hopefully, I'll be operational by next Christmas."

"You—my young friend—move far too quickly for someone barely old enough to shave."

"I notice you're not answering," Luke mused. "I'm guessing that means I'll need to grease a few palms to get the permits in order—as well as the road crews."

"Probably not," Colbin idled. "The town council's pretty much on the up and up. You might want to show up at a town meeting and do a meet and greet. And if I know ole Harvey Clemens, the road supervisor, he'll hit you up for a new plow or two if he thinks he can get away with it. Mostly, they'll expect a donation to fund a few projects in town." Colbin managed a wry smile, a musing shine in his brown eyes. "You might get your name on a new library or a playground over at the elementary."

"Well, hell, I can do without the name, but I can probably swing one or the other," Luke decided, already considering the library. "They don't have a library?"

"Oh, lord, what did I just do?" Colbin asked, raising his eyes to the heavens.

"Seriously," Luke said, generally serious. "Everyone should have a library."

"You—my friend—are about to make life very interesting in these parts."

"I'll think on it," he decided while he scanned the clearing, changing gears. "I think I'll put one of those portable sheds over there," he said, indicating a location by the pines on the north wall. "Maybe bring some tools and an ATV up. Don't guess anyone will mess with it, huh?"

"Not likely," Colbin said with a distracted note to draw Luke's gaze to see the sobriety back in the eyes.

"What?"

"I uhm . . . I just wondered how your brother's doing," Jim said grimly. "I just caught part of that newsbreak this afternoon."

Luke had avoided obsessing about the news coming from New Jersey, but the thought was never far from his mind. Five days and his brother remained in ICU or the equivalent of ICU if a private room, life support, private nurses, and a guarded room were considered Intensive Care. The last he'd heard, his family and several relatives were still occupying an entire floor of rooms in a hotel near the hospital. His father hadn't bought it yet, so that was something. They weren't moving in permanently. By now, though, Luke would have thought his brother was ready to be transferred. Every day that event was delayed gave him more cause for concern. Lucius MacDade wasn't the most patient man, and he'd planned on transferring Liam closer to home days ago.

His gaze listing toward the pines, the ridge, Luke wasn't certain how to answer Colbin. Only last evening, he'd responded to Gregor's email and received the latest update. "Guess he's doing as well as can be expected," he decided and found Jim studying him far more intently. "He's still in ICU, but I think they were lowering the meds today."

"I uh . . ." Colbin appeared more uncomfortable than a moment past, and Luke's tension hiked before Jim continued, "You haven't been near a TV or phone, have you?"

"No," he said quietly, his alarm rising as he studied the intent gaze. "Not since this morning." Not since checking out of the hotel in Roanoke and heading for his meeting with the realtors. "What have you heard?"

"There was a newsbreak around noon." Jim started, then seemed to realize he'd better continue quickly. "Apparently, they were about to downgrade his condition from critical to guarded, but he took a turn for the worse. An infection is what they said."

Introverting the words, studying Colbin, anticipating a jest, Luke shook his head and cast his gaze toward the ridge, thinking. His brother should be improving, not taking a god-blessed turn for the worse . . . and maybe it was time to return to New Jersey.

The contractors, damn it. He was supposed to be meeting with them. He checked his watch absently, realizing they should be coming up the fire trail about now. A short meeting then, he considered as he pulled his cellphone from his windbreaker, intending to make flight arrangements.

"You might's well throw that thing away up here, Luke," Jim commented, trying to sound amused—failing and sobering, "You won't get a signal on this side of the mountain. We're lucky to get through on the radio half the time." He was already unhooking his bulky radio from his belt. "If you want to make a call, I can patch you through my office."

For a split second, he considered accepting the offer, calling Gregor's cellphone, then thought better of it. Jim's office was only one town away from Freemont and too damned close to his mountain. The phone number would inevitably appear on Gregor's caller ID, and Luke wasn't ready to share his accomplishment, not even with the paperwork finally signed and recorded. Luckily, he was spared from making excuses with the distant rumble of an engine approaching. That was a good sign; the contractors had found the right trail . . . And fixing that lane might become a priority if he intended to haul equipment and supplies to this ledge.

Watching the truck bounce over the ruts onto the bent high-meadow grass, Luke pushed off the fender where he'd been leaning, Appreciating their punctuality along with their foresight to arrive in a lifted four-wheeler, he admired the pickup as they approached. The tall Ford made his Jeep look like a toy, but the little red devil fit the bill for his purposes.

As the healthy rumble of the engine died, Jacky Monahan stepped down from the front passenger seat, hitting his boots running—or so it seemed. Two years Luke's senior, the fellow dressed like a lumberjack in dark jeans, a plaid shirt, and genuine suspenders—unless one happened to notice his designer jeans, Doc Martin boots, and gold rings on several fingers, along with a diamond chip glinting from his left ear. He wore his hair neat and short, an apparent reflection of the older man—his father—who stepped down from the driver's seat. Both back doors swung open, and two other men stepped out as Jack loped forward.

"How the hell are you, Lucas?" Jacky demanded and threw himself into a bear hug that nearly knocked Luke back into the fender.

"I was better a moment ago," Luke said dryly but stifled a laugh as he returned the embrace. He hadn't seen Jack in four years, but they'd become fast friends over several heated arguments on the Debate Club.

'My old man builds hotels,' Jacky had said all those years ago. 'And amusement parks, and any other damn thing that's tremendously large—including skyscrapers . . .' And a few days earlier, Jacky had said, 'Hell, yes! My dad would love to build a resort. Just say where and when . . .'

Already, the elder Monahan had begun looking at the clearing as if sizing it up as he strode forward. With the confidence of a man accustomed to tramping through a forest as often as a boardroom, wearing a leisure suit and hiking boots, the gentleman came between the Jeep and ATV, nodding toward Jim before focusing on Luke. "I heard about your brother, youngster. How is he?"

"Honestly, I'm not sure," Luke admitted, seeing no reason to lie. "I'm heading back there when we finish here."

Again, the elder scanned the clearing, asking, "You intend to build a resort on this spot?"

Luke glanced off his old school friend, then to the father. "I think I mentioned to Jack, I want to start with my personal cabin," he said and motioned toward the back of the Jeep. "There's a second ledge, about five times this size, where I intend to put the Lodge. I have the blueprints back here."

"LJ," Colbin interjected. "I'll leave you to it."

"Shit, being rude," he realized and paused long enough to make introductions and receive a few. The other two gentlemen were part of Monahan's hierarchy—both project managers. Over the next hour, with the blueprints spread in the back of the Jeep, Luke outlined his plans, pausing to point out the layout regarding the rock formations and some of the older trees. "I don't want a single tree cut down or damaged unless it's necessary, Mr. Monahan. I'm leaning toward the organic architecture, a little like Frank Llyod Wright's designs."

"That might be impossible, youngster. Some of those roots could be in our way."

"Then we'll shorten the foundation and put deeper footers under the slabs," Luke decided. "I don't actually need much of a basement . . . which sort of leads to this area here. . ."

"The basement."

"More of a holding cell," Luke corrected. "There's a gas vein running through the center of the mountain, Mr. Monahan, and I own the proper rights to tap into it. I have an engineer working on a system to heat this cabin and the Lodge . . ."

"Hell," Jacky chuckled. "I should have known you'd have something else in mind. I'll go out on a limb here and guess you designed this system?"

Luke shrugged, "Something like that."

"You probably drew these blueprints, too, huh?" Jack mused.

"I had assistance," he admitted, not entirely sure why Jack wore such a bemused expression. In fact, Jack Sr. and the younger project manager, Ken Lin, wore peculiar expressions. The other seemed intent on the blueprints.

Jack harrumphed a sound and looked at his father. "Think I mentioned, Dad, my friend here has a creative streak a mile wide."

"An inventor, as I've heard mentioned," Sr. commented. "I think we can work with the schematics. How soon do you want to start?"

"Tomorrow wouldn't be soon enough, sir," Luke said and shrugged.

"We'll need a few days to juggle some numbers," the elder said thoughtfully. "We should have an estimate for you by early next week."

Luke reached into the back of the Jeep and brought out his leather binder, unzipping the case and extracting several sheets of paper. "I've jotted a pretty thorough list of supplies, estimated labor,, and equipment," he admitted. "Should give you a springboard. Most of the materials can be bought locally. There's a stone quarry and a lumber mill, both a few miles from here and I'd like to employ local talent when we can."

Monahan leafed through the pages, taking pause at a few places then looked to Luke. "If these numbers are accurate, we can work with this."

Jack commented, amused, "They're accurate, Dad. Trust me. He probably has that estimate tabulated to the last dollar."

"I wasn't certain about the equipment," Luke admitted, feeling odd as if he should defend himself then curious of the reason. He'd never tried to impress anyone nor found any reason to excuse himself—especially not for accuracy. "If you get close to that, you have the job if you want it."

"You're probably about ten or fifteen thousand over, depending on the availability of those beams and the cost of the stone, but we could probably get started on that lane straight away." He barely paused, "Why don't we take a look at where you want to set that Lodge . . .?"

An hour later, content with his decision to place the entire project with Monahan and Sons Contracting, Luke navigated the slightly more passable lane to wind off the mountain. Driving on autopilot, he reached the valley and subsequent town of Freemont. Four years . . . he'd driven into Freemont four years earlier on his way to meet a few friends at the ski resort several miles north, and he'd fallen in love with the mountain town ambiance, from gas light lanterns to wide sidewalks with lively storefronts. No fast-food franchises had found Freemont. A few bars, cafés, and diners complemented the single supermarket, gas station, car dealership, bank, and post office. The town boasted an elementary and middle school. High school students were bussed several miles east to a town where the modern age had caught up and caught on.

Despite Freemont's ambiance, however, the entrance ramp to Interstate 81, not far from the edge of town, had cinched the decision to sightsee in the nearby mountains. Subsequently, he'd found Skyler Peak with a deteriorated 'for sale' sign at its base. He'd needed to climb out of his rented Jeep, then, and dust snow off the faded letters, had improvised on a few of the numbers of the hand-written phone number and eventually found the correct series to reach the owner. Those first 53 acres had become the third acquisition of Sky High, LLC. Buying the land at the mouth of the only access road to Skyler Peak had helped when he began researching to find other owners. It had seemed like an omen—finding a mountain called 'Sky'-ler Peak when he'd only recently formed his Sky High, LLC.

The Skyview Lodge.

That it might become a reality even sooner than expected was another good omen; after all, purchasing the mountain was the only investment that hadn't offered a quick return. If the Lodge was up and running within the year, he would be almost a year ahead of schedule on his ROI. Not bad if the Monahans could meet their projections. Not bad at all.

At the top of the first mountain he climbed, Luke pulled to a wide berm long enough to make flight arrangements out of Roanoke, then phoned the hotel where he'd been staying and made arrangements to leave is Jeep in their lot and catch a shuttle to the airport.

At one a.m. in the morning, slipping into a hospital through the emergency entrance was child's play. But Luke was glad he'd opted for the disguise when he spotted the cigarette trailing from the open window of a nondescript white van. He probably would have made a decent spy if he were so inclined. Dressed in hospital scrubs—the color matching a lowly orderly—he'd donned a pair of clear glasses and taken time at an office supply store near the airport to create a badge. Displaying an authentic Southern General logo, the laminated nametag dangled from his uniform breast pocket on a small claw clip. Voila. Instant orderly.

At an unhurried pace, changing his walk to appear almost sluggish, he passed the guard at the entrance and managed a half-assed wave as he continued through the waiting room. Only four people occupied the four rows of chairs, and two were asleep. The triage nurse spotted him and buzzed him through, and despite his delight in his success, his frown was genuine. Hopefully, the security around his brother was more capable.

Thanks to the ongoing newsbreaks, Luke knew his brother occupied a private room on the seventh floor, and according to Molly Anderson, that floor was heavily guarded. Quite the reporter, that lady. She'd managed to report on every move the MacDades made, and although she hadn't succeeded in many interviews, she'd captured images of at least a half dozen clan members,

A few were mere shadows passing behind other more prominent bodies, and Luke wondered if the FBI—AIC Parsons—had identified a few of those fellows, then countered the thought. Men like Uncle Cyrus Macanders wouldn't be caught on film or by the FBI unless they chose to be so. Even on the sidelines of events throughout his life, Luke knew that not every member of the MacDade clan could be considered legitimate. In fact, he knew at least three who could have easily arranged to ambush the clan's heir apparent outside a sleazy hotel, and by now, his father had investigated that avenue.

Recognizing the casual stride of a young man in one of those shadowy newsflashes, Luke halfheartedly wondered if his father might already have discovered Liam's enemy or if one of the clan had decided to take matters into his own hands. Ryan MacDade was not likely here for a social visit, not if the rumors across the pond were any indication. That lad was in the business either of solving or creating problems, depending on one's perspective. And generally, his business involved guns.

Nearly a week without a single official lead—if Molly Anderson could be believed—was difficult to fathom.

Passing through the emergency department, where the pace seemed subdued compared to the Saturday morning past, Luke strode into the empty connecting corridor, appreciating the near silence. Somewhere ahead, an elevator dinged, but none of the telltale signs of patient rooms reached him, which provided a reason to bypass the first set of elevators.

With signs designating patient rooms ahead, Luke veered to the next set of elevators and pressed the call button. Stepping inside, he was already tugging the loose blue tunic over his head before the doors closed completely. Quick change. He stepped out of the loose blue scrub pants, gathered both items, and stuffed them into a paper bag he brought from his jeans—minus the nametag. He shoved the fake badge into his back pocket for future use.

When the doors slid open on the seventh floor, his curiosity enhanced, but stepping into the corridor restored his faith. Five doors away, two dark-suited gentlemen stood at military attention, already looking in his direction. One, the younger of the pair, remained rigid; the other, familiar face relaxed and might almost have smiled. Luke did smile slightly, striding forward, by-passing a shadowed open door wearing an overhead sign designating 'Patient Lounge.'

Did patients lounge? Or should the sign read 'Visitors Lounge.'

Liam's door stood open; soft light dissolved into the brighter corridor light. The steady beat of a heart monitor issued from the doorway, offering some relief, but judging the grim expression on the sentinels, Luke suffered the tension. Pausing, looking into the room to see a nurse hovering at the bedside, Luke wasn't altogether certain he should enter. To the familiar guard, Luke spoke quietly, "How is he?"

"Might be better asking the nurse," Kelly Finnegan, a man who generally stood in the company of Mason Eldridge, spoke in a lower volume. "Miss Natalie's inside, too, but I think she's just fallen asleep."

Luke nodded, then continued silently into the room. When he needed to be covert, he could be as quiet as a cat, and sure enough, the situation warranted his stealth. Natalie lay curled on her side under a stark white blanket, dozing in a recliner a single pace from Liam's opposite side. Even in sleep with the blanket pulled over her shoulders, she was attractive, her glistening hair in a ponytail tucked under her chin like a neck scarf . . . or a cat's tail. Sidling to the end of the bed, Luke barely acknowledged the startled nurse, who nearly jumped out of her colorful smock when she spotted him. Before she could more than squeak a breath, he uttered, "Shhh."

His brother looked nearly as bad as he had when last Luke visited . . . if not worse. Black patches stood under his closed lids, and his long black lashes nearly disappeared in the bruises if not for the visible quiver. In fact, beneath the sheet, the entire body seemed to be shivering, and rather than tiny dual tubes at his nostrils, he wore a full nose and mouth mask to feed him oxygen. In slow motion, that mask rocked as if Liam were denying something in his sleep.

They'd cleaned the blood stains from his fingernails. Lying at rest, one hand on his waist, the other at his hip, the fingers curled in the start of a fist, but even those capable digits seemed to be moving, twitching.

Lifting his gaze to the nurse, Luke recognized the sorrow on the lovely young face, the compassion apparent in her warm brown eyes and forced smile. Tanya R. couldn't be much older than him; however, she wouldn't be in this room if she weren't overly qualified . . . But that altered nothing of Luke's sudden hostility. How dare she look at him as if she felt sorry for him—as if she believed he was about to lose his brother! If ever he would like to strike a woman, never more than at this moment, and something in his eyes—like the color turning to blue flames—lent her reason to worry. In a voice barely above a whisper, he asked directly, "What's his condition?"

"S-table," she said in an equally soft volume. "His fever's still a little high, but we think the antibiotics are working."

Did she think him an idiot? Under no circumstances could the antibiotics be 'working' with less than twenty-four hours of doses. Shaking his head, he looked down at his brother, and just for a second, he believed the lashes lifted to emit a sliver of cobalt blue. His brother was neither awake nor aware of a damn thing.

Recording the vital signs on the monitor, judging the drip of liquids from several clear bags hanging over his brother's right shoulder, Luke saw everything he needed to see. His brother was nowhere close to surviving that attack . . . and in slow degrees, another thought surfaced.

With his affairs in order, he could afford to spend a little time in or around Trenton, New Jersey, and he had a good idea of where to start. So, maybe it was time to do some digging.

On autopilot, he departed the room, striding to the elevator and navigating a path to the first floor. Without a conscious effort, he read enough overhead signs to reach the parking garage exit and kept his face averted from the cameras by habit—belatedly, grasping his foolishness. Kelly Finnegan would report to Mason, if not directly to Gillis MacDade, both of whom would undoubtedly inform Lucius of his youngest son's visit. Not that it mattered.

If Luke had believed for a moment that his brother was unconscious, he might have saved himself the trouble of a disguise and visited in the daylight—providing he could avoid the press. The more he kept his bearded face from the spotlight, the better he liked it. Most of the fellows he dealt with, had no idea who he was even after meeting him. They just assumed he was some low-level pencil pusher for Sky High Limited, and that served his purposes just fine. He doubted some of them would appreciate knowing they dealt with a kid—and he knew he was still considered a kid by most standards. Eventually, he might grow into his intelligence and look the part of an executive, but that day hadn't come.

Finding his rental on the fourth floor more by accident than intent—or so it seemed—he glanced off his watch and decided it was too late—or early—to visit a strip joint. He could just return to his hotel and do a little research.

Without a conscious decision, Luke passed the front entrance of Southern General, not entirely surprised by the mounds of flowers and well wishes—and votive candles—still piled against the shrubs outlining the horseshoe-shaped entry. The tribute had continued to grow, Molly had pointed out for her viewing audience, periodically slipping dramatic shots of well-wishers into her broadcasts. For whatever reason, this young reporter had decided to turn Liam into a national celebrity—and what a surprise. In that first photo, Liam MacDade had worn the iconic handsomeness of a movie star, and Ms. Anderson had seen her ticket to fame via ratings.

It was working, too. Luke nearly sideswiped a parked car across from the entrance as he spotted three young ladies laying bouquets of flowers on the mound. Two o'clock in the morning, and these folks were delivering flowers? Shaking his head, recovering the listing wheel, Luke heard the slightly slurred voices through his open window and again shook his head.

"I'm tellin' you, if I wasn't married, I'd be sneaking on up there—"

"Getting your dam self arrested, too," another laughed. "You ain't seen the picture of all them security guys . . .?"

"That Natalie's one lucky lady . . ."

"Yea, an' she is one, too—a lady . . ."

The voices faded with the distance growing, and Luke was still marveling at the words when he sped past the white van, recording the sights though he couldn't see the driver clearly. A male, he judged if only by the hand flicking an ash off a cigarette through the open driver's window. A Chevy van, white, '03, no logos, but Luke recorded the license plate number. If the need arose, he could track down the driver.

At a legal speed, he left the hospital in his rearview mirror and headed for his hotel, vaguely aware of his stomach rumbling. He couldn't even recall when he'd last eaten a decent meal, and by all the closed signs, he'd missed his opportunity for dinner. Luckily, he spotted the neon glow of a twenty-four-seven convenience store and rolled into the lot.

When he needed fuel, he generally headed for the snack aisles and syrupy sodas, toward which he was destined when his attention halted, riveted. Snatching the tabloid off the rack, he continued toward the coolers in the rear, grateful for the foresight to wear the glasses. His hair pulled strictly flat into a ponytail, his too-blond locks toned down a few shades, and the clear lenses could deflect his eye color. Too blond, too blue. Liam was becoming famous over those attributes, and Luke had a niggling feeling he should dye his hair sometime soon unless he meant to suffer the fallout.

He wished his blasted cabin was done already. He could be safely tucked away atop his mountain, out of public sight and mind.

Well, if wishes were horses, beggars would ride . . . that was his mum's old line.

At the counter, Luke turned the tabloid face down without fanfare, and the young woman behind the counter still seemed to look at him a little too critically. If she recognized him, however, something in his direct gaze halted her from speaking. As he'd learned at a very young age, there was more than one way to become unapproachable, one being the clear and concise silent command, 'Back the hell off.'

He paid for several sodas, candy bars, cookies, and the tabloid, then left the store without uttering a word. If he got arrested for scaring the daylights out of her, it would be his own fault, but apparently, she was made of sterner stuff.

She would have to be made of sterner stuff to work the night shift not too far from where a man was beaten and stabbed, maybe shot, only a few days earlier.

Attuned to his internal thought, Luke navigated the route he'd recorded some time earlier and turned onto the street with the Fairmont Hotel's entrance blazing neon from two blocks away. Considering the details he'd overheard days ago, Luke scanned the neighborhood leading toward the hotel, judging a few neon signs—currently turned off with happy hour long gone. Not what he would consider a place ripe for a mugging. Row houses between mom-and-pop businesses, a deli, pizza shop . . . a supermarket past the hotel. More like a pleasant suburban neighborhood with cars lining the street on either side and trees botching the efforts of streetlights on corners.

He spotted the alley if only by the broken police tape dangling from the bricks at the entrance, like the streamers broken by football players trotting into a gymnasium for a pep assembly. Luke remembered bursting through the streamers a time or two, fulfilling his childhood fantasy to become a football star before deciding he would never be as tall as his middle brother, much less his oldest. At 6'4", Gregor could have played Pro ball if he hadn't preferred racing around an obstacle course at the mercy of a fourteen-hundred-pound muscle-bound animal.

Wide enough for a normal-sized car to pass through, the alley remained a study in deep shadows with a scattering of light designating the rear entrance. No direct light illuminated either end of the alley opening, and neither building boasted a lighted loading dock. At 2:30 in the morning, the only sign of occupancy remained the vacancy sign aglow under the neon announcing the Fairmont. Four stories tall, a city block long, the hotel entrance resembled Southern General with a circle drive leading to and through a covered portico boasting another neon, 'Front Desk.' While trying to imagine his brother—a study in wealth and sophistication wearing designer jeans, tailored shirts, and enough gold to weigh down a small child—entering this bland front entrance, Luke barely jerked the steering wheel in time to avoid hitting a curb. Some days, he shouldn't be allowed behind the wheel of a tricycle, much the less a rented vehicle.

Shaking his head, Luke continued past the hotel entrance, deciding either his brother was extremely bored with his life . . . or he was trying to punish himself for whatever he'd done to be separated from his wife. Even spending that brief time with them in the recovery room, Luke had grasped the integrity of their love.

A story there, too, undoubtedly. What had Liam done—or failed to do—to create that situation? And why not even consider that Natalie could have been at fault? Why automatically blame Liam? Hold him responsible? Natalie might have done something . . .

Not possible. Whatever problem had developed, Liam was responsible. Over and above the fact that he'd stepped out on a woman as fine as his wife, he'd probably have killed her if it were the other way around. If not her, then at least her paramour, and as far as Luke knew, there were no bodies found beaten to death in or around Lexington . . . not in a few years, anyway.

Liam was attacked, though, and might have been killed . . . to clear the path for a lover rather than suffer a messy divorce?

Natalie Callahan-MacDade would never win a custody court battle against Liam MacDade, and if she'd been caught stepping out—and survived—Liam would have demanded custody.

Was it possible? Had she initiated this ordeal to avoid an ugly divorce?

She'd been in that alley alongside Liam . . . suffering second thoughts? Had she hung around to see it through and suffered a change of heart?

"Shit," Luke muttered and set his course for his hotel, a fine hour away. That whole blasted scenario fell apart with a single, simple image of that long, cool drink of water leaning over the bed and weaving a spell to still the raging giant. She probably did suffer the knack—that fabled of all women's talents rumored to affect more than a few MacDade women in the past. The Callahan women likely carried the same affliction.

His own Gram had boasted that mystical talent.

And a shiver skittered down Luke's spine as he saw her, freeze frame, eying him as she held him on her lap. The smell of haggis hung in the kitchen despite the warm breeze blowing through the screen-covered windows. Blue eyes as vivid as a summer sky, she'd peered through him as her eyes changed, darkening as clearly as her gray brows furrowed. The lines on her face seemed to magnify as her lips curved into a grim smile. 'Ye dan look at the worl't ta same as others,' she had spoken in that weird mix of Gaelic and English. 'Nae, nae ye, wee bairn . . . Be a lonely road ye tae travel, but dane ye fret . . . come a day . . .' And she'd smiled more naturally then, her eyes dancing with delight. 'Aye, come a day . . .'

That day hadn't come yet either, Luke nearly muttered aloud, then corrected silently. Maybe it had. With the past dozen hours behind him, he took himself to the ridge, standing on that ledge and watching that hawk soar past the pine peaks nearly within reach. Maybe that day had come. His dreams were well on the way to becoming a reality.

At the hotel, Luke gained access with his key card at a side door and reached his room on the top floor without passing a single body. A hotel suite could be as comfortable as his one-bedroom apartments, and this one was well-equipped. He could have bought a frozen pizza and utilized the full-sized oven. Putting his sodas in the refrigerator, he considered finding some ice but opted against it. Warm soda was just as good. Cracking open a can, he arranged his workspace, connecting his laptop to the wall outlets and internet jack. As much as he liked visiting libraries and courthouse archives to research deeds and the like, he'd found the internet faster, more efficient, and far more pleasant without personal interaction. His Gram was right all those years ago. He looked at the world differently, but she was wrong about the other—he never minded the lonely road.

Even as the computer hummed to life, Luke reached for the tabloid. With a glance of the cover at the convenience store, he had recorded the details without needing to concentrate. Flipping rapidly through the pages, he introverted the printed words and pictures for later reading, then turned to the computer.

Where to start? Where to start?

Frank Pendleton.

Ah, and the young woman. Alecia Helms. Maybe Helms first.

14

The buzz of his cell phone shot Luke awake as quick as the ping of his computer, but it took him less time to find it on the nightstand alongside his head. Even with the heavy drapes drawn over the windows, the afternoon sun created a hazy glow within the room, and Luke needed little else to be irritated as he flipped the phone open. "Yes?"

"Mr. McDade, you have a message from a Mr. Frances Pendleton of Trenton, New Jersey," the nearly mechanical voice announced. "He would like you to return his call as soon as possible. The number is . . ."

Coincidence?

Luke recorded the number and snapped the phone closed. He'd shut down his computer less than two hours ago after spending the night and most of the morning visiting more websites than he cared to consider. At this point, Luke probably knew more about Frank Pendelton's life than Frank himself. By extension, he'd learned a great deal about the elder Pendletons as well. Why would the elder be calling him, though?

If Pendelton wanted to know about Liam, he could probably ask his son or watch the local news at any hour. According to an exasperated Frank, whose call Luke had returned at least twice over the past several days, the local stations were engaged in an airtime war, offering nearly hourly updates on the oldest son of the wood tycoon who was becoming as famous as the 'flipping Kennedys' according to Frank.

Luke had to smile at that. He could imagine his father's take on that comparison. The big guy probably loved it, considering the Kennedy's descent, which likely included a touch of Scottish blood. Probably three or four centuries back, but what was a few hundred years when the MacDade lines could be traced into the three-digit centuries? To hear his father tell it, they were probably direct descendants of William Wallace . . . and if he was slightly in the cups, he would begrudgingly claim a connection to St. Patrick.

After just such a claim, more than a decade earlier, Luke had begun a research project of that fellow and decided not to mention to his father that St. Patrick was probably not even of Irish descent, much less Scottish.

With a cup of coffee in hand, Luke settled into the chair behind his laptop but reached for his cell phone, where he'd dropped it in passing. By habit, he blocked caller ID before pushing the buttons to the Pendleton home. Not surprisingly, he recognized the butler's voice answering with a clipped, "Good afternoon. How can I help you?"

Smart. The fellow refrained from admitting the call's destination. "Luke McDade. I believe Mr. Pendleton's expecting my call."

"Hold, please."

If it took more than thirty seconds to locate the old man, the fellow would need to call the service again. Patience was not a virtue to be squandered, and Luke waisted very little.

"Lucas?" the lofty voice erupted.

"Just Luke. But yes. You left a message for me to call?"

The fellow hesitated, then asked, "How's your brother?"

If the question didn't sound forced, Luke might be more annoyed. Instead, he was instantly more curious. "Holding his own, sir," Luke answered, maybe lying, maybe not. "Thanks for asking."

"Are you there—at the hospital or in the area?"

"Is there a reason you're asking?" he asked directly, slightly annoyed without a definite reason.

"I'd like to speak to you, young man," he said with an odd note, sounding more irritated than Luke was becoming. "If you're in the area, I'd like to invite you to dinner. Mrs. Pendleton would love to see you again."

"Mr. Pendleton, what's this about?" Luke asked lightly, genuinely curious. He couldn't think of a single reason why this gentleman would want to speak to him, and although he and the matron might be kindred spirits, doubtful he'd made much of an impression to warrant a repeat experience.

"I'd rather speak to you in person," the fellow spoke as if irritated. "It's not something I'd like to discuss over the phone, and it might be worth your while to come."

Intrigued, as much by the clandestine nature of the words as by the edgy tone, Luke decided, "I am in the area. What time, sir?"

"If you can be here by five, we can speak before dinner. We sit down at six."

And not a moment later. So, whatever the fellow intended to speak about would take about an hour.

Glancing at his watch, Luke decided, "I can be there at five-thirty if that works?" Anything that could be explained in an hour would be better said in half the time.

Sounding almost agitated by his curt tone, Pendleton commented, "That would be fine. We'll see you then."

The line went dead even before Luke could flip his phone shut. In a paradox of curiosity and amusement to be bested at ending the call, Luke considered what he knew about the Pendletons.

Franklin Delany Pendleton, named after his grandfather, was second generation American; Frances and his wife were both first-generation, born to English immigrants. Frank's grandparents, newlyweds, hadn't traveled too far from Ellis Island before settling down. Comfortably well off upon arrival, Franklin the First had made a few wise investments in the manufacturing and shipping industry—and the parallel to his own heritage struck Luke funny and possibly explained Liam and Frank's friendship. Manufacturing and shipping with some land holdings to their credit, the elder Pendletons, including both immigrants—who currently resided in Florida—had managed to hold onto their fortunes and remain comfortably well off. Maybe not in league with Lucius or even Liam, but Frank could afford to 'scratch together' five grand to help Liam's mistress disappear.

So far, the mistress hadn't turned up nor contacted the police. Or if she had, then Molly Anderson's source in the Trenton PD was slacking. Even the mention of the Fairmont Hotel hadn't made a big splash.

Luke's gaze drifted to the tabloid on the end table where he'd tossed it in the wee hours. He needn't bother opening the front page to read the contents. One paparazzi had cashed in on a few photos, some possibly resurrected from another tabloid. The picture of Liam and their cousin Carmin was the most damning, depicting Liam with his arm wrapped around the glamorous young woman who'd capitalized on her tall, lithe MacDade genes. The implication remained apparent—Liam stepping out on his wife and meeting a secret lover—enhanced tenfold by a plethora of pictures depicting a family on the brink of collapse as Liam lay at death's door. The Fairmont

Hotel hadn't made the national news, barely mentioned, not by name, as somewhere nearby where Liam had been meeting a business associate.

If Liam had wanted someplace obscure to secret a lover, Trenton was probably as good of a place as any, what with his old college chum to help cover his ass. Luke could see how that was possible. Liam in the doghouse with his wife, calling his old friend to share a few laughs, and the conversation Luke had overheard between the old friend and mistress had evidenced that possibility. Frank and this Alecia Helms had been casual acquaintances—not strangers but not close friends, him not knowing her address. That the Emerald Club might be the last place Frank would hang out further suggested Liam had orchestrated the introduction between those two.

Questions. Only more questions, and in a momentary epiphany, Luke considered what the elder Pendleton might intend to discuss. Chiefly, a means to keep his son, and ultimately his family name, out of the public eye. Doubtful Pendleton had met any other of the MacDades to feel comfortable with such a discussion,

Automated, Luke checked the time, meandered to the closet in the next room, and woke to the sight before him, shaking his head. He'd packed three days ago on a brief layover in Lexington, and anticipating a few business meetings, he had packed with two goals—banking and hiking. When a twenty-year-old aimed to make an impression, he dressed accordingly. Two Armani suits hung in the closet, nearly identical aside from the color. Dark blue and black—and he'd worn the black to the bank. The dark blue could pass for black, and the pale blue shirt with the deacon's collar wore well with white-gold chains rather than a tie. Upper-crust business casual.

He could wear jeans . . . but the Pendletons, with their old-money attitude, might be far more at ease if he dressed appropriately for dinner. That he might be stealing a page from his father's book occurred to Luke as he gathered the matching accoutrements. His father wore suits. At any hour—at every hour of every day of the week—Lucius MacDade wore suits presenting a position of power. If his father even owned a pair of jeans, Luke couldn't recall seeing them.

Dressed for a semi-formal dinner, Luke rolled his rental into the circle drive and stopped at the entry. He half-expected to see Carl trot across the shadowy front porch to take his keys and park his car. The entire three-story Victorian gave vent to images of coachmen and servants hustling in every direction. The Pendletons had lived well, probably once employing a sizeable staff of servants to tend everything from coach horses to polishing silver. Either they'd changed with the times, or their finances had taken a turn in recent years. Three servants seemed not near enough to maintain this estate, and in passing, Luke had seen enough of the grass around the cast iron gate to know the apparatus no longer functioned or the gardeners were remiss.

The gardeners were definitely remiss.

The yard could use a good grooming, and the decline was recent, what with the tell-tale signs of weeds sprouting in the mulch and twigs gathering in the hedges.

At 5:27, Luke employed the brass knocker, timing his arrival to be comfortably on time.

The all-too-familiar Carl, appearing as aloof and somehow annoying as on previous encounters, held the door with a simple, "Mr. MacDade, you are expected."

Who would have guessed? With a bemused smirk, Luke commented, "The invitation would suggest as much."

If Carl appreciated Luke's somewhat lofty tone, nothing showed as he turned, indicating with a flagged hand. "This way."

Directed to the open door across the ancient-smelling parlor, Luke continued into the room as if he owned it, unimpressed by the continuation of the ancient ambiance. The room smelled of old cigars, baked linens, and dust from the velvet drapes covering two windows to either side of crowded, mahogany bookshelves. The bookshelves could double as bookends sandwiching the wide, mahogany desk. Behind which, Pendleton sat holding a cigar, sporting a brandy snifter in the same hand. Rather than rise, the fellow appeared to take in Luke's appearance from his casual pose, and clearly, he approved, even managed to appear impressed.

"Luke," the fellow said by way of greeting. "Please, have a seat. Would you care for a brandy?"

Damned social etiquette to dictate that he accept the offer or be considered rude. "That would be fine, sir," he commented as he settled into one of the two receiving chairs strategically placed opposite Frances. Rather like the chairs found in a bank manager's office or the dean's office in a prominent school—the upholstered chairs were about as comfortable as a dentist's chair with thinner padding.

Letting some of his curiosity show, Luke glanced about the antiques within view, appearing more impressed than he was. The MacDade homestead was filled with similar museum-quality lamps on brass poles and bases, with Tiffany globes filtering the light on the old tomes. But in his parents' house, the brass was shined, the colored glass clean, the ancient first editions protected from damaging light with indirect lighting on every shelf . . . And no matter how many cigars Lucius smoked, the rooms emanated the scents of lemon, and beeswax, or fresh mountain air.

As he accepted the brandy snifter without more than a glance and lofty nod, Luke focused on Pendleton, aware of himself being weighed and measured behind the wire-rimmed glasses. "I appreciate the invitation, Mr. Pendleton, but I have to admit, I am curious."

"I wonder if you have any updates on your brother's condition," Pendleton said. "According to the latest news this afternoon, he's still listed in critical condition."

"He is, yes," Luke answered with a touch of his heritage slipping into his words as he considered the latest update he'd received via email from Gregor. "He's suffering from an infection, though they've not isolated the type," he continued and might have admitted—that without isolating the type of infection, they couldn't efficiently target the antibiotic to the source. Thus far, according to Gregor, the doctors were administering a broad-spectrum IV antibiotic without a great deal of success. Liam was still more delirious with fever than ever coherent.

"When you see him, perhaps, you can pass on our well-wishes," Pendleton spoke as if distracted. "I've always liked your brother."

"I'll tell him," Luke answered offhandedly, only more intent. The fellow was stalling. For what reason and about what? "Sir, meaning not to be rude," Luke spoke while hearing the door closing behind him, aware of Pendleton dismissing his butler with a nod. "What did you want to see me about?"

The fellow hesitated a moment more, his lined lips pursed and eyes more sober. "Tell me, Luke, is it true you've followed in your family's business?"

More curious, Luke wondered, "To what are you referring, sir?"

Sighing, the older man repositioned, coming from his relaxed pose to sit squarely behind his desk. "Your family's been known to buy land. Woodland, if I'm not mistaken. Do you follow that pattern?"

Not the question he might have anticipated, considering how much more visible the manufacturing and shipping business remained. Even more so with Liam's latest infamy putting the MacDade holdings front and center. Anyone who hadn't heard about High Land Inc. or MacDade Industries before last Saturday certainly knew the names now. Considering, Luke commented, "I may have a few investment properties, but I don't buy land for stripper cut, if that's your question, sir."

"But you do buy land?" he asked.

"Sir, truly, what's this about?" *Not a strip club or soiled reputation.*

Again, the elder sighed, "Quite frankly, I have about a thousand acres of woodland in the Poconos. It's been in my family for years, and honestly, I see no reason to keep it," he said as if the idea of owning land, in and of itself, was appalling. "I'd just as leave part with it, and if you were interested, we might reach an agreement."

About a thousand acres—just like that? "You offered it to my brother?"

"I'm offering it to you, Luke, and frankly, I'd like to keep this deal between you and me for the time being. I'd rather you not even discuss it with Franklin."

A thousand hundred acres in the Poconos, and if Liam had passed on the offer—which is what it sounded like—the land was probably not worth a great deal. "What are you asking for it?"

"It's five hundred and sixty-two acres, and I'll not lie to you—a great deal of it consists of hillsides and cliffs. There might be some useable wood—mostly pine, some birch," he shrugged as if he could not care less. "Still, it might have some development possibilities. I've had it appraised recently. It's valued over one and a half million. I suppose I'd let you have it for a million even. That's less than two thousand an acre."

Seventeen hundred seventy-nine dollars and thirty-six cents an acre to be closer to the penny . . . and if it appraised at a million and a half, twenty-six hundred sixty-nine dollars and four cents was the current market value per acre. A loss of eight hundred eighty-nine dollars and sixty-eight cents per acre. Depending on the terrain—and wood—it could be worth either value . . . or a great deal more if the development possibilities were accurate.

With barely a few seconds past, Luke wondered, "How soon would you need an answer?"

"As much as I'd like to give you all the time in the world, Luke, I've been contemplating this for quite some time. I'd prefer just to have it done and gone," Pendleton said aloofly. "Suppose, though—given your current situation with your brother so ill— I could give you a few days, but I'd like an answer by early next week if possible."

Researching the appropriate parcel, checking the deed, and whatnot could take a day or two. He could probably take a drive this weekend and take a hike in the Poconos. "I can have an answer for you by Tuesday if that works for you, Mr. Pendleton."

"I've waited this long, I can wait a few more days," he spoke as if put upon. "Tuesday, then. Would you care to see the deed? I have the original as well as a recent survey."

Could it be that easy? "That would be nice," Luke decided in a voice as dry as kindling. Anything too easy couldn't, possibly, be true—or legal—but Pendleton brought a slight stack of papers from his desk drawer. Rather dumbfounded though nothing showed in his expression, Luke identified the documents, from a deed dating more than fifty years earlier and signed, sealed, by the first Franklin Pendleton, to a survey dated as recent as mid-June—less than three months earlier. Forcing himself to take his time to appear to study the documents, Luke recorded the pertinent data as if inhaling air. At the end of a few moments, he sat back in the chair, genuinely dumbfounded although nothing appeared in his expression. Pendleton could wait until Tuesday, perhaps, but in Luke's mind, the deal was done. He would take a drive on the weekend if only to satisfy his curiosity. Unless the land had already been stripped of either wood or minerals, it would be worth three grand an acre.

As always, functioning on dual levels, Luke surveyed the data in his mind's eye while accepting the elder's invitation to reach the dining room. He would have preferred leaving the brandy snifter behind but carried it with him, sipping rather than gulping as he made small talk with Cheryl Pendleton. The woman truly possessed a wicked sense of dry humor inherent to the English, and Luke resigned to pay attention if only to enjoy her quiet zingers aimed good-naturedly at her stoic husband.

Surprisingly pleased with the entire evening, Luke thanked both Pendletons for a pleasant evening and accepted Carl's escort through the parlor. No more did he start across the porch, emerging into the fading sunlight, still brighter than the Pendleton dining room, when he spotted the familiar black Lincoln rolling between the cast iron gates. Considering the senior Pendleton's insistence that he not mention the deal, Luke was grateful for the extra seconds to decide on the simple truth as an excuse.

A dinner invitation.

15

Pausing alongside the driver's door of the Regal, Luke waited as Frank parked behind the rental and slid gracefully from the car.

Already, Frank's mustache quirked with the curious smile, and his focus darted, down, up, and over the car hood, expecting to see someone else. Apparently, not believing his eyes, he managed, "Luke?"

"I thought you'd be here too when I accepted your parents' invitation," Luke commented, preempting the question, and letting his curiosity rise, Glancing to the car, miming Frank's expression, anticipating a passenger to account for Frank's tardiness.

"I wish I'd known you were—Liam?" His face drained of color; panic flashed in his eyes. "He's all right? Nothing's happened?" The words were rushed, as surely as the hasty step and clasp on Luke's arm.

Connecting the dots, Luke understood the panic. "No change that I'm aware of," he said smoothly and witnessed the relief.

"God," Frank huffed, glancing down at Luke's attire. "I just . . . I thought. Well, never mind what I thought. How is he, truly, Luke? They said an infection now. He is all right, isn't he? He'll be all right, though, right?"

"They have him on antibiotics," Luke admitted. "They'll probably not take him out of ICU until they get it under control." Refraining from mentioning his opinion of his brother's condition with a fleeting thought of how bad Liam had looked in the wee hours, Luke commented, "Other than that, they're not saying much."

"You went to see him, though?"

"I did," Luke admitted. "But I got in late, and he was asleep, so I didn't stay long."

"Any chance you're heading there now?"

"Not this evening," Luke answered as he considered his ulterior motive for this visit to the Pendletons. Speaking to Frank had become imperative after running into a wall concerning Alecia Helms. No known addresses, car registrations, no employment records, or bank accounts. If she'd ever paid a tax in her life, she had filed under another name. On paper, Alecia Helms didn't exist. "I wonder, Frank . . . do you think . . .? Well, this might sound odd," Luke feigned his discomfort and inhibition.

"What is it?" Frank asked, concern rising with his curiosity.

"I'd like to—that Emerald Club," he decided. "That's where Liam met that woman—Alecia Helms—isn't it?"

Uncomfortable suddenly, Frank hesitated, then agreed. "Yes. I'm afraid it is, but that's not where they met afterward," he added hurriedly.

"She's one of the dancers there, isn't she?"

More distressed, Frank withdrew his grip and glanced to the house, back, fearing to be overheard. "She was," he admitted quietly.

"You know he was with her last Friday night, huh?"

"Luke," Frank began sorrowfully. "I don't know how much you know about your brother's personal life, but well, I'd really rather not discuss it."

"I know he and Natalie were separated," Luke offered quietly, studying Frank's discomfort despite the feigned sorrow in his expression. "I don't know exactly why. Do you?"

Again, the hesitation. Then Frank sighed and sidled, leaning against the Regal. "I know Natalie believed he was cheating on her, but honestly, I don't think Liam was cheating at that time. He uhm . . ." His gaze listed, searching for answers in the shaded lawn. "I know he was worried about her." Appearing slightly uncomfortable to share Liam's confidence, he continued carefully. "He loves her, you know? I know it was a forced marriage at the onset, but I think he cares for her far more than he lets on. Alecia—she was just—I think she was just a fun interlude until Natalie took him back."

And that should make it all right? With a faintly bemused smile, Luke considered that other tidbit of new information. *A forced marriage?* In a split second, Luke calculated the dates—more than nine months lapsed between the wedding and his oldest nephew's birth. Did Natalie trick Liam into marriage, only claiming to be pregnant? That was one of the oldest tricks in the book, but surely Liam would demand proof by way of a paternity test, which should have foiled any false claims. And why the hell dig into this anyway? What Liam did or failed to do couldn't have been bad enough to have him lying at death's door.

"You're worried," Frank stated and appeared more distressed. "How bad is he, Luke? Truly? What are you not saying?"

"He does look bad," Luke admitted, wondering if that was the truth belying his interest. He was not, had never been, a candidate for the Mac-Dade security army. Sleuthing was not his forte. If there was anything personal about this assault, plenty of people existed within the MacDade organization—far more qualified and knowledgeable investigators—to discover the cause. And Lucius MacDade was far too well-informed to overlook that angle. By now, Gillis had probably torn Liam's personal life apart—not that it would take much effort.

Far too clearly, the image of Gillis, tall and solid as any MacDade among them, appeared in Luke's mind's eye. Even before becoming head of security—hell, as much as fifteen years ago—Gillis had hovered in Liam's shadow, and that image ignited in Luke's memory. His tall, lean uncle had forever hovered over them, all of them, but more so Liam. God forbid anything should happen to the heir apparent to the MacDade throne. Which was why this entire ordeal seemed nearly impossible to fathom. A slip in security. One lousy glitch and Liam had become a target. Gillis was probably beside himself to have failed so miserably.

A coincidence, that glitch? Or was there far more to this?

Damn it, Uncle Mase had been a mess, and that breakdown hadn't been staged. No way Mason Eldridge deliberately manipulated those circumstances to leave Liam vulnerable, and Mason would have needed to be involved since he was responsible for sending Artair to offer Natalie protection. Not even Natalie could have predicted that event—and on a dual plane, that eliminated her from the suspect pool. If she'd anticipated Artair being sent to her aid, she wouldn't have gone to that alley to either watch or intervene. Too many working parts to manipulate in that scenario, and although she might be smart, doubtful she was a criminal mastermind.

"Luke?" Frank asked, reaching and again clasping Luke's arm. The fear loomed large in his dark eyes and strained attempt at a smile.

Only a few seconds had lapsed. Belatedly, Luke considered his words and, judging Frank's genuine concern, admitted, "I won't lie to you, Frank. He's not well. Probably won't be well for quite some time between the infection and the injuries, but if anyone can pull through this, Liam's a likely candidate."

For a long moment, Frank remained on the verge of panic, but his tension ebbed in slow degrees, and he managed a wan smile. "I think I should be the one consoling you, Luke," he said with a slight strain. "He's not my brother, but I love him like one."

Why those words should hurt, Luke couldn't decide, and again wondered at his personal interest in this situation. He and Liam had never been close. From a distance, Luke had always admired him and looked up to him. And Gregor, too. But they were too far apart in ages and interests to be close. Big brothers. They had tormented him to no end throughout those early years, but in hindsight, Luke knew he was more to blame. He'd followed them around for as far back as he could recall—which probably meant since before he could walk. Whether he'd found them fascinating or merely interesting, he still wasn't certain. He just remembered watching them. Whether they were sparring in karate lessons, learning to ride, or just fishing and swimming, he'd trailed after them whenever he could slip away from the protective fold of his nanny—or mum.

"Luke . . .? What do you say I buy you a drink?" Frank interrupted again.

Drawn from his thoughts, Luke focused on the fellow's sorrowful gaze and realized his lapse.

"My Country Club's not far from here," Frank added with a faintly bemused gaze. "No strippers, I promise."

"I uh . . . I think I'd prefer the Emerald Club, Frank," Luke said hesitantly. "I know it sounds stupid, but uhm . . . I'd just like to visit where he's been."

For whatever reason, Frank appeared more sorrowful with a hint of understanding. "You probably saw enough last week to know it's not the type of place your brother would appreciate me taking you."

"Probably not, but I . . . I won't tell him if you don't."

"Lord, what is it with you MacDades?" Frank asked, besieging the sky as he rolled his eyes heavenward. A more pitiful smile kinked his lips as he commented, "You're as bad as your brother, you know? And, if you so much as snap your fingers or wink at one of the dancers, I'm dragging you out of there before she jumps in your lap."

This fellow seemed just a wee bit fickle in a comical sort of way. "Okay then, but I'm not covering my eyes—and neither are you, sir. I'll draw the line there."

"Oh, God, you even sound like your brother," Frank said as he pushed from his lean against the car, shaking his head. "Shall we go in my car?"

"I'll follow you," Luke decided and reached for his car door handle.

Barely two blocks from the Pendleton house, Luke glanced at the rearview mirror and identified a familiar dark blue Chevy. He needed only a second to recall the nondescript Malibu parked in a lot near his hotel.

Forever, he'd suffered a near-debilitating habit of recording sights, sounds, and scents, never consciously searching for the patterns or algorithms around him. Doubtful many people would notice a plain blue Chevy Malibu parked in a public lot, any more than a person might recall seeing five more of the same make, model, and year . . . or zoom in on the license plate to know it was the exact vehicle as though he'd taken a physical picture. The gift of instant recall was more like a curse at times, but it served him well enough to know he'd seen this very car on three separate occasions since arriving in Trenton last evening. Once in the hotel parking lot when leaving earlier, once on the drive to the Pendletons' house, and now. By no coincidence, he was being followed. More than likely, Kelly had passed the word, and Gillis had tracked him down. To believe that his life remained private was a fool's dream. Lucius MacDade had probably heard about Sky High Limited since its inception in 2003, and Luke had picked up a tail often enough after booking a room under his company name to know Gillis was keeping track.

The thought of Uncle Gillis tracking him sent a tiny shiver down his spine, and for a moment, Luke considered phoning Frank, changing course. Instead, he decided on a few evasive maneuvers and dropped from behind Frank on the first highway. He could reach the Emerald Club without following Frank, and if Frank took off before he arrived, it wouldn't be a problem.

Blending into traffic, Luke sped off the first exit ramp into a suburban neighborhood, not truly paying attention to his direction. That he might not have chosen the safest neighborhood occurred to him as he passed groups of black and Latino teenagers loitering rather than playing on two separate basketball courts with cyclone fences torn and gaping in every direction. Whether he'd found the ghetto or merely a declining urban street, he wasn't entirely certain. Windows wore plywood rather than glass, and graffiti covered nearly every available wall—public and private alike. Row houses formed a solid wall from one street to the next, and what remained of businesses wore scissor-style iron gates folded and waiting for the door signs to flip from open to closed.

Slowing for tight turns on the narrow, car-lined streets, Luke continued to watch the Malibu that had dropped back considerably, apparently falling for the ruse that their mark was searching someplace in particular and might stop at any moment. With little thought or concentration, Luke picked his moment, made a slow, random turn, and stomped the gas. He sped through two blocks, bypassed four alleys, then turned into fifth, raced the short stretch, turned, and doubled back on the next alley. This wasn't the first time he would need to lose a tail, and by now, Gillis was probably aware of the deliberate maneuvers, although, on the surface, it could appear random.

With several more turns behind him, Luke navigated the quickest route to the highway, and he was comfortably sure of flying solo by the time he pulled into a dark parking spot near the Emerald Club. He was likely slightly overdressed for this establishment, a thought to lend him pause and twitch a smirk on his lips. When it mattered, he was a stickler for details; visiting a strip club wearing an Armani did not fall into the 'it mattered' category.

Already amused, Luke found Frank waiting, leaning against his Lincoln under a streetlamp that had ignited with the slant of the descending sun striking the tops of buildings in any direction. The strip club resided between a strip mall and a vacant lot where trees offered an illusion of the suburbs. Muffled, the distant sound of a drumbeat lent evidence of a dance in progress, though unless one happened to see the front neon marquis with a naked silhouette climbing a pole between Emerald and Club, the music could pass for Big Band or Rock.

"Where the heck did you go?" Frank asked as he pushed off the side of his car. "One moment you were behind me then you were nowhere in sight."

"I got behind a Sunday driver and couldn't get around him," Luke shrugged. It had happened, once. Just not this evening. "Luckily, I remembered the way from the other day."

"Humph," Frank muttered as he flagged a hand to start them toward the front door. "I forgot you came here from my parents' estate last Saturday."

With a bemused smile, Luke commented, "Interesting place."

Again, Frank harrumphed and held the door. "Your brother said nearly the same thing the first time we came here."

'First time' implied there had been a second time. Just how often did his older brother visit a place like this . . .? And that was probably a foolish question. Luke could imagine Liam coming here to catch his paramour's act.

Rather than a booth, Frank traveled only as far as the end of the bar and slid onto the second high stool, leaving Luke the empty seat at the deep end, deliberately attempting to protect him from the mainstream while giving him a clear view of the stage. This fellow had inherited his mother's sense of humor if his bemused smirk was an indication. He seemed to find something vastly entertaining, and considering the man's lack of interest in the semi-nude dancer, he was probably contemplating the irony of his ongoing patronage of this fine establishment.

A busty, dyed-blond waitress eyed them both as she took their orders, lending a slight pause when Luke ordered Scotch before deciding. "Coming right up, sweetie."

When she turned, Frank leaned and spoke in the undertow of erotic beats. "Be careful, *sweetie*. If Bertie takes a shine to you, she'll likely drag you to a back room."

Eying Bertie, who wore tight black shorts and a white halter top showing as much skin as tattoos, Luke winked at Frank without serious thought, commenting, "Could be interesting, too."

Frank rolled his eyes, shaking his head, and even in the shadowy neon glow, his eyes emitted the dumbfound and awe. "One drink. That's all you're getting, my young friend. If you want a second, we are going to my Country Club."

Despite feigned innocence and amusement, Luke scanned the shadows, recording scenes from the dozen males scattered at the tables near the stage to others within the more deeply shaded booths. For a Thursday evening, the Emerald Club might not be crowded, but on this floor, at least, the audience was impressive.

What he might have intended to see or discern from this visit, Luke couldn't readily decide. Alecia Helms wouldn't be found here, and he doubted any of these women would talk to him. Losing something of his smirk, Luke found Frank still watching him. Studying him? "What?"

"I . . . can't get over how much you resemble your brother," Frank said directly, thoughtfully, and barely finished the words when a waitress halted beside them.

Already focused on Luke, her face under neon reflected an odd bewilderment as her smile wavered. "Gees! You have to be related to Liam," she said and eyed Frank. "He is, right?" she said as her focus spun toward Luke, flashing concern. "How is he? How's our Liam?"

Our Liam? "He's hanging in there," Luke said smoothly. "Do you know him well, then?"

"Oh, not personally," she said and seemed to connect too many thoughts at once—probably beginning with the fact that there was an ongoing police investigation with their own Alecia Helms front and center. "He's been in a few times, and with all the news and stuff . . ."

And stuff. Luke smiled slightly, letting her off the hook, wondering, "Has Alecia returned to work?" In the corner of his eye, Luke glimpsed Frank's surprise, but his attention remained on the waitress.

Slightly spooked, her gaze darted about, fearing to be overheard, and she spared a glance at Frank before answering. "I don't think she's planning on coming back." To Frank, she continued, "You probably know how it is. I mean the police and all those other guys coming around asking questions. Course, I doubt they think you were involved. Alecia though . . ."

Frank appeared genuinely interested and his lean face sobered considerably. "I don't think I'm following, Lyn. Do they think Alecia had something to do with that attack? Really?"

More uncomfortable, Lyn glanced toward the stripper—in that direction before her attention returned, bouncing off Luke. "I really don't know what was going on. I mean, I don't think she'd have agreed to anything to hurt him. She had it bad if you know what I mean? I mean we all told her not to fall for him, but hey—you can't always choose where your heart goes."

And Liam being loaded would have sweetened the pot. So . . . what if Liam was about to break it off? What if this young woman did, in fact, set him up to be robbed? Was that really any stretch of the imagination?

Absently scanning the smoky, shadowed atmosphere, Luke tumbled the detail through his mind, not overlooking a bearded face turned toward him rather than the dancer. Familiar. Damn it. Luke hadn't even considered that Gillis might have stationed a man at this fine establishment, no doubt in a position to see if Alecia made another hasty appearance. Without revealing his recognition, Luke continued his scan and reached a single conclusion—if Alecia Helms realized she might be losing her meal ticket, if Liam had even alluded to the idea of returning to his wife, that young lady could have enlisted a band of thugs to relieve Liam of his wallet which undoubtedly held a couple thousand in cash on any given day.

Considering the results of that plot, Helms had probably taken a vacation, and Luke could imagine her hitting up the only other wealthy fellow she knew for some quick cash. Five minutes with Frank, and anyone could judge him a bleeding heart. The fellow might not offer half his trust funds to charity, but he'd certainly lend five large to a friend in need.

Accepting the Scotch and exchanging a few offhanded remarks with the bartender and waitress, Luke analyzed the details as he knew them and reached a single conclusion—sooner or later, Gillis's men would track down Alecia Helms and God pity that poor young woman if she was—as it appeared—at the center of this ambush.

With a fleeting image of the television screen, the memory of those familiar shadows passing behind Molly Anderson, Luke swallowed a few hardy gulps of the whiskey. A police interrogation might be the least of that young woman's worries. Lucius MacDade wouldn't need to place a long-distance call to see justice done.

God help her and her accomplices if Liam didn't survive . . . and in an odd epiphany, Luke wondered at his sense of justice and morality when he would condone whatever measures Gillis would enlist even if it involved Ryan McDade.

PART TWO

Gets Burnt

16

For the first time in forever in Liam's mind, he was fully awake and aware of himself and his surroundings, but he had more reason to doubt than to believe. In slow-moving pictures, he recalled journeys to and from surgical rooms, remembered watching his blood flowing, some into tubes from a portal on his wrist, some at his waist to roll toward his back and lower regions. Panicky faces, anxious voices . . . and flames.

Brow furrowed, he rested in position to watch a cloud drifting across a blue sky, a sight he'd beheld on countless occasions. And why that sight annoyed him, he wasn't certain. Just a blasted blue sky and white puffy clouds . . . and he'd seen blackness through those drab brown curtains. Dark and light, day and night. A rancid smell filled his lungs and that, too, irritated him. At the motion, his attention shifted, and for an instant, he wanted to reach over that bar and strangle the little woman in his view. He could. Her neck would probably fit easily in his single palm . . . but he came to his senses—slightly. "Blue skies should accompany fresh air, don't you think?"

She managed a wary smile, wise woman that she might be, but when she parted her lips and spoke, Liam had more reason to doubt. "Feeling a little better today, are we?"

"I dinnae know what the hell yer feeling, but I'm fine."

From a distance away, a lyrical voice sighed, "Uh huh."

Tipping his head, Liam spied his wife rising from the recliner as if uncoiling from a nap. He might have known she was there. Seemed she was always there, just beyond his grasp.

A smile playing on her lips, she continued as she came forward. "Our wayward grouch is among us.

"I dinnae ken who yer calling a grouch, but—"

"Good morning, my love,"

That stopped him, and she might have spoken the words with that in mind, which was yet another irritation. "Aye, good morning," he growled.

"You might take note, dear, I'm not asking how you're feeling," she mused, and even with the weariness apparent in her drawn features, her eyes twinkled with natural mirth. "With all that growling, I'm fairly certain I already know."

"You look tired, Nate," he said and watched her lashes dip with the flash of irritation that forever amused him. His lips quivered uncontrollably, and judging her ire on the rise already, he thought it prudent to attempt to cover his smile. He managed to lift a hand and knuckle his mustache without hitting himself in the nose despite the heaviness in his arm. If he'd hoisted a Sequoia with his bare hands, he wouldn't be more bone weary, and the thought countered his slightly elevated mood. Far more sober, he studied her. "You do look tired. How . . . how long have we been here?"

"Too long," she answered while lifting a hand, brushing the hair off his forehead.

That action seemed far too familiar, and this view, him flat out and her hovering above him, seemed even more so. "How long?"

"Three weeks and two days," she answered directly.

Three weeks—two days. "Nearly a month? You are telling me—"

"Liam," she said haltingly and stilled her hand on his head. "You've had us scared spitless. So do refrain from ranting."

Well, that put him in his place. "I . . . I'm sorry."

A gentle smile touched her lips. "Well, maybe I won't mind you ranting just a little," she commented. "It's good to see you, m' darling."

"Aye, and you, m' love," he managed and saw the flicker in her eyes, surprise. Odd, these epiphanies in his waking moments. He did love her, this wild-eyed woman with wisps of honey-dipped waves catching the morning light at her temples. She wore her hair in a ponytail and flashed an image of how she wore those colored bands at her brow when she donned those skin-tight suits for her classes. If she had ever stepped from their house without a skirt over that suit, she wouldn't have gotten far, and he could think of a hundred ways he might have distracted her onto another course. Even weary, she was perhaps, the most attractive woman alive, barring none . . . and he should have been satisfied. That he might lose her, might have already lost her, played heavy on his mind.

On a slow-moving tide, Liam collected a few more thoughts than he cared to acknowledge, not the least of which was a conversation about a divorce.

"If you're truly awake, darling, would you like the bed lifted?"

Liam nodded distractedly, having heard that question a time or two. Unconsciously, he gripped, prepared for the fire that generally accompanied the motion, but no more than a twinge affected him as his view improved. Three weeks—and it felt more like years. Forever, he'd seen these canned posters, one of which was a reprint of an original painting that hung in his home office. Cheap cherry wood framed the doors and windows; resin-marble formed window ledges between the cotton drapes. A flat-screen TV stood dormant across the room within a circle of vinyl-covered couches. He'd seen his sons on those couches. His sons, his mother, brother, father . . . and others. At least several dozen others had stood above him, there and gone. None had stayed long, but they'd come in a steady stream.

And the odd memory touched him to recall Gregor clasping his hand in an iron fist, tears streaming down his handsome face, unchecked as he leaned on his forearms at the rail. 'Do not die on me, damn you . . . Don't you dare die on me and leave me to this mess . . . I don't want to be responsible for all these people . . . That's your birthright, damn you . . . Don't you dare leave me, Brother. . . .'

His focus through the glass, his attention caught again on a cloud drifting over the pale blue sky. Irritating. "I'm blasted sick of looking at that fucking sky."

A laugh stifled. In his improved position, Liam focused on his wife. She wore a soft beige sweater, cashmere to his thought, and blue jeans of an indeterminant brand, and she might as well be wearing an evening gown bedecked in jewels. "How the bloody hell can you make everything you wear, look like it came straight from Versace? How the bloody hell do you manage that, love?"

Her smile quivered more, betraying the sobriety she attempted to convey in her eyes. "I'm nearly certain there's a compliment in there somewhere. Though, with that cursing and the like, it's rather hard to tell."

"I'm getting blasted hard—" *Blast!* They weren't alone. He flashed a glance to the skinny nurse, who suddenly appeared preoccupied with something at her medical cart, and there was no hiding either the amusement to flash in his eyes or the integrity of his announcement. With the laughter alight in Natalie's eyes, he managed to lower his tone to admit. "Well, I am. And myself feeling like I've been dragged down the Devil's Staircase."

"Keep it up, lad, and I might take you there,"

Oh lord, but that was a loaded remark. Lifting a brow, Liam studied her attempt at sobriety and knew her intended meaning. "I . . . need a shower."

"Cold."

"Blast."

She laughed, unable to keep up pretenses. Leaning, she landed against him, burying her head in the nook of his shoulder, hugging him at shoulder and side. "Welcome back, mine own," she whispered at his ear.

Without conscious thought, he wove his arm about her shoulder and might have tried dragging her on top of him if not for his other hand locked in her grip. "Aye, good to be back." Content to merely hold her, he drew in the honeysuckle scent and caught a breath of heather on his tongue, starkly aware of the breath he'd craved when looking at the blue sky. "Aye, good to be back," he idled.

In slow degrees, she eased away, her eyes still shining with moisture as she studied him, and in an odd moment, he felt her there, touching inside of him, searching him. Odd, indeed, to suffer her weird talent and know the integrity of the same. "Finding else of interest?"

She retracted physically and mentally on the instant and looked as though he might have slapped her, so completely was her distress. She couldn't appear more embarrassed if she stood naked in a crowded room. "I uhm . . ."

He squeezed her hand, halting her liquid shine. "Settle."

That stopped her. She stared at him as if she were daft and that word beyond her ken.

Liam had heard that word often enough in his senses to have the lyric embedded in his mind for all time, and the stillness to spill over him was like balm on a wicked pain. Still, she looked at him, doubting and oddly afraid. "Natalie," he said quietly. "It's all right, truly. Whatever your means, it's not a thing I fear and nothing I'd be fool enough to reject or uhm . . . take advantage of, if you ken?"

Doubt still touched her eyes, but the revelation reached her on some distant plane as the smile eased into her lips. "You are better," she said quietly.

"Aye, weary. But the heat's doused, I do believe."

"We should probably call your father and mum. They only left here a few hours ago."

Considering a few lucid moments, he realized, "They've been here often."

"Your uhm . . . your father rented a rather large house a few blocks away," she said with a bemused smile. "Of course, he keeps calling it The Shack, as if twenty blasted rooms aren't enough."

"Please don't tell me he's moved our headquarters to New York."

"Not quite, but I think he might be thinking about buying The Shack. It's rather nice and sits on the Deleware. Might make a nice summer home."

"Good grief, I think you're serious," he said dubiously.

Her laugh alluded to a partial jest. "Well, he's mentioned it, but I don't think he was serious. More the fact, he was trying to bait your mum to distraction."

She sobered too quickly, and Liam understood he was the reason. "I uhm . . . I don't remember a hell of a lot," he admitted, feeling oddly inadequate. "I seem to recall being awake . . ." Divorce. A mention of a divorce. His sons in the room. He'd seen his daughter, too . . . her bright blue eyes searching him and her tiny delicate hands reaching for him. "Arabella . . . you held her."

A haunted shine lifted in her eyes as she nodded.

"I don't bloody remember much. Just blasted glimpses."

"Liam," she said haltingly and squeezed his hand. "You've been ill. So blasted ill," she said quietly. "They said it was a staph infection, and it hit you so blasted fast—" The spooked shine flickered yet again in her eyes. "We thought we lost you, damn it." The vibration in her grip reinforced the fear she'd endured, and he squeezed her hand unconsciously. "Don't ever frighten me like that again. Do you ken?"

The unspoken threat struck him rather funny and blast that twitch in his mustache! Before he could even lift a finger to smooth it away, her hazel eyes sparked fire.

"You think this is funny?" she asked with her ire on the rise. "Scare the hell out of an entire clan—two blasted clans—and you think—"

"Settle, lass," he managed and attempted complete sobriety, but damn, how he enjoyed seeing her temper. Far better than her sorrow or fear. "I can see clearly—you're annoyed with me."

"Annoyed?" she asked as if incredulous. "You've aged your poor mum by a decade. You have your both sons changing their career paths to become doctors. Your poor father's been growling like a wounded bear. We've been on the news more often than the blasted president, and you believe I'm—annoyed?"

Well, she put him in his place again and sobered him considerably. "I am sorry, lass, I didnae mean to inconvenience—" And the revelations slammed him. The fight. The hours spent before the fight. The news. Her being drawn into whatever twisted tale his father and Mason had concocted to save face. If he was not depressed when waking, it struck full force, now, and he wondered, again, how she could stand beside him still.

"Liam," Natalie interrupted. "I don't like it when you brood, and I'm sorry if I started that. I'm not annoyed at you, my love. I was terrified for you. Make no mistake there. We've all been terrified. Just to see you sitting here—even if you are brooding—is more the wonder and joy in my mind."

"How can you—" *Bear to look at me?* "We need to talk, lass."

"Suppose we do," she sighed. "But not with you just returning from Heaven's gate," she decided. "I'm calling your parents, and you, m' lad, are going to rest again before chaos descends."

"I . . . I'd like to get a bloody shower," he realized and flashed a glance toward the skinny nurse who'd been far too often in his glimpses in all manner of humbling motion. She perked up at his words, which struck him a low blow. "Standing," he said in a low tone. To be bathed by a woman might not disturb him if the woman was his wife, and she stood under the shower with him . . . and if he had the strength to act upon those ministrations. In his present state, he wasn't equipped to follow through, but he damn sure refused to be hand-washed by a stranger while lying down.

"Liam," Natalie interrupted. "You might want to rethink that decision. You've barely stood up in the past several weeks. Might be you'll need to regather your great strength before—"

"You assist me," he decided. And this time, she paused. "I've been afoot." At least he was reasonably certain that the skinny woman—and a stout male—had helped him rise a time or two. "There's a chair or the like in there," he recalled.

"Liam, you have IVs and uhm . . . there's that PICC line."

He had tried to ignore that second site of tape and tubes at his arm, but he supposed the reality was upon him. Far too often, he'd seen bags of medicine hung above his head and tubes connected to those dangling lines. The tube, as he'd heard, traveled up his bicep, through his vein, and directly into his heart. A nightmare of itself to think of some foreign line availing his heart to all manner of deadly ills.

"Ma'am," the nurse intruded. "If he truly feels up to getting a shower, we can cover those lumens, and there is a chair in the shower if he needs to rest. I could assist him if you'd prefer."

Liam flashed her a doubting glance and tipped his gaze in time to see Natalie's eyes flicker. Was there just a touch of venom in that gaze? Perhaps a hint of protectiveness or jealousy? Would she let this stranger . . .? Blast.

With a bemused shine quick in her eyes, she decided, "I'll help you, my dear, but if you try any funny business, I'm going to clout you."

"Well, hell," he muttered, eyeing her for the jest. He would likely get clouted.

After more than two full weeks in intensive care and another week of sleeping, more often than not, a lesser man would have diminished. Liam Mac-Dade had paled only in complexion, and Natalie couldn't help but notice that little else had changed. As proportionate as an ivory sculpt, his muscled shoulders flowed into his broad chest, amply adorned in a mat of soft blond curls. The same color as his hair, high and low, Natalie had noted the first time she'd seen him in his altogether. A sight to stir any sensible woman's blood, but she held careful rein under his watchful eye. That she might be nervous, and by his smirk, he knew it, bode not well on her—or him. Sitting as sturdy as a blasted lord holding court, he feigned a helpless expression . . . right up until she used the handheld showerhead to douse him.

Sputtering a curse, he dipped his head under the spray, and Natalie almost regretted her attempt to drown him. Standing clear of the overspray, she continued to soak him from head to heel. The bathroom was far too small with such a large man in attendance. No matter her effort, when she began dashing the cloth over his broad back, she brushed against his thigh and knee. Keenly aware of the physical contact, even without the warm water soaking her jeans, when he cleaved her hip and drew her legs against him, she nearly forfeited her task.

"Liam," she started with the proper amount of gravity, but she caught his blue eyes oddly conflicted when he lifted his gaze. Vulnerable. He appeared vulnerable. And strangely hurt. And her attention flashed to the wicked, jagged scar which had only begun to heal recently. "You're hurt," she decided and met his fleeting gaze. "I don't think you were ready—"

"Sadly, that's true, or I'd be standing, not sitting like some blasted lame duck."

In a glance, she read his distress, finding him already half-risen. At least that hadn't changed. She could still roust him without much effort but now was not the time. "Settle, lad, or I'm liable to turn that fancy knob to the far right."

"Lord, but that's a wicked thought," he groused. "And a thought here, you'd likely give me a blasted heart attack."

Worry fleeted in her eyes. "We need to hurry this, my dear. Sit still."

"Lass, I didnae move a muscle . . . Well . . . maybe one."

"Damn you, settle," she snapped and slapped the washcloth on his chest.

Subtly, he moved, leaning against the smooth tile wall to avail himself of her ministrations. "Uhhh . . .? Lower?"

"Good grief, you're impossible," she muttered, desperately trying to control the rampant thoughts igniting. And again, he knew his effect, flashing a glimpse of pearly whites beneath that soft mustache. If she were less a sensible woman, she would take advantage of his vulnerable state, but alas, he wasn't quite up to par, no matter what his head inclined. Sighing, she halted her hands, one at his shoulder, one dipping toward the bottom of the hourglass formed in fur, and met his gaze. "Maybe you better take this cloth, m' love. I'll wash your hair—"

"Aye," he idled with a more wry smirk.

"The hair on your head, dangit," she said, irritably, and favored him with a heated shine. "And we'll return you to that bed unscathed."

"I'd rather be scathed."

"Liam," she sighed. "There's no denying where this could go, but we're not going there, just now." Seeing the quick regret and memory of their celibate marriage in his eyes, she sighed, lifting her hand to touch her fingertips to his beard-stubbled jaw. "We'll get there, love," she said simply, stating a fact. "But not today. Not with you as weary as everyday past."

Whether he doubted her words or merely resigned to the weariness, he wore the shadows in his eyes as he nodded and took the dripping cloth from her grip. "Aye, I think you're right."

Cupping his cheek, stilling his weary gaze, she slid her thumb over his lips that never fully scowled. She'd prayed for this moment, to have him looking at her through eyes nearly as dark blue as a midnight sky and as clear as crystal. Tingles spread through every fiber of her being as she grasped the reality of his repair. He was alive and aware and on the road to recovery at last. "I have missed you, Liam," she said softly, honestly.

"I've put you through hell," he idled grimly.

Whether he meant the past weeks or the past months, she wasn't sure, and it didn't matter. "We're coming out the other side, love. Let's hold to that."

"Aye, I'd like nothing better, my love. Can you truly forgive me?"

With the stillness in his cobalt eyes and the firm set of his slightly curved lips, he awaited that answer with every weary bone in his considerable body.

"Aye, Liam MacDade, I can and have," she said quietly, and for a long moment, he seemed to doubt before the smirk quivered on his lips and a weight eased off his brow.

"You are a wonder, woman," he said almost wistfully. "I just wish you weren't so damnably right at this moment. I don't think m' lad's up to the task my mind's suggesting." And him leaning against the tile wall wasn't so much arrogance as it was necessary. "I am tired."

"Let's get you rinsed and dried before we need Tanya R.'s help."

"She probably wouldn't mind."

"I'm sure she wouldn't," Natalie mused, recalling at least one overheard conversation concerning a wayward giant in their midst. Not a single blasted nurse in attendance minded ministering to their charge, whether helping him into clean clothes or bathing the sweat off him. Was it any wonder he was a blasted rogue? With a wink and a smile—hell, nearly at death's door—women fell under his spell.

"Nate," he said as she reached for the handheld showerhead that had continued spewing warm water and filling the small basin at their feet. "You look as tired as I feel. I wouldn't mind if you'd rather sit this one out. I have a feeling there's not much that lass hasn't already seen here."

Far and too much, she might have mentioned, but doubted he was of a mind to grasp the teasing in her words. "I don't mind, honestly, darling. I promise not to drown you again, and I won't touch that cold water knob."

"I always knew you were a kind and gentle woman," he said wearily.

"Probably best to hold your breath a moment."

Careful but quick, Natalie rinsed and dried him, though he assisted when he could. By the time he stood in the pale blue pajama pants and a clean diamond print gown, his color had paled, and his actions had slowed. Still, he insisted she step out so he could attend his private business.

"I'll be right outside the door," she agreed and stepped out, worried as the seconds turned into minutes. She was about to knock when the door opened, and despite the hospital attire, she was stunned by the transformation. He'd shaved and combed his wet tangles into order, and the weary amusement in his eyes was an honest reflection of the man she'd married. "I was beginning to worry," she admitted and scanned him from head to toe and back. "But it was worth the wait, so I see."

"Found the mouthwash," he said and quivered a natural smile. "Maybe you won't be feart to come too close, now, eh?"

"Mmm, you mean like this?" In a single step, she closed the distance, slipped her hands about his waist, and need not stand on her toes as he met her halfway. Oh, and the fire to flash through her system as she tasted the spearmint on his lips, on his tongue, and felt the warmth of his arms encircling her shoulders and waist, drawing her to rest against the length of him. Never had she doubted how well they fit together, no matter the difference in their height. For such a tall, solid man, he was whipcord lean, without an ounce of muscle wasted on his sturdy frame. Weary, by no means weak, he held her in an iron grip, drawing her deeper into a kiss to stir the rampage at her core. Only a genuine sense of his exhaustion lent her pause to withdraw before she might have climbed his trunk to satisfy her own insatiable needs.

On a breath, his eyes the color of polished cobalt, he uttered, "What say we send the li'l lass on an errand . . .?" He paused to draw breath, finishing, "And lock that door for an hour or so?"

"We," she needed a breath as well to continue. "Need you well, mine own, as I don't think an hour will suffice."

"Blooody hell, lass. You're incinerating me here."

She drew breath, deciding, "Let's get you to bed."

"Ahhh man," he huffed and rolled his eyes, sounding as young and American as he was. "You're slaying me here."

Stifling her laugh with an effort, she kept her arm about him while sidling under his arm, all too aware of his weight coming against her. Not nearly as healthy as he appeared, he needed her help to start toward the bed but veered, deciding, "The recliner."

Barely, she settled him into the chair when she stated, "I am phoning your parents, now, Liam—"

From behind Natalie, the low voice idled, "No need, lass."

Pivoting a half turn, Natalie found Lucius leaning in the doorway, looking as though he were holding the building aloft by the doorframe. How such a large man could arrive so blasted quietly was a mystery—one she dare not attempt to solve with the fellow glancing between them with a lifted brow, a pensive set in his bearded lips. If Liam resembled a Highlander Lord, this man was undoubtedly the King of his Highland castle. Catching a glimpse of Liam's shared surprise, Natalie wasn't consoled. He, at least, had the excuse of his illness for delaying that phone call. "I uhm . . . Well, we were about to call. He's feeling . . ." *Better.*

The brow arched higher and, but a second longer, he held his pose before pushing off the frame, emitting a deep rumble of laughter and lighting the joy in his moist blue eyes. On his son, his attention riveted as he crossed the room, circling the bed. When it looked as if he might drag Liam from the chair—which apparently crossed Liam's mind as well as he seemed to brace for impact—Lucius leaned and landed an immense palm on the damp head, scuffing the combed hair into a riot of curls.

"Here, now, Da! That's attached—"

"So it is," Lucius mused and used his massive palm to tip Liam's head until their identical blue eyes met and merged in mirth. "By the fair and merciful Good God, it's good to see you, m' boy."

"Aye, likewise, sir," Liam spoke in natural rhythm and respect.

"Was our Natalie to mention you were coming aboot last eve, but I didnae expect to find yerself fully turned so soon." He favored Natalie with a warm and wondrous shine, nodding. "I dinnae know why I even doubted yer fine self. Yer far more bloomin' accurate than all those doctors we're paying."

Uncomfortably, Natalie glanced toward the space across the empty bed where one or another of the private nurses generally lingered. The room was empty except for the three of them, and still, she suffered a mild discomfort. Too new, too disconcerting to have the MacDades' belief and acceptance, but they seemed only to take her talent in stride. She gleaned the two sets of identical eyes mirroring an almost peculiar intensity—likewise disturbing. They both grasped her discomfort, and neither appeared to understand it.

Her husband seemed even more curious and befuddled; his caught head started to tip a fraction before Lucius scuffed his hair and slicked the damp locks back as if to restore order to the riot of waves.

The effort to return order to the soft blond locks failed, and Liam's resemblance to either of his sons, especially with the flicker of amusement lancing his eyes, was far more visible.

That the expression of innocence filtered down from the elder to the younger only amused Natalie more. How these devils could portray such vivid mirth was yet another mystery. No matter the circumstances, they could flit from laughter to rage and back again quicker than most people could change slip-on shoes.

"Aye," Lucius idled, studying Liam with a soft shine. "Thar's life in yer fine eyes and my joy to finally see it there."

"I uhm . . . I've heard I've been gone a while," Liam admitted. And the sobriety in his low voice couldn't be mistaken, any more than the sudden intensity directed at his father "I di-on't even want to think about how much paperwork is stacking up."

"And you shouldn't," Lucius stated bluntly.

"We had . . . damn it. We had several contracts pending."

Natalie glimpsed the elder's amusement and, like polar opposites, the younger's dismay. She understood both expressions.

"Aye, we did," Lucius barely kept the vibration at bay.

"I din—don't see the humor here," Liam said as he tipped his head against the recliner cushion and studied his father with sincere dismay.

"Well, not humor exactly, but simple truth. This is the first time in weeks that yer seeming to remember we have a business to run."

"Well . . ." Apparently, Liam wasn't certain what to say to that and appeared slightly more dismayed as the weariness dragged at him. "We do . . . and the Pendleton deal—"

"Is on hold," Lucius stated, sober on the instant. "It'll keep. As will most others. And I have Mason tending to anything pressing. Much as I appreciate yer interest here, son, you need concentrate on regaining your strength."

He nodded, but his gaze remained sober, pensive. "We should discuss a few things."

"Aye, I'm sure we should, and will upon a time," Lucius said just as soberly. "But this isn't it."

"I'm nearly certain, I've heard that a time or two," he idled and favored Natalie with a slightly weary smile. "But I am awake," he said while including them both in a glance.

"Liam," Natalie sighed. "You are awake and exhausted. Nothing is pressing that can't wait another few hours or a day."

"The uhm . . . urgency might only be in my mind, love, but it's there. I uhm . . . I need to speak with my father. Could you give us a few moments, and uh . . . shut the door there?"

The urgency, founded or unfounded, was palpable in his eyes, and the conflicts were likewise visible. She wouldn't argue a second time. "I'll just go and check on your breakfast then." Without a first or second thought, she dipped and brushed a kiss on his furry lips, skimming her fingertips over his clean-shaven cheek. Before he could reach and draw her deeper, she slipped away. "Don't be too hard on yourself, darling," she said and wondered at her words even as she fleeted a glance off Lucius's peculiar gaze and turned to the door. *Don't you be too hard on him, either,* she might have spoken aloud.

17

Waiting until Lucius settled into the second recliner, positioned at an angle so they could speak without craning their necks, Liam began. "What have I missed? Besides closing the Pendleton deal?"

"As I said, nothing that can't wait."

"Da-ad," he started and suffered the distraction of the brogue to slide too quickly off his lips. It was not as if he minded speaking with the brogue, but unlike his father, he'd been born on American soil. Seemed almost a betrayal of his heritage to adopt the auld country dialect, even if he'd been raised on those flowing notes.

"Aye?"

"Bloody hell," Liam muttered and realized that curse was just as bad. He sounded more British than American now, and that, he could blame on far too many relatives across the pond. Which could account for his thoughts flitting. "We had . . . I remember a lot of faces visiting here." And that was not exactly what he'd meant to say.

"Aye, a goodly lot of the clan stopped by," Lucius said, sobering, intent. "I'm not beating around a boosh, here, lad. There were too many times we thought you passing. Aye, and yourself in line of succession. You had visitors. Most to say some prayers over you."

A smile flickered on his bearded lips and fired his eyes. "Yer Aunt Matilda was here," he mused. "Blasted you with some fairy dust from the homeland, so she said, but the nurses here weren't so pleased when—well, I dinnae think they minded cleaning you up so much as they worried that ye'd suffer some other wicked ill from the dousing. To be honest, worried me some as well. I'm still not certain what the hell she put in that mix. Near to sent the lot of us sneezing to our own end."

The quiver tickled his mustache, and he brushed a knuckle on his lip to collect sobriety. But then, thinking of his sprite-like elder aunt and the effects she could have on the unsuspecting, he couldn't fully contain his amusement. Standing no taller than half his chest high, she wore the innocence of a child in her rounded rose-colored cheeks, and she was given to wearing men's trousers and shirts, generally with cuffed hems over army boots. She lived in the old country and walked with a crooked stick jutting a foot above her curly gray hair. He hadn't seen her in some time, not since making his rounds more than a year past, although he'd visited the Highlands this past spring.

"I di-don't remember her here," Liam admitted, disappointed to have missed her again.

"Aye, well," Lucius swung sober. "No surprise. You were near to under. So maybe yer aunt's dousing brought yer fine self back, after all."

"A-I need to know, Da-ad," he said and held his gaze steady despite the weariness tugging his head to the cushion. "What were the police told?"

More suddenly, his gaze intent but unfathomable, Lucius countered with a question. "What do you remember, lad?"

Therein lay the crux of his worry. "Not enough, I'm afraid. It uhm . . . I've worked out that it was an ambush of sorts. I remember two little blokes behind me . . ." He let the images scroll in sequence before continuing. "Aye, two, and the one to speak sounded reasonable, save for the handgun he held at my side." His focus found his father. "Was uhm . . . I don't remember if I was stabbed or shot. Seems I've been told both."

"Aye, both," Lucius confirmed. "Luckily was that bullet to pass through, but probably not so lucky that it might have initiated your decline. The knife wound nearly hid the blasted bullet wound. Aye, but yer here and a fine sight. So, and we dinnae need worry aboot else at the moment."

"How . . . Er why the bloody hell did you drag Natalie into this?"

"Excuse me?"

"Please tell me that was Mason's idea. Not yours," Liam said quietly, hovering on a precarious precipice. The answer could be a turning point in his feelings toward his father—a defining moment. If this fellow had dragged Natalie into this scheme to avoid tarnishing the MacDade name, Liam wasn't sure he could forgive him.

"Well, it was Mason's idea, but uhm . . .? You need to continue here, Liam. How much do you recall after those two approached you?"

Relieved, Liam drew a calming breath. Thinking, remembering the music drifting from open doors on the next block, the shuffle of soles on pavement, shadows, the nightlife . . . "They had help," he considered, listing his gaze though his internal sights held his focus. He remembered, "'Step into our office,' the one with the gun spoke and nudged me toward the alley opening." He focused on his father, shrugging slightly. "I don't remember actually seeing the others," he admitted. "Wasn't planning to step into their fecking office. Turned about before fully stepping into the shadows. S'pose that's when I got shot," he said indifferently, remembering. "Wasn't a large gun, probably a li'l .380. Sounded more like a firecracker pop than a serious weapon."

"Aye, was a .380. They found the casing in the alley."

Liam nodded. "Aye, didn't really feel any pain from that. Was the knife to make an impression, and by then, seemed like bloody flies swarming. I'd down one, and another took his place," he remembered, drifting his gaze, and in his mind's eye, he remembered. "There was another lad, there, then. I . . . I remember thinking it might be my end." His gaze landed, finding his father, but the confusion lingered in his mind.

"Another lad?" his father urged.

"Aye," he remembered with some effort. "I . . . I thought maybe a woman at first. The body was kicking and spinning, er . . . uhm, so I sort of remember." He shook his head, shrugging slightly. "Mine thought it was a boy, though. Tallish, thin fellow . . . wore glasses, I think. Was round reflections, and I didnae think it was an alien to be glowing so. Thus, I'm guessing, was a boy with glasses. Did uhm . . . he come forward?

"I uhm . . . What did the lad do there, kicking and the like?"

"I'm guessing he saved my life," Liam admitted. "If he's come forward, I'd like to repay him. And if not . . .? Has he?"

"What uhm . . . Did he say a thing to you? Have ye thought of why he came to yer aid?"

"He was not part of my assailants," Liam knew. "But no. I don't remember any words exchanged. The next I knew, I was waking—" And his attention riveted with where this had begun. "And Natalie was there when I came from surgery. Her—dressed to the nines . . . Why the hell did you let Mason drag her into this?"

"I'm still not following this train of thought, son. What makes you think she was dragged into this?"

And his father would make him say it, undoubtedly. Well, and the facts were the facts. "I was not where I should have been." He admitted and knew he couldn't exactly stop there, not when Mason certainly knew the facts, and hence, Lucius as well. Sighing, Liam shook his head, disgusted with himself and his circumstances. "No excuse for it," he said grimly then met his father's calm gaze. "Save for the fact, Natalie and I haven't uhm . . . Well, hell. You know we haven't slept together in months. No excuse, but . . . hell. I'm no angel, never claimed to be. It's one thing for her to suspect I was satisfying my selfish needs in a blasted cheap hotel, but another to drag her face through it."

"Aye, we're on the same plane there, but I'm still not following this train, lad."

"I'm guessing here, mind, but I figure Mason meant to squelch the fact that I was engaged in extramarital affairs. Our separation wasn't public knowledge, after all. So, I can certainly understand the scramble to save face, but Goddamn it . . . What the hell were the police told? What . . . does she know?"

For an unnaturally long moment, Lucius merely studied him, perhaps weighing his words. "Ye're looking weary," he decided.

"Da, I need those answers," Liam said quietly. "I'm fairly sure I'll need to speak with the police soon."

"Aye, in time. When your head's clear."

"Unless you answer a few of my questions, I doubt that will happen," he admitted. "I have a sense, she knows far more about the facts than I do. She's said we've made the news . . . More often than the president, as I recall. And that can't be good."

"Well, you are a MacDade, and no secret, the heir to the fortunes." His father shrugged. "Bound to be headlines."

"How bad, sir. These headlines?"

"Facts as they're known by the media," Lucius said at last. "You were leaving a business meeting at that hotel when you were assaulted. As far as the press and the like are concerned, it was a random act of violence," he barely paused. "The police have the name of your uhm . . . friend. But so far, she's not been found."

His attention riveted. "Alecia's missing?"

"Liam, how much do you know about this Miss Helms?"

"She's flexible—damn it," he uttered. "A dancer, actually." His gaze landed. "Exotic dancer, s'pose I should admit. Not a superstar in any regard."

"Filled a physical need, then, aye?"

"This is na-ot a conversation I'd like to have with you," he admitted. "But I sense you are headed in a direction that I might not like and need to go. Aye, she filled a physical need, and if you blasted need to know, I was getting bored. Too predictable—damn it. So, she's gone amiss, and I don't need to be a brain surgeon to ken you—er the police—figure she's involved in that ambush."

"Aye."

"And Natalie—she knows that as well?" he asked, hoping not to receive that answer.

"Aye, she knows," Lucius said and eyed Liam more intently. "That bothers you."

"More than I care to consider," he admitted grimly.

"Why is that, lad?"

"She and I," he started, and therein, the confusion took a stronger hold. In every waking moment, she hovered at the edges of his mind, if not front and center. "We've . . . not been close," he said resignedly, meeting his father's intent gaze without malice. If ever he'd held his father accountable for his loveless marriage, that time had passed. Like every eldest son with scant few exceptions in MacDade history, Liam had determined to honor his duty and perpetuate the lines. *Still* . . . "I'd not meant to hurt her."

"There's a connection here, but I'm hard-pressed to find it." Lucius prodded.

"You—or Mason—asked her to dress as if she and I were together on the town, maybe that I left her in one hotel while I conducted business in another. Am I close?"

"Aye, perhaps," Lucius idled. "As I said, we've managed to keep the media believing that you were on business. A few tabloids caught wind of your actual business, but their credibility came into question. And might be yer wife's participation there. She's a photogenic sort, our Natalie."

"Aaa-aye, she is that," Liam agreed, more weary with his concern. "And she was photographed . . . When—and in what circumstance?"

"Yer worrying far too much," Lucius said simply.

"Not near enough when I'm thinking you're worrying too little," he decided. "Is she in these blasted tabloids regarding some sordid affair? Er in the legitimate press in some reference to the same? How the bloody hell badly have I screwed up?"

"Ahhh, I see then," Lucius said in a feigned gravity, one brow lifted. "A wee bit of guilt rising to the surface here."

"More than a Goddamn little," he admitted, and although his ire was rising, little else changed in his pose. He was tired, and this conversation was sorely trying his patience. Just a fleeting memory of those wicked months after Arabella's birth nearly derailed his thoughts. Natalie had seemed fairly recovered . . . "Da-ad," he nearly growled. "I need to know how badly I've hurt her." *If this set her back—*

"Aye, fresh back from an early grave, and you're wondering how badly you hurt yer lovely wife—aye, and the two of you are not close."

"I'm not well, you know," he admitted, hoping to gain his father's sympathy and soon receive a straight answer

"Yer looking weary, and a mite peaked," Lucius said, appearing only more relaxed against the recliner.

"I should think you'd have a little mercy here," he grumbled.

"Son, you are weary," Lucius said more candidly. "So, and I'll mention—the publicity is bent toward yer favor. Our Natalie has countered any mention of any sordid affairs just by her presence. Only a fool would believe any man would stray from that stunning young lady."

Well, and that struck a chord.

"Lad," Lucius continued before Liam could react too severely. "You had yer reasons, and none have been made public. Our lass is in a fine position to be privy to the facts. She knows about your affair with this woman, and I think, perhaps, she blames her fine self, truth be known. If she'd been warming yer bed, ye'd nae have gone elsewhere."

"That's not fair," Liam stated, irritated again.

"Not saying I blame her, er you, but you wanted answers," Lucius reminded him with a subtle rise in his ire. "What you make of them is up to you."

What was that supposed to mean?

"Now, about this other," Lucius began on a different tract as if to derail his anger. "This other person—this good Samaritan to come to your rescue . . .? There's been no mention of him thus far, and at this late date, I'm seeing no good reason to change that."

"Other than the fact that I owe him my life," Liam commented.

"Aye, maybe so, but think about that a moment. With all the publicity, if uhm . . . this fellow wanted reward er glory, dinnae you think he would have come forth?"

Blast his father for sounding reasonable.

"I'm not saying we'll forget him, Liam, but what say I look into it quietly? My thought here, the lad might have his reasons for remaining anonymous. Could be he didnae want to be famous, er it could be he's wanted by the police . . . or uhm . . . maybe was yer physical state to alter that memory. Mason was there. He did mention seeing a body racing down the lane in your direction. So maybe you had a guardian angel, and the lad fled with the others. Either way, I think the police have enough to worry aboot."

Considering the possibilities, Liam nodded, his thoughts listing. "I uhm . . . s'pose you're right," he idled. "So uhh . . . what am I supposed to say to the police?"

"No more or less than what ye told to me, here. No reason to lie about a thing. They know about this Helms lass, and they know you were ambushed. They might want whatever descriptions you could give of yer attackers, but doubtful more than that."

"Those bastards were unremarkable, but I'll give the police what I can in that regard."

"Liam," Lucius said quietly, drawing Liam's gaze if only by the firm tone. "You need rest, lad. What say I help you back onto that bed?"

A raucous outside the door drew both their gazes, and Liam recognized the faint elevated notes of Micheal's young voice muffled through the wood. Weary or not, he needed to see them with only vague recollections of them peering at him from various angles.

Rising smoothly, Lucius paused, "The bed?"

"Think I'd prefer to see them sitting up," Liam decided, and Lucius cast an approving smirk before starting to the door.

Two rather large, colorful balloons bobbed through the door a half step before the sprites sidled through the opening. In a position to see both faces, Liam's chest ached with the clarity of mind to know what they'd endured. Both wrenched their necks to peer at their grandfather, then ambled a step. Almost in unison, they looked toward the bed . . . and the panic was there, etched in their widening eyes, parting lips. Fear blazed neon at the sight of that empty bed where their father had lay dying for too long.

"La-ads," Liam's voice broke uncontrollably on the lump in his throat, and with every ounce of his remaining strength, he battled the sting in his eyes. "Lads."

Both faces spun, and the fear vanished behind the joy igniting in their eyes. In harmony, they nearly shouted, "DA!" "Daddy!"

Balloons released and bobbed toward the ceiling as both boys sprung forward, evading their grandfather's intended clasp, their mother's hands.

Bracing for impact, Liam stifled a laugh as the pair parted, intent on ramming into his shoulders. Surprised and grateful, he watched them slide stop, landing one to either side of the recliner arms. Glancing between them, he grasped sense of them breathless, waiting, anticipating . . . and he merely opened a palm to either side.

"N—!" Natalie started.

Over the arms of the chair, both climbed. Their knees landed firm on the chair, only their arms drove forward, diving to strangle him in an embrace.

"Da!" Jamie huffed in the nook at Liam's shoulder, and against his cheek, Micheal's reddish locks jerked with a sobbed breath against his neck at his opposite side. "Mine-own-Da," Micheal heaved in spurts.

Hugging their quaking backs under either arm, Liam nearly buckled to his own sobbed breath while ducking his head between them. Drawing breaths of floral scents from their locks, his fingers slid into their curls, circling their heads to hold them close. "There, lads . . . No worries now," he idled and managed to blink the start of tears away, aware of Natalie hovering over Jamie's shoulder. Tipping his head enough to find her damp eyes glistening above the blond locks, Liam nearly lost all thought—so stunning was her pose. Caught in the strip of sunlight, her auburn waves appeared to glow . . . and the same ethereal shine lighted at the edges of the soft green sweater, refracting a rainbow of color in the fuzz.

"They've been worried, love," Natalie spoke, oblivious to striking him dumb. A smile played on her lips as she glanced between the buried heads, judging them safe from inflicting harm.

"Aye, so I'm seeing and feeling here," he muttered while scuffing a head in either palm. They were still shaking, Micheal close to sobbing, but whether his words or their good sense started them moving, both were attempting to withdraw. He held them quick, refusing to part so soon, and neither offered too much fight—luckily—before sinking into a more natural stranglehold.

"Well, and this was worth waking for, here," he mused. "Mine both arms full."

"I widnae mind ye staying awake for it either," Jamie rumbled in a muffled voice.

The simplicity of that statement, the integrity of the child's fear, nearly destroyed his tenuous rein. "Aye, and I will, m' lad."

Needing to be sure, Jamie lifted his head enough to spy Liam at close range, and perhaps, he saw more than he should. He rose slightly more, looking far more intent than a child of seven should ever appear. "May'en I could just sit here on this chair beside yer fine self?"

On the arm of the chair rather than any closer to the injuries, Liam understood, but it was the heavy brogue drawing his focus and vibrating a stifled laugh off his lips. "M' lad, I'm thinking here, you've been spending a good deal of time with yer grandad, eh?"

"Aye, Da, he's rented a wee Shack on the river," Jamie offered while easing to rest on the arm of the chair. In perfect balance, he sat sidesaddle, his blue-jean-covered leg dangling over the side, the other folded at Liam's thigh, his tennis shoe on the seat cushion. As arrogant as ever a lad, he rested his elbow on his knee and looked as if he might scratch his chin in a rendition of his grandfather. Pensive, his blue eyes spied his brother, and he reached, touching Micheal's shoulder above Liam's arm. "Micheal, let's we give our Da room to breathe now, eh?"

Had the lad turned into an adult in a few blasted weeks? Suffering an odd sway, Liam eased his arm aside as his younger son took his older son's advice and began sitting up. In a wet glance, the boy emulated his brother's pose except he landed his both tiny tennis shoes on the cushion and rested as if prepared to launch himself back into his father's arms. "Better, Da?" he asked carefully.

"Either way is fine, m' lad. I rather liked holding yer fine self, Dickens."

The smile enhanced on the soft lips, and his hazel eyes, like his mother's, shined with delight. He, too, seemed to scan Liam's face, searching for the reality. He barely thought to speak before sparkles flashed in his blue eyes, and his head spun, searching. "We brought ye balloons!" he said as he found them bobbing at the ceiling. Giggling, he looked to Liam. "Gran'da needs a get them down, now, Da. Lost the slippery buggers."

Liam chuckled and glanced at the bobbing balloons, reading the 'Get Well' wishes on both. Fleeting, he recalled other balloons—and flower arrangements—and the heady scent of too many blooms. With his thought, he scanned the room and noticed the absence of bouquets and overflowing vases, but he flashed a memory of flower-decked tables and ledges. As his father reached and plucked both wayward balloons off the ceiling, Liam suffered a hazy memory of a funeral. His focus shifted to find his wife's eyes upon him, and her smile faded. "Flowers," he remembered absently.

"Aye, Da," Jamie said gravely and drew Liam's gaze to find the dark blue eyes studying him suddenly. "But we didnae bring them."

"Uhhh." He was at a loss, but there seemed something serious a' mind here.

"Da," Micheal stated grimly, his young face as sober as an adult. "We're nae having none of that funeral business."

"Baby," Natalie said haltingly, and reached to the accessible strawberry blond curls, scuffing gently. "I told you about the flowers, sweetie. They were meant to help your daddy get better."

"Well, they didnae work," Jamie huffed in soft exasperation and found his father's confounded gaze. "You said it was like looking at yer own damn funeral with all them flowers suffocating you."

"Oh Lord," Liam muttered and glimpsed at Natalie's worried gaze before focusing on his son. "I have a feeling I might have said a lot of wicked things to scare the daylights out of—"

"Liam," Natalie interrupted. "You didn't," she said simply. "And I did explain to them how you were just having at a bit of raging." She quivered a smile. "Was rather by necessity we began taking the flowers with us. We barely had space to move about, and it was starting to look like a florist shop in here. Isn't that so, loves?"

"Aye," Jamie agreed stoically. "And smelled like one, too, Da. Gram'mum says it's because you have lots of friends, and we need be thankful, but I'll tell you, sir, the Shack smells like we opened two flower shops."

"We're gonna have to build a greenhouse, Gran'da said, just to hold 'em all."

"And the jet's gonna have to make two trips to get them all home," Jamie added soberly.

Stifling a laugh, Liam glanced between them, feeling somewhat like a pinball trying to keep up.

Spontaneously, Micheal leaned forward and wrapped his arms around Liam's neck, his voice barely muffled, "I love yer fine self, Da."

"Oh, Lord, I love you, too, my fine lad," he uttered and drew Jamie into his other arm, holding them both with equal pressure. "Aye, and I love you both more than breath."

"I love you too, Dad," Jamie said in precise English.

If he could just rest here, holding his sons for the next ten years, he would be content, but life had a way of intruding. At the edges of his mind, he gleaned the intrusion as candidly as he knew himself sinking and buckling to the weariness. More than half asleep, he barely understood Natalie slipping Micheal away and his father lifting Jamie afoot. The chair seemed to unfold of its own accord, and on some distant plane, he heard the voices whispering.

A soft panicky voice near to crying, "Waaake him up, Mummmy."

"Shhh," Liam managed. "Just need to rest a minute, son . . ." Or so he hoped he said.

"Your daddy's just sleeping, baby," Natalie whispered, and held Micheal on her hip, straining against tears to see the panic on his handsome face. Liam's words had stilled him, and he rested now, fisting the tears from his eyes as he looked down at his father, judging the integrity of her words. "He just needs to rest, the way you needed to rest after you caught that awful cold last summer. Remember, sweetie, how you were so tired you didn't even want to play ball with Jamie?"

"I 'member, Mum," he uttered, now, whispering not to wake his father.

Standing at her side, Jamie clasped his brother's shoe, commenting, "He's just sleeping, now, Micheal. We have to be quiet, now."

"We didnae even give him his balloons," Micheal uttered, looking at Natalie with his sorrow.

"He saw them, love," she assured him. "And he'll see them again when he wakes."

Megan held both balloon ribbons, now, and she battled a well of tears as she suggested, "Why don't we just hang them here on his bed?"

"Okay," Micheal muttered, and Natalie let him slide afoot. As both boys sidled to assist their grandmother, Natalie glimpsed Lucius studying his sleeping son, and by the tension in his gaze, she reacted to search Liam for a sign of distress. He was sleeping, this once, merely sleeping. She barely thought to question her father-in-law when she found him searching her with equal intensity. "Da?"

"What say we go find a cup of coffee?" he asked, and Natalie knew better than to decline. The small private waiting room had been turned into a fully stocked lounge—complete with a small icebox filled with assorted popsicles and a coffee pot with gourmet blend coffees in single-cup servings.

If he wanted coffee, he wanted privacy.

"Sounds good," Natalie said and favored Megan with a smile. "Can we bring you something, Mum?"

"Just had a tea, dear. Thank you, though."

Accepting Lucius's escort, she strode into the quiet hall, halfheartedly wondering where the nurse had gone. They were never too far away, and Natalie solved the mystery, spotting Tanya R. coming from the private station just past the waiting room.

Like all other of Liam's private duty nurses, she walked with purpose, dark hair pulled into a ponytail and an all-business expression on her lovely face. At the sight of them, the nurse hastened her stride, appearing worried, nearly breaking to run. "Is he—"

"He's sleeping," Natalie said before the woman could panic or Lucius could scare her more by his mere presence. As Natalie had noted more than once in the past three weeks, the staff at Southern General tended toward panic when any of the MacDade males graced their presence, but Lucius more so than any others.

A formidable man, her father-in-law, but Natalie had never found cause to fear him. Considering his posture at that doorjamb with her and Liam locked in that embrace, Natalie could imagine Lucius merely canting his head to send the stunned nurse fleeing.

By no surprise, Lucius pulled the door closed behind them, and perhaps, he truly wanted a cup of coffee as he sidled to the newly installed serving cart providing a stack of ceramic mugs. Not exactly fine crystal, but probably better than the industrial wares in the cafeteria—assuming a cafeteria existed. Natalie had heard one mentioned, but as regular as clockwork, a catering service arrived with as many meals as needed.

Without a need to ask, Lucius selected her favored brand and started the first cup brewing. He was brooding, she gleaned as she watched him choose another brand at random.

"I could get that," she offered.

"Sit, lass. We'll have this done in a blink."

And he needed a moment to collect his thoughts, she understood, and meandered to the window, merely scanning the busy street below. The day seemed brighter somehow. As though the sun had risen for the first time in weeks and streaked to reflect lasers off windshields and chrome. Another press release, she considered. One of more than a half dozen with the Chief of Staff insisting on offering the public updates, and still, several reporters, photographers, and well-wishers lingered just off the hospital property, waiting for that first big newsbreak.

By now, Dr. Ed Turner had likely rallied his troops, thrilled with the news he would finally impart.

Absently, Natalie accepted the cup handed into her view and managed a mere sip before she realized who stood at her side and nearly spilled hot coffee over her fingers with her start. Had she been so blasted deep in thought she could forget in whose presence she stood? Whether he meant to announce another press release . . .

She found his gaze, already doubting that message before reading the bemusement twinkling in his eyes. "I uhm . . . Thank you, Da," she said awkwardly.

"Been a long journey, lass. No shame in being weary."

"For you as well, but I think he's genuinely on the mend."

"Aye," he muttered, and looked out the window, appearing more pensive.

"Sir?" she asked with a sprinkle of tingles at her nape.

Sighing, he canted his head and spied her at an angle, his peculiar expression caught somewhere between curiosity and doubt. "Daughter, I need tell you. Your fine husband's as mixed and muddled as a man can get."

"He uhm . . . Well, he's lost more than three weeks. I don't think we need worry too much."

"Lass, following my lad's thoughts is like trying to catch a blasted pixie sprinkling fairy dust," he said gravely. "And I'm not so certain the past three weeks are the problem."

An odd sense of the man's unnatural befuddlement touched her far more deeply than his concern. "Sir?"

"I need to have mine thoughts put in order here," he said smoothly. "Tell me again how you came to be in that alley, will you?"

He was not a fellow who would need details repeated a second time, and his asking was more a curiosity than all else. "I followed him from that lounge. The Castaway," she said lightly.

"Aye, then you sat in the cab for nigh on three or four hours," he said while watching her intently. "And whence you saw him attacked, you raced to his rescue."

She nodded, wondering if he doubted.

"The problem is this, mo nighean," he said carefully and continued, "Mine fine son has no recollection of yerself in that alley. He's twisted and muddled the facts in his mind. He has himself believing Mason and myself somehow convinced yourself to enter into some blasted scheme to spare the clan a taint. And therein lies the greater problem. Do ye see where I'm heading with this?"

"I . . . wish I did, Da. I'm not following."

"Aye, there it is then. Mine own problem. Was blasted hard to keep up with his spinning wheels. I'm not certain if he's holding himself, my self, or Mason's self to blame for putting yourself in this circumstance, but he's bloody well blaming one of us."

She studied him carefully, as befuddled as he appeared. "Ere uhm . . . I'm to blame, then?"

He nearly flinched with his start. "Daughter, I didnae mean to imply any sooch thing, and my apology if it seemed thus," he said and offered the sincerity in his expression, as surely as his sudden concentration. "I think what I'm asking here, is if ye intend to set him straight?"

"Uhm . . . in what way do you mean, then?"

"Comes down to this, daughter, and mind, I'm not saying you must, but do you intend to tell him that you followed him? And thus, rested in position to rescue him?"

Leave it to this great bear of a man to hit upon the one question she'd been wrestling with for the past three weeks. Tilting her gaze through the window, Natalie drew a swallow of coffee, searching that answer . . . and suffering the intensity, as well as the patience in the fellow beside her. A conflict, to be sure. Especially when she'd believed Liam already knew.

"I'm truly not saying you must," Lucius said carefully, watching her still. "Right now, he knows he had help in that fight. He believes another lad came to his rescue, and he alluded to wanting to find his savior and offer reward. I uhm . . . might have convinced him to leave the fellow be and might have suggested I'd personally look into finding this Good Samaritan to repay him."

Natalie had turned her gaze about and found Lucius leaning at the table and studying her intently. "He thinks . . . Oh lord, I didn't even think about that foolish disguise," she realized. "I just assumed he'd already known it was me, but . . . he truly wasn't fully conscious by the time I reached him. But—" She focused inward, remembering those moments as she'd held him, begging him to live. "I know he heard me talking to him."

"Aye, but I think the sequence is muddled in his mind. Think he knows you were there when he came out of surgery, but I think he believes we were all there by then. He truly believes we convinced ye to play this part."

"But why the hell would that blasted matter one way or another?"

"Lass, comes down to him feeling guilty for hurting you, and there's not a thing he's accustomed to feeling."

"He's never had any qualms about his carousing . . ." Reining her irritation, Natalie averted her gaze through the window and sipped the coffee if only to swallow her ire.

"Aye," Lucius said quietly. "And I'm guessing this Helms lass is not the first one you've known about."

She shook her head, feeling the frustration that had set her on this path. "I . . . I know he's never loved me, not the way a man should love his wife—"

"Lass—"

"It's all right, Da," she said and sought his concentrated gaze. "Truly. We were both consenting adults and knew what we were getting into, so I couldn't blame him for searching elsewhere for what was missing. It's just that . . . if I thought for one minute that he'd be happier elsewhere, I'd not hold him to the bargain. And no amount of family tradition or pressure would change my decision. I'd let him go. And that's what I needed to know. What he'll need to hear when he's well enough."

"Lass, these affairs . . . They didnae mean a thing to him."

"Perhaps, but sooner or later, he'll find what he's looking for."

"Daughter," Lucius said grimly. "Tell me thus . . . Do you love him?"

More than life itself, she might have admitted, but answered quietly, "That doesn't matter."

"Aye, it matters a great deal, my dear, and it may be a thing he needs to hear."

How had they gotten into this conversation? Turning her gaze through the glass, distracted by the sound of a car horn in the distance, she followed the slow progress of a van . . . a white van on the street below. Surely not the same van from weeks ago . . . though it was possible. More than a few times, now, she'd glimpsed familiar faces loitering outside the hospital and on the streets near the Shack. Even with its cast iron fences and high hedges, a few industrious newsmongers had managed a few shots. Nowhere was truly safe from the paparazzi.

Sighing, she collected her thoughts and found Lucius watching her. What were they saying . . . *Ah, to tell or not to tell?* "What difference will it make to tell him that I was there?"

"Might ease his mind. Other than that, I'm not certain."

"He would stop blaming you and Mason," she considered.

"We're fairly sturdy lads, the two of us, lass. I dinnae mind him laying blame in my direction if it'll spare yourself an ill."

Therein lay the crux of it. If she admitted being there, she would need to explain her reason for the same, and what kind of fool would he see before him then?

"Daughter, there's nothing we need to mention to him right now. He knows that you know about this other woman and truth be, he's suffering the weight of hurting you. Mayet be he needs suffer that guilt a while—"

"I can't do that to him either," Natalie decided. "I'll speak to him. I'll give him the facts as I know them to be and let the chips fall. It's not fair to you or Mason. I got myself into this mix, and I'll weather his ire."

Lucius hesitated before nodding slightly. "Just mind, lass, he's likely to rage a wee bit whence he realizes the danger you faced."

"I'll just remind him, I wasn't the one to be stabbed and shot."

Lucius studied her, then emitted a humph. "Aye, that should do it."

18

The news of Liam's transition from critical to guarded condition had reached Luke only an hour ahead of Molly Anderson's announcement two days earlier but, by the time the reporter had appeared on the noon news, Luke had already boarded a plane destined for Trenton. For as often as he'd been traveling that route, he'd considered renting a helicopter or chartering a private plane for a week. The chopper would have made more sense. He could have scheduled a flight path to the Poconos and spared himself this latest drive.

Not a bad drive, though. By Interstate, Luke had reached his new acquisition in under two hours. Standing on a ridge near the summit of his new mountain, he panned his gaze over the blanket of trees spread along its flanks. With a keen sense of direction, he estimated the boundaries, judging a large portion of his immediate view now belonged to Sky High Limited.

Rather than the sense of accomplishment experienced when looking over his mountain in the Blue Ridge Range, Luke suffered an odd sense of discomfort. Something was wrong with this entire ordeal, from Frances Pendleton's initial offer to the simplicity of the paperwork in perfect order. Too easy. Too simple. Too much good hardwood from Eastern Hemlock to Eastern White Pine with enough Eastern Red Cedar thrown into the mix to justify Liam's interest and question his decline to purchase. Pendleton had sold the land at fair market value, but either the fellow hadn't accounted for the wood or he'd neglected to consider it. On the timber alone, High Land Inc. would have made a fortune, and Liam was no fool. One look at this land—hell, a simple flyover in the MacDade chopper would have justified the purchase.

Sliding onto the hood of the rented Jeep, Luke listened to the birdsong, the whisper of wind through the nearest pines, the drone of an airplane engine well above the mountaintop . . . A cluster of white clouds drifted across the pale blue sky. Sun streams speckled the clearing and sparked off the windshield and chrome. Breathing in the scent of damp earth and deadfall, Luke flashed snapshots of the past three weeks.

On every prior visit to Trenton, he'd stopped at Southern General. Wearing a half dozen disguises, ranging from a hospital orderly to an old man with a cane, he'd breached the hospital's security. Undoubtedly, his father knew of those visits. By the time Luke had reached the private wing on the 7th floor, he'd always dispensed with the disguise if only to gain quick access to his brother's room. No one ever stopped him or questioned his late night/early morning excursions, and Luke could only conclude that his father knew and approved his odd hours. His father never missed much—which only added to the curiosity over Liam's decision to forgo the Pendleton land.

Frances had never openly admitted that Liam declined to buy the land. But he'd never denied it either.

Only three days ago, Pendelton had phoned and declared—if Luke wanted the land, they needed to finalize the deal; otherwise, he was placing the property on the open market. Allegedly, he was raising capital for an investment opportunity in Jersey City, and therein lay the genuine curiosity.

Scoring through hours of news media archives from TV broadcasts to newspapers, Luke hadn't come across a single tidbit of information alluding to the city planning anything of significance. A few building permits were pending on apartment complexes and shopping malls; a new firehouse was receiving private, local, and federal funds; at least one college was hinting at a need for more housing, but they were soliciting their alumni to fund the project. The city was ripe for urban renewal and development, but nothing appeared pressing.

So, what was Pendleton up to? Why the need for quick, ready cash?

The fellow was current on his taxes, had no lawsuits or liens pending, seemed not to need bail money for any nefarious deeds . . . And Frank's upcoming nuptials shouldn't warrant the necessity of an extra million even if it was held at their Country Club.

Leaning back on the windshield, Luke drew his boots to the hood and linked his hands behind his head, watching the clouds drift overhead.

Liam had looked pretty good last night.

Luke hadn't needed a newsbreak or even an email from Gregor to determine that his brother's fever had finally dropped to a normal range. He still looked pale, and his features had sharpened with the subtle weight loss of ill-health, but he by no means appeared gaunt. For the first time since this ordeal had begun, Liam had appeared naturally asleep, not shivering or twitching or lifting his lashes to stare through shiny black eyes.

That was the worst.

Too clearly, Luke saw his brother's thick black lashes lifted, two black shiny orbs staring at him within the soft white light of a lamp above his head. Words . . . in Gaelic, Liam had uttered deliriously, but Luke had learned that language nearly simultaneously with English.

Aingeal bhàis. Angel of death.

In hindsight, Luke doubted his brother had recognized him, but that didn't stop the hurt. Even now, he felt oddly gut-punched and needed to refrain from rubbing his stomach. That he might be slightly more unbalanced than most other MacDades, he'd determined quite some time ago, though he couldn't put his finger on his strangeness. At times, like now, sitting on the hood of a rented Jeep, he believed himself as insubstantial as air. No real part of the physical world at all.

The angel of death.

But his brother was alive and on the mend, finally breathing entirely on his own power and starting to make some sense when speaking, according to Gregor. A testament, that, as his brother had resorted almost entirely to Gaelic in his delirium, and hence, probably sounded like he was speaking in tongues to the nurses and doctors attending him.

At the snap of a twig, Luke's attention riveted, but he maintained his attention on the sky. As much as he might not mind an encounter with either a deer or bear, he knew better. Nearly an hour earlier, he'd spotted the dark brown SUV for the third time, and he might not have given it a thought if he'd remained on the interstate. Seeing the car dogging him through several small towns had ignited his radar, but even that could have been a coincidence as the main highways were few and far between. Had he not heard the rumble die in the distance not long after he'd pulled into this clearing and killed his own engine, he might not have taken an interest.

Patience. When he needed them, he knew how to use them.

Hard though. He felt like a sitting duck. And depending on his visitor, he couldn't entirely rule out that scenario. If this was anyone other than a

MacDade security detail—like maybe the same miscreants who'd attacked Liam—Luke could be in trouble. Especially if there were more than a half dozen and they held guns. Otherwise, he could probably hold his own.

Once a sound was identified, it wasn't too difficult to isolate it from other sounds. Luke followed the soft snaps, aware of his stalker advancing from the left, close enough that if he turned his head, he would likely see a shadow progressing behind a wall of briars. One body, not a dozen, and this fellow was either a city boy or out of practice navigating a forest.

Uh oh. Another snap, this one closer, softer, and advancing from the right.

The stealth in that quiet footfall would suggest someone far more acquainted with the woods and equally adept at stalking prey. Not a street punk or city thug. And perhaps, far more dangerous than whoever had piloted that SUV.

At the muttered curse from the left, Luke reacted naturally to tilt his head, already looking toward his visitor when the familiar fellow bulldozed a path onto the fire trail a short distance away. Kelly Finnegan was out of his element. Wearing a sporty blue hoodie and jeans, he might pass for a hiker only until one noticed his walking tennis shoes or the disgruntled expression on his ruggedly handsome face. Average height, he carried himself like a middle-weight boxer, all sinewy muscle and solid physique with a bounce in his stride despite his forty-plus years. Arrogant, as all of the upper echelons of MacDade Security carried themselves, Finnegan adjusted his hoodie as if adjusting a suit jacket and collected his stride.

Donning one of his more curious smiles, Luke watched Kelly's advance while judging the man's darting eyes and obvious discomfort. All too clearly, he was prepared to draw his gun from the shoulder holster under the hoodie and likely shoot a rabbit or raccoon just for the sake of it. Finnegan was a city boy, Luke recalled. A cousin on his mother's side, like Uncle Mason, in whose company Kelly traveled most often. The absence of Finnegan on the eve of that ambush was yet another indication of how safe that tryst should have been. Only Artair had remained at Liam's side, and as Luke recalled, that fellow would likely cancel his own funeral to see to Liam's safety.

"I wondered if you might be headed here when you hit the Interstate," Kelly said without preamble. Glancing about as he came forward, his dark brows furrowed, and his attention riveted. "This is the Pendleton land, isn't it?"

"Any particular reason you followed me?" Luke asked as he tilted his head further without shifting from his comfortable pose. The second stalker had halted a short distance away, probably near enough to hear them.

With a hint of anger pinching his eyes at the edges, Kelly commented, "Following orders."

"I'm guessing my father's via Uncle Mason, but I'd still appreciate an answer, sir. Why?"

"You're smart enough to know why, Luke. Whoever attacked your brother is still out there, and until they're caught, no one's taking any chances."

"So, Uncle Gill's been monitoring my flights and hotel arrangements," Luke surmised.

Kelly smiled slightly, not truly amused if he'd ever suffered that condition. The most he ever managed was a smirk to pass for a friendly greeting. "For your safety and your father's peace of mind, I'd wager that's true."

"So. You're dropping pretenses?"

"Originally, I was told to keep my distance, but your uncle called en route," he said with a shrug. "I'm sure you know your father rented a house not far from the hospital, and there are plenty of rooms—along with ample security. Your father's extending an invitation."

"You risked life and limb climbing this mountain to tell me that?"

"I wasn't sure how long you'd be up here—and I wasn't sure that car would make the climb," Kelly said in mild irritation.

"It has four-wheel drive," Luke noted.

"That doesn't mean shit if the ruts are the size of ravines."

All pretenses were dropped as Kelly had just confirmed his surveillance vehicle, and his lack of surprise to be spotted was even more telling. Apparently, Gillis was aware of Luke's deliberate evasive maneuvers and, undoubtedly, enlightened his men to the probability of being spotted or lost.

But what about this other fellow currently as still as the cluster of hardy tree trunks within which he stood? Doubtful the fellow had hidden in the back of that brown SUV, and Kelly had driven close enough at one point to know only a driver had occupied the vehicle.

Was it even possible that a second car had followed him out of Trenton? Or that this stalker could be involved with those thugs who'd ambushed Liam? Did that mean Pendleton was likewise involved? The possibility of someone following him undetected was pretty slim, and aside from Pendleton . . .

Kelly had known this was Pendleton land. Had anticipated Luke's destination.

With the tension sliding down his spine, Luke lifted from his comfortable pose and skidded his boots to the front bumper, landing his forearms on his knees. Listlessly, he glanced about the slight plateau, not seeing his second stalker but sensing the presence if only by the absence of birdsong in that direction. Only a few seconds passed before Luke landed his piercing blue gaze on Kelly, and by the quick discomfort in the sharp brown gaze, Luke knew his effect. Whether it was a learned talent or inherent, he could mask every thought behind his eyes, and he'd seen the reaction often enough to know he worried the recipient of his direct focus. "How did you know this was the Pendleton land, Kell?"

He hesitated only a fraction of a second, far too startled to lie. "I came up here with Mason and Liam a few months ago."

"Pendleton offered the land to Liam then?"

"I'd imagine the sale's still pending," he commented.

"Excuse me?" Luke asked with a crawling sense of alarm.

"It's been in the works for months," Kelly continued. "I don't imagine that's changed."

As of three hours ago, it certainly had changed. The land currently belonged to Lucas McDade, and if Kelly wasn't privy to that information, then this second stalker had originated in Pendleton's circle. Other than Luke's Banker, Albert Milligan, who'd drawn the check from Luke's personal account, Frances Pendleton, and the two title transfer company reps—no one else should have known about the sale. Only Pendleton could have told someone about Luke's intention to visit the mountains. Just before leaving, Luke recalled Pendleton asking, 'Are you heading to the hospital now, then?'

'Maybe later,' Luke had admitted. 'I might take a ride up north while there's daylight . . .' An innocent admission, that, as he'd meant to avoid mentioning his habit of late-night visits to Southern General.

Was it a coincidence that Pendleton had pushed for the sale on the same day as Liam taking a turn for the better? After two weeks of intensive care and bleak updates on the local and world news, Pendleton had suddenly become impatient . . . because Liam might soon be in a position to finalize the sale?

Which made even less sense. Why had Pendleton offered the land to him while Liam lay near death . . . or was that too simple? If he feared Liam would die without closing the sale . . . rather than dump the land on the open market, he might have believed Luke was the next best bet for quick ready cash. He might even believe that he was still selling the land to High Land Inc. through Luke. If Pendleton had met Gregor, would he have offered Gregor the land?

Questions. Only more questions and Finnegan's new orders might have been designed for an irate patriarch to gain answers.

Damn it. It was only a matter of time before Lucius learned of that sale falling through and the land transferring to the wrong son. Sky High LLC was not in the lumber business, and in another scan of the immediate wood within his view, Luke judged the value double what he'd just paid. If he ever wanted to jump into the lumber business, he could turn a fine coin . . . and High Land Inc. would probably buy every last board.

That was never going to happen . . . unless he sold the land back to Liam.

Luke slid off the hood to his boots and decided, "Give me a minute, Kell, then I'll give you a lift back to your car."

Without awaiting a response, he turned in the intruder's direction, already searching the thickets ahead. Twenty feet into the briar patch, Luke knew the fellow was gone. He continued another ten feet, searching where he suspected the stalker had stood. Algorithms. Luke spotted the marred leaves, the twist of black earth where a boot had spun in a hurry—too much of a hurry to be too careful. Other signs existed, from a snapped twig on a sapling to an unnaturally twisted vine folded back on itself. Someone had stood twenty-five feet from where he and Kelly had chatted, and as Luke stood, taking advantage of the privacy to relieve himself—killing a few more moments as he listened—he heard the distant, distinct sound of a quad engine ignited further down the mountain.

Coincidence? Could this second entity be a genuine mountain dweller? Perhaps one squatting in a hunter's cabin or tent? Mid-summer, there were bound to be hikers and campers . . . and not unheard of—a poacher or two. Had he unwittingly interrupted someone sitting in a tree stand, waiting for dinner to trot up a well-worn path?

Again, scanning the briars and lifting his attention to the tree bows, he realized both the futility of spotting a hunter's hide with the foliage in full bloom and Kelly awaiting a ride off the mountain. Sighing disgust at his rising paranoia, Luke retraced his path to the fire trail where Finnegan stood leaning against the passenger side door, a natural scowl on his face. This righthand man to Uncle Mase always appeared disgruntled or simply ready for a fight.

Luke flagged a hand to grant Finnegan entry to the Jeep as he passed around the front end. The sooner he dispatched the bodyguard, the better. He would prefer not to explain why he was on this mountain. Not just yet. And sooner than later, Kelly would ask.

Navigating the ruts to make a three-point turn in the weedy trail, Luke held his thoughts to himself, and Kelly did the same, apparently adhering to the age-old custom of treating Luke with kid gloves. The past served him well. Few MacDade family members or employees engaged Luke in conversation, having been warned or ordered to leave him alone.

He hadn't intentionally set out to gain a reputation for departing rather than dealing with too many questions or commands, nor had he preempted how others would respond to his silence—not consciously, anyway. Sometimes, he just preferred not to speak when he could see no point in conversation.

At the mouth of the fire trail, he found the SUV waiting precariously on the side of the gravel road. Stopped, Luke glanced over to find Kelly watching him. Merely waiting, his gaze steady, Luke noted the fellow's discomfort rise in leaps and realized, belatedly, that he truly made this security guard nervous. Curious despite his vacant gaze, Luke needn't wait long.

"Can I tell your father to expect you, then?" Finnegan asked carefully.

"You could give me the address." Though it wasn't necessary. Dependable Molly Anderson had reported the MacDades' move from a hotel to the Franklin House, a historical site on the banks of the Delaware River. Twenty seconds on the computer would provide a detailed account of the house, its history, and its address. "If I arrive, he'll know I accepted, don't you think?"

Irritated, if the twitch in his cheek was any indication, Finnegan held his temper in check, impressively. "I'd like to ease his mind concerning your safety, Luke," he said carefully. "In fact, I'd be happy to escort you."

And spare himself the aggravation of trying to keep up, Luke knew and conveyed his knowledge with a slight smirk. "We're traveling in the same direction. If that counts as an escort, you can admit you did your job. When we reach 295, though, I'll expect to part company."

"This isn't exclusive treatment, Lucas," Kelly said in the tone most annoying, both condescending as if he were speaking to a daft child and superior as if he had a right to be condescending.

"There's your car," Luke commented.

"Your father's appointed security for all of you until we find Liam's assailants."

"Any luck with that?"

"We've made some progress," Kelly said, maybe lying, probably lying.

Any progress they might have made would have reached one of Anderson's newsbreaks. Luke had decided the woman possessed a direct pipeline into the Trenton PD if even half of her information was accurate. Canting his head to affect his curiosity and doubt, he wondered, "What progress?"

"It's confidential," Kelly offered the old stand-by.

Finnegan might know of progress, but doubtfully, he knew the details. Luke knew who would provide that information, however, and decided, "I'm fairly good at keeping myself out of harm's way, Kell. Take your car. I'll see you in Trenton."

Kelly seemed to grasp Luke would neither reject nor accept the offer of his services and resigned to his earlier position, believing himself capable of remaining invisible once they reached the interstate. "All right, then," he agreed and reached for the door handle.

Two seconds after Finnegan shut the door and took two steps clear of the Jeep, Luke pulled out, and less than a minute later, he left Finnegan in the dust. Literally. With a half mile of gravel road, Luke created a cloud between the trees, descending the mountainside and reaching the nearest town limits within minutes. Not a large town, but side streets existed, and Luke turned on the first block, circling a block and parking alongside a barbershop entrance with a clear view of the main street. Only two highways bisected the town, one leading north and south, one east and west. He'd arrived on a northbound two-lane, the quickest route.

Predictably, the SUV sped past, moving a little too quick for the quiet ambiance of the mountain town, and Luke decided he better wait a few moments more just in case Kelly attracted the attention of the local PD. Finnegan might just be mad enough to demand an APB on a little black Jeep if he saw it pass while routing for his license and rental car agreement.

Five vehicles passed on the main road before the sixth vehicle, a black Nissan with dark, tinted windows passed the entrance to the side street. Without seeing the front or back of the car, Luke couldn't be certain, but what were the odds of seeing the same make, model, and year with the same tint, the same dull chrome wheels . . . for the sixth time in two days? With the odds scrolling through his mind, Luke considered following his stalker and realized the impracticality of attempting discretion in a fancy black Jeep.

Time to go into stealth mode, Luke decided and waited a few moments more before pulling away from the curb. The odds were high that the fellow in the Nissan was following the fellow in the SUV, and both of them were headed on the quickest route to Trenton. Luke bypassed the junction for the southbound highway and continued another half dozen blocks before turning eastbound.

He would arrive thirty-two minutes later than his escort, provided he traveled at a median speed limit.

Finding a rental car agency had only taken a moment on his cellphone. In record time, Luke exchanged the Jeep for a nondescript Taurus and returned to his hotel.

With the first shadows of dusk spreading over the parking lot, he needed only a golfer's cap, dark glasses, and a hulking posture to avoid alerting Kelly in the SUV parked near the rear entrance. The dark sedan was nowhere in sight. Using his hotel key card, he entered his hotel through the backdoor and climbed the stairs rather than take the elevator to his room on the second floor.

Only once, on an earlier visit, he'd nearly run into trouble with the paparazzi and might have—if not for his disguise as a maintenance man. He'd walked past the two reporters stationed at the hotel entrance, affecting a limp in his sluggish stride and continuing past the service desk. Amused behind his gray-frosted beard, he'd offered the receptionist a few offhanded words and a wink. Ten minutes later, he'd checked out of the hotel and traveled another half hour before checking into a different hotel and offering a sizeable tip to keep his name from the public eye. No one, particularly newsmongers, paid heed to the missing 'A' when searching for any MacDades in the hospital's vicinity, but Lucius MacDade had simplified their job by renting the Franklin House.

Perhaps, there was more to that decision than mere convenience for their visiting relatives. Offering the reporters a central location had drawn the heat from the MacDades—and company—who wished to remain anonymous. Gladly, Luke reaped the benefit of his father's semi-deception, a benefit he shared with at least one other McDade.

Spotting Ryan entering the same hotel a week earlier hadn't been a surprise, but it had provided a sensible reason to continue his deception and remain incognito. If ever there was a cousin to avoid, Ryan McDade qualified, and the lad's continued presence didn't bode well on Liam's assailants.

Barely inside the door to his room, Luke noted the blinking button on the telephone base, signaling a message at the front desk. By now, Kelly had probably built a fine rage, and the fellow had likely already reported to his boss, who in turn had likely reported to the chieftain.

Tossing his hat and glasses aside, Luke reached the bed and engaged the phone to contact the front desk. Offering his room number to the perky receptionist, he spoke simply, "You have a message for me?"

"Hold a moment, please," she said pleasantly. Only ten seconds passed, with Luke preparing to hear his father's tirade before the perky voice returned and announced. "A package arrived for you this afternoon, sir. If you like, I can have it brought up for you."

"Do that, thanks," he agreed, already curious. A package? Not merely a message left at the front desk? And this afternoon—*after signing the papers*—not like a half hour ago?

By habit, Luke turned on the television to catch the latest updates, but in a rare moment, he found a game show rather than a breaking news story. He'd already missed the evening news.

Fishing his wallet from his pocket, he readied a tip for the delivery boy, timing his arrival at the door to coincide with the knock. Not much of a package. A cardboard envelope. The type used for sending mail—sans a mailing label or address. His room number and initials designated the recipient, and inside, another more cryptic white envelope wore the simple print-typed address designating—Lucas J. MacDade. A sheet of white paper unfolded to expose a typed line of text.

'I got information about your brothers attack Meet me at the emerald club 10 pm Come alone'

Considering the word use, lack of punctuation, and absence of capitals, either he was dealing with a slightly less-than-educated individual or someone posing as such.

Either way, he would accept the invitation-cum-demand, and visit

The Emerald Club at ten p.m.

8:14. He had plenty of time to make a few calls, only beginning with room service. It was a lot safer ordering in than patronizing a sit-down restaurant or a drive-thru. Even with his beard and long hair, he'd drawn too many second glances over breakfast. And it was a sure bet, that the MacDade face had become a little too familiar when even buying a hamburger at a fast-food drive-thru warranted a mention on the evening news as '. . . a MacDade seen earlier today in North Trenton.'

He was beginning to feel more and more like some blasted rare bird to be captured on film.

Maybe after this evening's rendezvous, he would make the changes that he'd contemplated over the past week. He'd come prepared, having stopped in Lexington to collect one of several FX kits that he'd put together more than two years earlier. For the hell of it, he'd gathered an arsenal of stage-worthy paraphernalia, including latex, spirit gum, and various hairpieces, from short gray wigs to black beards and mustaches, along with varied shades of tinted contact lenses.

'Tricks of the trade,' Ms Milsap, his drama teacher, had said years ago, and Luke had embraced those words literally and figuratively. Probably a flaw in his character, but he thoroughly enjoyed becoming someone else, someone old or young, hairy or even bald, once. With a skip in a stride or a slouch in the shoulders, he could pass his own mum without a second glance—and had on one occasion.

Carl answered on the second ring and lent Luke cause to imagine the fellow swooping across the foyer to spare the Pendletons a second of grief over the intrusive sound. "How can I help you?"

"You might take Mr. Pendleton the phone, Carl," Luke said in a friendly tone.

"I'm sorry, but Mr. Pendleton's not available—"

"Carl, this is Luke McDade. I suggest you put him on," he said in a less friendly tone.

"Mr. Pendleton's not here at the moment, sir," he said snootily. "Would you like to leave a message?"

Luke depressed the disconnect button on his phone and engaged the cellphone number that he'd used a time or two while blocking the caller ID on his own device. A handy thing—that caller-block feature. On the fourth ring, Pendleton answered, and in a split second, Luke identified the voice of a racetrack announcer. A horse race by the cadence of names and mention of "turning for home" to accompany the excited shouts echoing through the phone speaker.

"Yes? Yes? Who is this!" Frances demanded, sounding more animated and agitated than he had at any time in the past two weeks of communications.

A racetrack . . . only a half dozen hours after receiving a cashier's check for two-point-three million? Uh-huh. . . and was this the investment in Jersey City to underlie Frances Pendleton's need for ready cash? A vice . . . and an addiction . . . and it just might explain the visible decline of the Pendleton estate. The elder Pendleton wouldn't be the first heir to lose the family fortunes to the ponies or tables.

Only a second lapsed before Luke wondered, "Is this why you couldn't wait for my brother to recover and close the sale?"

"Who—Luke?"

"Mr. Pendleton, I seem to recall asking if you offered my brother your land, and I don't recall you mentioning you had a sale pending. Why is that, sir?"

"What's the difference?" Pendleton snapped. "You have the damned land, now you can all leave me alone, and I suggest you lose this number, young man. Our business is concluded."

The line went dead at Luke's ear—the equivalent of being hung up on—and Luke cocked his head and eyed the blank screen. What the hell was that? Less than seven hours ago, the old gentleman had seemed pleased with the sale, and three days prior, the fellow had phoned, nearly demanding that Luke deliver a check or forget the deal.

Five times in the past two weeks, Pendleton had phoned to check on Luke's decision, and Luke recalled his own hesitation, certain that something about this entire ordeal smelled fishy. He'd meant to wait, to speak to Liam when he was well enough . . .

Just what the hell was this about? Luke certainly hadn't pressured the old man into the sale. He had stonewalled the closing, in fact. With all the paperwork in order, he might have closed the deal two weeks past . . . And twice, he'd mentioned Liam to Pendleton, pressing for a reason to explain his brother's decision to reject the sale.

Only Friday, the old goat had huffed into the phone, 'I offered it—he didn't want it.'

'Any particular reason?'

'I haven't any idea,' Pendleton had huffed, sounding indignant. 'I'm offering it to you as a courtesy. If you don't want it, fine then . . .'

'I'll see you Monday.'

If Gregor hadn't emailed a progress report suggesting Liam was finally responding to the antibiotics, Luke might have stonewalled a little longer.

Buying land and finalizing a land deal while his brother lay at death's door hadn't sat well in his stomach . . . or mind.

'. . . you can all leave me alone . . .'

All?

Who was this 'all?' Who was pressuring Pendleton into the land deal?

One thing for certain—Luke was not the guilty party, and unless Liam was making phone calls between bouts of delirium, he was no part of that 'all.'

What the hell was truly going on here? And what the hell did the Pendleton land have to do with it? As far as Luke had determined, those thousand acres were just a nice chunk of forest that could make another fine lodge if he ever decided to franchise. Liam, however, would have seen it differently, and Luke couldn't fathom any good reason for his brother to decline that offer. The price was right. High Land Inc. would have made another small fortune on the timber alone, and as much as Luke might disagree with that enterprise, he knew his father's practices were far more environmentally sound than most.

Automated, Luke answered the knock, letting the waitstaff wheel the cart to the small table, delivering a tip as the fellow departed. If it ever became imperative, he could describe the waiter in minute detail, but presently, the man remained invisible.

Various scenarios scrolling through his mind's eye, Luke viewed every detail of the past three weeks, searching for discrepancies to explain Pendleton's actions. First and foremost, based on those few spoken words, Pendleton had been pressured—blackmailed?—into offering his family land to the Mac-Dades. Liam first, perhaps, because of his friendship with Frank. So, what came first? The old goat deciding to sell his land and remembering his son's old college buddy in the lumber business? Or an outside party aware of the Pendleton land . . . and luring Liam into the sale? Like luring him into an alley without the gun?

In that scenario, someone wanted Liam in Trenton, New Jersey. And that made no real sense. What would be the purpose? Other than claiming the title of New Jersey's capital, Trenton boasted no serious claim to fame.

Unless one counted the Lindbergh kidnapping, which hardly seemed applicable 76 years later.

Kelly had admitted that he'd traveled with Liam and Mason a few months ago to look at the land. A few months . . .? To buy land that Luke had bought in two weeks? Why had Liam dragged his feet on that sale? . . . Because he was having an affair with a stripper? Not likely. If he knew his brother even slightly, Luke knew business came first. The assignation would have been a side benefit to kill time between negotiations.

Frank at The Emerald Club speaking with that attractive young stripper . . . 'You knew it would never last forever . . .'

On the surface, those words could sound as if Frank had known of some clandestine preordained plan. But that scenario fell apart with the memory of Frank's concern and his insistence that Helms speak with the police.

Alecia Helms knew something—something serious enough for her to panic and avoid the police. Frank had given her the benefit of the doubt, but that was probably in line with Frank's nature. He wouldn't believe the worst about anyone. Rose-colored glasses seemed to apply to Frank's outlook. His fear for Liam was genuine, and he'd sounded distressed over the entire situation . . . Yet Frank had wondered if Helms knew anything. A natural consideration, that? To believe she might have seen something since she was with Liam in that hotel? Natural. Not an accusation as if she might know who was behind the attack. Either Frank hadn't considered the possibility, or he refused to entertain the notion.

Alecia Helms knew something, and the invitation to join a stranger at The Emerald Club had taken on a greater significance. Whether Luke should go as himself or in disguise remained the only question. Benefits existed to either. First—foremost—if Uncle Gillis maintained surveillance on the club, a wayward son might escape notice, and the likelihood of Gillis closing that avenue of investigation was slim. In the same respect, if Luke went incognito to case the Club, he might miss the rendezvous. Unless . . .

Well, he could make a quick change in the rental if he arrived early and took stock in the patrons, then returned as himself.

If Gillis's men spotted him, it wouldn't matter since Luke would likely turn any genuine evidence over to his father anyway. Providing there was actual evidence.

The evidence, Luke feared, might exist in the simple fact that some-one knew where to find him, someone—other than Gillis MacDade—who might have sent a far more clandestine car to follow Kelly Finnigan to that mountain. And therein, another quandary. If Finnegan had been followed and not noticed, the fellow was slipping, which was doubtful. Whoever had been hiding in those weeds, had driven to that mountain in advance, with enough time to rent or steal a four-wheeler, and the only way that would have happened is if the stalker had known Pendleton.

Unconsciously, Luke checked the time as he swallowed the last bite of steak from his plundered plate. He had time. He could make the changes. Weighing the pros and cons, he reached a single conclusion. Although it could be simpler to shave and apply a fake beard, he wasn't quite ready to make such a drastic, permanent change.

A spattering of gray hairs though . . .

Sighing, he resigned to make some changes and carried only his soda from the table, collecting his plastic case from the closet before continuing into the bathroom.

19

No one took interest in the old man ambling through the dull light. With an obvious struggle, he mounted the high bar stool in the corner, ordered a Bud on tap, and then commenced to watch the show. Behind the dull gray contact lenses, however, Luke scanned the patrons, taking a mental snapshot of every face in the smoky room. Only a dozen men occupied the tables nearest the stage. At least half of them appeared to be sharing a gab session with friends rather than watching the burlesque routine unfolding centerstage. The woman gyrating on the pole appeared to focus her efforts and seductive smile on a single gentleman seated at a corner table, and Luke paid closer heed.

A boyfriend, perhaps?

Had Liam sat in a similar position to catch Helms' act?

Somehow, Luke couldn't picture his brother in a place like this, but stranger things had happened.

No one appeared unnaturally interested in the entrance, not even the bouncer who rested at the end of the bar near the door. Only in passing, this muscled fellow had glimpsed at Luke, judging him by appearance and dismissing either a need to card or harass the old coot. He appeared attentive enough, his dark eyes moving through the shadows, taking in the sights and watching over the dancers, and the waitresses meandering between the tables. A Monday night crowd, not much different than the Thursday crowd that Luke had seen on his second visit. In twenty-twenty hindsight, Luke recalled seeing this same bouncer wearing a sports coat and jeans on both prior visits . . . an active-duty cop from Jersey City moonlighting for an old friend. Ty—or Tyler—according to Betsy, the bartender. The bouncer-cop whom Alecia Helms had mentioned avoiding when meeting Frank that first eve.

Inconspicuously checking the time while chugging the last of his beer, Luke maintained his ancient persona while collecting his change off the bar, pointedly displaying the old-man-style money clip with a collection of worn, folded dollar bills. Details. His liver-spotted hands sported crooked fingers and enlarged knuckles, suggesting the onset of arthritis. Even under a spotlight, doubtful anyone would recognize the gloves extending onto his arm under the sleeves of a faded blue shirt and oversized cardigan sweater. Under the short gray wig and fishing-style hat, he had mashed his blond hair flat, and under the bushy gray beard, his real bristles itched. He refrained from scratching, however, and nearly cursed his procrastination at shaving.

He had seen enough.

The fellow in the corner, drawing the dancer's attention, was yet another of Gillis's men, though doubtful one with a stellar career as he was more interested in the brunette on the pole than the door. About every ten minutes, he seemed to remember he was working and glanced toward the entrance. Avoiding him could be child's play even without a disguise, and by that fact, Luke reached a simple conclusion. Gillis didn't expect Alecia Helms to return to this establishment. Why his uncle would keep an incompetent in MacDade employ could be as simple as the vaguely familiar features. Another relative—but not one of his own, Luke grasped. This fellow resembled the Callahans, which might make sense if Natalie's father shared an interest in solving this crime regarding his daughter. Luke could imagine the older Callahan insisting on offering some of his men into MacDade service. Lord knows the security forces were probably stretched thin by now. Between guarding Liam in the hospital and securing this Franklin House location, most of the more trained men in MacDade service were likely working around the clock.

Maintaining his old-man shuffle, Luke bypassed the few men at the bar, a familiar waitress and the bouncer to whom he spared an acknowledging nod. Polite, the way most old gentlemen were polite. The bouncer offered a like amenity, along with a friendly half-smile in his black mustache—a jaded smile for all that the man appeared not much older than thirty, if that. A story there, no doubt, Luke considered, having spent a great deal of time studying expressions and mannerisms to be duplicated in various parts of plays. PTSD came to mind, and in a quick tabulation, Luke wondered if this fellow had been on the force seven years prior—in or around New York. Participation in the rescue efforts of 9/11 had left a mark, undoubtedly affecting officers everywhere but more so those closest to ground zero.

Luke remembered his own reaction to that ordeal, recalling the announcement over the PA system at St. Andrews Academy. By the time the plane hit the Pentagon, he and his fellow academy students were watching the disaster on a small screen in the basement-level gymnasium . . .

Recalling his disbelief, Luke ambled into the shadows on the sidewalk bypassing the parking lot, fading into the darkness of a vacant wooded lot. On dual planes, he remembered one of his professors consoling an older boy whose father worked in one of the Towers and another whose father and mother both worked in DC; while at the same time, he recorded the present sights in search of anyone lingering in the shadows.

He was alone on the sidewalk; a dog barked in the distance, music blared fore and aft . . . and both of his fellow academicians lost a parent that day.

The bouncer wore that look. The weariness of loss. The frustration of helplessness.

Rounding a distant corner toward the more residential neighborhood, positive he was neither being followed nor watched, Luke launched into a full sprint, enlisting the speed that had won him a few awards on the track team. Even in the old-man shoes, he was moving while stripping off his old-man jacket, the wig, the gloves. By the time he reached the rental parked in a shadowed space at the curb three blocks from The Emerald Club, Luke needed only to step out of his trousers, strip off his shirt, and change his shoes. Scratching his head and beard, he set his waves loose, then removed the spirit gum from his facial hair. Luckily, no one stood witness to his transition as he would likely resemble a prop in a horror flick, what with latex peeling from his cheeks, forehead, and brow. Behind the rental's steering wheel, he removed the last telltale signs of movie makeup and stuffed the evidence into black plastic, sliding it under the driver's seat.

At ten minutes to ten, Luke pulled into the gravel lot alongside the club. The vapor lights on three telephone poles barely reached the edge of the lot or illuminated the entrances—one for deliveries, one above a basement entrance, both denoted with red 'exit' lights above the doors. The 'x' and 't' were missing from the delivery door; the basement stairwell looked more like a movie prop depicting descending steps to the gates of hell.

If anyone occupied one of the dozen cars in the lot, they were either tucked behind the seats or as still as a marble sculpt. Luke locked the Taurus that he'd deliberately parked far enough from the light to conceal the color. If anyone spotted him or the car now, it wouldn't matter. After this rendezvous, he intended to accept his father's invitation and visit the Franklin House. Hopefully, Gregor would share genuine progress reports concerning Liam's health and the ongoing investigation. The police seemed to be failing miserably if Molly Anderson's newsbreaks were any indication. Those folks would be better off hiring her as a detective; she was certainly thorough when surveilling the MacDades.

Wearing jeans, a suit jacket and a polo shirt with several gold chains to catch the light—as well as the attention of any interested party—Luke strode alongside the club on the street-side sidewalk and let himself into the shadowy alcove. No longer attempting to remain incognito, he flashed a natural smile to the bouncer and offered a greeting like they were old pals. Three encounters might qualify for such.

"Flying solo this evening, eh?" the bouncer spoke in an inherently deep voice that cut beneath the drum and horn recital.

"Frank might be coming," Luke said offhandedly, glancing toward the stage—or more accurately, toward the surveillance man sitting near the action. The fellow was still engrossed in the brunette, offering Luke enough time to meander along the bar and slide onto a stool.

Apparently, it was Betsy's night off. The same strawberry blond who had attended the old man with little more than a glance hustled to him. Gold hoop earrings bouncing on her slight shoulders, she presented a bright smile while glancing over him—maybe homing in on his gold chains. "What can I get you, handsome?"

"Corona, hold the lime and the glass," he said with a return smile. Shifting on the stool, he turned enough to view the performance and avoid the security man. In a position to watch the door, he flashed back to his mental slides and compared this new image with his earlier scan. Three other people had arrived in his brief absence. A thin, black-haired fellow sporting a ponytail, black mustache, and wire-rimmed glasses had taken a booth near the door; another middle-aged fellow occupied a table equipped for four to the left of the stage; and a long-haired blond woman of indeterminant age had settled at the end of the bar where the old man had resided earlier.

The bartender delivered his beer and accepted the neat flat twenty that Luke thumbed from his Louis Vuitton wallet.

Slinkily, the blond slid off the corner stool and sidled to him. Without the benefit of theatrical training, the woman wore far too many cosmetics, from thick black liner around her eyes to fake lashes resembling three-quarter-inch long waxed horsehair. Fire engine red lipstick and stiff curls plastered to her temples completed the facial image, but she hadn't stopped there. She'd managed to complement the style with a tube top from the seventies and a short skirt with fishnet stockings. If she wasn't a hooker, she offered a stereotypical rendition, and Luke wasn't exactly impressed with the overall picture. Like most things lately, this disguise seemed wrong and a little too contrived. She wasn't Alecia Helms, but with her ample bust, blond hair cascading down her back, and her muscled legs, the resemblance would pass at a distance.

Even before she spoke, Luke knew she'd sent the invitation.

"Mind if I join you, honey?" she asked with a Jersey accent.

"Not at all," he said, needlessly, since she was already hoisting a rounded hip onto the stool beside him. Letting his gaze wander as if admiring her goods, he managed to maintain his faint smile and affect dismay. "I better mention, though, I'm supposed to be meeting someone here," he admitted, feigning a question rather than a statement.

"Funny," she said coyly and nearly batted her lashes. "Me, too."

This wasn't a fun game, and behind his curiosity, Luke's irritation was on the rise. That she intended to pose as Alecia Helms wasn't a doubt or surprise. Somehow, that young woman was involved, and this one could be standing in as a friend. If that were true, the connection to Pendleton would be confirmed, and all these pieces fit together with the land deal at the center.

Unless it was a means to the end—the end being the assault on Liam.

"Do uhm . . . is it possible you were expecting me?" Luke asked as if doubting. She could be meeting a genuine john in that getup. And wouldn't that just be a fine coincidence? Her, propositioning him . . . instead of offering a proposition?

How much did evidence cost these days, anyway? A few hundred? A few grand? Frank had given Helms five grand just over three weeks ago. Did she blow that already and decide on another means for a cash injection?

The woman was still looking at him through pale blue eyes, the pupils as thin as pinpricks despite the shadowed world around them. Leaning as if she might lay against him, she landed a hand on his thigh. "What do you say we go downstairs and talk business, Lucas? It's a little quieter down there."

For the second time today, pretenses were being dropped, and Luke was happy to have done with it. Cryptic messages, clandestine meetings, and wordplay might appeal to his sense of intrigue, but he wasn't fool enough to believe this ordeal was risk-free. Someone had tried to kill his brother, and until the reasons were known, doubtful any of them were safe.

By action alone, Luke agreed, collecting his change and beer, catching a bemused smile from the bartender, and offering her a wink. Let her make of this what she would. Doubtful any employees of the Emerald Club would be surprised by the antics of the MacDades thanks to Liam paving the way, and by now, they all knew Luke's identity despite the absence of his face on the evening news. Sooner or later, though, if he continued to show up here, he would likely land his mug on the cover of a tabloid with a title like 'Little Brother Walking in Older Brother's Footsteps.'

Boy, even silently, that headline was stifling.

Letting the lady lead, Luke escorted her to the stairwell and descended behind her with a clear view of the dark roots on her crown despite the dull amber glow on the steps. She carried an oversized cloth purse, which she cleaved to her hip as if fearing he might snatch it away and make a run for the exit. Purse snatching was against the law, he thought to mention, only more intrigued by the possibility of actual evidence inside that gaudy bag.

They settled into a booth furthest from the stage, and Luke noticed the ambiance had changed to accommodate an actual dancefloor where a half dozen couples were taking advantage of the softer music. As he'd noted on his first trip, conversations could be overheard, though not clearly from any great distance. No one sat within three booths or two tables from the booth she'd chosen, and aside from a dull votive candle dangling above the table, very little light existed.

The candle reminded him of the ongoing vigil in front of Southern General. After this latest battle with infection, the hospital had attempted removing the growing mound, but according to Gregor—and Molly Anderson—they weren't meeting with much success. For every flower, candle, or balloon removed, two more appeared, and even now, Luke couldn't quite grasp a reason other than the blasted photos that Molly Anderson seemed to be finding and exploiting regularly.

When Liam survived this ordeal, he was likely to find himself bombarded with enough actors' guild agents and invitations to make a serious actor green with envy, and he was likely to need more than Artie MacDade to save him from his fans. When Liam survived . . .

The waitress arrived and spared a curious glance to the woman in the corner before eyeing Luke to take their order. His companion was not well known if she was known at all. By the estranged glances she was receiving, his companion was not well known if she was known at all, and maybe only the vague likeness registered with the waitstaff.

Looking into the corner, to the shadowed face, Luke asked, ".What would you like?"

"I'll have what yer having," she said softly as if fearing to be heard.

He would have preferred just getting down to business, but apparently, she wasn't in a hurry. "In a glass with a twist of lime, then?"

"Na. Bottle's good," she said and reached for his bottle.

"I'll have another," Luke commented aloofly, and the waitress smiled more, apparently noting the difference between his formal tone and her sloppy slang. What possessed him to adopt the lofty effect, he couldn't fathom other than his unconscious desire to separate himself from this outrageously dressed woman. On the outside chance that he might gain insight, he couldn't afford to alienate her completely, but by God, he wouldn't stoop to her level even for fun.

His arrogance might have something to do with himself stepping fully into Lucas MacDade mode, a persona he generally avoided since he preferred to be seen as just another regular guy. In certain circles, the MacDade name could affect how he was treated, and that wasn't always an advantage.

As the waitress strode away, Luke barely shifted to offer the woman his attention, wondering, "What should I call you then, miss?"

"Alecia," she offered, possibly only awaiting the opportunity to provide that name.

Not knowing how deep Frank Pendleton might be in this affair complicated this situation tremendously. Luke would rather not admit seeing the actual Alecia Helms in this establishment a few weeks earlier, nor even allude to the possibility. "Alecia—Liam's Alecia?" he asked innocently, affecting a hint of natural surprise.

The woman smiled, showing an upper rack of somewhat crooked teeth that some men might find attractive, emitting character, and Luke found rather disgusting, emitting a lack of self-respect.

"I didn't know if he told you about me."

Should he admit, Liam hadn't spoken a word about her—or the real Alecia Helms, for that matter? "I uhm . . . I know your name's come up in the investigation," he said hesitantly. "The note . . . at my hotel? Mentioned information. If there's anything you can offer? . . . Do you know who they were—his assailants? Or uh . . . what they wanted?"

"Slow down, honey," she said in a softer tone. "We'll get to all that, but first I gotta make sure nobody followed you. I got somebody checking, so we'll just have our drink and wait til they call me."

The black-haired man upstairs was probably her accomplice, what with his proximity to the door and the fact that no one had lingered outside unless they were adept at surveillance. Behind feigned dismay, Luke masked his irritation, considering the probability of phoning the Trenton PD or those investigators, Harbinder and Lenmar. "I . . . I'd be willing to pay for any information that would lead to an arrest, miss," he said hesitantly. "I mean—if the information is good—I'd certainly make it worth your while."

"Oh, the information's good," she said while gaining confidence.

She apparently believed she was dealing with a moron, now, or a naïve idiot—which might be the case; however, neither she nor her accomplice upstairs appeared to pose a threat. If anything, they might be attempting to cash in on the MacDade fortunes. Anyone even remotely close to Helms could probably devise this plan, claiming to have information to extort a few bucks. The possibility of learning anything of significance seemed thin, but that envelope—arriving at his hotel—suggested a genuine connection.

As the waitress arrived with their drinks, the fake Alecia decided, "I need to use the lady's room, honey. If you could just sit right here a few."

As much as he would prefer to have this finished, Luke slipped from the booth and stepped aside like a proper gentleman while the blond scooted off the bench. Appearing agitated with the waitress in her path, the faux Alecia snatched the drinks off the tray. Elaborately scoffing, she leaned over the table and her oversized purse to set their drinks in place. The short shorts rode up the crack of her ass, bulging her bare cheeks to glow orange in the strobe lights. Even in an establishment where flesh was a commodity, this young woman's lack of morals or self-respect seemed over the top.

Embarrassed, Luke turned his attention to the waitress rather than be caught staring at that ungainly sight. Offering a wan smile, he handed the waitress a twenty, offering "keep the change," as though that should excuse his lack of good taste.

Grateful to be sliding into the booth and the shadows to conceal something of his identity, Luke reconsidered his need to be here. This entire ordeal seemed more like an elaborate hoax than any genuine extorsion technique. Why would this imposter even deem it necessary to pose as Helms? Was it a test designed by the real Helms to see if any of the MacDades would recognize her? That seemed possible, although it suggested more to the Pendleton connection.

Who knew where to find one Lucas McDade this afternoon? The message had been waiting for him at the hotel . . . and what the hell did that mean? Was it someone inside the MacDade security force . . .? Impossible. If anyone in the MacDade security force was involved, Gillis would have figured that out by now. More than likely, someone had followed Luke from the title office to his hotel, which suggested another connection to the older Pendleton—and the old coot probably wasn't directly involved. A pawn then . . . but in whose damned game?

Money, damn it. It always came down to money. And someone had spent a bundle to land Liam MacDade in a hospital.

In a position to see the restroom signs above a cove near the steps, Luke was beginning to wonder if another rear door existed when he spotted the short blond emerging from the shadows. By now, she'd probably spoken to her accomplice, and hopefully, this charade was about to end. He barely started to slide, to rise, when her hand touched his shoulder, and she smiled almost sweetly.

"Just slide on over, honey," she suggested and appeared far more intent suddenly, bouncing her glance off their drinks—his drink and back, with a cockeyed smile.

On two levels, suddenly, it occurred to him that he wasn't arguing—instead sliding deeper into the booth, and his senses were swaying, his vision wavering. In delay, he recalled taking several swallows from the new bottle . . . killing time, thinking . . . but it was becoming hard to think. His focus swaying, senses snapping, he tried shaking the strangeness away and caught himself listing, leaning. In delay, he tried pulling away from the distorted, plastic face in front of him, spooked and more confused when the beer bottle came to his lips. As much as he knew he should refuse, he gulped several swallows and watched the images distort, large and small, near and far. He was in trouble here, knew it in the back of his mind. Even as he tried forming the words, raising a protest and pushing, his hand snagged. His lips pressed to silence under red lipstick, and his body reacted of its own accord. He wanted, needed something . . . and the sensation rose from his crotch. The press and insistence of touch, the pulse of his own awakening registered and faded . . .

"Shhh, baby . . . shhh . . . No hurry now . . . just finish up . . ."

20

Four days had passed since Liam had opened his eyes and found daylight, but nothing had truly changed in his mind or sight. Between the constant vigil of private nurses attending his every need, doctors visiting to poke and prod, baths, meals, and medicine to be hung on the pole over his head, he slept. On rare occasions, he stayed awake long enough to enjoy his sons, tickle his daughter, chat with his wife and mother, his brother and father. Get-well cards arrived daily and were stacked on the stand at his side to be opened and viewed at leisure. Visitors were limited and screened before admittance, and none were granted more than a few minutes at a time, which still baffled Liam when he was awake to see them come or go. A few, he might not have minded seeing longer than a heartbeat, he considered as his gaze caught on motion outside the window. He knew he could be in trouble when a seagull soaring across a gray sky could offer intrigue.

Muttering a curse, Liam was only vaguely aware of startling the pixie nurse who arrived alongside his bed. At the sight of her peering over the bedrail, his irritation enhanced. "Who in his right mind hires a dwarf to care for a giant?" he asked of no one and belatedly realized what he'd said. More irritated, he caught the woman's smile and wondered if she were daft. Surely, she should be offended.

"Feeling better, sir?"

"Does it sound like it, lass?" Liam asked in a quiet voice.

"Mmm? I'd have to say, yes," she said as if teasing him, and in a flashing thought, he recalled a moment when he'd considered wrapping his one hand around her throat, squeezing.

Alas, he was not that crazy, though if he remained in this wickedly dull room much longer, he might welcome a padded cell. "Aye, maybe I am well, after all. Do I have a pair of pants in this room?"

"Your wife brought you some pajamas and slippers, hon. A nice robe, too, if you're thinking about taking a shower."

"That's a far cry from what I asked, pixie."

She suffered to appear apologetic. "I know you're getting anxious, sir, but you're not quite ready to run any races."

"I'm not a fucking Thoroughbred, and truth be known, I've never suffered a need to run a blasted marathon. I'd settle for a goddamn pair of jeans or blasted sweatpants, a sweatshirt, socks, and fucking hiking boots—"

"Ahhh," the voice came from the doorway, as lyrical and smooth as a symphony in that single drawn note.

His attention riveted, Liam watched his wife glide through the door looking as if she'd stepped off the cover of a fashion magazine—wearing nothing more than a pair of casual blue slacks, a matching jacket, and a slinky white top. Her hair tumbled over one shoulder as if haphazardly tossed aside, and a feather of silky waves swept across her intelligent brow. Her eyes, near to emerald, carried the wave of amusement to wash over her soft lips and flushed cheeks. She was either glad to see him or laughing at him.

"There's the raging beast we all know and love," she said whimsically, reached the bed, and ducked, apparently, intending a peck on the—

Not a peck on the cheek.

She landed her lips on his with a force to halt the breath on his tongue and with a cant of her head, tipped his own into greater intrigue. Ah, to be kissed senseless at the crack of dawn! . . . His hands slipped upward, one catching her ribcage over the rail, the other gliding into the wild tangle of curls at her shoulder. More. Only that thought held firm as a different fire ignited below the site of such constant flames in recent memory. He was waking—fully—to the randy devil rising beneath the sheet and his heart slamming a quickening beat . . .

And the blasted external bleeping of a heartbeat increasing was not his imagination.

A low growl started in his chest, but an odd warmth slid over his chest, sinking past the scar and skimming to embrace him, halting whatever thought crossed his mind. In dual assault, the tongue danced about his own, and the hand slipped over his shaft, drawing him toward the brink of release.

If he'd ever climbed higher, faster, the memory was lost. On a wild and wondrous wind, he tasted the mountains, the lakes, and streams, the honeysuckle and thyme . . . And she was with him there, tasting and breathing the same air, shuddering to the same vibrations as the world inverted . . .

She took his breath, stilled his raging, and held him as she took him over the edge . . . and for an instant or an eternity, Liam hovered on the brink, certain of a dream from which he'd prefer not to awaken. But he was waking—or awake. The eyes near emerald peered into him at close proximity. The ends of her hair brushed against his shoulder; an impish smile quivered on her slightly swollen lips . . . and her hand remained at his nethers, kneading the tremors from his shrinking self. Confusion reigned in his mind and quickened in his eyes, and she appeared only more delighted.

Barely above a whisper, she asked, "Feeling better, my love?"

"If . . . I felt any better, lass," he uttered on a breath. "I'd think myself gone to heaven."

She stifled a laugh, her gentle touch stilling him beneath the sheet and her eyes softening with an odd wonder. "I'm not sure this is proper, m' love."

"Little late for doubts, mine own."

Again, that soft laugh and devilment danced in the deep green eyes. "S'pose it is."

In genuine wonder, he gazed up at her, his fingers twining through her silken locks with the thought of drawing her to him. "I dinnae know what brought you, m' lass, but I'm glad you're here."

"You brought me, love," she said softly, and something in her eyes changed, enhanced with a sobering thought.

Likewise intent on the instant, Liam idled, "Ay-I brought you?"

Natalie withdrew her hand to his instant dismay and whispered as she rose. "Be still."

He'd heard those words before. His senses swayed with an effort to remember as she pivoted in a half-turn. At the medical cart, Penny M. feigned to appear fully engaged in rearranging her wares . . . or counting cotton balls. When Natalie spoke, the tiny woman nearly dropped her jar of tongue depressors.

"Would you mind stepping out, dear? And do shut the door behind you," she added and left no option for the woman to decline.

"Yes, ma'am," the sprite said, a little breathlessly, and hurried to escape. To her credit, she refrained from slamming the door despite her haste.

Amused and curious, Liam watched his wife turning, as unruffled as a duck in a downpour. If she was embarrassed, nothing showed. She appeared only slightly less amused than he felt. "I'd wager she'll have something to talk about in the locker room," she mused.

"They have locker rooms here?"

"Damned if I know," she said offhandedly. "Perhaps a breakroom instead," she idled, distractedly fumbling with the iron rail, finding the mechanism to lower it.

With a thought of where her intentions might lead, Liam suffered another twinge in his nether regions and wondered if he might not find the strength to muddle through. And wouldn't that just be something? Him—unable to go two rounds in ten minutes? But she was raising the head of the bed, and his curiosity rose by the same degrees. The woman had something on her mind—other than round two, much to his chagrin. At the elevated range, he watched her fidget to arrange the sheet at his side, then slipped her hip onto the mattress at his flank, already collecting his hand and lacing her fingers through his. She drew their both hands to rest on her thigh and studied him with a curious cant of her head, filling her lovely cleavage with wild wavy locks.

"I'm not so sure I want to know what's on your mind, love," he said honestly, quietly. "And on the heels of such a hello, I'd rather postpone it."

She smiled faintly, shaking her head slightly. "You've mentioned several times, Liam, we need to talk. And the moment's upon us. I can't stand to see you brooding so."

"My father broods," he said matter-of-factly.

"So, he does, and you follow in his footsteps, to be sure."

"I don't brood. I . . . ponder."

"Mm-hmm. And you're procrastinating," she noticed. "What do you remember of that evening, Liam?"

How many times had he been asked that question? He'd answered it at least a dozen times, several times in the past hour, alone, with at least one surly police detective, Det. Harbinder, asking the same question in different ways—all sounding somewhat accusatory. Sighing, Liam admitted, "Not as much as I should, Natalie." And not as much as he wanted to say to her.

"Liam," she said gently and squeezed his hand. "Tell me the truth, m'love. You won't shock me or hurt my feelings. I know you spent several hours with that woman—Alecia Helms—in the Fairlane Hotel. When you left there . . . what do you remember?"

She had spoken those words so simply, so utterly without emotion, it set him on edge. "I'd like to deny recalling that much, Nate, but it appears you have the facts in order. I uhm . . . I'd apologize if I thought it would help."

"Liam, the tabloids may distort the facts, but we both know where we stood when you decided to start seeing that young woman."

"Aye, but . . . well, damn it, Natalie, I still don't know what set you off," he admitted with a too-familiar frustration. "I thought maybe you'd met someone."

"You're a dope," she said bluntly.

Blinking his surprise, Liam canted his head. "Well, I don't see myself as such, m' dear. You're too blasted stunning for your own good, and any man would be a fool not to hit on you."

"Good grief," she muttered and shook her head, a smile quivering on her lips. "Where exactly did you think I'd have met someone? At the blasted grocery store? Ere hmm . . . perhaps, the boys' cafeteria at St. Andrew's? Ah, wait, my aerobics classes—that I haven't attended for over a year."

"I miss seeing you dress for those classes."

"Liam," she warned. "Just tell me true. When did you think I would have met someone? Especially six months after giving birth to our daughter."

"Well, it didn't stop us from—"

"Liam," she stated.

"All right then, I'm a dope. So why the bloody hell did you kick me out of our marital bed?"

"Because of the blasted phone call and those Goddamn pictures."

Stopped, stunned, he suffered the first inkling of genuine anger. "Please, continue," he said as he studied her angry gaze.

"The call came first, m' dear. A woman claiming to be your lover, telling me I should give you the divorce you so desired."

"Was that lass kind enough to offer her name?"

"No, one better, dear. The pictures arrived a day later."

"I'm nearly afraid to ask but fear I must. What of?"

"You . . . and a lovely brunette. A stewardess or some such, judging by her costume."

Suddenly, he felt as if he'd been punched in the stomach. "So, you receive a phone call and then pictures, and rather than ask me o'er the same, you tossed my clothes and the like into the guestroom."

"Yes, and I'd likely do it again as an alternative to knocking you senseless in your sleep."

"Humph." And she probably would have landed a telling blow or two, but still . . .? "Why the bloody hell did it matter to you anyway?" he asked in irritation. "You never seemed to like me all that much. Seemed to like our blasted arrangement in so much as you love our babes."

"You have a lot of blasted nerve," she snapped, her green eyes flashing. "Was only the blasted making of our babes to seem paramount in your mind, and after Micheal, I feared you'd satisfied your obligation and wanted no more to do with me."

His lips parted in denial, but no sound passed his surprise.

"You cannot tell me you remained celibate for all those years, and whence you did turn to me, you held back. Had I left it up to you, doubtful we'd even have Arabella," she stated, still angry. "You could barely stand to look at me." And the moisture flashing over her eyes was not from anger. "What was I supposed to think, Liam?"

"Lass, do uhm . . . do you recall the trouble you had delivering Micheal?" he asked quietly.

"It was a long delivery," she said offhandedly. "All went well."

"Lass, it was twenty-seven hours of pure hell on earth, and maybe you don't remember every minute of it, but I sure as hell do. There were times I thought I'd lost you, love—thought I'd sent you to the heavens, you and the babe both. I . . . I couldn't put you through that again," he said bluntly, honestly, squeezing her hand carefully. "If I couldn't look at you, it was pure and simple terror that I'd buckle to mine damnable needs and put you through that again."

She stared at him, doubting.

"Lass, do you uhm . . . do you recall when I mentioned maybe the need for birth control?"

"I . . . Yes, I do recall."

"I couldn't bloody stand being within ten feet of you without needing to take you. And even after that, I was afraid the blasted pills would fail."

"You uhm . . . started using condemns as well," she remembered hesitantly. "I uhm . . . just assumed you didn't want any more children with me . . . or that you picked up a . . . well . . . an ill from one of your ladies."

"Good God," he uttered. "Do you hate me that much?"

"I don't hate you, you big dope."

"Aye, that 'dope' again. And you wonder why I never fully understand you even when my head's not a bowl of mush?"

"If I hated you, we wouldn't have Arabella."

"That makes perfect sense. Clear as a bell how those two thoughts connect. As I recall, Arabella was one of those perfect storms. Faulty pill, faulty condemn."

"Lack of one. Pinhole in the other," she said quietly.

Stunned, yet again, he realized, "Well—dope, wears well."

"I had to do something drastic, Liam. I wanted a daughter."

"Bloody lucky we had a little lass then, or I might have caught on after the third or fourth son."

She had the nerve to quiver a smile.

"Lass, I'm not finding the humor here. I thought I'd lose my fucking mind for those nine months."

"You were too busy with the business to worry."

"Why the bloody hell do you think I sank my teeth into the business? If I didn't keep my blasted head occupied, I'd have probably blown it off."

"Really? You were that worried?"

"Aye, really," he admitted. "I've never been that terrified in my life, Natalie. If I'd lost you . . . I don't know what I'd have done."

"She was an easy birth. Slipped right out," she said.

A smile quivered on his lips as he nodded. "Aye, slipped right out. After putting you through three hours of hell and landing me on my knees in the hospital chapel. I think I repented for every sin I ever considered committing in those three hours."

Her eyes brightened with a high shine of amusement. "I sort of recall you appearing a bit weary when you held Arabella for the first time."

"You were glowing," he remembered.

"I do love you, you know," she spoke the words simply, honestly.

"I've loved you since we met at the blasted alter."

"Naa, you're lying now. I think I'd have known."

"Do you recall our wedding night?" he asked as the image of an angel rose in his mind. He'd known she was stunning at the onset, but in those moments at the altar, he'd believed her dropped down from some ethereal plane.

"I do, yes," she answered while stifling her smile.

She wasn't thinking about the alter, he could tell—and his thoughts followed her to their wedding eve. He'd been far too anxious to consummate their vows, and with the memory, his sorrow ignited. "I bungled that eve badly," he admitted. "I uhm . . . first didnae believe you could still be . . ."

"A virgin?"

"Aye," he admitted. "I couldn't imagine you remaining so blasted pure when you . . . Well, you didnae act shy in those first moments. So, what was I to expect? And as blasted stunning as you are—it just didnae seem possible. I thought you were blasted experienced. And it . . . and it made me mad." And she was quivering that smile again. "Aye, let me guess . . .? Dope?"

She stifled a laugh, nearly a giggle, and seemed content to let him muddle through.

"Lass, suffice it to say, I was in love with you when you glided down that blasted rose-cluttered carpet and landed in my hands. If it seemed else in your mind, it probably was my fault. Over and above the fact that I was young, arrogant, and hated both our fathers for being so blasted smug—I believed you were coerced into that union against your will. Under different circumstances, I believed we might have gotten along well."

"We got along well regardless," she commented.

"Aye, in bed," he remembered. "But even there, after that first eve, I felt like such a blasted ogre, I wasn't certain we'd ever go there again. Frustration, lass. Pure and simple frustration drove me then and sometimes now. I still can't stand to be this close and not have you beneath me."

"I didn't know that, Liam," she admitted, no longer laughing but wearing that gentle Mona Lisa smile. "I believed you resented me. Still do at times."

How . . .? His hand lifted their both hands, and he loosened a finger to brush a path along her lovely cheek. "How could you doubt, m' lass?"

Softer still, her hazel eyes turned amber as she studied him. "How could I not?" she asked softly. "There've been so many others, m' lad. I wasn't fool enough to believe you were faithful."

"I couldn't have you," he said and their hands sank to rest again on the silky blue cloth. "And maybe that's not a good excuse, Natalie, but it's a fact. And if not you, I needed someone."

For a long moment, she continued studying him, then lowered her gaze. When she looked at him again, determination had risen into the amber hue. "I followed you."

Not certain he had heard her correctly or understood the words, he held her gaze. "Uhhh?"

"The night you were ambushed," she continued grimly, squeezing his fingers in her grip, needing an anchor. "I needed to know if you were finding the happiness you were seeking and deserved. I needed to know if that blasted phone call held merit and if you'd be happier in another's arms. I couldn't bear to think of yourself trapped for all eternity in a situation you regretted or resented. I suspected you were seeing someone regularly, but I needed to know."

Perhaps, his mind hadn't cleared as much as it needed to. She seemed to be saying far more than her words explained. Followed him . . .? The ambush? Followed him . . . "How . . . how the bloody hell did you follow me?"

"A cab from the airport," she answered matter-of-factly.

"The . . . airport?"

"It wasn't hard, you know? I had your flight schedule. Clarice gave it to me. So uhm . . . I booked a slightly earlier flight and waited for you and Mason to arrive."

"And hailed a cab."

"I couldn't very well follow you in another limousine," she said sensibly.

"No, I s'pose not."

"That Castaway seemed rather outrageous."

He stared at her, wondering if he were still stoned. "Aye, it is that."

"Mason recognized me," she continued smoothly. "I suppose he knew where the evening was headed. As did I with that scant blond attached under your jacket. I needed to know, Liam, and I'd come too far to be put off by Mason's attempt to protect me."

"Ahhh . . .? Do explain, please," he managed, holding rein on his confusion.

"Well, he escorted me to my blasted cab and booked a room for me at the Bayfront. I think he even sent Artair ahead to see to my safety, but uhm . . . I needed to know if she held your heart or just your body."

"And uhm . . . did you find out?"

"S'pose so," she said offhandedly. "But not then. I was so blasted angry . . . But then, it was such a long blasted day. I fell asleep."

"Uh-huh. . . in the lobby of the Fairlane . . . er on the bloody street?"

"In the cab, silly," she said lightly.

"Oh, of course," he managed, near certain he was delirious again.

"Anyway, Mario knew you by then and woke me."

"Mario."

"My cab driver, Liam," she said as if he might be a dolt for not following this train.

"Aye, the cabby. Mario."

She eyed him with a slight cant of her head, sunspots shooting off her auburn hair despite the absence of sun. "Are you angry?"

"Angry."

"You keep repeating what I'm saying," she noticed and canted her head further. "Are you uhm . . . feeling poorly again?"

"I might be," he decided, not at all certain. The thought of his wife, his stunning wife, traipsing about in a blasted cab in the middle of the night, on a street where he had been . . . "Oh-m'-God," he muttered, fearing that he'd just caught up to what she was trying to tell him.

"Mario restored my faith in mankind," she spoke lightly, perhaps aware of his rising hysteria. "He did, you know? There are good people in the world, Liam."

"Bloody hell, woman! You were there. You were—where the hell were you?" he demanded and might have risen; instead, he gripped her fingers more tightly, which might have accounted for her wince. With a serious effort, he softened his handhold, but his gaze held her quick. "Do not tell me . . . oh Good Christ. That was you. In that fucking alley," his tone descended with his ire ascending. "You were—"

"Well, if you're through cursing, Liam, I might admit I was there. I saw those idiots approaching you, but well, I wasn't exactly close enough to see a weapon or the like."

"No."

"I was a half block away," she said in odd exasperation. "You couldn't exactly expect me to see a serious threat in those little fellows against your great height. And I was still angry," she said rather offhandedly.

His insides shook with the memory flash of those shadowy men, but it was not for his own safety he feared at this moment. It took his every ounce of effort to keep from breaking her slender digits with the rage slipping through him. "Aye . . . angry," he caught up again, fearing if he spoke too loud, he might be ranting or raging.

"I got there a little belatedly," she said with a hitch of sorrow in her eyes. "If I'd known those others were there—"

"God be merciful," he uttered,

"I didn't know how badly you were hurt until you started to fall," she said with even greater sorrow and squeezed his hand. "I did try to catch you, m' love, but I'm afraid I wasn't close enough."

On a carrousel out of control, the images scrolled through his mind at lightning speed . . . and confused him more with the image of a boy wheeling about. A jest, he believed in one instant, certain his father was behind this telling—as it certainly sounded like some wild and fanciful tale for which Lucius could be a mastermind. And in the next instant, he studied her intent amber gaze and read the integrity. Yet it made no certain sense. Unless . . . "You came after the lad—" She was shaking her head slowly and seemed to be waiting for him to halt the carrousel in his skull. "What—no?"

"There uhm . . . There was no lad, Liam," she said carefully. "Foolish, I'm sure, but uhm . . . I wore a disguise."

"F—oolish. A dis-guise." She thought a *disguise* to be the only foolish thing here?

"Well, I didn't do a lot of preplanning," she said, back to the huffed breaths. "It was just a silly hat and a jacket I picked up at the airport. And uhm . . . glasses."

"Oh-mi-God," he was back to muttering and halting his fingers from crushing her hand. "Have you uhm . . . lost your bloody mind, lass?"

"You are angry," she said dubiously.

"I don't—*know*—what I am," he said honestly. Numb, perhaps. To think of this wondrous woman . . . alone. *Angry. Furious. Scared witless.* "God almighty, woman, did I drive you toward this insanity?"

"Now, there's a question worth pursuing at length," she said offhand-edly.

"You could have been blasted killed! Has that once, ever, slightly, then, or now, entered your blasted mind, lass? In this bloody quest . . . Jesus H Christ, woman, you are mad—"

"Not as mad as you at the moment," she interrupted his ranting, herself as calm as a frozen lake, but her eyes spit amber sparks. "But I could be getting there soon, lad."

"Natalie!" he demanded. "Stop these infernal word games! I feel like I'm on a blasted carrousel in a fucking funhouse, and you think this is—is—I don't even know what the fuck you think this is!"

"It started out as a conversation," she said offhandedly, her gaze steady. "I'd meant to ease your mind, m' lad,"

"By admitting you entered a fray that could have left our children orphans?"

"You're being unreasonable," she said smoothly.

"I'm . . .? You truly are a mad woman," he decided.

"You had them well in hand by the time I arrived," she said with a hint of irritation. "And how the bloody hell was I supposed to know there were a dozen of them? It's not as if I could actually see into that Goddamn alley."

"So, you just blindly leaped—"

"Oh, settle," she said bluntly.

"Settle?"

"You were hurt, damn it."

"And you could see that but not—"

"I felt it, Goddamn it," she snapped at him, fire flashing in her eyes. "You were in trouble, and I knew it! Goddamn it, I knew it was coming. Something was coming at you, and I had to stop it. Do you ken, mine wretched Highlander?"

What stopped him more, her announcement or her address, he knew only the whirlwind paused within his raging mind. Highlander. She called him her Highlander, sounding like an endearment off her lips, even with the 'wretched' in the mix. Uncontrollably, Liam felt the quiver in his lips. With a serious effort, he attempted to hold back that smile, especially with her eyes flashing as much anger as discomfort. She was uncomfortable, though. As if she spilled that essence from her pores, he felt her rage shifting to distress, nearing fear. After all else that she'd just admitted with such casual indifference, to see her faltering at the mere mention of her gift was a more effective brace against his amusement.

'. . . Something coming at you . . .'

"You . . . you felt the danger . . .? When, Nate?" he asked though he thought he might already know.

She hesitated and started, "It doesn't matter."

"Aye, it matters, Natalie, and might explain more than you've mentioned already," he said carefully. "I don't think you're a madwoman, lass. And I dinnae think you needed a thing confirmed," he added, reading her greater discomfort as she started to shift her gaze. Squeezing her fingers, he drew her gaze to him. This . . . this odd fear, he had seen before and never fully understood it. "Do you fear your sight?"

"Liam—"

"It is sight," he said quietly. "I've known about your gifts since we met at the altar, love, and I know it bothers you. I've always wondered, but I was afraid to ask why you seem so uncomfortable . . . Did you know in advance that I would land here, and uhm . . . took it upon yourself to follow me rather than simply warn me?"

"I . . . it's not that simple."

"No, probably not," he said calmly. "But what came first, Natalie, the idea to follow me or the need to do the same?"

"I needed to know," she said irritably.

"Aye, needed to know that your fears were justified, but which ones, I wonder. The fear of my indiscretions, or the fear for my life."

"Both, damn it," she admitted softly.

"Aye, and both confirmed," he realized. "It was not my heart though, love. Never that I've lost or given to another. If nothing else, you can believe that."

"I know that, now, my love," she said quietly.

He needed to hold her, needed to be held by her. No other thought remained more firmly as he drew their caught hands aside and opened his free hand in invitation.

Nothing felt more real or right than to have her husband's sturdy arms wrapped around her, and for time eternal, Natalie rested against him, her head at his shoulder, her breath at his neck. She'd needed this moment. She'd craved it like air since they'd stood at the bathroom door four days earlier. If she never moved, it would be too soon with the weariness dragging at her soul. Here was the man she'd married—the man she'd missed for longer than she could readily recall. Perhaps, since before Arabella had been born . . . and recalling his reason for steering clear of her, she quivered a slight smile. If he weren't still so wan, doubtful he would have admitted to fearing a thing.

At the soft, wispy motion at her shoulder, her thoughts stilled, her attention riveted on his fingers playing with her hair. For all his great size, he could be gentle, and all too swiftly, she felt his thumb brushing over the knuckles of her caught hand. She'd missed this the most. The quiet interludes between their lovemaking. He was never hurried when they lay together, generally cooling between rounds. Too long, far too long had passed since they'd shared this intimacy—either in prelude or pause—and perhaps he was thinking the same thing as his palm slid down her back, rolling over her hip. She rested at an angle, still against him but careful not to land fully atop him. For a time, the mere embrace would need to . . .

But his hand was gliding still, sliding under her jacket, and she nearly feared to breathe with the riot of sensations igniting behind that subtle investigation.

Not a good idea, she realized abruptly and started a move—

"Settle, mine own," he spoke in quiet cadence as his thumb found the waistline at her spine.

"Liam," she uttered and tipped her head to spy his dark blue eyes upon her. He held her quick, that much she knew, and the whisper of a smile on his mustache clearly indicated where his thoughts had traveled. "M' love, this uhm . . . probably shouldn't happen. This isn't the time . . . Or place . . ." And it was becoming more difficult to think with those long lashes dipping over the bemused blue eyes, the hint of his smile enhancing, the warm palm gliding the cloth off her hip. "Liam—We've shocked that—poor girl once and—too—"

"If I let you rise," he said as he tilted his head to eye her. "Do you think you might slip over there and turn that lock?"

"Liam."

Oh, and there it was, that flash of pearly whites, a whisper of that impish smile to set her on edge. She loved him. The look of him when he struck these carefree poses with a smile playing on his lips, his eyes firing toward molten cobalt, his blond waves scattering over his temple as if caught in a quick wind. Too handsome, by far, this wily husband of hers.

"Natalie," he spoke her name with a reasonable tone. "What's good for the goose is good for the gander . . . and I'm remembering a fine awakening not all that long ago. I think it's only fair, I should bring you to the same level. I uhm . . ." With an almost sheepish smirk, he finished. "I've mastered the controls on this gangplank, and it's wide enough for the both of us."

How he could appear so blasted innocent and sound so blasted pleased with that accomplishment, as if it were a feat of incredible effort, she had little sense to wonder as he withdrew his hand from her hip and patted her instead.

"G'on with yer fine self, now, lass. I have an adjustment to make here."

On her feet, she caught his gaze and knew, at this moment, she would deny him nothing, let alone something she might want with equal fervor. Flashing him a wicked smile to have him blinking, she turned and crossed the brief floor. Only for a second, she held the nob and contemplated passing through, then pivoted the bolt lock and turned, finding him with the bed control in his hand.

As Liam watched her advance, he engaged the call button on the control, and waited for the harried, "Yes, sir?" "I'm shutting off the heart monitor. When the single line appears, be assured, I'm not dead."

Natalie stifled a laugh even as he reached toward the hovering machine. "Sir! Don't—wait, sir."

He pushed the button to disable the machine and silenced the bleeping. "Sir!

"Lass," he said again into the speaker. "If you have a do-not-disturb sign, hand it on the door, and do not attempt to pick the locks. My wife and I are engaging in a serious discussion, and I absolutely do not want any intrusions."

"Sir, you need your medicine!" the anxious voice erupted.

"It can wait," he said in a voice to broach no argument—the same voice to hold dominion in a company that spanned the Continental US and several surrounding countries—then released the control. "Now then," he began in an all-business tone and sent his gaze down her, up, his smile sliding into place. "What say you take pity on me and lose that jacket, my own? I'll deal with the rest."

"You will, will you?"

"Aye, there's nothing I like more than unwrapping a gift one layer at a time."

She lost the jacket with an economy of motion, tossing it aside and sidling, once again sitting sidesaddle, poised to engage in conversation. In dual assault, his hands landed, one skimming up her thigh, the other skidding at the small of her back, and she landed on his lap, welcoming every inch of his anatomy against her. One layer at a time, he was as good as his word, and in the hazy morning light, his eyes shined midnight as his palms skidded over her hips, her breasts, sending fireworks flashing at her core. In a slow dance as old as time, she moved with a careful rhythm, barely shifting despite the vibrations rising as he found her center and began the quiet strokes, stoking her flames. Careful. They were careful. His hand slid to part her thighs. His thumb caressed as she whispered kisses at his neck and braced her forearms to either side of his shoulders, careful to keep her weight and motion off his injuries. And when she was certain she could stand no more, she slid her hand to find his manhood pulsing and ready. Against her neck, his breath heated and sounds uttered, and when the moment came, she shifted over him, straddling him to take the length of his shaft. By sense alone, she rode the tide, keeping him near to still as she drew the blood of life from his loins and carried them both over the brink.

For seconds or minutes on end, they hovered, her panting breaths matching him as she held herself aloft, looking into his livid eyes. They hadn't lowered the bed. On her shins braced against his hips, she remained suspended over him, loving the look of bewilderment to slide over his handsome face, into his eyes.

"I—was wrong," he huffed on a soft, panted breath. "I *have* died—and gone to heaven."

"I'm not—" She drew breath, equally winded. "Calling a nurse—to revive you."

"Good. I like—this view—of heaven," he decided and skimmed his gaze downward, taking in the sights. His sweated palms rested on her hips, his thumbs pressed gently at the joints as if he might start her moving again, but his head rested against the head of the gangplank, his weariness apparent.

Leaning forward, resting her sensitive breasts against his sweated chest, Natalie drew his gaze. Without the need to shift but a fraction, she lifted one hand to brush the damp locks off his temple, as awed by him as ever a moment past. Even after three children and all these years, she still grew damp at the sight of him and wondered at her good fortune to be married to such a one as him. "I should hate you . . . for being so handsome."

Appearing bewildered, he suffered a smile. "Love, that was—not the—sweet nothings—I hoped to hear."

"No. But it's true," she huffed softly. "If you were an ogre—life would be—so much simpler."

"Would you—still love me?"

For a long moment, she studied him, wondering at his sobriety. "Do you doubt?"

In an equally long pause, he appeared almost amazed to realize. "No."

"I don't want you—" She spoke simply, only vaguely aware of her elevated position to hold him beneath her, between her knees. "In other women's beds."

"I cannot make pr—"

She squeezed her knees, and his eyes brightened with a wild amusement.

"O'right then—that's settled."

"You're a married man," she said reasonably.

"Aye, and uhm—m' lass has uhm—very powerful legs," he mused.

"Aye, and don't you forget it, m' lad."

"Natalie," he said in sudden sobriety. "I do love you."

Landing her lips on his, she merely whispered the kiss and confirmed her response. That she felt his lad twitch against her thigh confirmed his response. Enlightened, she lifted and read his faintly heated shine. "We're not doing that again, Liam," she said firmly. "I'm drawing the line here. There's no blasted way that we're repeating any part of this process."

"You're sure of that?"

"Liam, we need a shower."

"Aye, my own thought exactly, and I seem to recall there's a chair—"

"No. It's not happening. I refuse to take advantage of you a third time.'

"Fine then, I'll do the taking."

"Those ladies are going to think I'm nothing more than a wanton hussy."

"I've had my fill of those—"

Seeing the flash of surprise and distress, regret flaring behind his gaze, Natalie lost her sudden start and burst into a laugh, landing her forehead against his shoulder as she hugged him.

"Lord—I am a dope," he uttered, still distressed.

"Lad, that's not a mistake you'd make if you weren't exhausted," she said lightly. "And I won't hold you to account for it, as I'm fairly certain, I'm to blame."

"Aye, ye're to blame," he said and wore the downtrodden expression only a moment more as he realized she truly wasn't holding him to account. "God, woman, I truly do love you."

"Sooo, maybe I'll let you do the taking," she said and slipped off him and the bed with a dancer's grace. "Providing you can walk to that room without any help."

"Now, there's a challenge if I ever heard one."

And one he was all too well equipped to accept.

21

"Settle, kid . . . just settle down, now."

Luke might have heard that voice several times if once. At the outer edges of his consciousness, he recognized the quiet cadence as he tried rising, twisting, pushing against the pressure on his shoulder. Not the first for that either, though his senses were far and too muddled to draw a clear image. Shaking his hanging head, resting on his forearm and elbow, he collected details in sluggish stages, waking to the brown faux leather couch cradling him like a bladder in a funhouse attraction. As if his body were suctioned into the cushion, he couldn't seem to throw his leg over the stuffing, and he woke more to the swaying, vaguely familiar image of a black-haired man sitting rather oddly on a shiny wooden table. The funhouse images hadn't faded but enhanced instead, as his wavering focus trailed from the blue-jean-covered knees to the black t-shirt and kinked mustache. Dark eyes looked down at him from a canted angle, more intent than bemused despite the quirked lips. "Wh-where . . . ?" *Am I?*

"I'd ask how much you remember, but I don't think you're awake enough to answer," the bouncer from The Emerald Club commented in an inherently deep voice.

Only more confused, as though the fellow were speaking in tongues, Luke lost his precarious balance, and his head sank into the cushion. In sluggish degrees, he collected more details, seeing dull gray light glowing through beige curtains, a television atop a sturdy short bookcase—filled with DVDs and electronics, magazines, or books. Generic pictures hung on the walls with glass faces reflecting the dull light. He smelled coffee . . . and his head pounded, his stomach churned in a slow revolution. Again, he found the man watching him; the capable hand retracted to dangle from the wrist at one knee. Wrong . . . something was wrong here. . . the woman . . . a blond woman posing . . . and not alone. Another body, a male. Spooked, Luke found the bouncer studying him still. "Wha-at happened?" he managed.

"That's a damned good question, kid," the man said in a more reserved tone. "Why don't I get you a cup of coffee and a couple aspirin, and you rest a little while longer?"

"Where th-the hell am I?" Luke asked, afraid he might already know.

"My apartment in Kingston, New Jersey," the bouncer spoke candidly. "You're safe here, and there's no one looking for you at the moment, as far as I know," he continued carefully. "If you need to make a call, though—let somebody know you're all right—your cellphone and my landline phone are on the stand there."

As if his senses were moving through quicksand, Luke stared at the fellow for a delayed second before catching up. No one he needed to call. Not one single person would be concerned one way or another unless he disappeared for a few years. His gaze listing, squinting against the dull light and the headache thudding behind his eyes, Luke lifted a heavy hand and nearly smacked himself in the ear with his own sluggish appendages. Concentrating, he managed to skim his fingers into his hair and hold his head as if he might halt the swaying and pounding. Only once in his life had he suffered a hangover, and although this felt similar, he knew the difference.

No pictures.

Closing his eyes, he verified that simple discovery. And his skin crawled with the possibility. No mental images of himself standing on a table and singing an Irish ballad, nor dancing with a stunning blond prima donna, nor staggering through a garden . . . Only once, but memorable, that night of drunken revelry. He'd been safe that night, safe and young and stupid but aware of every last bit of tomfoolery when he'd suffered through the morning ministrations, including a lot of orange juice, aspirin, and toast. Janel Livingston, his latest lover, had tried giving him tomato juice, and he'd nearly vomited in her father's pristine porcelain tub.

Not a single snapshot of last night's binge assailed his drifting mind.

To the scuff of shoes, Luke lifted his lashes enough to see the bouncer setting a stout steaming mug and a glass of water on the coffee table. Settling onto the table, rather like sitting a stool, he shuffled an aspirin bottle between his capable hands. "One, two, or three?" he offered.

"Three," Luke decided and freed his head, again struggling to rise to his elbow. The couch still held him as if cleaving him in a wrestler's grip for which he had no strength to resist. He managed to balance long enough to accept and swallow the pills . . . belatedly worried. "If I start to feel funny . . ."

What? What would he do then? Nothing. It would be too late, as it had been too late last evening when he'd eyed the half-empty bottle of Corona . . . and that was the last clear image in his mind. Already lying down again, he found the bouncer, and there was no disguising or hiding his genuine fear.

"It's just aspirin, kid," the man spoke carefully, confirming his powers of observation. "But it wasn't last night, was it?" he asked more carefully.

An active-duty policeman . . . and there was no point in denying a thing. "I didn't take anything," he managed quietly. "Not by choice."

For a few long seconds, the dark eyes studied Lucas without betraying his belief one way or another. "What do you remember, kid?"

"Luke," he offered. "My name's . . ."

"Lucas on your driver's license, which is lying next to your phone," the bouncer stated and kinked a weary smile. "And I'll mention here, your days of patronizing The Emerald Club are over for a while—like at least six months if I read that date correctly."

At another time, maybe, Luke might appreciate the man's attempt at levity. Far too confused and worried still, Luke barely flickered a smirk. "No worries, sir. I've had my fill of that fine establishment."

"Tye or Tyler," he offered and tipped his head, studying Luke more intently. "Are you really feeling up to talking for a few minutes here, buddy?"

Luke nodded, doubting it but knowing he needed answers whether he wanted them or not. "I don't honestly remember what happened last night," he admitted with genuine fear rising. "And for a whole lot of reasons, that's troubling."

"I'd imagine so," Tyler said distractedly. "What exactly do you remember?"

How much should he admit? And how much could he afford to omit? Casting his gaze toward the curtains, starkly aware of traffic sounds flowing to suggest an early morning rush, he decided, "I remember coming to the club. Meeting a blond woman of questionable repute. Going downstairs where we could talk."

"I don't imagine you came there looking for a hooker—or not just any hooker. Is that about right?"

Luke focused on the intent gaze, grasping the simple truth. He needed help, and reaching out to his family, or father in particular, wasn't an option. At least not until he figured out what happened last evening. "How much do you know about Alecia Helms and my brother, sir?"

"Your brother came into the club a few times," Tyler answered grimly. "I know he was dating her, and I think she was a whole lot more interested in him than he was in her," he continued without prodding. "Alecia's what I'd call a gold digger," he said with a shrug. "And your brother didn't strike me as an easy mark."

"But they were dating," Luke commented or questioned.

"Probably the wrong term for it," Tyler corrected and reconsidered his direction. "Just how much about this do you know, kid?"

"Enough to agree, dating's the wrong word, and to admit, my brother's no fool," Luke said with a sigh. "I'd imagine he was physically attracted, and she fulfilled a need. He's married—as if I need to tell anyone that," he said disgustedly and sent his gaze to the curtained windows. "His marriage was on the rocks for a few months, and that's probably not an excuse, but then, he doesn't really need an excuse. I'd imagine his affair with Miss Helms was just that. An affair," he said and found the near stranger studying him. Luke shrugged and even that slight motion sent another thump through his skull. "He probably meant to compensate her financially if he didn't already, and that brings us to what you might know, Tye. Is she the type who'd hire a gang of thugs to mug him for a few thousand?"

Tyler's head canted more. "He lost a few thousand?"

"I truly don't know, but potentially, he could have," Luke admitted. "He's six-six and a black belt in Karate, sir. He doesn't flash cash, but he doesn't worry about carrying it either. I know he generally carries at least a grand at all times. It's uhm . . . it's pocket change."

Tyler blinked, but that was his only reaction.

"So? Was she the type?"

"She never struck me as the criminal type, Luke, but that kind of cash can seem like a whole lot more than pocket change to a young woman who maybe makes fifty bucks a night in tips if she's lucky."

"Did she hang with thugs, do you think?"

"I'd say no," Tyler said. "Not that I ever saw, but that doesn't mean much. I can only vouch for when she was working."

"Was she any good? I mean, as a dancer?"

"Better than some, not as good as others," Tyler said offhandedly. "I don't think she was at it very long before she started at the club. Dancing maybe, but no stripping . . . And I don't think she set your brother up," he decided.

"A particular reason?"

"I think she fell for him."

"As in—in love with him?" Which sort of coincided with what Luke had overheard three weeks earlier.

"Whether she was in love with him or his money, I couldn't say, but I doubt she would have tried killing the golden goose either way," he said lightly and seemed to realize his words. "Sorry," he added quickly. "I just meant—"

"I get it," Luke said smoothly, not taking offense. "But what if Liam was breaking it off? Do you think she would have reacted?"

"I . . . I could see her throwing a tantrum, making a scene," Tyler said thoughtfully. "She was street smart if you know what I mean. She would have either found a way to keep him or some of his money. As much as she might have wanted to keep him to herself—I think she was enough of a realist to know their affair would never last. Your brother, he's one smooth operator, but I don't think he ever deliberately misled her."

"He wouldn't, no," Luke said with a touch of his heritage. "He wouldn't see a reason to be else than honest, and he'd never leave his wife."

"Certain of that, eh?"

"I could offer you a dozen reasons why I am, but suffice it to say, I'm certain," Luke said with the pounding finally starting to ebb, though his muscles still felt sluggish and weak. He couldn't feel wearier if he'd run the Boston Marathon—twice. "What happened last night, sir? How did I come to be in your apartment?"

"Do you remember leaving the club?"

Studying the sober gaze, Luke tried to remember. "Leaving when?"

"That's one of the questions I'd like answered, buddy. The fact is, you went downstairs, and a short time later, you were gone," Tyler said grimly. "I generally wait around for the girls to leave, and it was a good thing I did last night. I came out around three and found you stumbling around the parking lot, looking for your car and mumbling about a Vette. You uh . . . you were wasted, kid, and not making any sense. I thought about carting your ass to the emergency room but considering all the publicity surrounding your family, I decided against it."

"I appreciate that, sir," Luke admitted.

"I'm not sure I did the right thing, Luke," Tyler said quietly. "I've spent the past several hours wondering if you were just drunk or if you were about to OD. Then rousting you to make sure you weren't in a coma."

Judging the level of weariness apparent in the bloodshot eyes, Luke commented, "I appreciate that, too, Tye."

"You said you didn't take anything," he said carefully. "But you don't recall drinking that much either, do you?"

"The bottle," Luke recalled in livid color—his gaze swaying to the label, questioning.

"Have you ever heard of Rohypnol?"

Luke's attention riveted, doubting. "The uh . . . the date rape drug? Rufie?"

"That's the one."

"You think—" The confirmation and concern appeared all too clear in the dark, concentrated gaze. Luke shook his head slightly, disbelieving even as he took a mental internal inventory of his anatomy, reaching a far more distressing conclusion. His body ached like one massive bruise from his thudding head to his toes, and he'd felt like this once before, too, not all that long ago after spending a night and day making love to a lovely flight attendant. The same—but different. If he tried, he could recall every instant of his time with Peggy, but last night was a blank. "I . . . I don't remember leaving that club. Or returning. And that's an effect of that drug, isn't it?"

"It is," Tyler said almost carefully.

With his thoughts quickening, Luke reached several conclusions, beginning with the reality of his foolishness and ending with the reality of what could have happened. Along with what might actually have transpired in his mental absence. Setting the fear and self-recriminations aside in his mind, bypassing the anger, he chose the more analytical approach. "Do you know the woman who met me at the bar?"

"Honestly, no."

"But she resembled Alecia Helms, didn't she?" Luke asked needlessly.

"At first glance, yes," Tyler said carefully. "Have you ever seen Alecia Helms? Met her?"

"I saw her once," Luke admitted. "Which was enough to know the woman posing as Alecia Helms last night was an imposter."

"You want to tell me why you were at the club last night?"

He needed an ally, and one with some practical experience dealing with criminals was a side benefit. "How much of what I tell you will you need to report, sir?"

"How much of it could be illegal?"

"I . . . On my part, none of it," Luke admitted. "But I think I've stumbled into something, and if last night's any indication, I'm out of my bailiwick."

"You think?"

Luke canted his still heavy head and looked at the more peculiar expression on the weary face, noting the black beard stubble that was truly impressive if it was a single day's growth. Sidetracked far too easily, Luke gathered his wits, commenting. "Well, I could probably muddle through an investigation."

With a kink forming in his mustache, Tyler shifted and lifted the coffee—his own apparently, as he took a few swallows and bought some time to think. "Tell you what," he decided. "Why don't you try resting a little longer. Then we'll start over from the beginning."

"I'm awake. The aspirin's kicking in," Luke commented as he began picking himself up. The couch presented a problem, like a living thing intent on holding him in its clutches, but he landed his feet on the floor, appreciating the hand to clasp his shoulder and aid his balance. "Shit," he muttered as his head dropped back onto the thick cushion. He wasn't rising further just yet. Rather dumbfounded, he found the dark eyes studying him still. "Are you sure I wasn't hit by a truck before you found me?"

"Wish I could say absolutely not," Tyler said in quiet concern. "What are the chances that I could convince you to visit an emergency room to get checked over?"

Luke considered a split second before deciding, "Slim to none, and Slim's already departed. I was kidding about the truck. I'd know if my bones were broken."

Discomfort flashed over the dark eyes; his concern obvious.

"I'd likely know if I was raped, too—or at least if a male had been involved," he added in a practical tone. "I'd imagine the Alecia imposter satisfied a few urges at my expense, and no, it doesn't thrill me," he added and noted the fellow appeared more critical in his observation.

"Maybe we better make that drive, buddy," Tyler said carefully. "If uh . . . well, we could probably pull some DNA if that's true."

"Sir, I won't pretend this isn't disturbing," Luke admitted. "But I'm not about to press criminal charges, and the collection of DNA would be a waste of time as well as mental energy."

"Luke, I know it's not easy wrapping your head around something like this, but the fact remains—you were victimized last night. Pretending that it didn't happen won't make it any easier to accept down the road. There are support groups and counselors—"

"I appreciate your concern, Tye," he commented. "And if it bothers me too bad, I'll probably take your advice and seek counseling. At the moment, however, I'd rather focus on finding this bitch and her accomplice."

"She had an accomplice?"

"She did, yes, and I'd wager it was the dark-haired fellow sitting in a booth just inside the top floor door, which brings us to another question. Did you ever see him before? Dark hair, pulled back, longer than mine. Wire-rim glasses, thin mustache. The glasses reflected the orange light, so I don't know his eye color, but he wore a dark plaid shirt, jeans, black shoes. Uh . . . Nikes. A watch, silver elastic band—generic brand. 10:03. Thin build. Nothing outstanding about his features. Mid-twenties, I think."

"I could probably put someone in a lineup with that description," Tyler commented. "Ten o' three? The time?"

"On his watch, yes, but I think it was closer to ten after. Might mean it was a windup watch, but the button was on the other side."

"You're telling me you saw all of that in that lousy light? Even his shoe brand? Or did you see him outside before you came in?"

"Just in the club," Luke admitted. "I did mention I'd remember if I'd seen anything," he pointed out. "He was already seated when I arrived."

"Something alarmed you about him?"

"It did," he agreed. "And the alias Alecia mentioned an accomplice. He was the likely candidate from the patrons upstairs."

Tyler hesitated, then decided, "Let's start over here. Why were you meeting that lady? I'm guessing she contacted you. Start there. When and how, where?"

"I could use that cup of coffee, sir," Luke decided. "And that's not where we need to start."

Tyler considered momentarily, glanced toward the end stand, back, as he pushed off the table. "Why don't you make use of that phone? By now, someone's probably worried about you." He barely drew breath before asking, "What do you take in your coffee? Or would you rather a cup of tea or a soda? Think I have some cola."

"Coffee's fine. Black," Luke answered and watched the fellow turn, stride toward an open arch toward a kitchen. In a quick pan, Luke judged the apartment predominantly male. No frills or knickknacks anywhere in sight. Sturdy lamps, heavy dark woods, beige walls . . . as utilitarian as his own flat, complete with generic scenic pictures on the walls. With two doors and a hallway opening off this central room, the fellow probably had a home office tucked behind one of the doors. Neat and tidy, Luke judged, spotting his shoes, side-by-side, alongside the couch on a dark patterned area rug of oriental design evenly placed to separate a love seat and armchair. The chairs held his attention as he wondered if he might escape the couch and opt for a more accommodating perch. Listening to the rattle of cups and slam of a refrigerator door, Luke climbed from the too-plush cushions and swayed into the sturdy faux suede armchair. The aspirin had helped, but he was nowhere near ready for any sprints . . . much less a marathon.

Catching his elbow on the armrest, his head on his palm, he tried rubbing the feeling of a bruise from his skull.

A roofie.

Damn it.

22

In hindsight, Luke recalled the woman's shuffle to use the ladies' room and knew he should have paid closer heed to her hands and that oversized bag than to the crack of her ass. The oldest trick in the blasted book . . . and he'd fallen for the diversion, recalling himself looking away, as embarrassed as the waitress to see the woman's crotch—as if he'd never seen pubic hair in his life. Never in a public place, he corrected, not relieved by that excuse. His thoughts distracted, he glanced at the electronics under the flatscreen TV, and his attention fixed. 11:47 a.m.? He'd lost over twelve hours?

Tyler returned, carrying two cups, minus saucers, offered one into Luke's hand and took his own, settling on the parallel loveseat rather than the monster couch. A tight, slight smile kinked his mustache as he glanced off the couch to Luke—but his gaze caught on the untouched phone. "Really, kid. You should probably check in with someone. I've seen enough of those newsbreaks to know your folks are probably frantic by now."

"They aren't expecting me," he said honestly and sipped the scalding hot brew without lifting off his palm. Resting the cup on his knee, he found the peculiar, concerned gaze. "Truly, Ty, they probably know I'm in the area, but they're not fretting over my absence."

"Kid, they have one son in the hospital in bad shape—"

"Trust me, if I phoned and said I'm all right, they'd be more worried," Luke said with a sigh, a slight shrug. "I'll see them soon," he added, then firmed his gaze. "If I paid you to moonlight as a private investigator, would that gain your confidentiality?"

"You know I'm a cop," Tyler said.

"I do, yes. I heard that the last time I visited that club. Active duty still, too."

"Then you know, I'm under some obligation to report a crime if I find reasonable evidence to support a charge."

"If I were to admit I took the roofie of my own volition, then there would be no crime."

"Did you?"

"You know better," Luke said and sighed. "Suppose it doesn't matter either way. If we find something illicit in this investigation, you can take the necessary steps. At the moment, it's all speculation on my part, and well . . . I've often been accused of being absentminded. Don't mistake that to mean, I don't notice things. Only that I don't always see a reason to notice." He shrugged. "I just thought I should be honest with you. I've observed things to concern me, and I haven't been able to connect the dots—which concerns me more. I'm usually good at puzzles, and that I can't solve this one, probably means there's some emotional basis for it. Perhaps, like you said—Alecia Helms falling for Liam." He shrugged his indifference. "I can't fathom how someone might react over an attraction to any extreme. I think Natalie, his wife, would probably just shoot him herself if she became annoyed with his exploits." Again, he shrugged, his gaze listing off the intent brown eyes. "Probably proves I'm not the most reliable soul to solve this mystery."

"Do you think she's involved?"

"Natalie?" Luke asked, finding the more blank dark gaze as the fellow nodded. "I'd say no," he said honestly. "But there's something there . . . I just can't put my finger on it."

"Why don't we start at the beginning, Luke? You said this didn't start with Alecia's imposter contacting you. So where do you think it started?"

"Actually, I think it started around April or May," Luke admitted.

"Which is about the time your brother and Alecia hooked up."

"Exactly . . . but I think I'm missing too many parts of this puzzle," he decided and gazed into abstracts in Tyler's direction. "I just can't see Frank taking Liam to that Club," he said absently and focused. "Do you recall how they met? Liam and Alecia?"

"I wasn't there, but it was pretty big news at the club," Tyler commented. "It's certainly not every day a millionaire walks into a cheap strip joint and takes an interest in a stripper. Although lately, we've caught the interest of more than one." Again, the slight smile, an attempt at levity, but Luke wasn't in a jovial mood. "Okay, so that wasn't funny considering . . . but honestly, your brother made quite a splash in our little club. I'm only surprised that no reporters caught wind of it sooner, although I think my buddy, the owner threatened to fire anyone who mentioned your brother's name—and for a while, no one even knew his name. I think most of the girls just thought he was an actor and decided not to mention him for fear of scaring him off." Again, the slight smile. "Actually, I got a kick out of it—the irony. Guys come there to drool over the ladies, and from the moment your brother walked in, the ladies were drooling over him. I think Alecia was the first to catch his eye, but any of them would have jumped in his lap—and you probably know the feeling." Abruptly, he was sober. "Is it possible that was the underlying motive for last night?"

"Excuse me?"

"Is it possible that bimbo just wanted to spend the night with you and knew she didn't stand a chance by ordinary means?"

"I . . . don't think so," Luke said hesitantly.

"How did she contact you?"

"See, that's where this gets screwy," Luke said. "I don't see how she was able to contact me at all," he admitted bluntly. "Unless she was in league with Pendleton, and even that's tricky. The only way anyone outside the MacDade security force could have known where I was staying was if they followed me from the closing back to my hotel. And I think I would have known if I'd been followed. I've always been good at spotting a tail."

"Start over. What hotel? What closing? And are we talking about Frank Pendleton—your friend?"

"He's more Liam's friend. They went to college together. I only actually met him three weeks ago at the hospital," Luke admitted. "And that's part of the beginning, but not the Pendleton I was referring to." Barely pausing, he continued, "I first thought Liam might have come to visit his old friend when his marriage hit a glitch—or the opposite, that Liam's visit and subsequent infidelity created the glitch in his marriage. I'm not so certain of either, now," he admitted, distracted by the digits changing on the electronics. Bouncing his glance off the 11:47 to the dull light on the curtains, he looked to Tyler. "It's near noon?"

Tyler glanced at the clock as well and nodded. "It's raining."

"Ah, that explains it. I was rather hoping it was dawn and your clock was wrong."

"Stay on track here, buddy," Tyler coached. "What do you think was going on?"

"I think the land had something to do with all this."

"Uh huh, and that land would be?"

"The Pendleton land," Luke stated as if Tyler should be keeping up. "I was led to believe that Liam was offered and rejected the Pendleton land. About a thousand acres in the Poconos, as it turned out. I knew there was something hokey with that scenario. Liam passing on that much timberland? I'm wondering now if Liam was lured here with that land deal—like a carrot to bait him. I think this entire ordeal was manipulated with the ultimate goal of ambushing Liam." And the second those words slipped out, he knew the truth of them. "I think Frank was manipulated into bringing Liam here. I think the old man might have been black-mailed. And I think Liam might have suspected something fishy, which would explain his backing out of the deal. What I don't get is why the old bastard offered me the land—as if he was forced into it."

"You said 'closing,'" Tyler stated thoughtfully. "You were referring to a land closing. You bought the land?"

"I did, yes," Luke admitted. "Frances—the elder Pendleton—called me a few days after Liam's assault and offered me the land," Luke said and paused to taste his coffee, hoping to clear his raspy voice and put his thoughts in order. "I think it was the same day Liam took a turn for the worse—it was the day after. I flew in on Wednesday; he called me Thursday morning. And I don't know if it was a coincidence, but I'd just decided to investigate Frank and Alecia Helms. I believed one or the other knew about that ambush. I ruled out Frank. Not so sure about Helms or the old man. In any event, I wasn't buying land with my brother standing at heaven's gate. So, I uhm . . . I stonewalled the sale for these few weeks. Pendleton pushed, though, and I knew Liam was on the mend," he shrugged and held Tyler's gaze. "Not fast enough, that mending, though, and I thought one of us should own that land."

"A thousand acres," Tyler said absently. "In the Poconos."

"A little over," Luke admitted. "Eleven hundred and fifty-three, to be precise. So, you can see why I wouldn't want Pendleton putting the land on the open market."

"Of course. So you just bought it."

"Exactly," Luke said with an odd relief to admit that, and Tyler seemed to understand the practicality of it.

"About how much would something like that cost? If you don't mind me asking?"

"It's public record. Or will be once it's recorded," Luke admitted. "Two point five million."

"Let's see . . .? So about two weeks ago, you get offered a thousand acres, and you manage to secure a bank loan on vacant—it is vacant land, right?"

"I think there are some squatters and old hunting shacks, but for the most part, it's just woodlands. But no, I didn't secure a loan. I paid cash—well, not cash exactly. I had a cashier's check from my bank."

"Of course you did."

Luke studied the peculiar blank expression, wondering if he was missing something. "You think that's relevant? I mean the cash angle?"

"Pocket change."

More dumbfounded, Luke commented with slight exasperation, "I didn't carry cash, and I wouldn't exactly consider it pocket change. I'm not generally foolish where money's concerned."

"Apparently, not if you have a few million lying around."

"It's not as if it's under my mattress," Luke said, wondering why he suffered an urge to defend himself again. Rather like speaking with Jacky Monahan on the ridge, defending his intelligence. "It was in a secure bank—FICA insured," he added.

"What was that you said—you're a little absentminded."

"I've been accused of it, but not where numbers are concerned," Luke said carefully.

After a moment, Tyler shook his head and drew a few swallows of his coffee, seeming to scan his living space before again focusing on Luke. "Okay, so you bought the land. When was this closing?"

"Yesterday morning," Luke answered, not certain of the fellow's peculiar expression. "I met Frances at the title company in Trenton, and we signed the papers. That's when I mentioned I might drive up to the mountains, and that's the only way . . . Well, that's not true either. My stalker might have followed me to the hotel, then followed Kelly to the mountains, but that doesn't seem right. He wouldn't have had time to steal a quad and get up there so quick if he was behind me—"

"Slow down," Tyler stated. "Who are we talking about here? Who's Kelly? And who's this 'he' following her and stealing quads?"

Luke stifled a slight smile. "Kelly's a 'he,'" he corrected and continued. "Kelly Finnegan. He's my Uncle Mason's bodyguard, but apparently, the family was hoping to keep tabs on me. By now, my father probably knows I bought the Pendleton land, and he's probably pissed unless Kelly was kept in the dark about the sale."

"You, my young friend, aren't making a lick of sense," Tyler commented carefully.

Feeling oddly hurt by that observation, Luke withdrew his gaze and sipped his coffee. Far too often, he was accused of lacking common sense, and after last night, he couldn't dispute it.

"Let me try to get this straight," Tyler said smoothly. "Pendleton senior lures your brother to Trenton to buy his land . . . and your brother stonewalls the sale?"

"I'm not sure about that," Luke admitted. "Kelly believed the sale was still pending," he added. "I didn't tell him differently, and I dropped him off at his car before he could ask what I was doing on the land."

"In the Poconos," Tyler said.

"That's where the land is, yes," Luke said, becoming slightly irritated with his patience waning. "I told you, Kelly followed me there from my hotel. I'm guessing Uncle Gill's keeping tabs on my coming and going from various hotels, but I tend to lose his surveillance vehicles when I hit the road." Luke shrugged. "I think they've come to accept that I'll turn up again when I want to. Anyway, I didn't think much about the surveillance yesterday. I wasn't even sure of the tail since there weren't that many roads cutting through the mountains. It could have been someone headed north, the same as I. Turned out though, Kelly had orders to approach and invite me to the Franklin House where the clan's staying." He paused a half beat. "The thing is, Kelly wasn't the only one on the mountain with me. I thought a poacher after I heard the quad, but then, when I lost Kelly in town, I spotted the same black Nissan I'd seen earlier in the day, and that's where this becomes more curious . . ."

"Uh, huh. Curious."

Considering a moment, he continued, "When I reached my hotel room, the message was waiting. The letter was in a plain white envelope inside a mailing envelope. No actual address on either. Just my room number and initials on the outside, and you need to understand, Ty—I generally opt for the VIP suite to ensure my privacy. Someone had to know my hotel and my room number to leave that message."

"What was on the message?" Tyler asked.

"Just to meet him—I assumed it was a male—at the Emerald Club, and he claimed to have information about Liam."

"So, you're thinking it was an inside job," Tyler summed it up.

Considering, Luke admitted, "That crossed my mind, but the problem is this, Tye. The only ones who should be privy to any of that information are two of the highest, most respected men in MacDade Industries. I truly can't see either one planning or executing an ambush on Liam."

"Your brother's in line to inherit your family fortunes isn't he?"

"No one would benefit from his death, sir," Luke said sincerely.

"You have another brother," Tyler said carefully.

"I do, yes, but if you're suggesting he could be behind this, you'd be wrong," Luke said bluntly. "Gregor would probably cut off his own arm before he'd ever hurt Liam," he continued as he read Tyler's speculation. "Seriously, sir. You can forget that angle."

"Money and power have a strange way of affecting people, Luke. Maybe your brother's tired of playing second fiddle."

"He's never played second fiddle," Luke said matter-of-factly. "He's next in line in name only. If he ever wanted to take the helm, Liam would hand it over in a heartbeat."

"You're certain of that?"

"I am, yes," Luke said honestly. "They've never been the cliché brothers, always competing against one another. I'm not even sure they're aware of their own dynamics, but I've always had a knack for seeing algorithms, and theirs is simple. When one excels at something, the other takes a step back. Liam at Karate. Gregor at horses. Liam at swimming. Gregor at football. Liam at business. Gregor at finances. They're both accomplished at all of those things and when they put their heads together, they're like equal halves of a whole."

"It's still possible—"

"You didn't say—do you know that black-haired fellow I mentioned?"

"I've seen him . . ." His voice trailed with an apparent thought, then focused. "I've seen him in the club a few times."

"What? What were you thinking? Remembering?"

"I've seen him talking to Alecia a few times this summer."

"And?"

"And he went downstairs last night," Tyler said carefully. "And I don't recall seeing him return or leaving through the front door."

Like spiders tap-dancing in the roots of his hair, Luke suffered the crawlies in his scalp. "So, then, he was the accomplice the imposter mentioned."

"That's one lead I can follow," Tyler decided. "Someone at the club probably knows his name, and I can run that through our system. Get an address on him."

"You never saw that woman though. Is that right?"

"Not that I recall, but she was gooped up pretty thick."

"I could probably sketch her—minus the goop," Luke offered.

Tyler considered and decided, "We need to take a break here. If you really won't let me take you to the emergency room . . .?"

"I appreciate the offer, but no. I'm fine."

"Probably not, but I won't argue with you," Tyler said in a more business tone. "You're close to my size. If you want to get a shower or bath and soak for a few minutes, I could probably find you a change of clean clothes. And I don't know about you, but I need some breakfast. I make a pretty mean omelet if you're interested."

This was certainly not the first time someone offered to tend to the basic needs in his life—like baths, beds, and meals. Under the circumstances—looking down at his wrinkled, untucked shirt and faded jeans, as far from neat and tidy as the sun from the moon—he probably looked even more desperate than he felt. Still, "If you wanted to give me a lift back to my car, I could probably get out of your hair or . . . you look tired—I could probably call a cab."

"We're nowhere near finished with this discussion, Luke," Tyler spoke in cop mode. "If you don't want a shower, that's fine, but I am making breakfast, and you're going to try eating a few bites. You still look a little too pale and shaky for my liking, and I doubt whatever you ingested is completely out of your system. Bluntly, buddy, you're stuck with me for a little while."

Maybe that was not such a bad turn. Luke wasn't altogether certain he wanted to be alone at the moment. And that was enough of a distress in his mind to verify the need. Generally, he preferred his own company, and he'd never feared flying solo. "This . . . something like this messes one up, doesn't it?" he asked absently and focused on Tyler, who managed not to appear too sorrowful. "I've never been a victim," he admitted, not positive whether he needed to be understood or to understand. "I don't particularly care for feeling either vulnerable or violated."

Tyler studied him more intently. "No one does, Luke," he said carefully. "That's one of the reasons I suggested speaking to a counselor or reaching out to a support group. You'll need to talk to someone about this."

"I'm talking to someone, now," Luke pointed out. "I couldn't imagine standing in a public forum and admitting an emotional investment, and honestly, I'd likely deny the entire ordeal if anyone ever asked. One celebrity in the family is far more than my parents need."

"Those groups are confidential, Luke."

"Sir, not meaning to be the bearer of bad news and to repeat something I heard recently, money affects people in strange ways. Even doctor/patient confidentiality can be bought for the right price." Sighing, he decided, "I'll accept your charity if the offer's still open, Tye. I could use a shower, and I wouldn't mind a change of clothes."

Sheffield set his coffee aside and pushed off the chair far more agilely than Luke and by no surprise, crossed the carpet and stood near enough to halt Luke's sway when he rose.

"Boy," Luke muttered, clasping the proffered arm by reflex. "This sucks worse than a hangover, and I thought that was the end all."

"Those frat parties are hell," Tyler said offhandedly, motioning toward the hall. "First door."

"I don't know about frat parties, but I went to a graduation party and tied one on once," he admitted and collected his balance, feeling as if he'd run another marathon by the time he reached the compact bathroom. Utilitarian. All the necessities, including a vanity mirror above the small sink, and one look at his reflection explained Tyler's concern. Through a blood-red haze, his eyes glowed neon blue like something found in a baby doll's sockets, with his complexion near porcelain white. "Shit, I look like a junky already," he muttered in disgust and caught the intent dark eyes in the mirror. "I think I can manage from here, though, if you don't mind."

"I'll just get you those clothes."

Nodding absently, Luke waited for the door to close, then turned his attention to his ministrations. The ability to function on autopilot served him well in tuning out the immediate details of his physical distress while tending to his business. When he stepped from the shower, two clean towels and a set of clean clothes awaited on the back of the commode. Black sweatpants minus any name brand or sports logos, a loose-fitting polo shirt, and a new pair of socks. Apparently, this fellow had been a Boy Scout, or he just rescued people as a routine. A new toothbrush, toothpaste, and a packaged comb rested on the sink vanity top; a plastic cup stood next to the mouthwash. Luke took advantage of the hospitality and then checked the medicine cabinet above the sink, not disappointed to find the eye drops along with various medicines from antibacterial creams to anti-allergy sprays for insect bites to bandages and gauze tape. A Boy Scout. The fellow was well stocked and prepared for any disaster, a mirror reflection of Luke's own cabinets in various locations.

A kindred spirit without the Boy Scout background, Luke considered while making use of the drops. He felt better, if not great, by the time he combed his hair and collected his dirty laundry, putting the bathroom in order no differently than he would in his own flat.

By the sound and smell of bacon frying, Luke was drawn to the kitchen and found Tyler at the stove, mixing a small bowl of eggs.

At a glance, Tyler sized him up and commented, "You look better. Help yourself to the coffee and have a seat if you feel up to it."

Like the living room, the kitchen was compact with a metal-legged table, three matching red vinyl chairs, and pressed wood cabinets. By the style alone, Luke judged the apartment within an apartment building rather than a duplex. A glance through the single window above the table verified his thought with the generic image of apartment windows visible through the gray curtain of rain. Generally, a good rain was soothing; presently, it only enhanced his lingering lethargy.

Sipping his coffee, he watched the water splatter the glass, following the trails down the window pane and listening to the continued traffic. A busy highway. The sound amplified beneath the ping of rain striking the glass.

Toast popped; eggs sizzled. Sheffield shifted and sidled, tending to the details between the stove, sink, and refrigerator. He knew his way around the kitchen. The omelet arrived with toast, silverware, and a refill of coffee. "Dig in," he suggested, then turned to the stove, repeating the process.

Bacon, cheese, chunks of ham, peppers, and onions—all mounded and sandwiched in a golden fold of fluffy eggs. With the first bite, Luke's attention riveted. That he hadn't eaten in over eighteen hours occurred to him as he reviewed the past evening in his mind. He'd spent nearly two hours on his disguise and he'd apparently done well. Clearly, Luke recalled passing the fellow settling into a chair across from him.

In companionable silence, they ate, and Luke managed to finish the omelet himself, comfortably full by the time Tyler rose and refilled both their coffee cups. At a glance, Luke found the dark, intent gaze and knew they needed to finish their earlier discussion.

"I called a friend of mine while you were showering," Tyler began as he returned to his chair, keeping his deep voice friendly. "Rohypnol probably wouldn't show up in your blood, but we could send a urine sample to a lab—"

"Which will only confirm what we already know and won't further our investigation."

"First off, you're not conducting an investigation, Luke. Second, the lab could confirm what we suspect. Third, catching your abductor—or abductors—is a police matter—"

"We've tread this sod, sir," Luke said with a sigh. "I'm not reporting them—not for this anyway. It was my own folly to be abducted, and when I catch this pair, I want them arrested on more than sexual assault. Whatever they're up to, it led to my brother lying in a hospital bed for the past three weeks, and I don't think he's entirely in the clear, yet."

"We do need to start at the beginning here," Sheffield said grimly. "Would you mind if I take some notes while we pick up that earlier thread?"

"I don't mind, and if you have paper and a pencil, I could work on that sketch," Luke suggested.

Sliding off his chair, Tyler strode from the kitchen but returned with a tablet, pens, and pencil. Delivering a few loose sheets of blank copy paper and pencil to Luke, Tyler collected the dirty dishes, setting them in the sink before settling into his chair. "All right, let's start back at the beginning. You said April or May—your brother's marriage was on the rocks."

"Either before or right after he started seeing Alecia Helms," Luke agreed as he began sketching, thinking. "I intend to ask him when he wakes up, but I'm not sure he'll answer me. Probably tell me it's none of my business, and he'd be right."

"You two aren't close?"

"Not for a long time," Luke said offhanded, distractedly. "Not really a huge surprise. There's eight years between us. We've always traveled in different circles, which is why last night seems screwy. Somehow all this fits together—"

"What do you mean by—it seems screwy?" Tyler interrupted. "Assuming you're referring to something other than the obvious."

"Everything points to someone knowing Liam—and me—and anyone who knows us, knows we're not exactly buddy-buddy," he admitted and looked over to find Tyler studying him. "Fact, sir, I haven't even seen Liam face to face for about two years," he admitted. "I graduated at seventeen and left home shortly thereafter. I attended a few family affairs for about a year, but after that, I . . . I went my own way."

"Just from your brother—? You mentioned the security guards trying to keep track of you," Tyler recalled. "You slip away from them?"

"I do, yes," he admitted. "I don't particularly like being followed, and no— not just from Liam. I talk to my mum. Haven't really spoken to my father in . . . well . . . not in five or six years." He paused, considered, and sighed. "Hell, longer than that," he admitted. "I've probably never actually talked to him. He's . . . a bit of a tyrant," he said and shrugged, judging Tyler's doubt. "We've just never gotten along. I've always steered clear of him and vice versa."

"I'm not sure I'm following you here, buddy. I mean, it's sort of natural for fathers and sons to bang heads eventually."

"I'm sure that's true, but my father and I have been banging heads since I was born, I think, but don't mistake that. I do respect him and admire him. Always have. He's a force to be reckoned with, but always at a distance."

After a moment, Tyler seemed to accept the words and continued, "So anyone who knows you—your family—knows you're not close, not with anyone in your family."

"I get along well with my mum," he confided and shrugged. "And it's not as if I don't like them or that I deliberately set out to alienate them."

"I'm not accusing you of anything," Sheffield said carefully.

"Good then," Luke commented. "But you're right. Anyone who knows us, knows I'm not around the family much—which could explain something else and point to someone close to the family."

"How so?"

"The land," Luke said thoughtfully. "Whoever used the Pendleton land to lure Liam . . . they had to know I wouldn't talk to any of the MacDades about that land offer, and I think Pendleton was forced, maybe blackmailed into selling that land. First to Liam, then to me. I think . . . If I was a betting man, I'd wager the elder Pendleton had a vice to be used against him."

"What vice would that be?"

"Gambling," Luke said lightly. "I uhm . . . I called Pendleton yesterday from my hotel room. I meant to ask him about my stalker—"

"Stop there," Tyler said as he seemed to doodle on his notepad. "You mentioned this stalker—him following you to the mountains."

"I think he knew where to find me. I think he was already waiting for me when I reached the mountains, and the only way that was possible, was if Pendleton had told him where I was headed. I went back to my hotel where I picked up Kelly Finnegan as a tail, but that Nissan was parked near the title company. That's where I first saw it. So . . . it had to be connected to Pendleton."

"You don't think you could have been followed from the hotel?"

"Unless my stalker used a dozen different cars . . .? No, I wasn't followed."

"It's not too difficult to follow someone without them noticing, Luke. There are a lot of techniques to avoid detection."

"I'm sure there are, Ty, but would you like me to tell you what shirt you were wearing the first time I saw you?"

"Excuse me?"

"I uhm . . . I have a photographic memory," Luke admitted indifferently. "If I tried, I could probably tell you the make, model, and color of every car I've passed in the past twenty years, and I'm not bragging, here. It's just a fact. If I'd seen that surveillance car once, I'd have ignored it. Even twice or three times—unless it was out of its element, like appearing near a title company, then in a mountain town two hours away. I don't forget what I see," he said carefully. "One of my teachers, a million years ago, called me an idiot savant, and I looked it up. It fits. I . . . I don't exactly see the world like everyone else, or so I've been told." He shrugged. "I notice things. Right, wrong, or in between. My arrival on that mountain was preconceived by that second stalker, and the fellow arrived with enough time to rent or steal a quad and reach the mountain lookout with time to spare. He was already in position near the most traveled ledge when I got there, or I would have heard him advance. Sound carries in the mountains. I heard Kelly's engine shut off a half mile away, and I figured my stalker heard it, too. I'm not sure what that stalker intended, but I have a feeling, Kelly thwarted his plan."

"So, we have someone who knew Pendleton—talked to him after the closing," Tyler spoke as he doodled. "And this Kelly Finnegan, on your family's payroll following you from the hotel to the mountains," he considered, then wondered. "Sound carries. You heard the quad start. Knew your stalker had departed?"

"I think he left right after Kelly arrived in the clearing. At least, that's the only time I heard him, and he was not more than twenty—twenty-five feet away at that point. If he'd arrived after me, I'd have heard him. He was stealthy, though. I only heard a twig or two snap."

"Did you mention him to the bodyguard? To Kelly?"

"No."

"So . . . You realized someone was stalking you, and you didn't bother mentioning that to a man who—I'm guessing—was there to protect you?"

"I . . . Well, I didn't think about it," Luke admitted, feeling a little foolish belatedly. "I'm . . . I'm accustomed to handling things on my own. Kelly following me was more of an inconvenience than a relief."

"It didn't occur to you that someone might intend to hurt you? I mean, considering that your older brother was attacked, nearly killed, three weeks ago."

"No, actually, it didn't," Luke said with mild irritation. "I didn't think the Pendleton land was any part of Liam's attack," he admitted. "Honestly, I was led to believe—by Pendleton—that Liam declined his offer, which is why—as I said—the whole thing seemed screwy. There's a lot of decent timber on that land."

"You found out differently—I mean about your brother wanting the land?"

"I don't know if he wants it," Luke admitted. "I thought one of us should have it, and the price was right." He shrugged. "If Liam wants it when he's well, I'll sell it to him."

"Is it possible there's something about that land to make it important? Maybe a gold mine or some shit on it?"

"Maybe coal . . . Hell, maybe gas, too. The Marcellus Shale runs through there. If something on the land was at the heart of this, though, I doubt Pendleton would have sold out at fair market. If there was the potential for a quick profit, Pendleton would have turned that dollar on his own or, at the least, withheld the mineral rights. No, I think the land was a means to the end. A carrot. Which makes me think Liam was truly lured here. Pendleton was pressured, maybe blackmailed, to offer that sale. The problem, as I see it, is who knew Pendleton had land to offer? Knew Liam and Frank's connection?. . And might benefit from . . .?" *From Liam's early demise?*

"This makes no sense," Luke decided. "No one stands to benefit if Liam's lost. His dying might destroy my parents emotionally, but my father would keep hold of the reins. It's not like he's over the hill, and the company wouldn't suffer."

"Maybe it's part of a financial coop?" Tyler wondered. "Is it possible, someone wants to take over the company and could succeed if—say, your brother's lost and your father's a mess?"

"My father would be a mess, and you'd never know it," Luke commented indifferently. "And that's not possible, anyway. My father does hold the reins, Tye. High Land Inc., my father's corporation, is family-owned. My father, my brothers, hell, probably me, too, to an extent, hold the controlling interest with nominal shares distributed between a few of my relatives. All combined, there are not enough shares to shift the balance of power from my father or even from Liam unless my father threw in against him, and that will never happen."

"So. We're back to who could benefit if your brother was lost."

"Somehow, these working parts fit together," Luke said as he added the final touches to his sketch. "The Pendleton land, the Alecia Helms affair, possible blackmail . . . my acquisition of the land, getting followed, baited and abducted," he considered. "Why come after me?"

"Blackmail . . . kidnapping."

"I'm not a kid," Luke commented.

"You're still a kid, just not a small child," Tyler said quietly. "Maybe they snatched you with a thought of ransom—" Tyler halted and tilted his focus to the sketch as Luke skidded and turned it on the table. For a long moment, he studied the rather bland feature, small eyes, short lashes, thinner lips . . . then lifted his gaze to Luke. "You're pretty damned good at that. I've seen police sketch artists with less talent."

"Do you know her?" Luke asked.

"No, but that doesn't mean anything. I could probably make copies and ask around the club, and I'll likely run this through the database. See if anything turns up. We're having a lot of luck with facial recognition programs."

Luke looked down at the inverted sketch and shook his head, "I've never seen her before, not even in passing," he knew and looked to Tyler. "Do you think she could have been hired by Alecia Helms? Maybe with some promise of cash?"

"Luke, honestly, I'd never peg Alecia as a mastermind. A little devious, granted. Manipulative, I could see. But of a nature to lure you to that club and have you drugged. . .? I don't see it. Any more than I think she'd set up that ambush for some extra cash when she could just as easily have stolen his wallet if he truly carried that much cash around."

"She wouldn't have known where to find me to send that note," Luke added, shaking his head. "I can't get past this stalker business," he said in mild irritation. "Not even Pendleton knew where I was staying, only where I'd be at ten yesterday morning. I think I might need to pay him a visit," Luke considered. "He talked to someone. About the closing and about me traveling to the Poconos, but that timeline is off. If someone followed me to the hotel, spotted Kelly, and followed at a distance . . . how did they beat me to the mountains? And if they just drove from the closing to the mountains, how did they know where I was staying?"

"We're dealing with two different entities," Tyler deduced. "Or one entity with multiple arms and motives."

"That takes money," Luke considered and pondered that thought, realizing his accuracy. "So, money's not the motive, not if this entity can afford to hire professional stalkers and set up ambushes and . . . My father would have already chased down the money angle. By now, his investigation team has probably tracked down anyone with means or motive."

"I think we'll need to speak to the detectives on your brother's case, Luke," Tyler said carefully. "We need to tell them about that stalker, the note, and about last night. Do you still have that note?"

"We're not telling them anything," Luke said.

"Look, I know this won't be easy—"

"It'll be easy because it's not happening, Tye," he said more quietly. "I'm not talking to those detectives, and neither are you."

"What we're discussing here could be directly related to that ambush," Tyler stated. "We can't afford to withhold that information."

"We can and will," Luke stated. "At least until I've had a chance to speak to my father or Uncle Mason."

"Don't suppose you intend to tell them about last night, do you?"

"I'll say enough to raise a flag, but I probably won't mention the roofie," he admitted. "I'd like that to remain between you and me—at least until I've had time to process it."

"You're likely going to need help with that, Luke," Tyler said carefully.

"I didn't mean emotionally," Luke admitted indifferently. "I was stupid and paid the price for my stupidity. I need to know the reason behind it and find out where it fits in this puzzle. Someone either wanted or needed to victimize me—and . . . and it feels like even that was directed at Liam—like whoever's behind that ordeal might intend to use it against him."

"I'm not sure I'm following this. You said you and your brother haven't spoken."

"That's a fact, but it wouldn't stop Liam from feeling responsible if he found out I was hurt because of him," Luke admitted. "You have to understand, Tye, whether my brother takes the helm of the company or not, he'd still be considered the heir to the MacDade clan, and with the chieftain title, there are certain responsibilities. Liam's been groomed from day one to hold that position, and he'd never take it lightly. Someone striking me to get to him . . . I could see that happening, and maybe therein lies another clue," he considered. "Whoever's behind this has to be close enough to the family to know Liam's recovering."

"I'd like to agree with you, Luke, but that's not necessarily true," Tyler said carefully. "A few of the local stations are keeping pretty close tabs, and at least one reporter seems to have a direct pipeline to your brother's condition," he added. "As of last evening, she was reporting that he's improving and he was moved to guarded condition."

"Molly Anderson," Luke guessed, and Tyler nodded. "I think she has better detective skills than some of the detectives on this case," Luke stated.

"I won't argue that. She seems to have the inside track, but the hospital's offering regular updates, too."

Luke considered a moment, then sighed. "I better get moving."

"Not necessarily," Tyler commented. "You're welcome to crash here for a while. I'm covering for Jack again tonight, and I usually leave here around five. I could give you a lift to your car then."

By habit alone, Luke always scanned a map when reaching an area. It took a few extra seconds for him to find Kingston and calculate the distance to The Emerald Club. A half hour depending on traffic . . . and Sheffield already appeared exhausted. "You look as tired as I still feel," Luke decided. "Guess I can wait a couple hours if you want to get some sleep."

"You could probably use a couple more hours as well, buddy. From what I've heard, it can take a good twenty-four hours for that shit to wear off completely."

"I'm guessing that refers to the weariness," Luke said in mild disgust. "I'm not disoriented or dizzy, which is a vast improvement."

Tyler managed another of his faint, kinked smiles. "I'd have to agree," he said and glanced down to collect the sketch. "I'm faxing this over to my office then hitting the rack for a few hours. If you need anything you can't find, wake me. Other than that, help yourself. There's some junk food—cookies and crackers in the cupboard. Soda in the fridge."

"Thank you—for your hospitality as well as breakfast," Luke said, and added, "You were right about your cooking skills. That omelet was outstanding."

"You're welcome," he said and started to turn but stopped. "I probably should mention, I made another call while you were in the shower, Luke. You were right about that guy last night being the lady's accomplice. He goes by the name of Johnny, and he was last seen with Helms about a month ago—puts it around the time of your brother's mugging. This lady," he said while flagging the paper. "Was never seen before yesterday, according to the girls working last night. We will find her, though. Him, too."

"I appreciate that," Luke said and refrained from reacting despite the tension gripping his stomach. Between that odd couple, he'd probably been half-carried through that exit door, but no images existed to verify that thought.

"If you start to feel funny, buddy, how about waking me, all right?"

"Will do, thanks again," Luke offered distractedly, and if Tyler had said anything more, the words were currently lost. A few phone calls . . . he should probably check in with Ken Lin, who'd been placed in charge of building the cabin and lodge. The main road to the latter had been cut a week earlier, and part of the driveway was already paved . . . and thinking about the groundbreaking for his cabin was a whole lot easier than considering what might have been done to him the evening past. If he landed in some sleazy magazine or tabloid, he'd have no one other than himself to blame . . . and that was an odd thought. Had something during that blackout triggered the impression of a camera?

23

With the rain falling in a steady stream, Luke had the park to himself, a detail he'd counted on when pulling through the main entrance. Less than a quarter mile from the highway, winding through trimmed lawns and clusters of trees, he found a gravel inlet that probably accommodated fishermen gracing the banks of the Deleware on better days.

In the front seat of the Taurus, Luke made the cosmetic transitions from pale brown to darker beard, from loose waves to short brown hair under a ball cap, to clear, wire-rimmed glasses with brown contact lenses. Tyler's clothes afforded him enough of a change from his usual attire. He needed only a pair of worn tennis shoes to complete the jogger-style.

A half-assed disguise by his estimation, but then, he shouldn't need much else to escape the notice of any nosey parkers . . . or any of his relatives who might be lingering in the area.

Why exactly he had opted for a hotel rather than the Franklin House, he couldn't readily decide, but avoiding his relatives seemed prudent.

Less than an hour after picking up his rental in the Emerald Club parking lot, Luke strode into a Courtyard Inn, slapped his credit card and driver's license on the counter, and requested a room.

The receptionist, a lanky young fellow with a bright smile and quick brown eyes, studied the laminated license an extra second, then lifted his doubting gaze.

Losing his smile, Luke feigned a side glance, lending the impression that he feared to be overheard. Not another soul stood in the lobby. Still, Luke spoke in a near clandestine whisper. "Desperate times call for desperate measures," he said carefully. "I've been hounded out of a half dozen hotels over that Liam MacDade character. I'd really prefer not to be mobbed by reporters if I can avoid it."

"You're MacDade—"

"I'm Mc-Dade," Luke said quietly. "And if you could keep my name from becoming public knowledge, I'd certainly appreciate it."

"It's against our policy to give out personal information," the man said confidently and hurried the registration, handing over the keycards. "You can access the hotel from the parking lot with this card, sir. I hope you'll enjoy your stay."

"I'm sure I will," Luke said loftily and strode to the elevator.

At least three other hotel receptionists had offered the same assurance, and still, the MacDade security had found him. The only questions remained—how soon and what approach might be enlisted this time. By now, Uncle Gillis was probably spitting nickels, and Kelly Finnegan was likely taking the brunt of Uncle Mason's anger. Lucius MacDade might not be anything other than annoyed. And if the latest news update concerning Liam's improvement was an indication, the big guy wouldn't suffer too grievously over his youngest son's evasive maneuvers.

Even as he settled into the suite on the fourth floor, the top floor, Luke wondered why he even bothered sticking around. He could just catch a flight to Chicago and disappear in the crowds of O'Hara before returning to Roanoke . . . but he'd really like to talk to Pendleton Sr. again before departing. That whole business just wasn't sitting right.

Sitting, then flopping on the floral quilt, Luke stared at the ceiling momentarily, then closed his eyes, still seeing the five hundred and thirty-two dots in the corrugated square of ceiling tile. Even with the gray light filtering through the drawn curtains, he'd recorded those black dots. Yet, he still couldn't draw a single image from the twelve hours between eying the distorted Corona label and waking in Sheffield's apartment.

If he were waking in the morgue—or merely lying there—that ordeal would make more sense.

What had anyone, least of all Liam's enemy, gained by slipping him a roofie and taking advantage of him?

If they'd meant to make him feel more like an idiot than a savant, they'd succeeded. What the hell had possessed him to believe he should meet with a possible killer alone?

The message had sounded like it was written by a moron, and it was possible, the messenger had counted on Luke's arrogance to gain his compliance. Clever bastard—or bastards—or . . .? Or again, the mastermind behind this ordeal knew enough about him and his disassociation from his family to know he would come alone.

In that regard, the person or persons behind this ordeal surely knew how Liam might react to any violation against a member of his family.

Pendleton might know.

The older—or younger—for that matter. One or both had been manipulated.

Or blackmailed?

Was it possible that father and son had both been drawn into this—or was the son just a side benefit? No. Not possible. Frank was a key factor since he was the connection to Liam.

Pendleton Sr. had been pressured into that sale . . . because of his son's friendship with Liam?

Pendleton playing the ponies. Pendleton playing the ponies . . .? Close a 2.5-million-dollar land deal and instead of taking the missus out for a fine dinner to celebrate . . .? Run to the racetrack where fortunes could be lost more often than won.

The ponies. The racetrack . . . and not all that long ago, Luke had thought about Jimmy Chandler. James Chandler, who'd come to the estate with his father . . . an abusive old man—who'd probably not been all that old except to a ten-year-old—who'd trained thoroughbreds at Churchill.

What if . . .?

Luke sat up unconsciously, reaching for his cell phone where he'd left it on the night table. What if the connection had been made at the track?

Halting his finger from hitting the button, Luke gazed into abstracts, thinking, wondering what had become of Chandler—the older or younger. What he remembered . . .

Liam had swooped from the loft like an avenging angel—or Batman in the flesh to a ten-year-old with a vivid imagination. For a split second, all motion ceased. Then Jimmy flew through the air, landing a dozen strides away and skidding on the cobbled floor. More growl than words, Batman transformed into a raging bear, and Luke could barely recall a thought to stop him, fearing for the repercussions as surely as he feared for James' life. Reaching, clasping the shirt sleeve, meaning to stop Liam—Luke had known his mistake too late. He never saw the hand slamming him against a stall door. He heard the horses clamoring and snorting within their stalls up and down the stable aisle. Shoulder already thumping, he witnessed a blur of motion, James scrambling, spider-walking and pivoting, racing toward the open barn door. And as the bear spun toward him . . .

Flash frame, Luke remembered his brother's shirt hanging open, flagging like a caped crusader as he wheeled about, but Luke wanted no part of his brother—not after their previous encounter to leave blisters on his behind. Up and moving, he'd fled toward the opposite end of the stable, not slowing or stopping until he reached their mum's Victorian gazebo.

Blinking against the memory, Luke realized that was the last time he'd seen James Chandler. Three days later, Milton Chandler had been fired and escorted—him and his son both—off the estate. Even then, Luke had believed Liam was behind the Chandlers' dismissal, and for a time, he'd wondered if the Chandlers might turn up floating in Froog Pond or if they'd actually driven off the estate. He'd considered hiking over the hill to the pond, but the thought of Gram MacDade's knack and her stories of talking to ghosts had veered his course. He hadn't much cared for running across either of the Chandlers in the flesh, much the less as ghosts.

For all that people considered him intelligent back then, he sure was stupid about some things . . . And sitting on the side of a bed, alone in a hotel room, wearing a lame disguise, contradicted the idea of his mental stability as an adult. He still believed in ghosts, damn it. To believe that people just lay rotting six feet down for all eternity seemed even more farfetched than an incorporeal image floating above ground.

So, if they were alive, what had become of them? The Chandlers?

Someone had once told him—ah, Uncle George MacDade, who ran a string of thoroughbreds from one end of the country to the other. Uncle George had once, a million years ago, said that racing gets in the blood. Whether betting or racing—according to Uncle George, once a body got hooked on the ponies, there was no turning back.

The Chandlers would still be hanging around the track—and at least five race tracks existed within a couple hundred miles of one another. Without a need for research, Luke cited several within spitting distance, from Parx and Penn National in Pennsylvania to Saratago and Belmont in New York to Pimlico and Laurel in Maryland, and that wasn't even counting harness racing. Uncle George had traveled in a pattern, hitting the meets and stake races up and down the coast for years.

'One of these days, Luche, we're going to make a run for the Crown . . .'

The Triple Crown—the coveted culmination of a lifelong dream, and Luke knew his father had indulged George in so much as he invested in several decent horses over the years. None had ever taken the Crown, not yet, anyway, but Lucius MacDade had always come out ahead on his investments.

Unconsciously, Luke pushed the buttons and held the phone to his ear.

After just two rings, the deep voice erupted. "This better be a wayward young man with a penchant for disappearing."

"That's probably me," Luke said lightly. "I didn't want to wake you."

"I'm pretty sure I told you to do exactly that, Luke," Tyler growled. "Imagine my surprise to find the couch empty and a nice note atop a folded blanket."

"Places to go—sorry. My friends usually call me LJ. If you're interested, I thought of two people you might look into."

"I'm interested," he commented. "And I have a pen."

"James and Milton Chandler," Luke supplied. "Son and father. I'm reasonably sure you'll find them living on or near a racetrack, but I honestly don't have much more than their names to go on."

"Who are they?"

Should he admit . . .? "A couple people from the past who might or might not have a score to settle with Liam. Maybe me, too," he said with a silent shrug. "Just a thought."

"Did you talk to Pendleton?"

"Not yet. Soon."

"Did you see your family?"

"Not yet."

"I thought that's where you were headed."

"I thought so, too, but decided against it," he said lightly. "Maybe another time."

"Damn it, then you didn't talk to anyone about last night, either. Is that right?"

"I'll probably talk to someone eventually," he decided. "Can you look into those names?"

"I can," Tyler stated. "You want to give me a number to reach you when I find out anything?"

"I'll call you tomorrow," Luke answered.

"Where are you?"

"Doesn't matter. I won't be here long," he said honestly.

"Damn it, kid, has it occurred to you—you could still be in danger?"

"Hasn't slipped far from my mind, Tye," he admitted. "If I think of something else before tomorrow, I'll leave you a message."

"LJ—"

Luke depressed the end button, waited for the number to clear, then pushed the next series. Sitting through a half dozen rings before the answering machine engaged, Luke hung up and tried the next number from memory, not surprised when Frances senior rejected the call. Becoming slightly annoyed, Luke punched another series of digits and sat through three rings before the breathless voice answered.

"Hi! Who's calling?"

"Hi, Frank. Luke McDade, here."

"Luke! Hello! How are you?" he huffed, then seemed to laugh. "Where are you?"

"Actually, not too far from Trenton. Any chance I could buy you dinner at the Rivers?"

"I'll buy. Just say when," he said lyrically.

"I can be there around 7:30," Luke decided. Just past sunset suited him just fine.

"I'll be there—Luke, how's Liam?"

"Coming around," Luke commented. "See you soon."

Again, he ended the call and engaged another number, and again, he was met with a brusque demand.

"Luke?"

"Hi," he said quietly, oddly out of sorts to hear Gregor's short tone.

Gregor drew a breath before beginning in a far more careful tone, maybe fearing Luke might hang up at any second. "Aye, hi. Any chance you'd like to mention where you are?"

"Where are you?" Luke wondered, curious at the absence of background sound to offer a clue. The voice carried a hollow tone as if Gregor stood in a tunnel.

"At the moment, in a john at the hospital," Gregor answered with the mere whisper of a brogue. "Any chance you're on your way here?"

"A reason I should be?" Luke asked carefully.

Never one to hide his emotions, Gregor spoke in barely restrained irritation. "Ach, well, yer elder brother might be awake enough to appreciate your visit—finally—and yer next elder brother might like to see yer pretty mug for a tick or two. Aye, but aside from that . . . I cannae think of a thing."

"Good then," Luke commented, distracted by a hint of something more in the tone. "Really, Gregor? He's improving then?"

"He is," Gregor answered, sounding mildly pleased, still irritated. "But he likely thinks he's hallucinating, what with his little brother coming and going in the quick of night."

"I don't like coming in the day," Luke stated with a slight edge, not entirely surprised by Gregor's knowledge of his late-night excursions. "He has plenty of company then."

Damni it. He'd just spoken more words to his brother than he'd spoken in the past year combined, which undoubtedly accounted for Gregor's slight pause.

"I notice you've managed to avoid the blasted newsmongers."

"You photograph well enough for both of us," Luke said distractedly, and again, Gregor paused with his apparent surprise.

"If you don't want to come to the hospital, what say you and I meet up somewhere? Have dinner or the like? A drink?"

For a half second, Luke considered accepting the offer, then realized the probability of Gregor attracting too much attention, over and above Uncle Gillis likely posting at least one or two bodyguards to see to his welfare. Fat lot of good that did, when a fellow could be too intent on avoiding the legitimate surveillance to realize when a genuine threat arrived. The same blasted thing had probably happened to Liam. He was so accustomed to being followed that he'd missed the signs of a genuine stalker.

Still, Liam was no more deaf, dumb, and blind to the possibility of an ambush than Luke had been unaware of his stalker . . . and it seemed suddenly far too similar. Liam's ambush, his own abduction. A setup from the get-go. Liam's assailants had been waiting for him in an alley, Luke's had baited him . . . and their enemy had counted on their audacity.

"Luke?" Gregor interrupted.

"I have to go," Luke decided. "Maybe another time—"

"Wait! Just hold on a second, Lucas," Gregor demanded. "I know Da invited you to join us at the Franklin House, and I dinnae need be a rocket scientist to know you've rejected the invitation. The offer stands though, and if all goes well, Liam will be moving there tomorrow or Thursday. Just saying, you might want to visit him there, and we're holding a room open for you if you want it."

"Don't, Gregor," Luke said quietly. "Don't hold a room. I won't be coming—"

"Damn, you, Lucas," Gregor said shortly. "Just damn you for not giving a damn about anyone but your own fine self."

Perhaps, Gregor had only demanded the halt so he could end the call first. As dumbfounded as he might be hurt, Luke closed his silent flip phone and sat staring at the curtained window. What did that mean, anyway? It was not as if anyone gave a good Goddamn about him. They'd been pushing him aside and avoiding him for as far back as he could recall . . . and he could recall falling out of his playpen to find his big brothers.

"Damn it," Luke muttered, and wiped his burning eyes with the heels of his palms. He was in no condition to see anyone in his family; not when he felt so blasted vulnerable already. Gregor's words shouldn't have disturbed him, not one way or another—

At least he'd remembered to remove his contact lenses, or else he might have permanently damaged his eyes—provided he hadn't lost them in the flood to mash from under his lashes.

Maybe, just maybe, he should cancel that date with Frank and return to his mountain. He'd already dragged a small camper and a shed large enough to house a four-wheeler to his ridge. He could hang out and commune with nature to watch the construction of his cabin rather than hotel hop in a blasted city. Between the Trenton PD, the FBI—providing they were still involved—and Gillis's security teams, someone should be making some progress, and his hiring Tyler Sheffield should be enough of a personal investment in this ordeal. He could always cross over his mountain peak and find cell or satellite signals to keep in touch with Sheffield if he was seriously interested in this investigation.

A fine idea . . . except that he needed to know how this Pendleton thing had begun. He needed to meet with Frank.

With the cover of dusk shadows, Luke had needed very little enhancement to alter his appearance. Wearing a bandana headband-style, faded jeans, a flannel shirt, and a pair of clear wire-rim glasses guaranteed to reflect light and mask eye color, he entered the River's Inn at exactly 7:30. Without a glance, he bypassed the hostess who was sidetracked by an arriving party—a party of six whom Luke had waited to follow into the restaurant with the diversion in mind. He found Frank in a corner booth and slid into the highbacked bench seat with his back to the door, appreciating the fellow's foresight to avoid the spotlight and reduce the possibility of being recognized.

Donning a bemused smirk with his dark eyes glittering in the candlelight, Frank scanned Luke's costume, shaking his head and appearing bewildered. "Interesting look," he commented. "I don't think I'd have figured you for the hippy style."

Luke shrugged, "Keeps the hair out of my eyes."

A problem Frank avoided with a slick cut and hair gel to sweep his dark hair into a modern wave. He'd dressed for dinner, wearing a sports coat over a loose-collared shirt and jeans, which might be his usual fashion, a reflection of Liam's style when caught in a few camera shots—made more famous by the industrious Ms. Anderson.

Either the young woman was infatuated with Liam MacDade. Or she intended to launch her entire career based on this single crime. According to her latest update filmed outside the hospital entrance—in front of the mound of continuing well-wishes—Liam was, indeed, moved to guarded condition. '. . . And might be looking forward to his discharge. . . Stay tuned . . .'

"I wasn't sure what you'd want to drink—"

The waitress interrupted, halting outside the booth. "What can I get for you, hon?"

Considering a heartbeat with a memory of a doctored beer, Luke decided, "Just a can of cola, a glass of ice, and I'd rather open the can myself. Thanks." Probably like shutting the barn door after the horses escaped, but better late than never. And so-the-hell-what if she looked at him with a peculiar glance. As she turned away, Luke lifted the menu and eyed Frank, seeing his fleeting curiosity. Not even a hint of understanding touched that gaze—not one sign of Frank guessing why Luke would prefer a closed can. Pendleton was no part of the roofie or the abduction.

Frank offered, "I caught the latest update this afternoon. Is he truly going to be all right?"

"Believe he is," Luke answered distractedly, not needing to eye the menu since he'd scanned it three weeks ago. Setting the leather book aside, he met Frank's gaze. "Would you mind much if I ask you a couple questions, Frank?"

"Not at all," he said with a friendly note. "Ask away."

"This might sound odd, but I was wondering—what came first? You contacting Liam about the land? Or Liam contacting you because his marriage was on the rocks?"

Frank sobered considerably, his curiosity as apparent as his sudden dismay. "I'd imagine it was about the same time," he said thoughtfully.

"Did you contact him? Or him you, then?"

More curious, he seemed to consider before offering, "I contacted him," he admitted. "My father decided to sell some of our land—mostly woodland," he said and shrugged. "When my father mentioned it, he remembered that I knew Liam and that your family is in the lumber business." He shrugged, "Father suggested I call him ... Yes," he remembered. "I called him, and he was growling like a wounded bear when he returned my call. That's when he mentioned he and Natalie had separated and decided he wouldn't mind paying me a visit." He stopped suddenly, too suddenly.

"What?" Luke asked. "What are you thinking?"

"Nothing, really," he said as he reached for his drink, lying.

"Frank?"

Seeming agitated, suddenly, he huffed, "I just thought if things had been different, if Liam hadn't come and met Alecia, then maybe—maybe he wouldn't be in the hospital."

Was that really all there was to it? Frank appeared genuinely distressed. Before Luke could ask, however, Frank commented.

"I'm surprised you know about that land. Did you talk to Liam? I mean, was he thinking about it? Asking about it?"

"Not that I'm aware," Luke admitted, studying Frank more intently behind the reflecting panes. Was it possible? Had the elder Pendleton sold that land without speaking to the son whose inheritance had just decreased? "Have you talked to your dad about that sale lately?"

"I . . . I haven't, but I'd imagine Liam's deal is still pending. My father hasn't said differently," he said offhandedly.

As if someone had punched him in the stomach, Luke suffered the blow, grateful for the waitress arriving with his cola, as much a diversion as a genuine need. How much more proof did he need of the elder's involvement in something nefarious? Or of himself being used in the scheme?

Popping the tab and pouring the soda carefully to avoid the foam, Luke concentrated on the physical motion, aware of Frank ordering dinner. When the waitress asked him, Luke ordered a steak salad to be polite, although he wasn't hungry what with information overload wreaking havoc on his internal system.

The waitress barely departed when Frank wondered, "Did your Uncle Mason mention the sale? I mean, did he say whether he's ready to finalize it?"

"You truly didn't know the sale closed already, Frank?"

He hesitated, then seemed to smile slightly. "That's a relief, then. I know my father seemed adamant about selling, even with all the complications. Apparently, that all worked out then?"

"You were all right with your father selling it?"

"I can't see any reason to hold onto it," Frank said, offhandedly. "We kept at least the hundred acres with the cabin—not that I'm big on camping, mind, but I might one day have a son I'd take fishing or hiking."

Another hundred acres? Not attached, but . . .? "Is that hundred acres near the thousand?"

"On the other side of the mountain, actually," he said as he drew another sip of his mixed drink.

Was it possible . . .? "Any chance you have a four-wheeler garaged there?"

Frank considered even as he appeared more curious. "It's been a while since I was up there, but I'd imagine so," he commented. "We had a boat and trailer, I think skis and things—yes, I'm pretty sure we have a four-wheeler. Did you want to use it?"

Pendleton Senior was in this ordeal up to his eyeballs, and Frank Junior was clueless. "You're not too involved in your father's business, are you?" he asked, thinking the same could be said of him.

"Actually, I am," Frank said, sounding slightly offended. "I'm CEO of Pendleton Inc."

"I meant his personal business," Luke commented. "I didn't mean to offend you."

"I don't share my business with . . . What's this about, Luke?" Frank wondered, more curious than defensive.

"Your father offered me that land, and I was led to believe Liam had turned down the offer. I bought it. We closed the sale yesterday."

Frank studied him with his doubt, then slowly eased backward into the bench seat, still holding his tumbler on the table but not drinking. Rather dumbfounded and doubting, he wondered, "You closed the deal for Liam?"

"I closed the deal personally," Luke admitted, watching for Frank's reaction and seeing the cheek muscle twitch with the sudden tension.

"I'm not sure I'm following this, Luke," he said carefully. "I know Liam was in town three weeks ago to close that sale. I believe he was supposed to meet with my father the day—the next morning, if I remember correctly. How did you come to be involved?"

"Your father called me . . . Actually, the day we went to the Emerald Club," Luke admitted. "He offered me the sale, and like I said, it sounded as if Liam had turned it down. I only learned after the closing that Liam might have had a sale pending. So saying, any idea why your father might be in such a hurry to part with that land? Is there something I should know?"

"It's prime timberland—what the hell did my father say about this?"

"Honestly, he said he just wanted rid of it, and if I wasn't interested, he was putting it on the open market," Luke shrugged. "I buy real estate. It seemed like a good investment, and the price was right."

"So, just like that, you bought it."

"He had the paperwork in order, which I found a little odd, but considering he seemed like he was in a hurry to sell," Luke shrugged. "It was on the up and up."

"You talked to Liam about this?"

Luke hesitated, then shook his head slightly. "He hasn't been in any condition to talk about anything, Frank. I'm not even sure he's in any condition, even now. That's why I wanted to talk to you."

"Why not your Uncle Mason?" Frank asked with an edge, genuinely irritated. "I should think he could tell you everything you need to know. He's been involved—"

"Frank," Luke interrupted quietly. "I didn't know that, and honestly, I probably wouldn't have talked to him had I known. I haven't . . . I haven't really talked to anyone in my family for a few years. That's not to say I would have undermined that sale if I'd known. I did ask about Liam at the onset—why your father wasn't selling to him—but honestly, I might have bought that land even if I had known—providing your father had no intention of waiting for Liam to be well before selling. He wanted the land gone, Frank," Luke admitted, thinking he better not mention his suspicions of Frances Senior's reason. "Maybe I should have asked more questions, but he wasn't in a forthcoming mood." Again, he shrugged. "It seemed—"

"I can't believe my father would do this," he said with an edge. Lifting his tumbler, he swallowed a hardy gulp before setting the glass aside, reaching into his jacket, and extracting his phone. "Let me just get to the bottom of this," he said with a firm voice befitting an executive about to make an important decision.

Deciding he could benefit from patience, rather curious to see what the elder would say, Luke killed a few seconds, refilling his glass and playing with the foam.

"Hi, Father," Frank began simply. "I know it's rather late, but I wondered if I might ask you something. . . No, everything's fine between Laney and me. Wedding plans are well underway . . . I was calling about that land, Father—the pending sale you had with Liam MacDade . . .?" Frank's gaze listed toward his hand on the table, apparently watching his slender, manicured fingers turn the tumbler in a slow circle. "When would that have been?" he asked quietly. "Father, I don't think I'm following this. You say someone from MacDade Industries withdrew the offer after Liam was assaulted? . . . Yes, I'm certain this is my business, Father, and I rather find it hard to believe anyone would have withdrawn that offer on Liam's behalf . . ."

Frank continued to study his hand, but his cheek muscle twitched, offering an indication of his descending mood. For all his whimsy, he might be hell across a boardroom table. "So, you offered the land to his younger brother for the same money, I trust? . . . I'm sure he didn't hesitate, as we both know that land held its value in timber . . ."

For a long moment, Frank remained silent; his dark gaze remained intent on his stopped hand. His cheek muscle pulsed with his anger, and when he spoke, the tone reflected nothing of his irritation. "Father, just for the record, I think this was an underhanded move on your part, and I think it has more to do with my fondness for Liam than with any sound business dealings. And make no mistake—this isn't over. I think you and I will talk about this again tomorrow," he stated and lowered his hand, folding the phone to disconnect the call.

After a moment, Frank lifted his gaze and commented, "He claims someone in your father's company called and canceled the sale, but he was lying. I'm more inclined to believe—he saw Liam's trouble as a means to destroy a friendship that I've valued for the past ten years. And for the record, Luke, it's purely platonic."

"It's not my business, Frank—"

"I believe I owe you an explanation, and that makes it your business," Frank continued quietly, intently. "I remember you, you know," he said with a more natural, fond smile curving his lips. "You were a beautiful child, and you've grown into an even more handsome man, by no surprise. I don't know if you remember me, though."

"You and my brother were college roommates, as I recall."

"We were," he said fondly, his eyes lighting with a soft spark. "And the simple fact is, I fell for him hard. If he weren't straight as an arrow, I would have pursued him in earnest. He is, however, straight. And I value his friendship too much to ever broach this subject."

"Then why tell me?" Luke stated, genuinely curious, if not annoyed.

Frank cocked his head, more amused if his expression was any indication. "First, I don't think you're the type to judge. Second, I feel I owe you an explanation. My father was lying, Luke. He always goes on the defensive when lying, and he was agitated, which likely means he was thinking about my preference toward male company."

"You're engaged to a woman," Luke said bluntly.

"Yes, I am," Frank said in a musing tone. "And I'm genuinely fond of my fiancée," he admitted. "And yes, she knows my inclinations. We've worked it out. The point is, my father doesn't approve—never has. And as much as I've denied Liam and I are anything more than friends, my father seems to know, that if ever there was one to hold my undivided attention, Liam would qualify." He shrugged. "I think, with the wedding coming, my father wanted to make certain Liam and I were fully parted, and he saw this as a means to that end. Your brother is likely to feel that I've betrayed him, and . . . I hope you'll clear that up if or when you speak to him. Had I known about my father dragging you into this, I would have put a stop to it."

Frank might have tried, but doubtful, he would have succeeded. There was far more to this land deal than Frank knew, and Luke had a feeling that the conspiracy had begun about four or five months ago. Possibly, before Liam's separation—before the land offer—before meeting Alecia Helms, who might have been involved in something from the onset. One certainty, Frank was not privy to whatever had driven his father to part with that land but . . .

Gambling. A gambling debt? The racetrack?

Chandlers.

He was still missing something, and speaking to the elder Pendleton was far more imperative.

The waitress arrived with a basket of fresh bread and butter, a carafe of dressings, and whatnot for salads. As soon as she departed, Frank commented, "For what it's worth, Luke, I am sorry for getting you into this. I know the sale's final, but I'd be willing to buy the land back if you wanted out from under this whole mess. I do know you're not on the best of terms with your family. Liam mentioned it a time or two—which is why I was a little surprised that you knew about the land." He shrugged, though he appeared apologetic. "If this complicates things for you, I'd truly like to make amends."

"Not a complication," Luke commented. "I made out well enough." And if Liam wanted the land, Luke would sell it to him. "I was just curious, is all, and I couldn't reach your father."

"If you don't mind, I wonder if I could ask you a question, Luke?"

"You can ask," he admitted.

Frank appeared amused, guessing accurately, "But you reserve the right not to answer. So, I just wondered—what did your family do to alienate you—or you to them?"

Well, and that was direct. "I don't think there was any one thing, to be honest, Frank. We just—we were never close, and I guess I reached an age where it didn't matter."

"I know it bothers Liam," he said rather carefully as if belatedly aware of treading on dangerous ground—somewhere between breaching his friendship and being a snoop. "I was glad to see you at the hospital," he added quickly. "But I have to tell you, it scared the hell out of me, too. I feared the worst, and I already knew from those damned newsbreaks that it was bad. Anyway, I'm just saying, I'm glad you put your differences aside and came to be with your family."

And in the next second, Frank seemed to realize that Luke hadn't exactly been with his family—not when they met that first morning in the hospital lobby, not anytime later when the family was followed to and from the hospital.

"You uhm . . . you have been to see him, haven't you?" Frank asked hesitantly.

"I've visited," he admitted and concentrated on buttering a slice of warm bread. "But he's been sleeping."

"So . . . you haven't talked to him?"

Luke took a bite and chewed, looking at Frank through the candlelight reflections, seeing the discomfort sliding into the expression, tightening the smile in the thin, dark mustache.

"I don't imagine it's my business, Luke, but I just meant, if you do speak to him, tell him I'm worrying about him, will you?"

"I will," Luke said. "You should try this bread. It's pretty good . . ."

24

Perhaps, hotels existed where the staff understood the meaning of discretion.

Rolling between the frozen-open cast iron gates of the Pendleton estate, Luke stole another glance through the rearview mirror, almost amazed to realize that he hadn't been followed. Without the need or desire for a disguise, Luke slid from his rental in front of the shadowed porch, halfheartedly wondering if he might be tossed out on his ear. Frances wouldn't be pleased to see him.

Engaging the bell rather than the polished brass knocker from a Dickens' era, Luke scanned the manicured lawn, noting the lingering signs of neglect with more weeds spurred to life from the recent rain. Not much of September remained. In a couple of days, it would be October 1st, and before long, the leaves would be changing on his mountain . . . both of his mountains.

At the door cracking open, Luke's attention riveted, and the arrogance in Carl's posture annoyed him even before the man spoke.

"Mr. Pendleton is not in right now—"

"Carl, do refrain from lying," he said in a priestly tone. "I know Mr. Pendleton is here as I just spoke with Mrs. Pendleton. Do tell him, unless he'd like me to return with a few police detectives, I must see him now."

Carl blinked as if slapped and arched his thin neck as if raising his head from a tortoise shell rather than a suit jacket. "Excuse me—"

"Take him my message, Carl. I'll wait."

Little more than a minute passed before the door opened again, and an indignant Carl flagged him inside. "Appears Mr. Pendleton had just stepped out onto the rear veranda—"

"Save your lies for someone who cares, Carl," Luke said as he stepped into the dismal foyer. Stealing a page from his brother's—and Frank's book—Luke had dressed semi-casual, wearing jeans, a white jersey, and a black jacket with bright white tennis shoes of a brand to be noticed. He liked shoes—always had—having decided long ago that a lot could be said about a man just by the shoes on his feet. Something Freudian about that, certainly. Luke often changed his shoes three or four times daily. Either Freudian . . . or simply influenced by the past since he'd always been the smallest body on the estate and spent a lot of time looking at shoes.

His father wore black, from shined oxfords to Doc Martens hiking boots.

Frances Sr. wore brown oxfords, shined despite the wear wrinkles visible within the shadows under the desk where his feet poised, solid on the musty oriental rug. Frances was as far from relaxed as a man could be, although he leaned back, effecting a comfortable posture. That, too, a ploy.

"Glad you could see me, sir," Luke said politely, not awaiting an invitation to settle into the chair across from Pendleton.

Pursed, his lined lips would imply anger, but something slightly more critical belied his tension, something akin to fear. "How dare you come in here threatening some nonsense about police, young man. That you've aroused my curiosity is the only reason I've agreed to see you—"

"Perhaps you should ask Carl to step out, sir?" Luke interrupted in a calm, quiet voice, his deep blue gaze as steady as laser light. "I should rather hope to keep our discussion confidential."

Pendleton hesitated momentarily, then flagged his hand, "Leave us, Carl."

"Sir—"

"That will be all, Carl," he stated in curt dismissal.

The time for pleasantries had passed. Proper etiquette, bedamned. Luke waited, slightly amused behind his steadfast gaze as the butler barely restrained his indignant sniff before departing. The fellow probably would have enjoyed pouring a drink if only to drop it in Luke's lap. As the door closed, Luke commented, "I think we can drop pretenses now, Mr. Pendleton."

"We certainly can," he said snootily. "How dare you come into my home making some asinine threat—"

"It's not a threat when it would have been fact," Luke interrupted quietly, his gaze steady and his smile far from friendly. "I don't know exactly how deeply you're involved in my brother's attack, sir, but you are involved."

"I'm most certainly not—"

"I'm supposing you were blackmailed into offering my brother the Pocono land," Luke said and witnessed the flash of fear as clearly as the hostility to verify his words. "Who contacted you, sir? And when?"

"I don't have to—"

"We can speak here, in private, and I'll try to keep your name out of this, Mr. Pendleton, or I'll go to the police and offer them everything I know," Luke interrupted again, granting no quarter for the man to recover. "I do know you were forced into offering Liam that land that ultimately led him into the trap three weeks ago," he continued, watching the distress compound in the red-lined cheeks. "Like I said, we can discuss this here, quietly. Or I can contact the police and let them sort this out. I'd prefer to handle this discreetly, as I'm reasonably certain you weren't behind that assault."

"I certainly was not, and I resent that implication."

"Whether you were aware of the ultimate plan or not, you implicated yourself in an attempted murder, and unless we sort this out, that fact will become public knowledge."

"How dare you—"

"You can drop the theatrics, sir. You're not that good at them," Luke said, his voice void of inflect and eerily quiet. "Five months ago, you lured my brother to Trenton with the offer to purchase land. Now, you will tell me who contacted you to make that offer."

"I don't know," he said, angrily.

"Explain," Luke stated. "How were you approached? And bear in mind, I know about your gambling habit. You like the ponies, Mr. Pendleton. Maybe a little more than they have liked you over the past year. I'm betting you have a bookie, but you're not against visiting any of a half dozen tracks within a hundred miles of here. Is that how or where you were approached?"

Angrily, he began, "They contacted me by phone. And before you ask—no, I don't know who he is. I do have a bookie—or had one—I'm not using anyone now . . ."

The dam broke on those simple lines, and Luke listened to the diatribe unfolding over the next half hour. Silently, he introverted the words, judging the older man's mannerisms as Pendleton unloaded five months of stress.

Behind the wheel of the rented Taurus, Luke navigated on autopilot, finding a park on the Pennsylvania side of the Delaware. Sipping a cola that he couldn't recall buying, he gazed into abstracts. Late afternoon sun streamed over the rapid brown current, passing through his line of sight as he continued scrolling through the words, connecting dots.

". . . They knew my son's affiliation with your brother . . . and if not me, they probably would have used Franklin to get your brother to come here . . . They knew about our land, but that probably doesn't mean much . . . I offered to sell it a few years ago to a breeder I'd met at Saratoga . . ."

"Let me guess . . . George MacDade?"

"I don't know a George MacDade," Pendleton said offhandedly, then, "No, wait, I do recall hearing about him—a relative of yours, I trust?"

"He is," Luke admitted, feeling sick with the thought of Uncle George behind this, already hoping he was wrong.

"He generally runs stakes horses," Pendleton said with an easy familiarity. He'd definitely spent time on or around a racetrack. "He does well, too," he seemed to remember with an oddly fond smile. "On a lark, I once wagered on his horse—deciding it had to do well if it was attached to the MacDades. Your family's rather lucky. I won a few thousand on his horse. A cousin, is he?"

"Who did you offer the land to, sir?"

Brought back on track, Pendleton's mood soured, lips pursed. "Think his name was Timmons, but honestly, I don't recall. I met him in the clubhouse, and we shared a few drinks and a love of horses . . ."

Love of gambling, Luke corrected silently, then and now. "So, how would the mention of your land become public knowledge if it was just a random meeting?"

"I was contacted a few months later by someone looking for prime farmland," Pendleton had shrugged and reached for his half-empty glass. "As you know, the land's not exactly suitable forto farming, though I suppose with enough clear-cutting, there could be pastures."

If only to keep him talking, Luke had slipped off his chair and moved of his own accord to pour himself a bourbon and bring the bottle to refill Pendleton's tumbler. The conversation had relaxed enough by then, the older man had remembered his manners to offer his thanks for the drink, not seeming to consider that the bottle came from his own stocked cabinet.

"So, word traveled, then, that you had a sizeable chunk of land," Luke urged.

"I'd guess so, but that was a few years ago, mind . . .? I don't know who contacted me about this land last spring . . ."

"You said they phoned you. Private line or home phone?"

"Initially, through the business line," Frances said, forthcoming. "And . . . honestly, I thought it was someone from your brother's company." The agitation was back. "Or Liam, himself, pressuring me into that damned sale, what with my son's upcoming nuptials."

"You found out differently, then?" Luke had asked, not entirely certain how Frank's marriage connected to Liam buying land.

"Actually, no. But . . . I've had a few suspicions."

"As in . . .?" Luke nudged.

"As in, I still think it's someone in your family doing this," he said in agitation.

"Why did you offer me the land, Mr. Pendleton?"

"Because they contacted me again," he stated, irritated. "I was told to offer it to you. I think they wanted me to stonewall again, and I just wanted done with it," he said in finality. "It's yours and your problem now. My debts are paid, and I'm out of it . . ."

The only thing Luke had accomplished was to compound the questions and curiosities. Old man Pendleton didn't believe for a second that his blackmailers and Liam's assault were connected. Unless he was a far better actor than Luke imagined, the man suspected that someone in Mac-Dade Industries wanted that land and used blackmail to acquire it. A viable conclusion, except for one major flaw to which Luke was singularly privy. Anyone who knew his penchant for buying land—in or outside MacDade Industries—likewise knew that he didn't associate with the MacDades even on a personal level, much the less in business.

Whoever had drawn him into this plot had done so for a personal reason . . . as a slap in the face to Liam? Hurt him physically—ambush him, attempt to kill him. And when that had failed, strike at his business savvy? Undermine Liam's potentially profitable business venture . . . and use his own wayward brother to do it?

What had Frank said? Liam was bothered by their separation? How much more bothered would he be when he found out who had bought the land?

And learned about his wayward brother's abduction conducted by someone posing as Alecia Helms?

"Damn it."

Helms was still involved. Frank had admitted last night that he'd suggested the strip joint—allegedly to help Liam over the rough patch with his wife. And what was that rough patch about? Why had Liam and Natalie separated, if not over Alecia Helms?

Questions, only more questions.

To the quake at his ribcage, Luke jumped slightly and muttered another curse as he identified his phone vibration. He recognized the number before accepting the call, speaking simply, "Hi. What's up, Tye?"

"Just checking on you," Sheffield said smoothly. "And checking in," he added. "How are you feeling? Get any rest?"

The question caught Luke strangely off guard. This near stranger wondered, with genuine concern, over his wellbeing? "I'd imagine I'm fine," he said in a more guarded voice than intended. When people pretended to care, they generally had an ulterior motive. He'd suffered enough feigned concern to last him several lifetimes between nannies in the early years to tutors to the MacDade security forces treating him with kid gloves. Plenty of false concern for the benefit of the elder MacDades, and that never even included the relatives who treated him differently, the youngest son, fawning over him or lavishing him with gifts to gain the chieftain's favor.

"You don't sound fine, kid. Where are you?"

"You mentioned an update?"

"Why don't we meet for drinks? I'll buy you a soda or a milkshake, and we'll discuss it."

More bewildered and bemused, Luke commented, "I don't think a milkshake—or soda—would sit well on the bourbon I've been drinking all afternoon."

"You do recall, I'm a cop, right? And you're a minor? Technically, if you're drinking and driving, I might be under obligation to arrest you."

"Uh-huh, and I'm stupid enough to meet you if I'm half-kicked," Luke mused.

"You know, I memorized your birthdate just so I don't arrest you the day after your birthday by accident," Tyler said, sounding sober, then huffing a laugh. "Please, ease my mind here and tell me I'm not working for an underage lush."

"Humph, you want me to lie to you straight away?" Luke asked.

"Well, hell," Tyler muttered into the phone, then sobered in the instant. "Seriously, Luke, how are you today? No lingering headaches, nausea, chills?"

Truly bewildered by the sincere concern, Luke spoke distractedly. "Seriously, I'm fine, Tye, but uhm . . . Thanks for asking." Odd, very odd, this jaded fellow. Perhaps, that was the reason behind his weariness, a deep ingrained sense of concern for his fellowman. "Someday, you'll have to tell me why you seem so jaded, Tye."

"Hell, that noticeable, is it?"

"It shines through on occasion," Luke commented.

"Humph, well, it's not a huge secret but rather a cliché," Tyler offered. "No matter how many criminals I collect off the street, three more are waiting to take their place. Most of the time, I feel like I'm trying to plug a hole in a bucket with too many leaks. That's the story of my life."

"You're not married? No kids?"

"Tried the first. No luck on the second. Which was a blessing considering my marriage lasted about six months."

"That sucks," Luke decided. "Were you in love?"

Tyler huffed a laugh. "More in lust for about three months. We were young. I was fresh out of the academy, and she decided she didn't like being married to a cop."

"You never tried again?"

"I know better," Tyler commented. "Have you satisfied your curiosity yet?"

"Not even slightly, but I apologize for prying."

"You're not sorry, and honestly, I'd be disappointed if you were," Tyler spoke in a musing tone. "I really don't have any deep, dark secrets," he continued. "I enjoy being a detective, but the shine wore off a long time ago," he said more quietly. "If you want the truth, I think I watched one too many kids get hurt. Criminals—hell, just about any nutjob out there seems to prey on kids and that wears on a man's soul."

"Ever think about changing professions?" Luke wondered.

"Think I'm already there, as I seem to be moonlighting for a rather young eccentric," Tyler mused.

"Boy, didn't take you long to decide on that label," Luke uttered loud enough to be heard.

"Wasn't meant as an insult, just an observation," Tyler said without retracting his words or apologizing. "You're not the typical twenty-year-old, +and I'd wager you're well aware of it."

"I am, and you know I'm not insulted," Luke commented honestly. "I've been called worse. So, how would you like to be head of security at a resort?"

"Excuse me?"

"I'm building a resort in the mountains, and I'll need a security force," Luke said offhandedly. "Probably not a big force. About a half dozen men or women. I've researched it, but I don't want to spend much time on it. You'll have to do the background checks and the like when the time comes."

"Uh huh," Tyler said more carefully than any time past. "And this is in the Poconos?"

"No. More like the Blue Ridge. It'd involve moving a few hours away, and I didn't even ask if you have other family around here. Anyone you wouldn't consider moving away from or the like?"

"You're serious."

"I am, generally," Luke admitted. "You can think on it for a few days .. . actually, maybe more like a month. I don't think the Lodge will be fully livable for about six months, depending on how fast and hard the weather sets in. My cabin has a few extra rooms, and it should be inhabitable before Christmas." He paused a heartbeat, considering, "You wouldn't be able to moonlight at the Emerald Club. But I'd match your earnings, and of course, it would include meals and lodging if you want it."

"Let me get this straight," Tyler said haltingly. "You're seriously offering me a job . . .? Without even looking at a resume or running a background check?"

"You're a detective," Luke pointed out. "And I don't think you're a crooked cop. What else should I know?"

"I think just keeping you out of trouble could become a full-time job," Tyler said distractedly. "But if you're serious, I'll think about it and let you know. In the meantime, I owe you an update to justify that check I got this morning, and I really would prefer to meet in person."

"Are you working tonight?" Luke wondered.

"No, and even if I was, I wouldn't suggest meeting there," Tyler commented. "I have a friend staking out the club in case our imposter or her accomplice shows up—which reminds me. That sketch of the accomplice was pretty impressive as well. If you ever consider moonlighting, my captain would probably hire you."

"Wouldn't work," Luke commented soberly. "I'd have to see a criminal to sketch him. Did I mention that one of the regulars there is on my father's payroll?"

"Excuse me?"

Not a MacDade . . . a Callahan, Luke reconsidered with the image flashing neon despite the shadows within the club. Clearly, he recalled the man sitting near the stage in a position to watch the door but far more enchanted by the stripper. And she'd been attracted to him, offering him a coy smile and keeping him in her sights. He probably tipped well—

"LJ? Which regular are we talking about?"

Callahan . . . one of the Callahans . . . Natalie . . . almost at the onset, Luke had wondered if Natalie were involved in that ambush and ruled her out at the same time.

"Luke?"

"Huh," he huffed thoughtfully. He'd ruled out Natalie's participation, but what if . . .? What if somehow the Callahans had gotten wind of her and Liam separating? The new baby. With Arabella's birth around Christmas, it was possible the Callahans were visiting and would know if there were problems in the family.

"Hey," Tyler stated. "Where are you?"

"Shh," Luke uttered, running the scenarios through his mind. What if Liam had been stepping out, and Natalie mentioned it . . .? And that's where the theory fell apart. According to Frank, Liam hadn't been stepping out on Natalie before meeting Alecia. But Frank had said she'd believed that Liam was cheating on her, and that might have been at the heart of their separation, which meant the Callahans might have heard about it . . . "Damn it, the timing," Luke uttered. "That's the problem. It's the timing."

"Clue me in here, LJ. What are we talking about?"

"The land offer and Liam meeting Alecia—it was too close together. Unless those two details were entirely unrelated—which was improbable as all hell—they couldn't have pulled off a conspiracy of this magnitude over a couple days or a week."

"Why don't we take this from the top," Tyler commented. "Are we by any chance talking about those two fellas you asked me to track down?"

"The Chandlers?" *Where would they fit into this?* "You learned something?"

"I did," Tyler admitted. "I'd still like to meet somewhere and discuss this."

"I can't meet tonight, Tye, and tomorrow, I'm leaving."

"Leaving for where?"

"I have some business to attend," he admitted. "Did I mention Liam's probably getting discharged tomorrow?"

"No, you didn't, but Molly Anderson alluded to the possibility," Tyler said, sounding amused again. "That lady has some kind of inside track, I can tell you."

"Goes without saying," Luke agreed. "What did you find out?"

"Milton Chandler, unless there are two of them hanging around racetracks, passed away about six years ago. I managed to talk to a fellow who knew him—another trainer—which was how I found Chandler to begin with. He was still training horses at Laurel until about three days before he died. He had Cirrhosis of the liver. The son hung around the track for a little while afterward but disappeared eventually. I haven't been able to pick up his trail yet."

"You tried other tracks?"

"Yeah, I did, but so far, no cigar," Tyler agreed. "I got the impression, the boy was not well-liked," he commented. "How did you say you knew him?"

"His father worked on my father's estate when I was a kid," he admitted.

"Oh, then—like yesterday?" Tyler asked in a grave tone.

The words, in conflict with the tone, drew Luke's attention more than the content. "Huh?"

Tyler chuckled. "Never mind. So, tell me why the father—or son—might have a score to settle with you and your brother?"

With the image of Liam swooping from the hayloft, Luke considered how much to tell and decided, "I'm probably making more of it than it was, and I'm probably way off base even considering them guilty of a thing. Honestly, it was just a thought of Pendleton and his gambling problem to make me think of them. You needn't waste time tracking Jimmy down."

"I'm going to spend a little more time on it," Tyler decided. "Now, which one of the club's regulars is on your father's payroll? Or should I take a wild guess? The scruffy looking guy who hangs out right of center stage, generally ogling the ladies just short of drooling."

"Probably the one if he has longish brown hair, wears plaids and faded jeans in the latest country-style fad," Luke admitted. "And I think he's just on loan. Not one of my father's regular employees."

"About how many guys does your father have on his payroll?"

"Honestly, I don't know. Probably about a dozen, maybe more counting the estate and the office complexes. Why? Is that important?"

"Maybe," Tyler said distractedly. "Generally, when I see your folks on TV, they have several able bodies flanking them. Is that normal protocol?"

"Ah, I see," Luke commented. "You're wondering if they have a lot of enemies? Or my father, in particular, and the answer could be, yes," he admitted. "I don't think you become as successful as my family without rubbing someone wrong. But if you're wondering if they're into anything illegal to warrant an attack? I'd say, no. The recent heavy security probably has more to do with Liam's condition and the unknown."

"As in, you don't know if this attack was meant for him, personally, or your entire family? And considering that attack on you Monday night . . . Have you talked to anyone about that yet?"

"No, and I'm not going to, Ty," Luke said grimly.

"Buddy, I know it'll be rough, but I think someone besides you and me needs to know about this," Tyler said carefully. "It could verify that your brother wasn't the single target, and that's something those investigators need to know."

"That's where you and I disagree," Luke commented. "My assault was a direct strike against Liam."

"Explain," Tyler stated.

"I believe that whoever came at me, they meant for me to run to the investigators and muddy the investigation. It wasn't about me, personally, and that ambush was personal. If it was random, they'd be caught."

"LJ, it was personal," Tyler said with sincere concern. "It doesn't get much more personal, and you damn well know it."

"To me, yes," Luke admitted. "But it could as easily have been Gregor, or God forbid, one of my nephews if they were left unattended. I was a random choice, and we've already established—Liam's enemy has done his research. Anyone who looks closely enough knows I generally dance to my own drum. I was an easy target."

"Which is why you shouldn't be running around alone, LJ," Tyler stated. "Have you even considered that you're still a likely target?"

"I won't make the same mistake twice, Ty," Luke admitted. "If I get any more messages, I'll be sure to call you, and honestly, I'm not following any pattern to be ambushed."

"You, my young friend, are taking this far too lightly."

"Ty, I've lived with a threat over my head from the day I was born," Luke said with a sigh, genuinely weary. "The moment anyone knows my name and affiliation to Lucius MacDade and company, I'm in jeopardy, and that's not saying he has any serious enemies," he pointed out. "The fact that he's loaded and could afford to pay a sizeable ransom—and would—has made me a likely candidate for a random kidnapping from day one."

"You're considering the Lindbergh kidnapping, which, I'll mention, didn't happen all that far from here."

"Exactly," Luke admitted. "Me, my brothers, and a number of my cousins have always had bodyguards and a learned protocol in addressing strangers. On five separate occasions in grade school, I was escorted to my classes in a private academy because someone threatened some member of my family. We, the MacDades . . . I think all of us were born with a target on our backs. This isn't truly any great surprise other than the fact that someone got close enough to do damage—to Liam—and to me, to be honest." And that was the longest he'd spoken about his personal life to anyone in a very long time. "The bottom line, Ty—I'll be careful. Right now, I have to run."

"LJ . . . keep in touch," Tyler said.

25

Long after the call ended, Luke rested behind the steering wheel, reviewing the conversation while watching sparks dancing over the muddy water. The river was still running high and fast from the previous day's rain. A lot like his thoughts. Muddy. He couldn't even remember when he'd last shared something of his private life with anyone . . . until he actually thought about it.

Chandler . . . with Jimmy Chandler, years—ten or nearly eleven years ago—Luke had admitted his concern over the escorts in St. Andrew's Academy. He'd been lying on a bench in his Mum's gazebo alone, reading . . .

A chemistry book, Luke remembered, seeing the pages open on his raised thighs. Forever, he'd been carrying books to one of his Mum's half-dozen gazebos. Wadding his jacket as a pillow against the arm of the bench . . . the oriental-style-bench, with its cast iron and teak wood. Luke had often wondered if Mum set this gazebo so far from the house because his father wasn't thrilled with oriental design. Still, his father had indulged his mum to have the peaked roofs erected and benches fashioned in teak, along with importing some of the hardier bushes. Already, the trees had begun to turn livid orange and red, reflecting a bright glow through the delicate screens and scrolled iron posts. Against the soft orange glow, Luke squinted slightly, inhaling the words and compounds as easily as he drew breath . . . and he heard the footfall. Rising from a hypnotic state, Luke spotted Jimmy through the shrubbery before he strode up the steps.

Not entirely surprised by the interruption, Luke tipped his head and spied Jimmy with a faintly curious smile. He'd become accustomed to Jimmy joining him, and he never truly minded. His arrival was more of a fleeting irritation than concern after enduring the past week of constant company and supervision.

"Funny finding you here," Jimmy said as he continued onto the gazebo, strolling leisurely across the shined planks.

Not a chance visit. The boy had arrived stealthily, verifying who rested on the gazebo before advancing. Luke knew the boy would never risk climbing the steps so boldly or enjoying the gazebo without invitation if he thought he'd encounter either of Luke's brothers or mum.

"I didn't know I was lost to be found," Luke said simply.

Jimmy twitched a smirk and swung onto the bench alongside Luke's feet.

Resigning to the interruption, Luke closed the book on his thighs and started skidding his boots to the floor. He'd dressed for the hike through the garden, although he'd considered traveling further into the upper forests when pulling on his jeans and boots, wearing his jacket. The weather wasn't cool enough for a windbreaker at these lower levels, but toward the peaks, the wind and thin air could be a problem for a slight body—and his body was slight enough to be frostbit rather quickly. He'd even shoved his lined leather gloves into his pocket, along with several health bars. The hand landed on his boot, halting him, startling him to find Jimmy smirking still.

"Don't get up on my account," Jimmy said lightly. "You look comfortable."

"Aye—" He started with the Scottish word, a lingering effect of visiting his relatives in the motherland over the summer. "—I am," he corrected in a breath. Enough MacDades were speaking the brogue, and most sounded angry when they did; Luke had decided some time ago that he'd rather not be one of them. "But I don't mind the interruption," he'd added while skidding his foot from under the clasp.

Jimmy clasped his knee instead. "Really, I didn't mean to bother you."

"You're not, then." Dangit. "I probably should be getting back to the house soon anyway."

"What's your hurry? We could just hang out for a little while."

It would probably be rude to leave straight away. Fleetingly, Luke recalled Mum coaching him to be more sociable. She worried about him, he knew. MacDades were supposed to enjoy the company of others . . . which, to Luke, meant they needed to tolerate people. He tolerated a lot of people, he'd once admitted to her, referring to himself accompanying her to the shelters and fundraisers for the underprivileged. He never minded helping others, although he'd often heard the underlying awe when others spoke to him as if he were royalty or the like. Even at the Academy, he was often treated differently, and this past week was even more distressing than most.

Despite the clasp on his knee, Luke rose and repositioned, scooting sideways, dragging his knee onto the bench to face Jimmy. "I don't need to hurry."

"Whachu reading?" Jimmy asked, leaning to read the title.

"Nothing important," Luke said while tipping the book toward the bench behind him. Jimmy never seemed to resent him for his intelligence, but Luke had become accustomed to hiding his interests—not to mention, he probably shouldn't be caught with one of Liam's books. This one had just been lying around, though, left haphazardly on an end table in the great room, and how could he pass up a book with a microscope and beakers on the cover? So far, he'd recorded a half dozen experiments—

"Lemme see," Jimmy said and made a quick move, maybe to grab the book, but Luke pivoted by instinct, off the bench with the book in hand, already wheeling.

At the last second, Luke transitioned the offensive move to defensive and deflected the calloused hand while recording the shock in the brown eyes, the grimace of instant pain from the strike. In trouble again! The words shouted in Luke's mind as he launched forward, grabbing Jimmy's arm as the taller boy staggered backward. With an 'oomph,' Jimmy landed on the bench, clasping his wrist and gasping breath.

"I'm sorry!" Luke cried as he settled beside the injured boy. "I'm sorry, James! Are you all right? Did I hurt you?" he demanded as the boy blinked against a quick sheen of tears. "I'm sorry, James!"

"How—how's the hell come you did that? I wasn't meaning nothin'!"

"I'm sorry," Luke said miserably. "I didn't mean to hit you, just . . . I just . . . you grabbed and . . . I'm sorry!" Too fast! Gregor had played at slapping him not long ago, and Luke had deflected the hand even before Gregor had pulled the strike. And Gregor had claimed Luke was getting too fast for his own good. Like being too big for his britches, which was more just a joke since everyone said he would be the smallest MacDade ever made. But being 'too fast' might not have been a joke. Worriedly, Luke studied the wrist, the red streak where he'd landed a blow . . . which might have broken the boy's wrist if Luke hadn't halted the strike. Blinking tears from his thick lashes,

Luke found Jimmy staring at him. "I'm sorry," he said again. "Are you all right? Do we need to call an ambulance?"

"How come you're crying? Did you hurt your hand?"

"I didn't mean to hurt you, James," he managed sincerely. "It's just been . . . well, all week, I've had to worry—it's no excuse. If you want to see my book—it's not really *my* book. It's Liam's. And he'll probably be angry if it's damaged. If you're careful though . . ."

"Liam's huh?" Jimmy asked with a different note, interested. "If it's his, it's probably about girls, huh? What . . .? A bunch of naked girls?"

Uncertain whether to be amused or embarrassed, Luke pivoted and reached for the book, shaking his head. "No. It's just a textbook," he managed, trying to ignore the thought of Liam's legendary interest in girls. Even at nine, Luke knew Liam would never need a book about girls. They were always hanging on him and shoving their half-naked parts at him.

"A textbook, huh? About girls—"

Luke presented the chemistry book in time to halt Jimmy's further banter. In Luke's opinion, the chemistry book was more interesting anyway—but then, Jimmy had just turned thirteen. According to texts about the human anatomy, sex was a natural infatuation for boys—and girls—at that age. "Chemistry," Luke said with genuine delight. "It's really very good, too," he added, seeing the doubt and disappointment in Jimmy's dull brown eyes. "There are some really good experiments we could try if you want."

"What—like foaming volcanos?" Jimmy asked in such a chiding tone that Luke decided he might as well keep his interests to himself. "I get enough of that crap in school," Jimmy further verified his lack of enthusiasm.

Considering, motivated as much by Jimmy still rubbing his wrist as by the camera dangling, as always, from a nylon cord around his skinny neck, Luke gained inspiration. "Actually, it could probably teach us how to develop that film in your camera. It's just a chemical reaction with liquids and the effects of light. We could probably make our own dark room. We'd need some plastic bins and certain chemicals . . . and I think some special paper and a red light."

Jimmy almost appeared interested for a moment, then, "Na. Why'd we want to go to all that trouble when I can just drop the film at the drug store when Pa takes me to town? They send it out, and I get it back in a few days."

"But you could have it right away," Luke pointed out, thinking it might be fun to build a dark room. The wine cellar . . . would be great if Jimmy would agree to come into the house. But Luke knew the boy would refuse. The only time Luke had ever invited him, Jimmy had ended up with a black eye after asking his father for permission. 'Pa says I gotta stay outa the big house. It's not my place . . .' "Maybe we could use the lab," Luke considered, thinking of the laboratory in the stable that housed the breeding equipment and medical supplies. The room was sealed well enough to keep dust and contaminants out, and it wasn't breeding season. Their vet might need the sonogram equipment to check the mares and babies, but probably not much else. "I could ask Mum for permission, and she could likely get whatever we need."

"Just hold on," Jimmy said while lifting, fingering his camera, and fidgeting with the lenses. "I could see maybe doing that someday, but not right now," he said and lifted the camera, covering half his face to spy Luke through the lens. "I just like taking pictures . . . Your eyes look even more blue when I zoom in—"

The picture snapped, and Luke blinked, drawing back as if slapped. "That's not likely to be a very good picture, James," he said soberly.

"Bet I could sell it to one of those rags at the supermarket," Jimmy said with a smile, his brown eyes lighting with mischief as he lowered the camera. "I bet they'd pay good money for a picture of Lucas MacDade's big blue eye."

"I don't think my father would approve of that," Luke said and almost felt bad as quickly as Jimmy's smile vanished. "I . . . I didn't mean I'd tell him, James. Just . . . people are always taking pictures of us and the like, and well, now wouldn't be a good time for it is all,"

"I didn't say I was gonna do it," Jimmy said defensively. "You don't have to tell anyone I even took that shot."

"I won't and . . . I'm sorry, James. It's . . ." Dangit, now he needed to explain. "It's just that this week's been bad," he admitted with a sigh and fidgeted unnaturally, turning sideways, dragging his leg onto the bench to face Jimmy more directly. "Something is going on that nobody wants to talk about," he said bluntly and found Jimmy's more curious gaze. Shrugging, he continued, "My father sent two bodyguards to follow me around school."

"Why? What did you do?"

"I didn't do anything," Luke said indignantly, instantly wondering if he was wrong. At times, Jimmy's way of looking at things could be distracting. "They were there to protect me," Luke sighed. "They've done it before, and it doesn't usually bother me, except that I don't know why they were there this week."

"What d'ya think? Somebody maybe gonna kidnap you?"

"Like I said, I don't know, but . . . maybe," he admitted.

"Guess that's possible," Jimmy said as he lifted his camera again, eyeing Luke through the lens.

Luke turned his gaze toward the garden, scanning the flowers if only to avoid reacting to the sense of Jimmy's teasing. At times, he wasn't the most tolerant of Jimmy Chandler's chiding and sneering since he knew it sometimes stemmed from jealousy. Jimmy making a joke of kidnapping was just that—a joke. But Luke knew too well—it was a genuine threat. From as far back as he could remember, he'd been cautioned about speaking to strangers and forbidden even to talk to other children without his mum or escort's approval. Never was he permitted to go anywhere alone, even to a restroom in public, which was a good reason to avoid the public.

"Guess . . . maybe it really is possible, huh?" Jimmy prodded. "I mean, with your old man being loaded. Somebody might want to snatch you and hold you for ransom. He'd probably pay big bucks to get you back, and then there's no guarantee he'd get you back. I heard how mostly kidnappers only wait 'til they get the money, then murder the kidnapped guy so he can't identify them. There was a movie about that I saw once."

Luke looked at Jimmy far more intently, wondering if Jimmy was still teasing or merely stating a known fact. Luke knew well enough that most kidnap victims never survived. "I don't think that's funny, James. I mean if you're trying to be funny, it's not working."

"I ain't," he said soberly, then lifted the camera over his eye and snapped another picture.

"Dangit, stop that," Luke stated, tense and irritated, suddenly.

"Hey," Jimmy said haltingly as he lowered the camera. "So, I'm sorry. Okay? I didn't mean to scare you. Just saying you gotta be careful."

"I know that," Luke said defensively. "And it's not like I'm scared. I just . . . so, maybe I just don't like having people follow me around in school. I doubt anyone could walk in and grab me out of a classroom. Anyway, it doesn't matter. Until my father says differently, I'll have to just accept it."

"That stinks," Jimmy said. "You probably get picked on and shit, huh? Like maybe some guys—or girls—saying how you're too dumb to find your way around the school and stuff."

If Jimmy were trying to make him feel better, it wasn't working. Rather indifferent, Luke commented, "No, I can safely say, that's not happened. They just don't come too close because they know it could be dangerous for them, too," he continued quietly. "If a criminal managed to get the better of my bodyguards and me, and one of my friends stood too close, they could be taken by mistake." Luke shrugged. "I'd hate to be responsible for someone else getting murdered because of me."

"Yeah, that would stink, too," Jimmy said and studied Luke a second longer. "Wanna go do something? Maybe hang out in the breakroom and watch some TV?"

Hanging around in the lounge just so Jimmy could eat a few candy bars was not what Luke would consider fun. "We could go for a hike instead? Maybe climb the mountain. I have some granola bars we could share."

"The kind that tastes like cardboard, or the good ones with chocolate chips?"

Scooting enough to gather his coat, wishing he hadn't suggested the hike, Luke produced a half dozen bars from several pockets. The good ones. Mum never bought anything but the best, chock full of vitamins. The hike was no longer in the cards, but at least they weren't stuck indoors watching the 'idiot box'—which his father called the television even when watching the news stations. Jimmy preferred those goofy sitcoms or cartoons, and there was only so much of that crap a guy could tolerate when he could be hiking or experimenting—or reading about either one . . .

If anyone knew how one Luke McDade felt about being kidnapped,

James Chandler qualified. Blinking the past from his mind's eye, Luke refocused on the muddy water, and in one blinding flash, he realized . . . James Chandler—Johnny now—was the fake Alecia Helms' accomplice.

26

D éjà vu.

With a sense of familiar flashing through his mind, Liam caught and halted the glossy print sliding from the manila envelope on his lap. Nearly ten years had passed since the first time someone had offered him a half dozen unsolicited photographs. Those had been amateurish compared to this fine photograph.

Resting in the recliner, dressed in black silk pajamas and a thick fur robe, nearly relaxed for the first time in longer than he could readily remember, Liam drew the print from the fold. It wasn't alone. At least two others started to follow the leader, and with every fractional inch to emerge, his temper rose. Not the work of an amateur. Even in the dull natural light from the window over his shoulder, the image glowed with every contour of bare flesh twining in minute detail, but the facial expressions were interesting. In the photo, he appeared fully engaged in the moment, while in retrospect, he knew himself to be daydreaming while kissing the porcelain flesh mounded before him.

Fascinated, intrigued, he studied the familiar rounded face glistening from a sheen of sweat. Her thick black lashes dipped to emit only a thin line of murky blue. In the photograph, her fingers twisted in his hair, appearing stubby—which was a detail he'd never noticed before now. Likely, a trick of the camera and a credit to the photographer meant to mute the fire-red gloss of her long fingernails. Possibly, the nails buried in his curls created the illusion of stubby digits.

He needed a haircut. Or a trim, at least. Even a month ago, he might have been slightly overdue for such.

His anger smoldering, Liam turned the first photo under and studied the next. Rather than himself caught between the immense white mounds, he'd been captured looking up from between milky-white knees. The film had captured his peculiar expression as he'd tried to decide what the young woman meant to accomplish by wrapping her legs around his head. In memory flash, he recalled trying to discover if she was practicing a yoga move. The lotus position, possibly.

And the next . . .? An almost boring moment captured him hovering above the young woman, prepared to lance her with himself more than ready for full thrust. Boring, but still artistic, as it clearly depicted his swollen member and interest in the wanton face beneath him. She'd been panting, then, and nearly begging him to take her. Her red nails had dug into his biceps, and were he a lesser man, she might have scarred him.

Well. And he'd wondered what price he would pay when ending that romance. Herein lay the answer.

Turning the photos right-side under, Liam tipped the envelope, intending to find the ransom note.

Empty.

Likely, a note or a phone call would follow.

The opposite of the sequence Natalie had endured five months earlier. First, the call, then the photos. Of him and Cicely, he knew by Natalie's reference to a costume. He'd only seen Cicely twice, and both times he'd accompanied her from the airport to her apartment via limousine—which had thrilled her. Atlanta, he remembered. She lived outside of Atlanta. Peachtree or Peachpit, Georgia . . . a far enough distance from the airport for him to close the curtain and enjoy the privacy of the tinted windows en route. The last time he'd seen her, they'd just arrived on an International flight. He'd been hungry . . . and they were both looking forward to a little R and R . . . And the paparazzi had spotted them . . . Only one industrious lad had trotted after them as they'd entered the restaurant . . .

And Liam hadn't asked Natalie about those photos.

Only partially tipped in the recliner, his heel hooked on the bottom cushion, Liam slid the photographs into the folder and studied the envelope. Unremarkable. The envelope was postmarked from Jersey City and addressed to him c/o Southern General Hospital. The words were typed, which hadn't alarmed or alerted him to the contents. If this envelope had reached the headquarters in Lexington, Clare would have considered it just another unsolicited proposal for one investment or another, and depending on her mood, she might have opened it. Generally, the unsolicited offers landed in the trash; those of interest she passed to him. This one would have reached him.

The timing of this bit of apparent blackmail was not a huge surprise.

At least five, maybe six days earlier, the hospital Chief of Staff had announced Liam MacDade's miraculous return to the living realm. For dramatic effect, Ed Turner had waited for the scheduled conference, then milked the podium, according to Natalie, to build suspense before stating their esteemed guest had been moved to guarded condition and was expected to fully recover. Turner had gone so far as to mention the MacDade children were with their father when the patient awoke for the first time.

Recalling Natalie's outrage to have their sons exploited by Turner and the Press, Liam almost managed a smile. His wife's temper could become legendary if she needed to endure much more publicity.

His started smile soured as he considered how she would react to these photos. And he should have asked about those photos that she'd received. She hadn't said if they were pornography or just another candid shot of him escorting a strange woman as others to reach the tabloids over the years. With that mention of a costume, he'd assumed the pictures were innocent and G-rated. Now, though? There seemed something far more sinister at work.

Pictures? An anonymous call? More pictures? An ambush that nearly killed him?

Somehow those events were connected. But how? And to what end?

Blackmail seemed the most obvious, but that made little sense for the obvious reason. If Natalie had reacted and demanded a divorce, the blackmail would have been a moot point. No reputable publication would publish porn, and what the hell would he care if some idiot alluded to an affair with his marriage on the rocks?

Truly, none of it made sense. It wasn't as if High Land Inc. would collapse over some lousy pictures or bad publicity. At most, if the clan was annoyed with him, he might be asked to step aside and let Gregor take the helm no differently than if Liam had died, but the chance of that happening was slim to none. Lucius MacDade had built the present dynasty from the first tree up, and no one alive would dare to change the line of succession—no matter how morally corrupt the successor might be. The tradition of fortunes passed from eldest son to eldest son might be as old as time to the MacDades, but their wealth had been won or lost throughout their history. Lucius truly had built this latest windfall from the ground up over thirty years; no one in the clan would dare attempt to destroy it when so many now depended on it.

To the motion at the door, Liam tilted his gaze, and his attention riveted. Of all the people he might expect to see at the crack of dawn, Lucas MacDade was, perhaps, the last. But here he was, tall and as lean as a sapling, appearing more like a California beach bum, with his white-blond locks brushing at his shoulders, than an heir to a dynasty. Perhaps, more like Jesus, Liam corrected as he noticed the slightly darker blond beard and mustache, and his thoughts created a kink in his mustache.

"You look better."

Half afraid that he might be imagining the body halted several steps away, Liam fleeted his memory of this fellow hovering at the edges of his mind . . . and personifying the grim reaper.

"Aye . . . feeling better," Liam managed while sliding his gaze down and up. He appeared real enough, wearing blue jeans and a blue sweater that enhanced the neon blue of his eyes. Like his own, the color could change with his wardrobe, and more so than any others, Lucas resembled him—physically. There, the likeness began and ended. Lucas had become such a sober and quiet young man . . . or perhaps, he had always been.

Presently, Lucas appeared as tense as a rabbit in a fox den despite his effect of nonchalance. His thumbs hooked at his jeans pockets, a black leather jacket caught at one hip in the crook of his wrist, he stood in solid balance on a pair of hiking boots. His focus shifted, scanning the room and confirming Liam's belief that the lad hadn't been here before this moment . . . Unless he was merely confirming that they were alone.

Perhaps, with dawn barely breaking, the lad had expected to find Liam asleep. Doubtful the lad knew how one older brother had always adhered to a schedule of rising before dawn to attend to mundane business affairs—like opening junk mail from the previous day.

"You could sit," Liam offered and nearly mentioned saving him from a stiff neck. Whether Lucas would take that as a jest as intended or become offended, Liam had no idea. Sadly, it occurred to him, that he had no idea what would or wouldn't set this young man to growling. And the feeling of walking on eggs, here and now, almost tipped his own precarious balance. He hated this feeling of estrangement. He should know this brother as intimately as he knew Gregor. He should be able to laugh and joke, to wrestle him to the ground, or spar with words.

Rather than sit, Lucas sidled and leaned casually at the bed, resting a hip at the bed rail, keeping the jacket hooked at his other hip as if posing for an advertisement in a men's fashion magazine. He could be a model. He bore that look, young, lean, and handsome, with the MacDade smirk kinking his mustache without a hint of genuine mirth.

"You look good, Luke," Liam said honestly and noted the smirk enhance slightly. "Well, you do," he said with a thought of the irony. Him, judging his brother sound, while he rested in a hospital suite.

"Thanks," Lucas said in a natural low rhythm. "You, too."

Well, and they had covered that topic. *Now what?* "How've you been?" *Which sounded just as blasted lame.*

"Fair to Midland," he said idly.

Uh-huh. Wore that one out, too. "So . . . what have you been up to of late?"

"This and that," he answered.

"Don't s'pose you'd care to elaborate? Seems to me, it's been a while since I last saw you." Two years and six months, give or take a week, Liam calculated while watching the speculation behind the blue eyes. This brother was a thinker. Far more calculating than either he or Gregor.

"No," he said smoothly. "Don't suppose I would," he said and eased onto his boots as a prelude to departure. "I'm glad to see, you're on the mend," he continued without prodding. "Wasn't sure I'd be granted access, what with all the security, but I don't put much stock in those daily news briefs."

"Had to see for yourself, eh?" Liam said offhandedly, uncertain if he was annoyed by his brother's evasive tactic or amused by the same. Either way, the fellow was leaving.

On his feet, Luke freed his right hand as he stepped forward and proffered his palm.

A handshake? From a brother that he hadn't seen in two years? Liam locked his palm and barely started the pressure to pull him down into an embrace, but Luke drew back with such sudden alarm that Liam released him. "Lucas—"

"Take care, Liam," he said lightly. "See you again."

A reflection of those early awakenings, Liam considered as he gazed at the door where the image of his younger brother remained more like a retina stain fading. There and gone. A fleeting motion. The boy arriving and departing in an eyeblink. Someday, damn it, he would discover what set this course in the brilliant mind. Surely, something . . .

His gaze drifted and snagged on the envelope, and as if via Fisher's fence, the memory surfaced. Not a large manila envelope ten years ago. Clearly, he recalled the small white envelope, one generally used for sending a letter through the post. No address or postmark. Not even his name scrolled across the open space. The envelope had been hand-delivered, and the bearer had stood before him, hands hooked in the back pockets of thin jeans, stringy brown hair tipped to one shoulder as the boy had needed to wrench his neck to meet Liam, eye-to-eye. More curious than alarmed, Liam remembered asking, 'What's this?'

'Might want to have a look for yourself,' the boy commented, sounding unnaturally smug.

They'd stood on the cobbled stone just inside the stable. The fresh scents of alfalfa and sawdust carried on the soft breeze wafting through the open aisle. Behind the iron rails to either side, more than a dozen horses munched their morning feed, evidence of the boy's father already making his rounds through the stables. Six in all, the stone barns ranged from foaling stalls to stallion quarters, but the main stable in which they stood housed the working hunters and jumpers, from Thoroughbreds to Hanovearians.

He'd arrived for his morning ride, and with the spring meet advancing, Liam hadn't appreciated the interruption. Like all else in his life, even at seventeen, nearly eighteen, he'd maintained a somewhat grueling work eth- ic. Adhering to schedules—whether training for a Cross Country meet or studying for dual exams, one to pass high school, the other to finish his second semester of college—he'd rarely dawdled. To have this somewhat odd child of thirteen handing him an unmarked envelope and appearing far too arrogant, yet again, had annoyed him.

Even in hindsight, Liam recalled his own arrogance, remembering a barely restrained urge to backhand the boy and wipe the twisted smirk from the pouty lips. Doubting his father would appreciate him smacking their barn manager's son and considering the child's delicate features, his good sense had overridden his annoyance and stifled his reflexes.

If only to indulge the lad, Liam had used a pen—a habit he still enlist- ed—to slit the flap open and spill the contents, catching the half dozen pho- tographs in his palm. Even at a glance, he recognized the subjects captured on the prints. Not snapshots like those featured at an arcade, but more of a style to be tucked into a family album. The grainy photos, 2" x 3", might have been developed at the local photo kiosk without cropping or editing.

Clearly, the camera had captured the scotch-patterned quilt, the golden hay in a strip of sunlight from the loft vents, and the two naked forms twined under similar stripes of daylight. In the very first shot, the photographer had captured the faces, not quite glowing but glistening enough to suggest the effort expended. He and Lisa Robertson—her below, him above—poised in the natural act, and a half dozen poses had followed, rumps and busts exposed in fine form. The camera angle hadn't changed, and judging by the position, Chandler had hidden within the loft quite a distance away and across the open space above the runway. Later, Liam had climbed into the opposite hayloft and found the budding photographer's hidey-hole, confirming his belief that the lad had used a telephoto lens.

Whether he was amused or annoyed, even now, remained a mystery, but Liam remembered looking at the boy with a lifted brow. Judging by the youngster's smug, wry smile, the lad expected something, but what exactly, Liam had wondered. A backhand had seemed in order then, surely, but still, Liam had refrained. Speculating, he'd asked, 'How much do you want for these?'

Pale eyes oddly glittering, the boy had commented, 'Those are free, but if you're wanting the negatives, maybe something.'

Blackmail. Still undecided between amusement and annoyance, Liam scanned the pictures again, considering what action he should take. The lad had overstepped, but another thought had intruded on the heels of that revelation. He remembered the day, a few weeks earlier. He and Lisa Robertson had climbed into the loft . . . and all too well, Liam recalled handing this lad a twenty-dollar bill to see that a certain younger brother was occupied for a time.

His memory paused; Liam considered the past with the eyes of the present. Lucas had followed him and Gregor around nearly from the moment he could walk. Wherever they traveled on the estate, the little lad had dogged their heels, and seldom had Liam minded. Generally, either he or Gregor had swung the little fellow to a shoulder and carried him or tossed him between them like juggling a basketball without the dribbling. Even at nine or ten, Lucas was small enough to be bandied about between his teenage brothers and seemed only to enjoy that tussling. But there were places that Liam had preferred not to take him—or let him follow—like the loft.

That revelation, the mere thought of his nine-year-old brother huddled in that loft watching him and Lisa coupling, had snapped Liam's precarious rein on his temper. He'd clasped a wad of the dirty t-shirt and lifted Jimmy against the stable wall, ignoring the fright in the pale eyes. 'Where the hell was my brother when you took these?'

Stammering, no longer smug or arrogant, Chandler appeared more fragile as he grappled uselessly at Liam's arm. 'House . . . h-house—y-your m-m-mom called—for h-him.'

'You're positive?'

'Y-y-yes! H-hon-est!'

That he might have been choking the boy had occurred to Liam as the round face had flushed red and his dull brown eyes had bulged to saucers. The lad was not breathing just right, either. A fragile sort, their Jimmy Chandler. So, and Liam had let him catch his footing, and the boy stood heaving breaths and battling tears, nearly collapsing against the wall. If only to apologize, certain that he'd come too close to hurting the boy, Liam had decided and pulled his wallet from his jodhpurs, digging a twenty from the fold. As an afterthought, he changed that to fifty, halfheartedly hoping his father wouldn't hear about him choking their stable manager's son.

'For these,' he'd said, indicating the photos in his hand, and handed the fifty into the trembling slender fingers. His gaze locked and steady on the terrified brown eyes, Liam had continued simply, 'I don't give a damn what you do with the negatives, but I'd suggest thinking long and hard before trying to sell them to a tabloid . . . And you might want to rethink blackmail as a career choice. I'd wager it could be dangerous . . .'

Had the boy heeded that advice? That was the question rolling over in Liam's mind.

That he might have been staring at a black television screen for several moments occurred to him only as he realized he wasn't alone and his breakfast had arrived. Waking more to the natural sounds, he heard a radio playing at a low volume, the nurse skidding ceramic plates and silverware on the tray. Voices trailed from some distant place, and an elevator announced its arrival with an echoing ding.

Still, Liam lingered in the half-waking world, recalling he and Lisa sharing a laugh over the photos and determining to share them—her three, him three—although he teased her to suggest she reimburse him twenty-five for her half. She'd repaid him tenfold in the comfort of the boathouse behind her house. Fond memories, indeed. Quite the spring, that one.

Photographs. He wondered absently. What had become of those three photos—then recalled tossing them into the fireplace within a few days of receiving them. What need for photos when he held the memories clear and dear?

"Sir, if you're finished with these?" Tanya R. intruded and started to gather the scatter of cards and envelopes on the recliner and his lap.

"Leave them," he said in a voice deeper than intended.

As if bitten, her hand recoiled before touching the envelope, and she bumped the serving cart in her haste. Hot coffee plopped over the rim of a cup, red Jello jiggled, and Tanya grabbed the glass of orange juice a split second before it tipped into the loaded plate of eggs and bacon. Not fast enough, that recoil. In a stopped instant, she stared at the orange sprinkle—like decorations on a cupcake—atop over-easy eggs.

Into that stopped second, the sigh came from the doorway, and Liam tipped his faintly startled gaze to find his wife shaking her head, starting forward. How she always managed to arrive within these mini disasters, he had yet to confirm. His lips twitched with the start of a smile, and her eyes brightened in mirth.

"Terrorizing these fine ladies, yet again?" she asked.

"I didnae do a thing," he said while fleeting a skyward glance to notice Tanya R.'s more distressed expression flashing toward Natalie, clearly seeking salvation.

"Lord," Natalie said as she looked at the plate. A quiver in her lips, she reached automatically to the young woman's elbow, offering solace. "No worries, dear," she said while nudging the nurse and cart away. "I'm sure he won't mind a little flavoring on his bacon."

"I uhm . . . No," R. decided quickly. "I'll just have another brought," she stated and took charge of the cart, starting it away.

"That coffee's unscathed," Liam said and regretted speaking when the woman jerked. The cart stopped and plopped more coffee over the rim. Lifting his gaze to Natalie, he mocked distress, managing an innocent expression that brought a laugh off her lips. "Grab it quick, will you, love? I dinnae think it will survive much more."

With a visible effort, Natalie stifled her laugh and plucked the coffee cup from the tray, favoring the nurse with a Mona Lisa smile. "Forgive him, dear. He's not generally such a bear."

Holding his tongue for fear of wearing either the juice—still too close for comfort—or the coffee, though it rested firmly in his wife's capable hand, Liam waited until the woman moved several paces toward the door before accepting the cup, meeting Natalie's bemused eyes. "I didn't do a thing," he repeated, far more amused and at once, captivated. How she could appear stunning wearing another simple ensemble of brown flowing skirt and another soft beige sweater, he couldn't fathom. The skirt hem hovered at her calves, offering only a hint of her long, slender legs, but his thoughts tilted toward how swiftly he could breach that fine thread. Sliding under that silky cloth—

"Settle," she said and drew his gaze to find her green eyes glittering.

"You cannot waltz in here with your fine self dressed for success and not expect to meet with some," he said.

"My dear, I'm wearing a skirt nearly to the blasted floor," she mused. "I'm dressed for warmth."

"Ahh, well we can arrange that too," he idled and masked his smile with a sip of coffee.

With her smile threatening to become a laugh, she lowered smoothly to rest on the arm of his chair, dipping to land a quick kiss on his lips.

Apparently, the morning for hit and run. He barely lifted his free hand before she caught his fingers and landed their interlocked hands on her lap—on the *outside* of that lovely skirt. Sitting up, she studied him with a slight tip of her head, her soft locks spilling over one shoulder. With the amber hue of her eyes, he sensed her looking past the surface of his gaze, and his thoughts stilled. A sensitive, this lovely wife of his, and though she might not read his thoughts, she hadn't arrived at this early hour, alone, without a reason. Himself, to be that reason. On his lap, the envelope seemed to gain several pounds, becoming a lead weight.

"Something's troubling you, Liam," she said gently, sober despite the lingering curve in her glossy lips. "I thought, perhaps, the thought of finally leaving this blasted hospital could account for your distress, but that's not it."

"Don't suppose I could just claim to be maudlin?"

"If it's not something you want to discuss, that's fine, love," she said lightly. "I just needed to see you."

So simple and direct, those words. He sipped his coffee while searching her enchanting gaze, wondering, "Did you fear a thing, in particular, love?"

With the discomfort flashing, she considered the words before answering carefully, "I wish it could be that simple." She rested in a position to cast her gaze toward the window, her brow troubled as she looked to a place he would never see. "I don't think the trouble's past," she said quietly and tilted her gaze to him. "I truly wish I could look into a crystal ball and see what lies ahead, but it doesn't work that way for any of us."

"A lucky thing, that," he said quietly. "Life would be boring as hell if we foresaw the future," he added and squeezed her fingers in reassurance. "I think we'll leave that to the good Lord and just be glad that you possess a sense of things to come."

"I keep thinking, Liam, I'm reacting to what's past," she said with genuine dismay. "You've been so blasted close to the fey. If I wasn't just a wee bit paranoid worrying over you, I'd consider myself daft."

"But that's not what yer fretting over, is it?"

"Something's still . . . damn it, Liam," she sobered more and focused directly. "I still feel like there's something just beyond our ken, and . . . and it's not natural."

"A ghost then?"

She appeared hurt, suddenly, as if he were teasing her.

"From the past, Natalie, or the future," he added and watched the transformation of emerald to amber and back again with the wonder high in her eyes.

"I . . . possibly, both," she answered softly.

"We'll get to the bottom of it either way," he decided and lifted her hand to kiss her fingertips. "What say you bring that phone over here, love, then give me about ten minutes? Maybe you could ask that flighty woman to bring us breakfast and convince her not to throw it at us."

The amusement washed over her eyes in an instant. "You make them nervous."

"I didn't do a thing," he repeated honestly, bewildered as she rose to his bid. "Seriously," he added. "I don't even think I've cursed at that one."

As she collected the phone from the stand near the bed, she vibrated a laugh and met his gaze as she turned, losing control in a huff. "Love, they don't know whether to run to or away from you."

"Aye, now yer having me on," he groused.

Setting the phone on the stand, she shook her head and flashed the humor in her gaze. "I think I'll shave you bald in your sleep."

"What—the hell you say," he snapped, seriously spooked by that musing shine. "Why the bloody hell would you think sooch a thing?"

She nearly giggled. "That might thwart some of your admirers. But doubtfully all of them," she added and sighed. "Guess you get to keep that unruly mop."

"Well." Unconsciously, he swiped the hair off his brow, still wary of her high shine. "That's something. Unruly mop . . .? S'pose that's true."

"You, sir, are sooch a brat," she mocked the brogue and dipped, stealing a kiss to soften the blow. "Ten minutes. Do you want the door shut?"

He nodded, "Thanks, love."

No fool, this wife of his. He watched her flow from the room even as he lifted the phone to the arm of the chair. Something had happened between them. Something he was still hard-pressed to fathom. More than once over the past several days, he'd caught himself thinking he was imagining her love—and his own.

Shaking his head, he turned his attention to dialing the first number.

After the second ring, a familiar husky voice barked, "Aye."

"Aye, yerself, Gillis."

"This better be the resurrected," the deep voice growled.

"Well, hell. Suppose I asked for that," Liam mused.

A husky laugh erupted, then, "How the 'ell are ye, lad? Good ta hear yer fine self!"

"Good to be heard," Liam idled, and the fellow reined his exuberance by half. Aside from rising to the head of security, Gillis had been a part of the family for as long as Liam could recall, one of the many who'd passed through this hospital room more than once over the past month. If Liam had heard correctly, Gillis had personally inspected the security for the Shack and, as usual, handled the complex security details.

"What can I do for ye, lad?"

"I need a bit of research done on a fellow, Gill," Liam began simply. "You might recall the family name Chandler. The elder, Milton, worked for us years ago. Our stable manager, about ten years back and several prior."

"Aye, name rings a bell," he growled. "I was still working on the estate then."

"Wondered if you might locate him and likewise his son James. The lad should be about twenty-four or twenty-five."

"Does this have a thing to do with yer current fix, Liam?"

"That's what I'd like to know, Gill, and I'd appreciate it if you'd keep this to yourself for the time being. Call me directly with whatever you find."

"Ye're knowing yer Da has me doing some research too, lad, and if there's a connection, I'd need to share sooch with him as well."

"Speak to me first," Liam said quietly and understood the silence on the line as Gillis judged Liam's firm command.

"Aye, I didnae mean to suggest otherwise, lad. Is there a thing else I can do for you?"

His gaze lifting to the envelope weighting his lap, he considered momentarily, and decided, "Aye. These are our men hanging about this facility?"

"They are, the most of them, aye."

"Any I should know?"

"Be yer own cousin, Artair, I put on the detail with yer fine wife."

"I need a man who can be spared to deliver a package to you, Gill. Possible?"

"Lad, I can probably do ye one better. I'm on the detail to see yerself and company to the airport later this afternoon."

"Lord," Liam muttered. "Do tell—you're at this manse, the Shack, then?"

Gillis MacDade rumbled a laugh, which probably turned his cheeks rosy. "Aye, yer Da decided it was easier tay rent the house than a hotel."

"How the bloody hell many people does that Shack accommodate?"

"Don't rightly know, lad. Been folks coming and going. Guessing thirty at any given time, not counting yer immediate family. Security's been a bit of a nightmare."

"All right then," Liam said distractedly. Coming and going. Even with a security detail around the clock, keeping an area of that size safe could be impossible . . . and a dozen miscreants hovering in an alley? "Gill, shut it down."

"What was that, lad?"

"Shut it down," he said more firmly. "That Shack. I want my sons and my daughter on the next flight home. I'll speak to my father after we finish, but I want you to contact Mason and get my bairn home. Then clear everyone out of there."

"Lad, what's rattling ye, here?" Gillis rumbled in alarm.

"Simple fact, Gillis. Whoever set me up now knows I'm alive and on the mend. Whatever the intentions here, I don't want anyone caught in the crossfire."

"Lad, we have security—"

Liam jammed a finger to disconnect the call, counted to five, and lifted his finger. At the dial tone, he punched the buttons to reach his father's cell phone. Lucius was never keen on using a mobile device, but he'd begun carrying one as soon as it was of a size to fit in a pocket.

Five rings later, the low voice growled, "Aye?"

"What the hell were you thinking opening a Goddamn hotel and leaving my bairn vulnerable?"

"You better slow down, lad," the deep voice commanded. "What makes you think I'd open a Goddamn hotel, and how do you believe I've left your bairn vulnerable?"

"That Shack. People coming and going. I don't give a damn if they're clansmen or blasted strangers off the street," he snapped, barely controlling the anger vibrating through him. *The photographs, damn it. And Natalie's premonition. The threat hadn't ceased—*

"Liam," Lucius started, then tempered his demand. "What set you off, here? What's happened to rile you?"

Photographs!

"I want my bairn sent home," he managed while pulling the edge from his voice, forcing calm through his system. "I want them home and safe from harm's way."

"I don't like the way you sound, and I don't think this is delirium talking, here. Have you received a threat?"

"We can discuss that when you get here," he decided, drawing a calming breath, not even entirely certain what had set him off. The panic lingered inside of him. "Send them home, Da-ad. And . . . I need to speak to that detective—Lonnigan. The sensible one of that pair."

"Slow the hell down, Liam, and make some Goddamn sense," Lucius growled. "Who threatened you, and are you all right?"

"I'm fine, Goddamn it. Just . . . damn it. I'm fucking overreacting. I know it. And you probably know it. It just fucking hit me, my bairn could be threatened, could be harmed, and their traipsing around a Goddamn hotel—"

The knock interrupted, and Liam halted his rant before the door cracked open. Not quickly enough could he retract the rage in his eyes, not that it would do any good. By Natalie's spooked shine, she sensed his panic. She entered and shut the door on the cart in her wake. Through the door, the muffled rattle of flatware and ceramic drew Liam's attention. In a heartbeat instant, he identified his breakfast suffering his wrath, yet again.

"Liam?"

His name echoed in stereo. The husky voice in his ear, the gentle voice from his wife as she rounded the bed toward him.

Calm. Still. Be still . . . those words would forever act as a balm in a fit of rage. "Damn," he uttered and recognized his panic reflected in her amber eyes. "Damn," he said again as the apology lifted in his voice. "I . . ."

27

Heartbeat hammering, Natalie studied the sorrow etched on her husband's face. His panic had flowed, a living, breathing entity sailing through the hallway to reach her in the patient lounge. On the surface, now, he appeared calm, but his eyes told a different tale. Spooked. Something had spooked him terribly, and the shorthairs lifting at the nape of her neck didn't bode well for their immediate future.

Holding the telephone receiver to his ear, he managed, "I'm sorry." But his words were directed toward her, too. "I'm—I am overreacting. I uhm . . . I need to know they're safe . . . ." His focus listed as he listened to the voice on the line. "Aye—I know that, but . . . I want them home. Send them to your house, though—you have more security than we do . . . I'm not fucking being unreasonable."

Natalie lifted the base of the phone and settled on the arm of the chair, aware of the vibration of his growing rage. In a single motion, she grasped his hand over the receiver and locked his gaze as she drew the instrument from his ear. "Settle," she said calmly. She needed both hands to pry the device from his fierce grip. His eyes glowed nearly midnight hue despite his attempt to temper the flame. Lifting the receiver to her ear, she heard the deep voice—

"—The bairn are as safe as if they're resting in your own sturdy arms!"

And here was more raging. "Sir?" Natalie interrupted and heard the drawn breath, feeling the vibration as if she stood between two electrical towers. "I uhm . . . I don't know, exactly, what's happening here, but I think we all need a moment."

In her ear, Lucius growled, "What the bloody hell happened there? I haven't heard him that panicked since we refused to roust you from a sound sleep. What's been done?"

"That I know of, nothing, Da," she said honestly, but recalling their conversation, she wondered if she might be the cause of his raging. "I think it's just hit both of us that our little ones should be sleeping in their own beds and returning to some semblance of normalcy."

"Normalcy?" Lucius growled in an elevated tone, probably reflective of his raised eyebrow.

"Aye—yes," she caught herself adopting the brogue and suffered a faint smile at her husband's accuracy. The longer they spent with Meg and Lucius, the stronger their Scottish brogue would become. Already, their sons sounded as if they were born in the old country, and Arabella had begun using 'Mum.' Collecting her thoughts, looking into Liam's silent rage, she spoke calmly. "They've already missed nearly the first semester at St Andrew's. Not that they care, mind, and I'm sure Mother Margaret doesn't mind, but it might help them both to realize their dad is truly getting well."

"Humph," Lucius harrumphed, leaving little doubt that he was not so certain—either of her reasoning or his son's repair. "When put that way, it makes sense," he growled. "But I dinnae think that's what our lad was railing aboot, I'd damn certain never risk those babes."

"I know that, as does he," Natalie interrupted quietly. "I think he's going stir-crazy," she said lightly, recalling a conversation she and Meg had shared the previous evening at the Shack. Liam, in his twenty-eight years, had never spent so much time in a single room, let alone a bed. "I think we'd all be glad to get home and regain some normalcy."

"About that," Lucius said in a lower tone, sounding apologetic. "I just spoke with Dr. Cavenaugh a bit ago. Seems that bloodwork didnae come back just right. He wants to keep him there another day or two."

"Damn," she uttered, then wished she'd kept her mouth shut. Liam was far too quick not to grasp that changed tone. His head tipped; his eyes flickered wariness.

"I'm sorry, daughter," Lucius said. "I planned to tell him when I got there and will. Doubt he'll be too happy with that news."

"No, I'm sure not," she said with the evidence staring her in the face. He was already angry. That news might tilt his precarious balance.

"Was a thought I had though," Lucius continued in a lower tone. "What say you, we bring our lad here to the Shack? My thought, he needs some fresh air and a different view. We have that parlor room with those fine French doors. We're within throwing distance of that blasted hospital if he needs a thing. His mum thinks it's a fine idea."

Quivering a smile, Natalie wondered when these plans were put into play—ten minutes or ten seconds past? "A fine idea," she agreed. No matter the material comforts the hospital had attempted to provide, Liam MacDade was no more equipped to handle sleeping on a vinyl-covered mattress than he was conducive to eating Jello with every meal. With the cant of his head and the curiosity overriding his rage, he was calming. "I'll speak with him."

"Good then," Lucius decided. "I'll make the arrangements . . . and you can tell the unruly devil, I'll keep your bairn here at least until they see him before I send them home."

"Will do, Da," she said and lowered the receiver to its cradle. Under the deep blue gaze, she considered postponing the news and realized the unlikelihood.

"Well?"

"Yes, well," she said and managed one of her more sober, matronly gazes, as close to scolding him as she could manage without notching his rage higher.

"You should have let me finish talking to him," he said irritably.

"You, sir, need to calm down."

"I'm calm," he stated.

"Lucky those nurses aren't in here at the moment," she stated and watched him blink his surprise. "You'd have those poor women fleeing to the high heavens, what with your blasted raging."

"The hell you say—"

"Aye, well, look at you," she said, raising her ire to combat. "Growling and snarling like a blasted grizzly. What if our boys stepped into this room and saw you in such a state? They'd think your fine self a step from mad."

"Aye. I'm mad," he said darkly, his blue eyes flaming.

"You're stir-crazy," she snapped.

"That may fucking be—but it has nothing to do with my Goddamn raging."

"Huh! So, you admit, you're raging."

"What the bloody hell are you so mad about?"

"We're not going home today," she snapped, holding his halted gaze. "Your father's arranging to have you moved to the Shack. He's keeping our children there until you arrive, then he's putting them on a plane for home, as you apparently ordered."

His blue eyes darkened another shade, and the curve of his mustache appeared more snarl than smirk. "We are going ho—"

"Not," she stated.

"The hell if we're not. I'm not staying in this goddamn hospital—or in some fucking Shack. We're going—"

"You'll like it there," she stated. "There's a fine view of the Delaware, and we'll be sleeping in the parlor. If the weather warms a bit, we can open the French doors, and you can meander onto the veranda . . . or to the dock to do some fishing."

"Sounds just wonderful," he said darkly. "Remind me, and we'll vacation there some other fucking summer day—"

"Liam," she said with a sigh of exasperation. "We're staying."

"The hell we are."

"Fine then," she conceded. "You're staying in this fucking room then."

He stared at her, either at her curse or her words. "Lass, that's—"

"The end of it," she stated and rose off the chair, lifting the telephone receiver.

"That's not the blasted end of it—who the hell are you calling?"

"Your father," she snapped and avoided his hand, stepping from his reach. "He needs to know you're not going anywhere so he can cancel those travel plans."

Liam slammed his heels into the recliner base and rose—and the recliner bottom jumped out and caught his ankles. Growling like a raging bear, he spun with stunning grace for a man of his size. In one smooth motion, he clasped the bottom of the recliner in one hand and flipped the entire chair to slam it upside down in the same space. The end table rocked; the lamp tumbled and rolled over the next chair, striking the tile floor and exploding the decorative glass bulb. Apparently, not satisfied, he slammed his stocking foot into the internal mechanisms of wood and hinges, shattering the frame with resounding snaps and crackles.

Barely three steps away, Natalie watched, fascinated as he flashed his feral gaze in search of something else he might break and settled on the veneer end table. Well, and it was not of a quality to withstand a tornado. Vaguely aware of a voice in her ear, Natalie watched Liam lift the stout stand in one hand and slam it to the floor. All four spindly legs disintegrated into kindling.

"What the hell is going on there, lass! Gillis—get yer men to that room!"

"Uhhh," Natalie uttered, merely watching as Liam kicked the crumbling stand against the wall. He was good with his feet. As graceful as any master of the Arts. Or a dancer, perhaps. The wood split under the direct hit, and as Liam spun his blind gaze toward her, she commented, "Think you killed it, m' lad." Nodding slightly, struggling to keep the smile off her lips, she watched him blink. "I'm sure that other chair could use an overhaul."

In her ear, Lucius demanded, "Natalie, lass! What's going on there?"

"Rearranging the furniture," she said quietly as her husband blinked again, only now appearing to regain partial sight. "Let me call you back, Da," she decided calmly, lowering the receiver to the base. In mere seconds, the midnight hue melted toward cobalt, and he blinked yet again, his focus returning. "Feel better, my love?"

He barely parted his lips to attempt speech when the door burst open, and his reaction was instant. As the two suited men entered, one after the other, Liam spun. Poetry in motion, he pivoted and sent his foot flying to be caught by the first, but Liam merely used the fellow as a springboard and continued to pivot in midair, slamming his other foot across the security guard's jaw.

"Liam!" Natalie demanded as he landed on his feet. He might have followed through and slammed a fist into the second man if the first hadn't spun under the kick and rammed the second. Both security men staggered as one, and behind them, a female cry pierced the silence.

"Liam!" Natalie demanded and launched forward as his hand dropped to his side, and he gasped a breath.

Hurt. He was hurt!

Halting his sway, catching him at the waist, she lanced the collecting guards and commanded, "Help me! The bed!"

The second man, Conrad, recovered quickly and leaped to her aid, catching Liam's other side, taking far more of his weight as he buckled with a hissed curse. "Easy, sir. I have you!"

In staggered steps, they reached the bed, and Liam cursed soft breaths as he accepted their assistance to land on the mattress. He was hurt. In slow motion, he folded sideways and wrapped his arms around his waist, drawing a knee to add protection.

"Oh God," Natalie huffed as she clasped his shoulder and felt the tremors. Tears flashing in her eyes, she found Conrad. "Get Dr. Cavenaugh."

From the buried face, the deep voice growled, gasped, "No."

"Yes, ma'am,"

"You're hurt!" Natalie stated with as much fear as anger in her mind.

"Mi-minute—just need a—minute," he heaved.

"You just couldn't stick to the furniture!" she heaved, her voice vibrating, close to sobbing. "You just h-had to—" *To what?* What had he thought was coming through that door?

"Pro-tect y-you," he heaved, rocking as if he might land fully on his head. "Fuck."

Lying over him, Natalie twined her fingers in his already damp hair and held his head still, his body still against the vibration and shudders. He was hurt. No other thought remained clear as her tears spilled. "Shhh, baby," she whispered. "Shhh, m' love."

Terrified or not, at least two nurses flew into the room and attempted to take charge, trying to unfold him. He was having none of it, and neither security guard deemed to help at the risk of hurting him.

"He's going to hurt himself!" one of the nurses heaved in exasperation.

"Lass," Conrad said grimly. "That ship sailed."

"Dang you! Help us! We have to lie him flat."

"You need to wait for that doctor, lass. His wife has him fine," Conrad said reasonably.

"Ellen!" the same nurse stated. "Page Dr. Turner!"

"No!" Natalie stated and lifted her drowning eyes, blinking the hot tears away. "Dr. Emmerson or Dr. Cavenaugh! And get him something for the pain!"

Beneath her, Liam growled, "Nooo—just give me—a minute—"

"Liam, please—you're hurt," Natalie huffed.

"No—pain med-cine," he heaved and struggled to draw clear breath, then in a firming voice, managed, "Conrad—clear this room."

Three simple words, and he might have dropped a hammer. If only to soften the blow, Liam skimmed a hand free of the fold and found Natalie's hand at his head, dragging it down to brush a furry kiss on her knuckles. "G-go, love . . ."

The Crown Prince of the MacDade clan had spoken, and neither of the security detail would reject his command. Gently but firmly, Conrad clasped Natalie's elbow, and his dark eyes wore as much apology as determination. Too well, Natalie understood his predicament. As long as Liam remained reasonably coherent—which the command evidenced—neither of these fellows would deny him. Even Ethan, with a trickle of blood at his lip, accepted the order; catching Tanya's elbow, he eased her from the side of the bed.

"Stop! What the heck are you doing! He's my patient! He needs—"

"You need to step outside the door, miss," Ethan said grimly.

"Liam!" Natalie snapped.

"g-Go, love," he managed almost firmly.

With a glance at the woman trying to yank free as Ethan nudged her toward the door, Natalie realized the futility. If not before this moment, Liam had just claimed dominion. If she wasn't so blasted worried—and irritated—she might be relieved and impressed. Three little words, and the security men, who'd become almost invisible over the past month, had come to attention, more than a little prepared to jump to his command. Still sputtering, Tanya attempted to catch the doorframe, and unconsciously, Natalie caught her hand, startling and stilling her. "We'll give them a moment."

"Mrs. MacDade!" she huffed as she collected on her feet outside the door, prepared to launch inside—until the door closed. Eyes wide with confusion and panic, she nearly sputtered, "He needs to be checked! He's not healed! He needs—"

"A moment," Natalie said as she brushed at her eyes and cheeks, shivering.

"Ma'am, please! Tell them—"

"As long as he's able to command those men," she said and focused on the stricken woman as she finished, "We can't tell them a blasted thing."

"But he's not thinking clearly! He's hurt—"

"Aye—yes," Natalie said quietly. "But he's not delirious."

"He's going to be," the nurse said and appeared to question Natalie's sanity. "Ma'am, we can't just stand here."

Irritated suddenly, Natalie snapped, "Then go find a blasted cup of coffee. Until my fine husband orders that door open or his father arrives, we're not breaching that door."

"You can't be serious!" she decided. "I'm getting Dr. Turner!"

"I wouldn't advise it," Natalie stated.

"Someone has to do something," she stated and started to turn. "Our hospital security—"

"Who the bloody hell do you think you have in that room, miss?" Natalie asked shortly and froze the woman in a half-turn. "The man is second in command to a billion-dollar empire. Do you really think he'll give a damn about your hospital security?" She let the words begin to sink in. "He damn well knows he's hurt, but he's neither delirious nor unconscious. If he needed or wanted our help, he'd ask for it." And in her own words, she found solace. "When Dr Cavenaugh arrives, he'll gain entry. Whatever that fellow advises will determine Liam's course of action."

"But—"

"There are no 'buts,' Tanya," Natalie assured her. "If you truly believe you need to enter that room, I suggest you call the National Guard. Anything less would be futile."

Lips parted, the woman darted her glance between Natalie and the closed door, then toward the motion erupting down the hall. Unfortunately, three more gentlemen from the private security force stepped out of the elevator ahead of Dr. Emerson and his assistant, both of whom attempted to pass the security men. Voice rising in irritation, Emerson demanded, "Excuse me, gentlemen!"

As one, a human blockade, the three men occupied the space ahead of Emmerson, appearing deaf and dumb. Not entirely surprised, perhaps, just a trifle amused, Natalie recognized at least one of the fellows who managed a wink to her as they advanced. She knew, before the three reached the door, what they intended. Only Artair entered; the other two turned and put their backs to the faux wood door.

"Dr. Emerson, thank God you're here," Tanya started. "I think Mr. MacDade could be hurt. I think he might have torn his incision, but he ordered us out, and now those men won't let us in."

"Mrs. MacDade?" Dr. Emerson started while attempting to reach past the shorter of the guards. "Gentleman—step aside."

"Sorry, sir," the taller, leaner man spoke in a faintly apologetic tone.

"If I have to call security—"

"Doctor," Natalie said with a sigh. "I would prefer we not have a donnybrook in this hall, so I'll ask you to wait."

"Wait . . .? What am I waiting for?"

"Dr. Cavenaugh would be my guess," she said calmly, waking to the sense of the flames ebbing from her lower abdomen. Still shivering, though. He was always so blasted cold, and according to Craig Cavenaugh that might linger for a while. Between the blood loss and the blood thinners to prohibit clots, his blood was likely the consistency of water.

"Ma'am," Emerson began carefully. "As much as I know you're all comfortable with your private physician, we can't afford to wait. If he's torn that incision, he needs—"

"Dr. Emerson, I understand your concern—believe me—but those two gentlemen and the others in that room are paid well to take orders. They are worth every penny, as they are very good at what they do," she said and glanced between the pair. Both glimpsed her with a twitch of a smile to express their appreciation. Sighing, she collided with Emerson's irritated gaze. "If my unruly husband faints, we'll gain access. Short of that, however, we're not entering that room until his orders change."

"I don't think you understand the seriousness, here, Mrs. MacDade, but you certainly should. You know what he's been through—"

"I certainly do, doctor, and when he sees fit to grant us entry, I intend to have a few words with him about that. In the meantime, doctor, you can get comfortable or go about your business. Either way, don't condescend to me."

He stared at her as if she'd grown two heads and might have protested, but the elevator dinged, yet again, intruding.

To Natalie's relief, she recognized Dr. Craig Cavenaugh walking off the elevator as if he hadn't paused for the ride. In his normal style, wearing blue jeans and a checkered shirt beneath a white lab coat, he looked like a lumberjack playing doctor; his casual, long stride and capable build only added to that persona. He was not tremendously old. Probably, no more than his late thirties. But as Natalie knew, he was the second Cavenaugh to wear the title of personal physician. From supervising the health and welfare of the immediate and somewhat extended MacDade family to overseeing the health issues of over two hundred employees, he was invaluable to the clan. Still, he neither wore his importance on his sleeve nor his face. Lean and capable, the fellow generally wore a smile, and confidence seemed to drip from his pores without a need for arrogance.

"Natalie," he said smoothly upon approach, his focus darting to judge the gathering and reaching the appropriate conclusion. "Dr. Emerson," he acknowledged as a professional courtesy. All too clearly, the physicians had butted heads.

Before Emerson could puff, Natalie said, "Glad you're here, doctor."

He lifted a single brow. Perhaps, the only visible sign of some distant relationship to the clan. "I was on my way—what happened?"

"I'm sure you'll see in a moment," she said lightly. "But I think we should have moved him a few days ago."

"Dr. Cavenaugh," Emerson started but stopped, possibly stunned.

At a mere nod from Cavenaugh, the taller guard, Morgan sidled and rapped his knuckles on the wood door before reaching for the doorknob.

"Doctor," Morgan acknowledged and opened the door enough for Cavenaugh to pass through.

As a courtesy, Cavenaugh told Emerson, "Give me a moment." And into the room, he went with the door brought shut in his wake.

The human door closed before Emerson could part his lips, and Natalie truly felt sorry for Emerson. That she owed the fellow her husband's life softened her irritation over his arrogance.

"Dr. Emerson," she said quietly. "We'll just give him a moment. If Liam's torn something, I'm sure we'll know soon enough."

"You do realize, if he has torn that incision, he'll likely need surgery again," Emerson said with a careful rein on his arrogance. "That wound hasn't healed nearly well enough after that infection. We'll need to run some tests before we can prep for surgery."

"Let's keep a good thought," she managed and held herself together—literally—with her arms laced at her waist, wanting to pass through that door even more so than the physician. If Liam had, as she suspected, hurt himself with his shenanigans . . .? Blind rage. He'd been no more in control of that fit of rage than a grizzly could be held accountable for raging in a cage. She should have insisted on moving him after his waking. Letting him prowl this private ward, hadn't been near enough to relieve his building stress.

Seconds turned to minutes. By the time the door opened, Natalie stood on the brink of hysteria and nearly launched through the opening at Artair's invitation. Ahead of the others, Natalie drew breath as she found Liam resting naturally against the raised headboard. A ruse, that casual pose. Clearly, she sensed the pain lingering beneath his dark blue gaze, but his arm rested at his waist atop the sheet, his hand appearing loosely held over the incision site. One raised knee leaned at the bedrail beneath the sheet—in a position to be drawn against that wound. Faint, the smile kinked his mustache, more apologetic than amused. The man was no fool. Wild and unpredictable, but no fool. He knew the price of his madness. Without a word, she reached him, slid her hand under the palm at his side, and clasped his hand as she leaned and kissed his furry lips.

His grip firmed, carefully, and his clear blue eyes held as she lifted. "Think I—owe you a few more apologies," he said in soft strain.

"How bad are you hurt?"

He started to shrug and winced slightly. "Craig says I'll likely live."

Cavenaugh added, "Despite yourself." Without pause, he continued toward Natalie. "We're scheduling a few tests, to be sure, Natalie. Starting with some bloodwork." To Liam he stated, "And you are going to accept a mild pain reliever."

"I told you, I'll handle it—"

"And I told you, if you don't behave, I'll have your father order these gents to hold you down while I shove a needle in your ass," he said firmly, his dark eyes as serious as his profession dictated. "I am not about to let you ruin all of Dr. Emerson's fine handiwork. Do you ken?"

"Aye," he said in lower volume, his gaze firming with his descending tone. He was not accustomed to being threatened or ordered, not when he was reasonably sound.

Unconsciously, Natalie squeezed his hand, drawing the heat of his gaze. Thrilling, that heated shine, as thrilling as all else about him. His arrogance was genuine, his confidence unparalleled, his mind, sound, and body nearly so. Quivering a smile, knowing her effect, she spoke softly, "The fact that he's willing to threaten you, darling, should tell you everything you need to know. I don't think he'd risk life and limb to relieve his own ill, do you?"

"You—just have to make sense, don't you, Nate?"

"One of us needs to be the voice of reason, and you're not it at the moment."

"Aye, and thanks so much, for pointing that out," he nearly growled, but his eyes flickering toward the stack of broken furniture—which resembled a mound of kindling in the prelude to a bonfire—countered his irritation. The distress fleeted yet again. He wasn't accustomed to losing control, and that, atop all else, disturbed him. "Aye, clearly the voice of reason," he said with a feigned smirk. "So, and if you're thinking I need a bloody painkiller, I'll see it done."

"Then see it done, my love," she said gently if only to counter the blow.

"Aye, and if I ripped some bloody hole in myself, then you'll want me to agree to surgery, too. Is that so?"

"Let's we cross that bridge if we come to it, Liam" she decided. "For now, I'd just like to see that strain lifted from your eyes."

"If he sends me under, here, and I wake after a bloody surgery, I won't be too pleased, my dear."

Cavenaugh interrupted carefully. "I'm not ordering a sedative, Liam. It won't knock you out unless you exhausted yourself and you need to sleep. But it will be a natural sleep. If—and I mean *if* you need surgery, we'll discuss it."

For a second, he seemed to doubt, then cursed, "Bloody hell. Give me the blasted shot, then, but it's not going in my ass."

As if he knew he was on borrowed time, Cavenaugh ordered the nurse—one of three now hovering inside the room—and likewise Emerson into motion. The sedative, bloodwork, the return of the heart and blood pressure monitor—to which Liam growled—and more tests which would become an ordeal with the security detail to accompany him from the room. As good as his word, Cavenaugh refrained from ordering a sedative, but the Demerol was enough to soften the strain and allow Liam a calmer breath.

At one point within the harried activity, Liam growled, "I should blame my fine father for this . . . him and his blasted raging. Passed that into the lot of us."

"Dinnae blame me, lad," Lucius said as he came into the mix, stop-startling a half dozen people who had somehow missed the arrival of a 6'6" fellow towering over them. "Yer maither has the temper."

Stifling a laugh at the words and Liam's mocked surprise, Natalie grasped the simple fact, that Liam hadn't missed his father's arrival and had meant to be overheard. If Liam made the staff nervous, Lucius still terrified them, and the poor nurse drawing blood fumbled the tube she'd just filled. Luckily, she grabbed it in mid-flight.

"Easy, miss," Liam coached. "I dinnae have a lot of that to spare."

"Sorry, sir!" she said breathlessly. "Just one more."

Liam flashed Natalie a bemused glance, a smirk, and shook his head. "And we still didnae have breakfast—er more than a few sips of coffee."

"Your fault," she mused. "But if you behave for a little while, we might try again.'

"Aye, maybe before lunch. I'm hungry." And just that fast, his slightly hazy eyes darkened, and he was no longer thinking of food.

Shaking her head, she refused to be baited. "Maybe lunch, then. How about a chicken salad?"

"A wrap . . . Maybe chicken," he decided, still not talking about food.

"I'll give you a chicken wrap, you big dope," she said and barely moved a hand to clasp his hand on the rail.

Therein lay the problem with pain relievers. Without the constant reminder of pain, he reacted. He might have meant to catch her hand to tug her into a kiss and moved far too quickly. The wince flashed through his eyes, his hand dropped to his side, and his focus followed as if more curious than alarmed by the pain. "Damn."

Damn, indeed. It was the first serious indicator that a problem existed beneath that capable palm, and Natalie knew, heart aching, that it was not to be the last.

He knew it, too. His gaze found her with an apologetic shine. "I have a feeling lunch will have to wait, my love."

She nodded. "So, it will."

28

Before his connecting flight departed, which only accounted for his stopped pose by half, Luke needed to make a phone call. If he hadn't been so blasted irritated, he might have placed this call before departing New Jersey . . . Well, and not *irritated*, exactly.

Honesty. If only with himself, he could admit the distress that chased him to the airport and followed him to Chicago. What bothered him more, his brother's grip latching onto him, the instant tug, or his ability to yank away, he still couldn't decide.

Again, he caught himself flexing his fingers, forming a fist.

"Damn it," Luke muttered aloud, grateful for the roar of human traffic noise to cover his insanity. Doubtful, most normal people suffered hours of distress, feeling phantom sensations over a blasted handshake. Not even a full handshake. He'd barely clasped that immense capable hand when he'd recoiled against the tug, and Liam—if he were truly as awake and aware as he appeared—probably considered his youngest brother a flipping idiot—minus the 'savant.'

"Damn it," he uttered again, trying to shake the feeling of inadequacy to steal over him. Sooner or later, he'd need to accept Tyler Shefield's advice and speak to someone about that abduction. Practically speaking, he knew he was suffering the latent effects of vulnerability, and reacting to a blasted handshake ranked right up there with the penultimate ill-effect of trauma.

For the millionth time, Luke replayed that scene, from his surprise to find Liam sitting up and appearing as sturdy as ever in his designer leisurewear to the sound of his brother's deep, resonant voice issuing off the mustached lips. That Luke might have preferred listening to that smooth baritone for a dozen hours, if not a few more moments, had occurred to him as he'd fled from that hospital in the wee hours.

He was stalling—still—he grasped and glanced at the telephone hovering below his line of sight. With plexiglass partitions between the half dozen payphones, he would need to strain to hear the gentleman standing in the next stall, even without the human raucous amplified within the corridor. If he stepped into the nearby restroom, he might reasonably engage his cell phone and hear the recipient of this call. But even as he considered that thought, he countered the practicality. No way would he make this call from his personal phone without blocking the caller ID. And if he blocked the call, the recipient would fail to answer. He'd tried that once in the heat of a fine rage—placed the call and masked his number, only to hear a blasted generic answering service voice commanding him to leave a message after the beep. Like him, his father would no more answer a blocked call than he'd record his own voice to leave a message.

A payphone with a Chicago area code was a reasonable solution.

Sighing, Luke brought coins from his jacket pocket and began filling the slot. He probably should have phoned last evening . . . or even this morning before departing. If not for that sense of being followed and his blasted preoccupation with that handshake, he might have made the call. He would let it ring five times—

On the third ring, the deep voice erupted, cutting through the background roar with no trouble at all. "Who the bloody hell is this now?"

Uh oh. That deep raging tone, the absence of a brogue, the short demand—? Luke slapped the receiver into its cradle and held the instrument in a death grip as if he feared a hand would reach through the line and propel the earpiece to his head. Maybe that phone call could wait a while longer. Maybe until he landed in San Antone . . . or maybe . . .? Luke drew a breath and collected the returned coins from the slot, depositing them in rapid fire. From memory, he dialed the second private number . . . and listened through five rings, which could mean Uncle Gillis was on another line or screening his calls. Muttering a curse, Luke hung up and tried the third number. Somebody would surely answer his blasted phone, and with the decision made, Luke listened and waited through seven rings before slapping the receiver down.

For a half second, he considered abandoning his quest, but the thought of Liam sitting so blissfully unaware of the continuing threat changed his mind. If nothing else, his father could direct the investigation or decide how to proceed. Sighing, steeling his nerve, Luke dialed the first number, again, prepared for the whiplash effect of his father's rage.

On the second ring, the deep voice answered far more tempered and controlled. "Aye? Hello."

"I uh . . . it's me. Luke," he managed in a reasonably sound voice.

"Wondered, aye," the deep voice sounded more guarded, restrained. "Ye've left the area then, aye?"

"I have," Luke admitted and controlled his natural instinct to panic with the barely guarded voice in his ear. "There's something . . . Well, I've come across information that might help the investigation."

"Go on, then, lad," Lucius urged carefully as if speaking to a man on a ledge.

Was his father gifted with Gran's second sight? Luke barely drew breath before rushing out with it. "I think this attack on Liam's coming from the past, Father. The Chandlers—that stable manager from years ago, his son. The older man's dead, but the younger one—he's in Trenton, and he's been there for several months. He uses the name Johnny, now. He was James—Jimmy, then. I don't know how the puzzle pieces fit—but he's involved and connected to Alecia Helms. That's all I've been able to find out, and uhm . . . maybe Uncle Gillis can dig deeper."

"How the bloody—how the hell did ye come by this, lad?"

"I uh . . . I had time," Luke admitted as if that should explain everything in minute detail. "I don't know if Uncle George is involved, but there's some connection to the racetrack and uhm . . . that elder Pendleton. The younger one's all right."

"Is he, now," Lucius said with careful rein.

"I think so, yes," Luke decided, relieved to be passing on the information now that he'd begun. "It wasn't random, Father. But I'm sure you already know that, or you'd have those bastards tracked down by now. I uhm . . . I wondered about Natalie's family, too, if they weren't somehow involved," he admitted. "But the timing's all wrong, and I don't see how they'd connect to Chandler. Anyway, I wanted you to know—"

"Lad, why don't you come on back here, now, and let's we sit down for a chat?" Lucius interrupted in a careful low pitch. "We have a room here at the Franklin House for you, and we'll be staying on a few days yet—"

"I'd like to, I would, sir—if I think of anything else, I'll try to call," Luke slapped the receiver in its cradle and drew breath, feeling even more the coward than he had in some time. Why was that? Why did any encounter with his family make him feel even more inadequate than usual? He couldn't claim an entire lack of emotional investment—not when the mere proximity of these MacDades seemed to send him into a tailspin. He hadn't suffered such a condition of insecurity or turmoil in more than two years.

Collecting his carry-on from the floor at his feet, he slung it over his shoulder and continued toward his departing gate. Something happened though . . . something between reaching the gate and striding away from the rental agency counter to find the economy car that he'd just rented.

Behind the wheel of a white Camry, he drove through the loops to escape O'Hare Airport traffic and set his sights south. With any luck, he should be sailing onto his paved lane, climbing his mountain before dinner.

Why had Lucius MacDade sounded like he stood on the brink of a fine rage when answering that first call? Very few things in this world would tip that great bulk of a man toward raging, and a threat against his family stood at the top of that list . . . And was it his imagination, or had the fellow identified Luke as the caller by that instant exodus from that connected phone line?

Maybe that was the widest chasm between him and his father—what Luke considered a practical retreat, his father might consider cowardice. Why subject himself to more of the MacDade ranting and raving—or arrogance? For as long as Luke could recall, he'd remained at the mercy of those blasted giants, and he was no more tolerant of their antics now than then. Why should he subject himself to their growling and the like, when he could hang up a telephone or avoid calling altogether?

What had set that giant near to raging?

Absently, Luke turned on the radio, hitting the scan mode and letting a dozen decent songs pass before he pressed the button to find an AM station. Without fully considering his actions, he continued the scan, passing big band and orchestra music, commercials . . . and slammed the stop button at the sound of a monotone voice on a news station.

Not long—not long at all before . . .

". . . in Trenton, New Jersey this afternoon where Liam MacDade, heir to the Fortune Five Hundred company, High Land, Inc. is once again undergoing surgery for complications due to the assault he suffered nearly a month ago . . . The hospital has not yet released a statement about the exact nature of this ailment, but his condition is reportedly stable. Stay tuned for further updates . . . and in World news this afternoon, Dublin is once again under assault from active members of the IRA . . .”

Luke switched the radio off, fumbled in his jacket, and brought his phone from the inside pocket. In rapid glances, he identified the appropriate number and pressed send.

“Where are you, LJ?”

“Hello to you, too,” Luke commented. “No one has telephone manners anymore. Just because I didn’t block the call, it doesn’t mean you should act like we’ve been talking for an hour.”

“I’ll try to remember that, kid,” Tyler stated. “Concern overrode my proper phone etiquette. So, hi. How are you? Where are you? What are you up to? Just call to shoot the breeze? Or would you prefer to ease my mind and mention you’re within spitting distance so we might have a face-to-face?”

“Everyone wants to see my face today for a chat,” Luke said absently. “Unfortunately, you—like the last fellow—are destined for disappointment. I’m not even in shouting distance. So, what’s up? Have you found Chandler—or Johnny? Who as it turns out, are one in the same. And what has Molly Anderson announced regarding my brother’s condition?”

“You know he’s in surgery?”

“I do, yes. Just heard,” Luke admitted. “What happened? Any clue? He seemed well this morning.”

Tyler hesitated a heartbeat before answering. “You could probably find out if you phoned your family directly. Right now, the hospital reps aren’t saying what happened, only that it’s a minor surgery. Even Molly seems to be in the dark now, though I doubt that will last. The lady’s probably bribing the surgeon as we speak.”

“She does seem to be a tenacious little fox,” Luke considered. “So, we might just wait for the update at noon.”

“Ooor, you could call your family, which I’m guessing you haven’t done.”

“You’d have guessed wrong,” Luke commented. “I spoke to my father briefly. Dropped the Chandler affair in his court. If there’s anything to be learned, I’m reasonably certain, he’ll find it.”

Barely pausing, he continued, “I wouldn’t mind, though, if you’d continue investigating. You know the area. I’d imagine if anyone can locate Alecia Helms, you’re the likely fellow and uhm . . . I’m guessing you’ll cross paths with MacDade Security in that regard. If you should meet success, you could pass her location to one of them. The head of the force is Gillis MacDade, not that you'll likely get a direct line—or you might if you mention my name. Just be prepared for some ranting in my regard, and I'd appreciate it if you refrain from mentioning that you might know where I am."

"LJ, I have to ask here," Tyler said carefully. "Regarding your family—I'm guessing you have some serious trust issues there, so is it something I should know? Some underlying reason why you prefer not to associate with them?"

"You mean like something illegal?"

"Something like that."

Luke considered the implication in an eyeblink and admitted, "Nothing illegal, Tye. High Land Inc. is a fully legitimate enterprise. And my father's as straight up as they come. I uhm . . . I just truly prefer flying solo, and my reasons are personal."

Tyler hesitated, then seemed to accept the partial explanation. "All right, then, I'll keep looking for Helms, and as for Johnny—I think he's in the wind. I found his last known address, but it wasn't much help. He was renting a room not far from the Emerald Club. There was one tidbit of interest, and it rather confirms your thought that he's in this up to his gonads."

Luke waited and needn't hold his breath.

"The night your brother was ambushed, a Mr. J. Channing rented the room right next to your brother's room in the Fairlane, and I spoke to the registration attendant from that eve—the description fits."

"Humph."

"Doesn't do us much good providing physical evidence of his involvement," Tyler continued. "But like I said, it confirms your theory even if we can't link him directly to the assault."

"Directly or indirectly, he's involved, and I keep circling back to the track," Luke considered. "The big problem, and mind you, it might be my arrogance speaking, so I'll let you decide—but I uhm . . . I just can't see Jimmy as the mastermind of this endeavor."

"Your arrogance figures into that—how?"

"He just wasn't that bright, Ty. Sneaky, I'll grant you, but I'm not even certain he attended grade school when he lived on the estate. I . . . I think if someone offered him the opportunity to settle a score, he'd jump at the chance, but I . . . I can't see him physically assisting in that assault. He was a scrawny child and not that brave as I recall."

"A lot can change in a few years, LJ. Maybe he grew a set."

Luke considered and shook his head. "No, not possible. He was coerced, and I'd wager, him and Alecia Helms both."

"So, we still don't know who's behind this, or uhm . . . behind your assault."

"One in the same, I'm afraid, Tye. Even with Jimmy in the mix, someone else was pulling his strings. Someone with enough clout to blackmail the Pendletons—father and son both, I think—and arrange for my mishap."

"Did uh . . . don't suppose you mentioned anything about your *mishap* to your father, did you, kid?"

"No, and I'm not going to. Nor are you, sir. I offered my father enough to further the investigation, and I'm sure when he connects the dots, he'll see justice done."

"I uh . . . I'm not sure I like the way that sounds, LJ, and bear to mind, I carry a badge. If you're even implying that we could have some vigilante justice—"

"Let me rephrase," Luke said in a quieter tone. "He'll see justice done."

"Damn it."

"Would it help if I mention . . .? He's responsible for bringing the FBI into this investigation at the onset."

"It might," Tyler said grimly.

"Then consider it mentioned as a fact, and Ty . . .?" Luke hesitated. "I wasn't implying that my father would take matters entirely into his own hands. As far as I know, he's never killed anyone—or uhm, had them killed. So saying, doubtful this will be the exception." At least Luke hoped that to be true. "So, Tye? Did you give any thought to my proposition?"

Tyler considered a half-second before deciding, "I've been looking for a change of scenery. Send me the details. I'll need a couple weeks to tie things up here and conclude this investigation, but yea, it sounds like fun . . ."

Long after the phone disengaged, highway miles stacking up in the rearview mirror, Luke wondered if he'd just lied to his new head of security. All too clearly, he recalled a few too many innocent tales about his father and Uncle Mason's affiliation with the IRA. Twenty or thirty years ago was not that long, and some of those lads might have long memories. Whether the modern chaps would be for or against justice in Liam's regard was the question, and in Luke's idling thoughts, he could see the wind blowing either way. His father—his clan—probably had just as many friends as enemies across the pond, and to believe those factions impotent was a fool's dream.

And Ryan McDade's presence in the States might not bode well for anyone's future.

EPILOGUE

Kicked back in the chair behind the ancient oak desk in the Franklin House study, Lucius McDade gazed through the crack in the heavy drapes He was far less interested in the fading daylight through the glass than in his internal kibitzing. Smoldering, a cigar jutted between his middle and ring finger; a thin smoke trail rose from the edge of his filled Scotch glass. If anyone stood in witness, he would likely be considered brooding, and the observation would be half true.

Not for a moment had he forgotten that brief chat with his youngest son despite his panic over his eldest. Something hadn't sat just right about that short exchange, over and above the fact that the lad hadn't phoned him directly in . . . well . . . ever. Not once in twenty years had his youngest son taken advantage of the phone lines, not land lines or cell tower conduits, to contact him directly, and by that singular detail, Lucius grasped the importance.

The Chandlers . . . Jimmy Chandler. Only vaguely, Lucius recalled that scrawny child of yesteryear, always sneaking about the estate, believing he might be invisible when naught could be further from the truth. Had the boy ever fully acted out of line, he might have learned the extent of the estate security, from camera surveillance to footmen on constant watch. Lucius had never taken his family's safety lightly . . . and at the time of the Chandlers, Gillis had already begun his stint as head of security on the estate. If anything untoward had ever happened, Gillis would have handled it . . . and was that somehow relative to what Lucas alluded to?

Doubtful.

Lucius need only recall a few hours earlier when he'd mentioned the name to Gillis to doubt any particular incident stemming from the past. Gillis had remembered the elder—and younger—Chandler, but more by way of a man recalling a face from the past . . . And yet, Gillis hadn't seemed surprised when Lucius had ordered the expanded investigation in the Chandlers' regard.

Well, and that was being handled. The other though . . . George MacDade, the Pendletons . . . the Callahans?

Sighing, Lucius swiveled the chair a half turn, set his drink aside, and brought his cell phone from his suit pocket. No more than two weeks ago, George had stopped by the hospital and spent an overnight in a room upstairs. A coincidence, or was there more to that visit than the convenient proximity to one of the tracks where George stabled several horses?

Only two rings passed before George's generally mild-mannered voice came through the line with a huffed, "Lucius? Liam—?"

Bloody hell. "He's recovering," Lucius stated swiftly, grasping the sincere panic in his younger brother's voice.

"Good God almighty, when I saw your name come up—! Well, never mind what I feart. How is he? I heard on the news, he was back in surgery! Was just three days ago I talked to Mason! What the bloody hell happened? I thought he was finally on the mend—"

"Settle, lad, draw breath," Lucius coached as the first honest smile quivered on his bearded lips. His brother's fear and concern were genuine. The lad was not involved in that ambush. Of that, Lucius was certain and more than grateful that his youngest was mistaken. "My lad's on the mend but had himself a bit of a setback this morn. Was but a wee tear in his intestines and patched up quick. Course. it added time to his recovery, but couldn't be helped."

George huffed a breath and sighed, "That's damn good to hear, and a fine thing you calling to let me know."

Lucius almost felt bad for not calling for that alone. "Fact, m' lad, was a bit of other business I had a mind to ask oover if ye have a few minutes?"

"If I didnae, I'd make them," George said smoothly, relieved but now curious. "What's on ye mind, mo bhrathair?"

"Ach, well, there's been a few names mentioned recently regarding a racetrack, and I wondered then if ye might know them," Lucius said honestly. "The first being Pendleton. Believe the lad's first name is Frances."

"Not ringing any bell, Luche," George said thoughtfully. "Is the lad a trainer or owner, do ye know?"

"I'd say neither," Lucius admitted. "But he may have some financial interest in a horse or two. More than likely, his greater interest is in the wagering."

"Ache, well then, I dinnae think I'd know him, but I can ask around if it's important," George offered. "What track does he favor, dae ye ken?"

"I'd think Monmouth or Delaware Park to be the closest, but I dinnae know for certain. Aye, could be Belmont or your Laurel there."

"Does this have a thing to do with Liam's condition?" George asked in a far lower, more intense tone.

"I cannae say for certain, George, and I'd rather keep the details between us if you learn a thing."

"You said that lad's the first. You have a second in mind?"

"Aye, well, and you'll probably recognize this one, but a thought, you might know if he's favoring a track of late," Lucius said lightly. "Be the name, Kirk Callahan, er his oldest boy, John"

"Well, now that you mention it, I did see the elder—be your daughter Natalie's ayr as I do so recall. Had a thought he might be looking to invest in a horse not so long ago."

"You talked to him?"

"Ache, no. Was a race day, and myself fairly occupied. Thought I might look him up after, but I didnae find him again."

"Where and when was this, do you recall, George?" Blast and damn. He'd just alarmed his brother by the absence of his brogue, and there was no accounting for it.

"Aye," George said in a far lower tone. "Was an easy one to remember, that. Was April 12, the last day of the winter meet at Laurel, and myself trying to get horses ready to ship to Pimlico for the summer."

"Humph," Lucius muttered. "April."

"Luche, what's this aboot, here? Are you saying what I'm thinking, lad?"

'The timing's all wrong . . .'

Or just about right if Pendleton and that land business was the start of this.

"Luche?"

"Aye, we're on the same page, bhrathair, but do me a favor and keep this to yourself for a time, and dinnae put too fine a point on asking about Pendleton. I'll no doubt have a chat with that fellow, personally, come a time."

"Luche, if you find out that either of those lads had a thing to do with my nephew's condition, you'll let me know, right?"

His brother had lost the brogue as well. A smile kinked Lucius's bearded lips. "I will, indeed, George. You may rest assured."

Signing off, Lucius considered the details, aligning what he knew with what he surmised, and the pictures were forming rather rapidly with flashing memories of the Callahans coming and going over the past four weeks. The whole family, from Kirk and his lovely stoic wife, Nadine, to the two younger girls and two younger boys, the entire clan had arrived that first Saturday evening at Southern General. Natalie's siblings had stood front and center at that candlelight vigil . . . But Kirk had come and gone, along with his wife, allegedly to check into a hotel. Neither had opted to stay with their daughter throughout that wickedly long day and night. Only the youngest lad, Tomas, had stood most often with his sister, his young face as distressed as Natalie and all others when looking at Liam on life supports in those hellish hours.

As if Lucius had taken a snapshot, he recalled Kirk Callahan standing furthest from the bedside, his cheek pulsing, eyes fixed and stunned . . . in concern, or terror . . . *or guilt?*

Ach, well, and there had been times when Lucius had ventured that thought, even spent a few ticks wondering if his lovely daughter-in-law might have taken matters into her own hands in her randy husband's regard. Aye, the lad might have needed a good throttling a time or two, as stubborn as a MacDade to ever walk, but that lass was far more apt to clout him with her own fine hands than to set these wheels in motion. That wondrous lass had the knack, without a doubt, and her reasons for being in the right place at the right time were sound.

Kirk though . . . ?

Sighing, Lucius realized his subconscious was at work as he found Kirk Callahan's name already front and center on his cell phone. Hitting the send button, he lifted the device to his ear, turning a blind eye to the faded light between the dark, paisley drapes.

"Lucius?" the husky voice erupted, a little anxious, worried. "Liam–? We heard about that surgery. He's come through all right, though, right?" The hurried pace of his words clashed with his generally deep southern drawl and further evidenced his guilt.

For a moment, Lucius considered reaching through the aether and snapping the lad's neck, and just the thought of it lent him pause to realize his suspicions were confirmed. "Aye, he's come through, Kirk, but far from all right, to be honest. The lad's lost nearly a month of his young life and not completely out of the woods yet."

Perhaps, the absence of his brogue enlightened Callahan; perhaps, the content . . . but the hesitation was telling. "I uhm . . . He's a strong one, your son, Lucius. I'm sure he's going to pull through this and be just fine—"

"Lad," Lucius interrupted in a deeper tone. "We've known each other how long? What say? About twenty years or more, aye?"

"Uhh, about that, I'd guess," Callahan spoke more warily. "Twenty-five years more like—"

"Aye, was just after you took the reins of your father's trucking business and set your sights on expansion. Aye, and I did my part, handing you the contracts to expand your routes nationwide."

"Ahh, you did yes—"

"Was near on ten years ago, we considered the benefit of an alliance between High Land Inc. and K.L. Trucking. Aye, and more of a jest, the thought of our eldest to eldest."

"You brought it up," Kirk remembered or accused with a soft edge in his southern twang. "Our Scottish lineage and some mention of a seer in your lines if I remember correctly."

"Aye, you do then, remember, the knack involved," Lucius said with a careful rein. "And you mentioning your daughter suffering that affliction, though I think you considered it a hoax—or a curse."

"I admitted she had some funny ways—"

"So, saying, Kirk, when you planned this ambush on m' lad, did you once consider that our stunning daughter might be inclined to join that fray and risk her life and limb—"

"Here, now, Lucius," Callahan spoke in a voice leaning toward outrage. "I don't know what you're implying—"

"Aye, lad, you do, and it's not an implication. Merely a fact," Lucius said in careful control. "My question is this, lad—why? What set you on this path to destroy the father of our clan?"

"I'll not even justify—"

"Lad, unless you would prefer to face a federal grand jury, you will, indeed, justify and answer me now," Lucius spoke calmly and waited. The silence dragged through the phone line for several seconds before Kirk huffed a short breath, and his control snapped.

"If you bloody well need to know, Lucius, was my daughter wailing to her mother about her loveless marriage just after our Arabella was born! Her to say—she was nothing but a cow to be bred and her holding me to account for getting her into it. He—your lad—was making a laughingstock of the lot of us—what with his carousing! I might of forced her to marry him, but I damn sure didn't sell her to you—or him—and I wasn't about to force her to continue with the farce—"

"So, your intention was to make her a widow, then?" Lucius spoke in a lower tone, his body poised for detonation.

"They were just supposed to teach him a lesson—"

"With guns and knives—"

"Lucius—"

"Lad, I would suggest you steer clear of me and mine over the next few centuries. For my daughter's sake, you are still breathing, but that could change," Lucius said in a softer, deeper pitch. "Aye, and you need to bend your knee to the Almighty and pray m' lad survives this circumstance else a legal defense will be the least of your worries."

"Lucius, I'm sorry! I couldn't stand by and do nothing! My daughter was suffering—"

"Aye, idiot," Lucius remembered those months after Arabella's birth—his daughter-in-law's suffering, his son's suffering, as well. Liam had come to him with his questions and concerns, and Lucius had suggested enlisting Craig Cavenaugh and a full-time nanny. Meg had suffered the same blasted malaise after their third born. Postpartum depression, Lucius knew, now. He'd known then only that his wife was a stranger for most of those first months after Lucas's birth . . . And there were moments when he'd feared for the infant's life. He'd needed all his great strength to weather that storm with his Megan.

Gazing into abstracts, Lucius disconnected the phone, recalling Liam facing those same fears and taking responsibility to work from his home office. 'I need to be there, Dad. She'll barely look at our lass—and it's as if our lads don't even exist.'

Muttering aloud, Lucius recalled himself consoling Liam then, 'She'll come around, lad . . . Just give her some time.'

She had been coming through the worst of it, Lucius remembered. She'd begun smiling again. Even laughing at their lads' antics and appreciating the boys doting on their baby sister. Liam had started to relax and even mentioned his intention to return to the headquarters . . .

And he'd been as befuddled as a man could be when Natalie had dumped his clothes in their guest bedroom . . . befuddled and disheartened.

'. . . I had a call the other day from my old friend, Frank . . . His father has some land for sale up in the Poconos. Might lay over a day or two in Jersey and see what's what. Sounds like some money to be made . . .'

'Thought you meant to cancel yer trip . . .'

'You said yourself, there's something brewing in the Highlands, and I'd rather it doesn't spill across the pond . . . Besides, I doubt my fine wife will even notice I'm gone . . .'

"She'd notice, lad," Lucius muttered and reached for his Scotch. Despite her father's meddling, the lass was in love with the lad, and at long last, the two seemed to grasp that singular detail. So, maybe someday, with Liam on the mend, Lucius might reconsider his need to remove Kirk Callahan from the land of the living.

Time will tell.

EXPOSED IN THE CROSSHAIRS

Turn the page for a sneak peek at the second episode of The MacDade Brothers Mysteries!

EXPOSED IN THE CROSSHAIRS:

He Who Rides

The last thing Liam MacDade recalled clearly was Dr. Craig Cavanaugh hovering above him, telling him they needed to make a minor repair. Several things had changed since then although he recognized the drab beige walls, the white—yellow—tile ceiling, and the dull curtains. Rather than dark brown, a plush beige recliner stood nearest the bed, and the lovely woman curled in its nook, drew his attention. She appeared to be dozing, and for a moment, he merely enjoyed the view, watching her long lashes flutter on flawless cheeks. Picture perfect, this wife of his. In the soft lamplight, her hair glowed nearer to gold than auburn and flowed in wondrous waves and curls over her shoulder. A ponytail, he noted and ventured a thought of tugging it to wake her.

With a thought of Natalie dozing, his focus drifted further and landed on the window between the curtains. The reflection of the lamp told the tale. Beyond the glass, the day had turned to night, and in an odd epiphany, he wondered how many days he might have lost. Time. He had lost time, again, but how much time? Struggling to remember, he collected hazy images of seeing his father, his mother, Gregor . . . all of them come and gone. Not his little ones, not Jamie or Micheal, or Arabella. Home. Someone, maybe his father, had mentioned sending the little ones home.

How long ago?

At the glimpse of motion, he rolled his head enough to spy the familiar pixie face of RN Penny Morgan with her attention currently directed to the monitor bleeping above her head. She was such a tiny thing. No taller than his ribcage—maybe only slightly taller than his incision.

Either the beeping alerted her, or she felt him watching. She turned more completely, lowering the clipboard out of sight, and smiling at him over the bars. Whispering, she commented, "Hi, honey. Welcome back."

"Errr ye trying to be funny?" he managed and saw her eyes light with delight.

"Nope. Not at all," she said softly. "It's good to see you, hon. Are you thirsty? How about a little water?" she asked, already reaching toward the movable cart beside her.

"Bourbon. On the rocks," he decided and again her eyes glowed with delight.

"Afraid we don't stock that, hon."

"We can change that," he managed, all too aware of the scratchy feel in his throat. Anesthesia. The last time he'd felt like this, he'd learned it resulted from anesthesia. He wasn't as parched as a desert. Time. Time had passed. "How long."

"How long, sir?"

"Have I been gone?"

She appeared worried suddenly and he suffered an inkling of not wanting her answer. "Not too long."

But the brown skirt was gone. Looking toward his sleeping wife, he scanned the pale green sweater and emerald slacks of a practical cotton. The beige sweater and skirt were gone, and he had a sense of seeing her wearing blue jeans and a T-shirt. Time. "How long?"

"Four days," Natale sighed and drew his focus to find her watching him now. "And if you even think about reacting badly to that news, I'm going to clobber you."

"Four—"

She rose in a single fluid motion and arrived at his bedside, leveling her hazel eyes on him with a direct and fierce shine. "Days," she finished. "The surgery went well. You only managed a small tear and Dr. Emerson was kind enough to repair it, though you haven't been the most gracious patient. You really should be nicer to that fellow when he comes around. We've put him through hell, you know."

"Slow—down, woman. I'm not even certain, I'm awake—"

"Oh, you're awake, and you know it," she said as she eyed him with a soft, musing shine. "Might not want to be, but so it goes. You're awake, and already irritated."

"Maybe that," he admitted. "I was—leaving here."

"And we will, probably later today or tomorrow," she said simply. "The only question is if we're shipping your behind to a rehab facility in Kentucky or moving you to the Shack for a week or two while you let those stitches heal."

"Other options," he stated in a rasping voice.

"None," she said flatly, her gaze steady. "Either you ride in a limo to a nice little mansion ten minutes from here, or you ride in a limo to a private airstrip ten miles from here, and from there, fly to a nice little resort facility not far from our home. I'll be happy to accompany you to either one, but either way, you are grounded, until you are truly ready to follow the blasted rules, take your blasted medicine, and let that great tower of a body heal properly. I won't tolerate another blasted temper tantrum, do you ken?"

"You sure—do—get testy, woman," he growled.

"You've not seen me testy, man, but God knows, that's coming if you don't behave."

"I've not done—a damn thing."

"Humph," she retorted. "Which one will it be?"

"Homeward bound," he said bluntly.

"You—lad—are not listening," she snapped. "The only other blasted option is to tie you to the blasted bed and keep you in a blasted coma for a month."

"Aye, well, ye'll play hell trying that one," he growled. "If I'm able to move to a fucking resort, I can damn sure get home." And he needed—his attention caught on the somewhat stunned tiny woman on the opposite side of the bed. She held a glass of water trembling in her hand and appeared as if she might douse him. "If that's far me, pixie, hand it over," he rasped and managed to lift a hand. "And put this goddamn bed up — I can't give this lass a proper dressing down when I'm lying flat."

"You're asking for it, lad," Natalie said shortly, and he found her gaze studying him with a spark of amusement.

"Aye, I need a drink," he growled. "Then we'll see what's what."

She stifled a laugh and sent her gaze to the worried woman. "You might as well do as he asks, dear, that's if he were actually asking,'" she added and caught his gaze. "All your damn fussing and fuming."

"Well."

At least the bed was rising, improving his view of his lovely wife. He barely spared a glance to accept the glass, nearly ramming the straw up his nose as he brought the glass to his lips and muttered a curse as too many revelations tumbled through his mind. He wore another mound of bandages at his waist, an IV in the back of his hand, the tube still at his biceps, a catheter in his nether regions . . . and it occurred to him. "I'm back to bloody square one."

"No, you're not," Natalie stated, drawing his attention to find her far too aware of his declining mood. "It just looks bad, love," she said more carefully. "Dr. Emerson was able to repair the damage with orthoscopic surgery. You have a tiny incision, and if you behave, we truly can leave later today."

"I look like that gadget lad again," he commented with a thought of Micheal's early assessment. His son had likened him to a blasted cartoon character.

"Those tubes and the like will be removed before we go," she said simply. "Aside from the one in your arm. You'll still need those antibiotics twice a day, probably for another two weeks." She barely paused for breath, asking, "So, have you decided?"

"Home."

Appearing truly disheartened and apologetic, she sighed, "Liam, that's not an option. We know you too well, my love. You might spend a few days resting and recovering, then you'll be at your desk or out riding a blasted horse or jumping into the helicopter and going who knows where. You'll be bouncing the boys about and nowhere near content to keep them on your knee."

"Natalie," he said quietly, reasonably, and opened his hand to draw her palm into his over the rail. "If it's truly been over a month, there are things I need do. Things needed tended. I had a half dozen contracts pending, not to mention the one to bring me here. Was close to closing the Pendleton deal and I need speak with that elderly fellow."

"Liam, there's my point," she said gently. "If we go home, you'll dive in with both feet, and you're not blasted ready."

"I can—can not lie abed for weeks or months, love."

"I'm not asking you to, mine own," she said in a voice near to pleading and the moisture glistening on the surface of her hazel eyes touched him deeply. "I don't want to lose you. Do you ken? I want you here for me, for our babes. I can't . . . I can't stand to see you hurting so, Liam. I want you well, and if you won't give yourself time to heal, you won't get well."

She truly was on the brink of tears. With his slight tug, she leaned over the rail and came under his arm. Feeling the sob break against his chest, he tipped his head to rest within the auburn silk and drew in the scent that forever took him to the Highlands. "Ah, lass," he uttered. "What I wouldn't do for you," he said and twined his fingers into the loose locks at her quivering back, holding her tighter. "The Shack it is."

"Thank you," she huffed against him, sniffing, trying to recover and it occurred to him, he'd never seen her cry, not before these last weeks. Even in fuzzy memories, he knew she'd wept for him, but never before. "It won't be so bad," she whispered, hugging him more, heaving soft breaths. "You'll see . . . it won't. We'll be okay."

Odd, he wondered in a strange epiphany, who was she attempting to convince? "Aye, we'll be okay." Just as soon as he knew what Gillis might have discovered. A month—he'd lost a month. Surely someone knew something by now. Gillis, Mason, the police, that asinine Det. Harbinder or the other one, Lenmar . . . someone knew something. And this Shack better provide the privacy he would need to catch up.

Acknowledgments

As always, thank you to Anne Graff and Mary Trunick for their tolerance of endless technical questions about everything from computer glitches to medical jargon. Thanks to David Graff for sharing his knowledge of weaponry. Thank you to Sr. Barbara Graff who offers her unconditional support and her spiritual influence—even when the storyline veers toward the dark side and keeps her up at night. Thank you again to Andrew Grueber and William Grueber, who continue to assist when modern trends, social media, and technology threaten my tolerance. (I do have patience. Honestly. If you don't wear my boot print on your butts, it's not likely I'll stomp on my phone or computer.) Thank you once again to my friend and cover collaborator, Bruce Sanderson of Sanderson-Decello Design, for his patience and natural gifts. And my thanks to Suellen Brady for her stamp of approval on this series (although you are reading on a higher plane, now, your words will continue to guide and inspire me to get it right.) Last, but not least, thank you to my West Coast cuz, Mary Lou Shimada, for her continued support and encouragement.

I love sharing these adventures with all of you!

For the latest news and updates from
J. K. Grueber visit:
Jkgrueber.com

"Thank you for reading!" J. K. Grueber

www.ingramcontent.com/pod-product-compliance
Lightning Source LLC
Chambersburg PA
CBHW020343010826
48973CB00005B/1254